May your goals be as lofty as Marcus's! Anne ♡

"*Anne Baxter Campbell has created the perfect hero—with his flaws and all. She has created the perfect heroine—one who doesn't want to fall in love. She has created the perfect story—one filled with conflict that will keep you turning the pages. A masterful portrait of the First Century painted with both history and romance.*"

Fay Lamb

"*Author Anne Baxter Campbell has done it again, releasing yet another page-turning thriller, laced with romance and tension. Don't miss it!*"

Kathi Macias (www.kathimacias.com), author

First Edition

Published by
Helping Hands Press

ISBN: 978-1-62208-513-2

Printed in the United States of America

The Truth Trilogy Book Two

Marcus Varitor, Centurion

Anne Baxter Campbell

Dedication

This book is dedicated to my older son, Brett James McMorris.

When he was a small boy, he always wanted to be The Captain, The King, or The Six-Star General. He bravely led where no boy in his right mind would go, and now as the youth pastor for two churches in Ft. Jones, CA, he's in charge of a scad of boys and girls who probably constantly challenge that authority. I'm so very proud of the man, husband, and father he has become.

Acknowledgments

First and foremost, thank You, Lord God, for Your help and inspiration.

My hubby, Jack Campbell has to be the most tolerant and helpful man who ever fixed a meal for a wife who totally ignores him in favor of a laptop.

There have been so many other writers, organizations, and friends who have helped me along the road with my writing and with this novel. Kathi Macias and Fay Lamb constantly inspire me to make more of the time God gives me. A host of critiquers helped polish the work, and I constantly bless God for them all.

Among the books and so forth that I've dug nuggets from, the Bible was highest and best. The *Complete Works of Josephus*, the journals of Pilate, the Atlas of the Bible, several Time Life books about Rome, and countless Internet sites were invaluable. I spent as much time in research as in writing—such fun!

Also, I want you to know: Any mistakes in the text belong squarely on my shoulders. I appreciate feedback, and if you find things that are iffy, ucky, or just plain wrong, let me know at **anneb1944@aol.com**. You could also let me know if you liked it.

Glossary

Adonai—Lord, as in God. "Adoni" is lord, as in a landowner or human master.

Amorphae—Large clay jars used to store or transport things such as grain

Atrium—The main entry/room in a Roman Villa.

Aurius (plural **aurei**)—A gold coin worth twenty-five denarii

Borasco—A severe storm.

Centurion—A Roman army officer, the leader over a century.

Censor—An officer who was responsible for maintaining the census, supervising public morality, and overseeing certain aspects of the government's finances. A censor could remove a senator for what he considered immoral behavior.

Century—An army unit of eighty men.

Circus—Rome's center for entertainment such as gladiator fights and chariot races. It would later be replaced by the Roman Colosseum.

Consuls—Two elected Roman senate leaders who appointed new senators to replace ones who left or died. In some cases, they also made the decision to remove a senator who seriously violated the rules.

Contubernium (plural **contubernia**)—An army unit of eight men.

Cubit—The length of a man's arm from fingertip to elbow, approximately 1.5 American feet. (A "hand" is the same as what we measure horses by, approximately four inches.) Varrus, at 5 cubits, would stand seven feet six inches tall.

Culina—The kitchen in a Roman villa.

Curia—The Roman senate building.

Decanus (plural **decani**)—A Roman army officer, the leader of a contubernium.

Denarius (plural **denarii**)—Roman silver coin for one day's wage for a worker or soldier

Dov—Bear

Ephah—20.8 quarts

Gerah—1/20th of a shekel.

Garum—A sauce made of a small fish and used as a condiment.

Hallel—A song or reading of Psalms 113-118, or sometimes Psalms 145-150. These are often sung or recited on special holidays. The Great Hallel is usually Psalm 136 and is recited or sung after the lesser Hallels at the Passover meal.

Ides—the thirteenth or fifteenth day of each month.

Kalends—The first day of each month.

Lanista—Owner and/or trainer of gladiators

Libra (plural librae)—The Roman pound, approximately 3/4 of an American pound. Varrus, at 500 librae, would weigh about 375 pounds.

Ludus—A place of training, in this book training and practice for the Circus.

Mango, **Mangones**—Slave seller.

Metretes—Greek unit of measure, about nine gallons.

Peristylium—The decorative garden area of a villa.

Persona non grata—A person not welcome.

Portico—The front porch of a Roman villa.

Pratorium—Governor's house.

Proselyte—A Gentile who has converted to the Jewish religion

Quadrans—A Roman copper coin worth very little

Sheckel—4 days' wages; 10 gerahs

Triclinium-- the dining room in a Roman villa.

Villa—A Roman home. It might include not only the house but garden and stables.

Wadi—A stream that flows only in the rainy season.

Chapter 1

In the sixteenth year of the reign of Tiberius Caesar, in the month of Junius

Decanus Marcus Varitor stood at attention in front of the tribune, his gray-fringed helmet under one arm and the other raised, his heart skipping one or two beats. Had Rufus sent for him to say he'd granted his friend Julius's request to also assign him to Caesarea? Probably. Getting out of the heat of Jericho and Jerusalem to the cooler seaside city would be welcome. Being in the same city as Meskhanet would be nice. Maybe not much chance he'd be there as soon as he wish, but... *Still, Adonai, may it be soon.*

He remembered clearly the day he and Julius had witnessed the Man called Jesus being baptized. When Marcus heard that thunderous Voice from heaven, it was enough to convince him that Voice had to belong to a powerful God. Marcus, together with his friends Julius and Cyril, had become a Jewish proselyte.

For a year, Marcus ignored his urge to indulge in Jericho's flesh pots and taverns. And for a year, he'd attended Sabbath Day meetings with other proselytes, but there were no other Romans in the group. Most looked on him with suspicion. It would be reward, indeed, to leave Jericho for Caesarea. It hadn't been just his lifelong friends who had moved there, but all the rest of his friends had followed Julius.

Including Meskhanet. Ah, yes, Meskhanet. Her name wove tapestries of recollections through his mind and made him forget the heat, the smell of too many people and animals jammed into a city, and his aching arm.

Marcus's rust-colored hair clung in sweaty strings to his head as he remained at attention.

Tribune Marcius Rufus glanced up from his writing. "Ah, Marcus, be at ease—sit." He nodded toward the only bench in the sparse room. He brushed his fingers through thinning iron-gray hair and scowled, emphasizing already deep wrinkles. "I suppose you wonder why I sent for you."

Marcus dropped his arm from the salute and sat. "Yes, sir."

"Centurion Julius desires for you to be transferred to Caesarea where he is."

"Yes, sir."

"You knew? Yes, I suppose he would have told you."

"Yes, sir." Marcus's heart skipped a beat.

"However, I've thought it over, and I'm not inclined to pursue that idea."

Marcus held his face expressionless, but his stomach fell. "No, sir? May I ask why?"

Rufus scowled even more fiercely. "I have use for you here, that's why. I don't intend to lose all my men at once. And I've seen a steady improvement in your conduct, Marcus. What brought about this change?"

All his men? Who else had left? No one Marcus knew of.

What would the tribune say if Marcus said the change in him was because of conversion to the Jewish faith? That might not generate a positive reaction. "You could say I decided to mature, sir."

"Mature? Whatever it is, you should have done it a long time ago. I've got an assignment for you, and depending on how well you carry this load, there might be a promotion at the end of it. What do you think of going into the wilderness, out of this accursed heat?"

"I'd like that, sir." Maybe Rufus wasn't so bad after all.

"I want you to take your men up into the Samarian Hill Country near Sebasta. I hear Barabbas stirs up trouble there. He wants to lead the Jews into rebellion. Your job is to arrest him and bring him back here for trial and execution. And if he should die in the process, you'll save the empire a few coins." Rufus rubbed two fingers together.

"Yes, sir. None of the rabble-rousers have enough sense to keep themselves out of prison. He won't be hard to find and bring back." Should he kill a man just to save Rome the cost of a trial?

"Good. Choose horsemen. You'll need to be able to move fast. Two other contubernia will join yours, Linus's, and Servius's. You will command. Leave tomorrow. This Barabbas is dangerous. I've been told he kills even his own countrymen, not just Romans. If you're not back in three weeks, I'll send other troops after you. See that this doesn't happen, Decanus."

"I will do my best, sir. Will that be all?"

"Yes, yes, go. I have far to go on this pile of parchment. Sometimes I wish the written language had never been invented." The tribune straightened himself on his chair, groaning as he stretched his back.

Marcus stood, saluted, and escaped the stuffy confines of the tribune's quarters.

While it wasn't what he hoped for, at least he would escape the heat and boredom of daily guard and patrol duties. He rejoined his troop of men and led the way back down the dusty road from Jerusalem to Jericho.

Meskhanet showed up in his dreams again. Not so pleasantly this time. She screamed in terror as four faceless men pulled her toward a thick stand of cypress.

He panted with the exertion of running after her, but he couldn't run fast enough to reach her. She faded into the mist, arms outstretched to him and her face contorted with fear. He called her name over and over. *Meskhanet! Meskhanet!*

"Meskhane-e-et!" His shout awakened him and he sat bolt upright in bed. Sweat soaked his blanket. His heart pounded.

Marcus shook his head. "Dreams." He stood and walked to the window. No moon this night. He caught the faint shadow of a man below, walking back and forth by the gate.

Brutus, he assumed, since the man had guard duty that watch. Did the man hear his outburst? He hoped not. Brutus didn't need any more fuel to burn him with.

What a temperament Brutus had. No friends. Brutus chased attempts at friendship away with snide remarks, coarse humor, or a rough fist. No one escaped the edge of his constant anger, at what Marcus was at a loss to know. Some of the men also told him of Brutus's activities behind his superiors' backs, and Marcus was his present superior. He shook his head. Although Brutus had a cruel streak with his fellow men, he had a tender side with the horses. What a creeping conundrum.

Marcus turned from the window. There would be no more sleep for him this night. He knelt beside his low bed, the stone floor hard beneath his knees.

When the early morning sun touched the top of the hills, Marcus strode to the stables. Tsal, glossy black mane undulating in the light wind, nickered at him from the fenced corral, his head stretched forward as far as his neck would go. The board bent before the horse's weight. Marcus stepped to Tsal's head and stroked his soft muzzle.

Marcus chuckled at the horse's impatient whicker. "Yes, I brought you an apricot. Did you doubt that I would?" He held out the withered fruit in the palm of one hand and stroked the stallion's neck with the other, marveling at the gentleness of this beast that could flatten him with one stomp of his great hooves. He slipped the rope over the horse's head, opened the gate, and brought the animal out. He enjoyed grooming his own mount, seldom leaving it for one of his men to do. He hummed as he ran the rough cloth over Tsal's flanks.

Other men arrived, scratching and yawning, leading their own mounts out for a good grooming before they left. Brutus caught his mare with a treat, too. Marcus could hear the soft murmur of his voice. Almost sounded like a fond father with his baby daughter. Marcus shook his head. Could Brutus be gentled? Doubtful. Yet—if he would assign grooming duties to any of his men, it would be to Brutus. It didn't matter how much Brutus hated him, he would care for the horse as though it were his own.

"Mount up." Marcus led the men through the gate, a stirring of excitement in his gut as he anticipated the coming conflict, and he had no doubt there would be conflict. Barabbas would not return with them without a fight.

He and his troop of eight rode up the Jericho road and met the other two contingents outside the Jerusalem gates. Servius sat his horse with eyes narrowed and lips pressed together. Small wonder. He'd been in charge of previous expeditions and doubtless thought he should be again.

Marcus pulled Tsal in front of the gathered horsemen. "I want you to keep in mind that we want to bring Barabbas in alive, but if it comes to one of our lives or his, we will bring him here over the back of his horse. His rabble is of no consequence. If they scatter, let them go. If they wish to fight to the death, it's on their own heads."

He turned his horse and led off at a trot. As he rode, he breathed a prayer for the men under his command. He knew the following days would be filled with hard rides, sparse food, and perhaps scant water, in addition to deadly skirmishes. The wilderness did not forgive incompetence. The lives of these men could rest on his decisions. He blew a puff of air out of pouched cheeks and breathed another prayer for himself.

Five days into the search, and not a trace of Barabbas and his friends. Lots of old campfires that might or might not have been Barabbas. Camels, horses, and men, hoof prints and foot prints in abundance, one brushing out another. What did these men ride, or did they? Donkeys and horses in addition to camels? Animals used for packing or riding? The answers could mean the difference between merchants, herdsmen, or thieves.

He took his helmet off and ran his fingers through dripping wet hair as they plodded along, his gaze scraping each rock and bush they approached. He thought they would escape the heat on this jaunt. He mopped his face and hair with a piece of cloth pulled from under his girdle. Where was Barabbas?

A shout sounded from the rear of the column. He pulled Tsal around amid clangs of metal and more shouts. He set his heels in the horse's side and urged him into a run, drawing his sword with one hand and readying his shield with the other. A band of ruffians burst from behind a rise, some on camels, some on donkeys, some on foot, maybe fifty of them screaming at full volume. They threw rocks, struck with wooden staves, and launched thick spears. Some even had swords.

One of the Romans fell from his horse, a spear protruding from his throat. A brigand jumped onto the horse's back with a victory shout, a shout cut short when Marcus's sword thrust through the man's ragged tunic.

A hand pulled at his leather skirt.

Jerking his sword free, Marcus swung it toward the hand, but the man pulled him off Tsal and jumped onto the back of the stallion. Marcus hit the ground with a thump that knocked the air from his lungs, but he lunged to his feet, sword aimed at the thief's chest.

Tsal screamed as the brigand's spear jabbed his rump. He whirled and arched his back, neck bent and teeth bared. The attacker fell and rolled out of the way of the horse's hooves—and into the point of Marcus's sword.

"You earned that. No one rides Tsal but me." Marcus raised his sword in triumph and turned to fight another man.

Less than an hour later, the battle was over. Four of the bandits stood bound and sullen, twenty more lay on the ground, the thirsty dust absorbing the blood almost faster than it flowed. Marcus examined each of the dead men, but they looked so much alike to him—dark hair and beards. Any one of them could be Barabbas as far as he could tell. Did they have him? He'd find out.

Marcus strode to the four prisoners and tilted his head toward their dead companions. "Bury them."

"With what?" One of the men, taller than the others, spat a response through lips scarred by a thick line running from left cheek to right chin.

"I don't care if you dig with your fingernails. What are you called?"

"You don't call me anything, Roman."

"It matters not to me. If I name you Barabbas, I will collect a reward for you."

"I am not Barabbas."

Marcus shrugged. "Start digging, Barabbas."

"I am not Barabbas. Hah! You will never catch that one."

Marcus narrowed his eyes and dropped his voice to a flat, deadly tone. "I say this for the last time, start digging. If you and your little girls haven't finished by sundown, you will join your companions wherever they lie. The jackals might feast on many bones this night. And until you tell me your name, it shall be Barabbas."

One of the other brigands pulled on their leader's sleeve and whispered something in his ear, gesturing toward the pile of dead men. The man scowled, grunted, and nodded, casting a sideways glance at Marcus.

Marcus turned to the soldiers. "If these rag bags have not finished by the time the sun sinks behind those hills, kill them. Let them use your shovels, but stay out of their reach."

He strode back to Tsal and stroked the horse's body, checking him for injuries as the stallion nickered and nuzzled for a treat. Marcus frowned at the thin line of blood crusted below the wound on Tsal's rump. Not wounded badly, but wounded.

Marcus rested his head on Tsal's withers. One soldier lost. Considering how many the brigands lost he should be grateful, but the tightness across his temples didn't feel like it would relax soon.

None of these were Barabbas. There was nothing in the murderer's description that included such a prominent scar as their spokesman had. And that man said they would never find Barabbas—which meant the fugitive was still free, somewhere. Where?

He lifted his head. "Brutus. To me, now."

Brutus stopped to urinate against a tree and sauntered to Marcus, a defiant glint in his eyes. He stopped in front of Marcus, feet spread, his arms crossed over his chest.

"Take over the care of Caius's mare," Marcus said.

Brutus raised bushy eyebrows. "Is she mine, then?"

"No, not unless yours dies or is hurt. But she's your responsibility until someone needs her. Understood?"

Brutus grunted. He walked to where the mare nudged Caius's body with her nose.

Marcus could hear the man talking in gentle tones to the mare as he led her to the other horses and tied her next to his.

This was as good a spot as any for their camp. Marcus set ten men digging a perimeter for their camp and two more on latrine duty. They had a good view to the south and of the trail before and behind. Sentries there and a couple on top of the rocky slope to the north would see anyone who tried to get to them from any direction. The grass looked sparse, but they could supplement the horses' grazing from the feed the soldiers brought with them. The cook had a goat roasting, and the sumptuous smell set Marcus's mouth salivating and his stomach growling.

Marcus grinned to himself as he listened to the men grousing about their empty stomachs. As the commander, he couldn't do that. Pity. More fun to be one of the soldiers who could complain and sneak glares at the cook or commander. He chose a low rock, high enough to provide a backrest but not high enough to hide an enemy, and lowered himself to the ground to wait for the cook to tell them the food was ready.

Marcus woke the next morning to a red sky. At least it shouldn't be as hot, but they could be making a wet camp this night. He could hear their bound prisoners whispering among themselves, faint hisses and grunts. Plotting their escape, no doubt. He lay still in his blankets for several minutes. Let them think they were unheard.

When the early deep gray and red became daylight, he yawned and stretched. Standing to his feet, he yawned again. This time loud enough to wake the camp. The prisoners were instantly quiet.

"Get up, Lucinius. I'm hungry. The rest of you, roll up the camp. We have horses to exercise this day. Vibius, to me."

The soldier who had been on guard with the prisoners trotted across the clearing to Marcus and saluted.

Marcus led the way to their horses. "Vibius, the prisoners were whispering this morning. Did you hear them?"

"Yes, sir. I couldn't hear everything, but I swear I heard one say 'Barabbas' and then 'Jerusalem.' They spoke in Aramaic, and I don't understand much of that language. They whispered, too, which made it more difficult."

Marcus chided himself for not taking lessons in the language with Julius. "Does anyone in camp know Aramaic?"

The soldier shrugged and shook his head. "I don't know, sir."

"Never mind, I'll ask Servius and Linus. Send them to me, please. Then take your horse to where you can watch the prisoners while you groom him."

"Yes, sir." Vibius saluted again.

Linus and Servius strode around the fire pit to him. Linus saluted. Servius did not until Marcus saluted them.

Marcus kept his voice low. "Decani, I think we have a plot working among the prisoners. No, don't look toward them. Our problem is that they speak in Aramaic to each other. Do you know if anyone in your troops understands the language?"

Servius shook his head at the same time Linus nodded.

"I do, sir. My mother is a Jew."

"Good. I'm going to post you as their guard today. I think it's safe to assume they think none of us understand the language. Wait a while, then relieve Vibius. When we set out on today's trek would be the logical time. We'll also need to work out a signal with the other guards for when the prisoners act as though either they suspect the current guard or as though they are about to start something. Is there anyone else who knows the language? I don't even know if anyone of my own understands it. Suggestions?"

Servius snorted. "You might try asking." His bushy gray brows drew close together.

Marcus gritted his teeth, took a deep breath, and continued. "In talking to our men, we have to make sure it's only two or three at a time. Talking to all the troops at the same time means raising our voices to the point the prisoners might also hear, and they understand Greek as well as we do. Not all of the troops understand Latin, so that's out. Ask your men a few at a time and report back to me before nightfall. I will question my men in the same manner."

Servius snorted again and walked away. Linus glanced after him then back to Marcus and shook his head.

Marcus nodded and shrugged. He strode to where two of his men stood waiting for their breakfast.

Chapter 2

Meskhanet sent frantic silent prayers to Egyptian goddesses Nut, Bastet, Mut, Tefnut, and Shu, as well as Yahweh, the Jew's God. Loukas said Yahweh was the only God, but surely she needed more help than one god could provide. Barabbas was the one reason she hadn't been raped yet. It was only that he wanted her for himself that stayed the clutches of the others, and he said he would have her this night. She pulled again at the ropes around her wrists and winced at the pinch.

Where were Loukas and Joanna? Were they dead? Perhaps better if they were. Otherwise, Joanna would probably be suffering the fate Meskhanet most feared. And Loukas, beloved Loukas, husband of sweet Joanna, tortured? They didn't deserve this. Where was their God when they had needed Him?

She shuddered. Soon Barabbas would come for her. Joanna said to save herself for her husband, whoever that might be. She didn't want to be Barabbas's wife nor his concubine either. Not that evil man. She watched him butcher Levi, the old servant who acted like a father to her. He cut one of Levi's hands off then the other. Levi had moaned when that happened. But then Barabbas cut Levi's ears, and he had screamed. She could still hear his screams fading as his blood ran out on the greedy earth. *Ah, Levi, I wish it had been me instead. At least your pain is over.*

Hers would soon begin. Begin? These ropes hurt now. She didn't hold much hope that the thug would be gentle with her nor spare her life once he finished with her. He had boasted of the number of Gentiles and traitors he had killed. So why did he kill Levi? Levi was born of Hebrew parents. Maybe because he served a Greek master, Loukas. Loukas had converted Judaism, but proselytes must still be Gentiles to Barabbas.

Her thoughts returned to Loukas. Did he live? Where would he and all the others be? Prisoners in a different tent? Dead? Free, out in the hills? She hoped—oh, she hoped they were free.

She heard footfalls outside the tent. She closed her eyes. Maybe he would think she slept. Maybe he would be too tired to, to… *O God of the Jews, You rule over the Jews, please stop him, don't let him… Please, please, please.*

The footsteps halted at the flap of the tent, and voices murmured. A woman's voice? Or perhaps a man with a high-pitched voice? And the other voice sounded like Barabbas the Beast. She felt the hair rise on the back of her neck.

OGodOGodOGodOGod. Help me!

The murmurs and footsteps faded, and Meskhanet released her held breath. Her intent focus on the tent flap gone, now she could smell and taste the dirty rag that covered her mouth and feel the ropes that bit into her wrists and ankles. She understood the ropes, but why the rag? She could scream until her lungs spewed out of her mouth, and no one in this camp would help her.

Meskhanet rubbed her face against the dirt under her head trying to loosen the rag, but all she did was scrape her skin raw.

She'd heard no loud voices since they brought her here after Levi was killed. Brought her blindfolded, but they'd removed that rag after they were in the tent. Where were they? In a city? She held her breath and listened.

There—a faint bleating. Distant voices. A bell? Or the clang of metal pots. Yes, that had to be it, a shepherds' camp. And someone cooking.

Her stomach rumbled, but the taste of the rag in her mouth made her gag.

No, no! She couldn't vomit, not with the rag in her mouth. She would die. But didn't she wish a few moments ago she wished to die instead of Levi?

The night wind played a grief-stricken song in the cedars, and an owl hooted. A shadow played on the tent wall, flickers of firelight making the shadows jump. Meskhanet saw one big shadow move closer to her tent. It grew larger, broke into two shapes, then shrank until they disappeared from view. She sighed in relief.

A lion coughed from somewhere nearby. The tent flap moved. Meskhanet inhaled, eyes feeling like they would burst from her head. It moved again, and a dog's nose showed itself, then the head. A snarl wrapped itself around the dog's muzzle.

"Eummmmmph." She couldn't stop the muffled scream. The dog laid its ears to its head and disappeared. If her heart weren't pounding so hard, she'd laugh. Was she a child, to be frightened at night sounds and wandering dogs? And the dog was frightened of one small bound woman?

All seemed quiet now. She hadn't heard anything for an hour, two hours. She couldn't see the stars to know the time, but it had been dark, very dark for a long period. Her eyes felt heavy, but she feared sleep. What if Barabbas returned? What if another dog came, one not frightened by a bound woman's muffled scream? Or a lion or bear? Still, what could she change by staying awake? Nothing.

So tired, so tired....

What's that? A scratching noise behind her startled her. A tearing sound. She tried to twist to see, but her arm had gone to sleep where she laid on it. With some effort, she rolled to her other side. Sharp stabs of returning sensation ravaged her arm.

Nothing. Dark, but she still should be able to see if it was the tent that ripped. Maybe the sound of her movements frightened whatever had been scratching. The dog again? She lay quiet, stilling her breath, but again the night was silent.

She needed to urinate, and she wanted a drink. The rag in her mouth felt dry, not even damp from saliva. Meskhanet sucked on her tongue, trying to generate even a little moisture. Had they forgotten she was here? Surely they would allow her to relieve herself soon. If they didn't, she would be lying in a puddle.

No more sleep. Her gaze darted toward the least insect hum or distant night bird's cry.

After a time, the morning light began to reveal shadows in the tent. There, on a bench, a water jar. She rolled painfully to the bench, grunting as her weight landed on her bound wrists. Now what? Could she get to her knees? Yes, there, she did it. Moving her face over the jar, she breathed in the moist air. *Water!* Carefully, she hooked her chin on the lip of the vessel and slowly tipped it to the side. It wasn't heavy, so it couldn't be full. She had no way of catching it if it fell to the ground, and it could break. *Oh, please don't let it break.*

The jar fell with a thump, and again Meskhanet used her chin, this time to stop the jar from rolling. Water sloshed onto the bench and floor.

She scooted to the neck of the jar and lowered her face to the wet bench and let the rag soak up as much of the water there as it would. She pushed her head as far as it would go into the jug, tilting downward with her chin to make the water slosh onto her face. Gratefully, she sucked the water from the cloth. It might not taste good, but it was wet. She sloshed the water again and again until it no longer reached the edge of the jar. She lay back on her side and rolled to where she had been before.

And now she needed to urinate even more than before.

Faint noises of the awakening camp reached her ears. Soon. They should come get her in a little while. But if they didn't....

Meskhanet began scooting toward her feet, wriggling to maneuver her tunic upward with each move. Footsteps approached the tent and she stopped moving. Now what? She hurried to scoot her tunic back to her ankles. She sat with her back to the center pole of the tent when a woman entered. Meskhanet made urgent noises.

The old woman seemed startled to hear another person in the tent and squinted in Meskhanet's direction. "Who's there?" The old woman's voice quavered.

"Mph mph."

She limped close enough for Meskhanet to see gray kinks of hair escaping her mantle. "Why are you tied up? Where did you come from? Whose prisoner are you?"

"Mph." Could the woman not see she was gagged?

"Oh, I see. Hmm. I cannot see how it would hurt to loose your mouth." The woman pulled at the cloth, then walked around behind her and untied it with many tugs to Meskhanet's hair.

She coughed and spat out pieces of what, she didn't know and perhaps didn't want to know. "Thank you."

"Now, who are you?"

"My name is M-, uh, Martha."

"Martha? You do not look Hebrew." The old woman's eyes narrowed. "You do not sound Hebrew, either."

"I-I am a Hebrew slave from, from the far south, Rhinocolura . Who are you?"

The woman shrugged. "I do not know Rhinocolura. Huh." She paused. "I am Rebecca."

"Please, Rebecca, would you help me? I must relieve myself. I have lain here since yesterday."

"I do not know whose prisoner you are. You might be a savage murderer."

"I am not, I swear. Even if I were, my ankles have been tied so long I don't know if I can walk. I cannot attack. And my hands are tied. That, too, would stop me from hurting you. I am a prisoner of Barabbas." She lifted her head to gaze to Rebecca's eyes. "Would you help me?"

"Huh. I am the mother of Barabbas." She pulled a knife from the folds of her tunic.

Meskhanet gasped and pulled back. "No, please!"

"Hold still, Martha. I cannot cut the ropes while you twist around."

Meskhanet obeyed. Her swollen hands and feet stung with returning feeling.

Rebecca nodded. "Rub them. It will help."

Meskhanet lifted herself using the tent pole, biting her lip as her hands and feet protested.

Rebecca stepped forward and put her arm around Meskhanet's waist, pulling Meskhanet's arm around her shoulders. "Come, Martha. I'll help you to the latrine."

For an old woman, Rebecca's grip felt strong.

When they returned to the tent, Martha sat on the bench, lifting the water jar to its proper position. "I'm sorry I tipped it over, but I was so thirsty—I had to get a drink."

"How did you drink with that rag in your mouth?"

The day passed in slow plodding moments. Marcus saw no life, other than herds of sheep on any valley or hill with grass. The shepherds watched them with interest. Marcus smiled. Probably more entertainment than they'd had in a month. He waved and the shepherds usually turned their backs. Some waved back—usually the young boys but seldom the grown men.

Their camp was dry that night. Without fresh water, they would have to use the large skins of water carried on the backs of mules. The mules would be happier, but he hoped they'd find water tomorrow. Two nights without water would stretch their resources. Three would be disaster. Marcus reclined against a rock and picked a dry stalk of grass to chew on while he watched the prisoners from the corner of his eyes.

Brutus stood next to them, fixing the bound men with a baleful glare. They were wise to remain quiet. They must recognize a guard who would enjoy an excuse for mayhem.

When Brutus sat next to a tree, two of the brigands ventured a whispered conversation. Marcus hoped Brutus could hear, but the soldier gave no indication. Brutus yawned and dropped his chin to his chest.

Marcus hoped the man was acting. He had to be. How would he ever dare sleep? So many of this cohort hated him, he must wonder how many would love to stick a knife in his ribs while he slept. In addition, the rules governing soldiers gave little lenience to sleeping guards.

A soft snore escaped Brutus's lips. If that didn't convince the prisoners, what would? The two who had been whispering before scooted closer to the other two, and the whispering resumed. As darkness fell, the sibilance sounded like one deer following another into piles of dry leaves.

Brutus grunted. "You—get back to where you were."

A yelp gave evidence Brutus backed up his order with a prod, probably his spear.

Marcus raised his head and caught Linus's gaze. Without a word, he jerked his head in Brutus's direction.

Linus walked past Marcus and up to Brutus. "You are relieved. I'll take over now. Report to the commander."

"Yes, sir."

Marcus stood and moved to the fire, and Brutus sauntered to his side.

"You wish a report...sir?" Brutus's response, as usual, was tainted with a sneer.

Marcus stood and led Brutus out of the prisoners' hearing range. "What did you hear, Brutus? Anything useful?"

"They are planning an escape."

Marcus sighed. "I knew that, soldier, without understanding a word of their language. So how is it they plan to escape?"

Brutus's eyes narrowed. "They didn't tell me, Decanus."

"You said you could understand Aramaic. Were they not speaking Aramaic?"

"I couldn't hear them." Brutus shifted his eyes in the direction of the prisoners.

"I don't believe you. Are your ears stopped? I could hear them speaking from where I was. Now which is it, soldier? Did you lie? Or did you hear their plans?"

The bushy eyebrows creeping across Brutus's forehead shot upward, then lowered back into a scowl. "Sorry, Decanus. I did hear part of what they said, but I don't speak the language fluently. Brothel whores don't speak in fighting terms." His lips curled into an I-dare-you-to-challenge-me sneer before he continued. "They said something about a canyon and a sheep camp. I heard Barabbas named a few times. They will try to get one man freed, probably the one with the scarred face. Two of them will fight each other. One will call for help from one side. Scar face plans to run from the other side. They said he was the fastest of the four men."

"You heard enough. Bind the prisoners together with a rope around their necks and tied behind their heads. Free only one hand at a time. One hand on one prisoner. Can you do that? See that you don't speak any Aramaic around them, even now." Marcus stared at Brutus through narrowed eyes for a few moments then turned and walked away.

He kept his visage fierce, but inside, he grinned. Brutus had flinched. It was all Marcus could do to keep from shouting his triumph to the camp. If only Julius and Cyril were here, they would have raised a glass together and laughed until their sides ached.

Marcus turned back to watch Brutus, arms crossed, a scowl and a jerk of the chin emphasizing his command.

Brutus stomped back to the prisoners. He and Linus retied each of the prisoners so that one hand could be freed at a time, then tied all four together at the neck. Narrowed glances passed between the captives.

They weren't idiots. They knew they'd been found out. Or at least suspected they had. Now what would they try? Marcus felt sure they wouldn't give up.

Nor did they. The commotion after the moon went behind a thick cloud made it obvious something was happening.

Marcus jumped to his feet, sword in hand, and pulled a brand from the fire. "To me!"

An arrow swished past his head. He dropped the brand and charged in a crouch toward the prisoners. The arrow came from that direction, and someone had to be near there to shoot it. One prisoner was gone, the rope that had been around his neck lying on the ground in a puddle of liquid. Brutus lay on the ground, and Linus held the remaining hostages, still bound, at spear point.

One of the men brought a torch. Brutus wasn't dead, but the oozing bulge behind his ear indicated he connected with something. He groaned and sat up, both hands holding his head.

Daylight revealed more of the story. Although Brutus insisted someone must have snuck into the camp, it appeared that when he let a prisoner loose to relieve himself, the man had butted Brutus with his head, grabbed the soldier's knife, and freed himself. The scar faced captive and Brutus's knife were gone.

No trace of other arrows or footprints leaving the camp other than the one escapee. Where had that arrow come from?

He'd have to come up with another plan. This one hadn't worked.

Chapter 3

Marcus led his troops through a long, narrow canyon. He and the rest of the troop cast tense glances to the rim of the canyon and the boulders scattered here and there. The scouts reported the canyon clear, but there were too many places to hide. He'd give his last gerah to know where Barabbas hid, and he'd wager that same gerah the man knew where Marcus and his men were.

If it were him, he would attack from behind rocks at the end of the canyon and send another band of men to flank him. Which is why he'd separated the troops into three groups spaced not quite a mile apart with horns to alert each other should an attack occur. The prisoners rode in a line between the men in the center troop, one leg tied to the horses they rode and the other to one of the soldier's horses. If they tried to escape, the horses would pull them to pieces. Even Servius seemed to approve of that idea.

Brutus, too. Marcus kept a wary eye on the man. Brutus might deliberately spook one of the horses—even his own—for the joy of seeing someone torn asunder.

The first sign of trouble didn't come from Brutus. A rumble sounded from ahead of them. Another from just behind them. Rocks tumbled down the steep slopes, missing the last two men by a couple of cubits. Faint shouts cut short echoed from the hillsides. Marcus signaled his trumpeter to blow, and blow again. Silence. No hoof beats, no clank of armor, no ringing of steel on steel.

The canyon walls erupted with ululating cries and brown-robed men. Dozens of them. Horses reared and men tumbled. Brief screams from the prisoners probably spelled disaster for those men, but Marcus was too busy to check. His sword tasted the blood of three of the brigands. Tsal reared, and a sword meant for Marcus connected instead with his horse. The splash of warm dark liquid from the charger's deeply cut neck told him his charger would not carry him into any more battles. As he rolled clear of the stallion's fall, his helmet fell from his head, and he didn't bother to pick it back up.

With a growl, he turned his sword on the man who had struck Tsal, slashing the man again and again even after it was certain he could feel no more blows. Angry tears ran down Marcus's face, but he didn't care. A blow to the side of his head put an end to further revenge, and he collapsed to the ground amid a red shower of stars.

Meskhanet followed Rebecca to the well where shepherds had gathered several herds of sheep. If she and Rebecca wanted unsullied water, they'd better hurry. A separate group of men seemed in a hurry too. They herded no sheep, but they galloped several horses and camels in their direction from nearby hills, whooping like madmen. The alarmed sheep milled and bleated, almost breaking away from their herdsmen.

Rebecca turned to watch, shading her eyes against the sun. "My son returns."

The oncoming hoard must have realized the difficulty they caused, because they slowed and stopped a half-mile from the camp, although they continued what sounded like victory shouts. The sheep calmed and followed their keepers to a large pen. By turns, the herders led their sheep into the enclosure, counting and checking each ewe, lamb, and ram as it passed through the gate.

Once the sheep were safely corralled, the men rode into the camp with much less fanfare. They led two mules, each carrying the body of a Roman soldier, and several more with what looked to be enough supplies to last every one of them at least two weeks. One of the bruised and bloody men slung over a mule's back moaned. Meskhanet might have to rethink her first idea that the two were dead.

The prisoners were hauled into a tent, and two sound thumps indicated the soldiers dumped them onto unyielding ground. Humorless laughter, scufflings, and grunts from inside the tent might have meant they were being trussed up much like she had been.

A wave of pity passed through her heart, but she could not reveal that. She knew not all the Romans were evil. Loukas's friends Julius and Marcus had been kind and friendly, but she shuddered at the memory of one not so friendly.

Rebecca grunted. "Romans. Barabbas will not let them live long, and what time they have left will not be pleasant."

Meskhanet cast a sidelong glance at Rebecca. "You think they will be tortured? For what? Your son should already know the location of all the soldiers, shouldn't he?"

Rebecca turned to her. "What? You would have them treated with mercy? What mercy have they shown our people? No, he will not be looking for information. Just entertainment. Barabbas will be our next king, you know. A prophet anointed him."

"A prophet? Do you mean Jesus?" Her heart quickened.

"Yes, Jesus bar Elias. There are many named Jesus. Even my son's given name is Jesus. You have heard of this prophet Jesus, son of Elias, Martha?"

"I saw a Jesus in Jericho, called a prophet by many. I do not know his father's name. That Jesus healed a friend of my…my master." A tear rolled down Meskhanet's cheek, and she brushed it away.

"You shed tears for your master?" Rebecca raised her eyebrows.

"He was a good master. He treated me well." She gulped back the gorge that rose in her throat. Had Barabbas tortured him for entertainment too?

"My son does not kill Jews…unless they serve the Romans." She spat again. "Such as the tax collectors. Was he a tax collector?"

"My master was a physician." She didn't mention that Loukas wasn't a Jew. Anyone who looked at him would know he was Greek. Even if they did not recognize his Greek accent, they would know. At home and on this move to Caesarea, he wore Greek togas, and his broad shouldered square frame shouted "Greek." Or used to. Another tear escaped, but Rebecca didn't seem to notice. Good.

Rebecca grunted. "Water. We came for water. Let's try to find a place where the mud didn't stir up so much."

The walls of the tent spun, but that was impossible. Walls didn't spin unless he'd consumed copious skins of wine, and Marcus's mouth was so dry it had to be a week since anything liquid passed his throat. He closed his eyes. It whirled worse. Why did his head hurt? He knew why his shoulders hurt. Arms tied behind your back at the elbows for hours would do that. Legs tied, too, but not as painfully. But his head must have been split by an axe.

He groaned under his breath and opened his eyes again. It seemed like an hour passed before the world stopped spinning. His eyes still wouldn't focus; there were two of everything. He squinted. The dark tent seemed to contain another person bound in similar fashion, but the man didn't face him. Marcus wondered if the other prisoner was alive. He didn't move.

Marcus tried to speak, but all that came from his throat was a hoarse noise. He cleared his throat and spoke with a low voice. "Ssssst. You, Soldier. Are you awake?"

No response.

Marcus shifted onto his stomach and turned his head to the side. The shoulders hurt infinitesimally less, but his head still washed in agony. He tried to remember what happened. The last he remembered was…was Tsal. Oh, no, not his beloved black. He had such plans for that beautiful, brave stallion. Another year as a war horse, then put him with brood mares. That plan would not come to pass now. But then, that could itself be a moot idea. He might not survive this captivity himself. But at least if Tsal had survived, these brigands might have given him the chance to be a breeding stallion.

He must have dozed. The tent was no longer dark. He couldn't see the lump where the unconscious man lay. He heard a hiss behind him and felt a hand on his back. A sibilant whisper, and then someone cut the ropes from his hands.

The faint whisper sounded neutral. Marcus couldn't tell if the voice was a woman or a man. His hands and arms felt numb, but they were free. He heard the rustle of movement and a faint grunt. A sibilant voice sounded again from where he knew the other man lay. More movement, then a glimpse of light as someone pulled up a corner of the tent and left. He rubbed his hands together until the feeling came back then crept to the other man.

"Can you move?" he whispered.

"Some."

"Follow me. We're going to get out of here."

"Can't. Leg's broken."

Ironic. It sounded like Brutus. Of all the men in his troop to live through this ordeal. "Wait here. I'll try to find a way out, and I'll drag or carry you if that's what it takes."

He crawled to the door flap of the tent, raised one corner, and looked out. One guard sprawled prone in front of the door. Sleeping? He wondered. The person who'd freed them might have knocked the guard unconscious or killed him. He grasped a weed growing at the edge of the tent, pulled it loose, and tickled the guard's ear with it.

A snort and a slap destroyed the unconscious theory. Now what? Marcus waited until a soft snore let him know the man was again asleep.

He turned to his companion. "I'm going to have to make another way out—cut the tent or dig out from under it. Did our rescuer leave the knife?"

"How would I know?"

Marcus exhaled sharply. Only Brutus could put sarcasm into a whisper.

"She or he might have told you." Marcus felt the ground. Nothing. He shrugged, moved to the tent wall, and tugged. The fabric tore in his hand as though someone had made cuts in it. Or maybe the seams and material were old. *Thank you, Adonai, whatever the reason.* He continued to rip the wall until the opening was big enough to thrust his head through and then his upper body. No one in sight.

He returned to Brutus. "As soon as we're outside I'll lift you over my shoulder. Whatever pain you feel, don't make a sound, not even if you're dying. If you do, I'll drop you right on that broken leg and run. Is that clear?"

"Yes."

"Can you pull yourself with your arms, or do I have to drag you over there?"

"I'll get there." A sound of scraping and soft grunts accompanied Brutus's progress.

"Let's go." Marcus grasped the man's shoulders and pulled him through the opening. He drew a deep breath and held it while he hefted Brutus to his shoulder and rose to his feet. *Adonai, the man weighs more than I do. Why did I do this?* Marcus blew out his held breath and staggered between the tents as quietly as he could.

He sniffed the air. Where were the horses? He could smell the sheep, so the horses would probably be nearby. "I'm going to set you down here in the shadows until I find horses for us," he whispered. For all the sound the soldier had made, he might well be a corpse.

"I'll be here." Brutus made a pained gasp as Marcus set him on the ground.

Marcus dropped to his belly and squirmed across a clearing, stopping to smell the air every few cubits. Marcus spied horses not five cubits from him. One of them leaned its head over the pole fence and whickered at him.

"Quiet, fool horse," muttered someone from the other side of the corral. "You wake Barabbas and he'll eat you for breakfast."

A low giggle followed and soft murmuring voices, one male and one female. Marcus grinned. The guard might be too busy to notice if he took a horse or two. When he got to the corral, he found a rope hanging on a post. He lowered one pole after another without a whisper of sound and led a large bay horse slowly across the clearing. As he thought would happen, a few others followed.

Marcus looped Brutus's arm over his shoulder and raised him to a stand. "Astride or belly down?" he whispered.

"Astride."

Marcus lifted Brutus by his good leg. He could the soldier's teeth grinding as Marcus moved his broken leg over the horse. "Stay low over his back in case anyone looks this way." Again he led the horse with slow steps, hoping the soft clopping would sound so natural no one would notice.

He spun at the sound behind him. From the clatter he knew one of the other animals must have kicked over some cooking pots. Jumping to the horse's back behind Brutus, Marcus said a quick prayer that this steed was trained by Romans and set his heels in the horse's side.

Shouts from behind him let him know the camp was awake. The sound of hoof beats could mean enemies or just loose horses following the leader, but he didn't take the time to look behind him.

The shouts became more distant while the horse ran on. A riderless horse came up alongside them and passed them, a pale horse with a white mane and tail. It began leading the way. It looked like Linus's mare, but in the dark it was hard to tell. Still…this gelding he had chosen for Brutus and himself was willing to follow. Linus's horse had been the alpha mare in their herd. Made sense.

So, if this horse was Linus's mare, maybe she would lead them home to Jericho. He smiled at that thought and let the horse have his head. The horse he and Brutus rode began to slow. They'd have to begin walking or trade horses. He slowed to a trot, hoping the other horses would follow suit. They did, and although the mare neighed a protest, she also slowed. Would she let him catch her? He pulled the gelding to a stop, and the other horses milled around them, blowing and snorting.

Marcus chuckled. Even one of the enemy's donkeys had followed, a jack maybe hoping for a few colts from a few pretty mares. Had even one of the horses stayed back at the enemy's camp? In the light of the newly risen quarter moon, he didn't see anyone on their trail.

Brutus must have lost consciousness, because he lay heavily against Marcus's arm. If only they had a wagon. Now what would he do? He couldn't take the time to catch the mare, not with Brutus unable to stay on a horse by himself.

He looked around. Caesarea should only be about nine or ten miles from here, and Loukas should be there by now. He could get help for Brutus and maybe see Meskhanet at the same time.

Smiling, he guided the gelding at a walk toward the west. Once more, the herd turned with him. The alpha mare objected, taking a few steps to the southeast, then turned her head and neighed for the herd. The gelding wanted to follow her, but obeyed the direction from Marcus's legs as the rest of the herd trotted after the mare.

Chapter 4

Meskhanet stretched, feeling every sore muscle and scrape. Where was she? Oh—at Barabbas's camp. In his mother Rebecca's tent. And her name was now Martha, not Meskhanet. She'd have to remember that. And a Jew. May the Jew's God help her remember not to speak in Egyptian or mention the wrong god's name. That would be a fatal mistake.

Her skin crawled as she remembered the two Romans who had been thrown in another tent. Did they still live, or had they perished last night? She had awakened to the commotion, the sound of horses' hooves and shouting. Maybe they escaped. She hoped so. Hours later, more hoof beats. Either the horses returned or they were found and brought back.

She looked over to where Rebecca had lain down, but the woman wasn't there. Meskhanet—Martha!—rose from her bed on the ground, rolled up the dirty blanket, and set it aside. She lifted the tent flap and stepped outside. She could smell fish cooking.

A group of women gathered around a pot on the fire. Shepherds called their sheep from the pen and led them into the grass-covered hills to the east of them. Lambs jumped here and there, chasing each other but still following their herds. Sounds of laughter and men's voices blended with the bleating into a cheerful cacophony.

Martha walked with hesitance to the group of women. Where was Rebecca? Oh, there, talking with her son. Barabbas glanced in her direction and frowned then continued arguing with his mother, milling arms and jabbing fingers punctuating their conversation. Despite their obvious disagreement with each other, their voices were low. Was she the topic of their discussion? Maybe Rebecca would talk him out of bedding her, since Rebecca thought she was a Jew. That would be against their laws, wouldn't it?

"Who are you?" One of the women who had been around the fire strode toward her, a scowl of suspicion darkening her face.

"I...I am Martha. I'm Barabbas's prisoner." She backed away a step.

Rebecca and Barabbas turned toward them. He strode the few steps between them. "This is my mother's slave, Martha. She is under my protection, Nomah, so do not harm her."

His growl and scowl seemed enough for Nomah. The woman backed away, pulling a scarf across her frightened face.

Martha couldn't blame her. She wanted to run, too. It was only because she felt frozen to the spot that she did not.

Why had Rebecca taken her part?

Why had Barabbas?

Barabbas jerked his head toward his mother. "You are in my mother's charge, woman. I do not believe you are a Jew, but she says you are. Therefore, you are her slave. See that you do not try to leave this camp, or I will test that improbable story when I track you down." The scrutiny from his black eyes seemed to bore holes through her.

Martha held the cloak Rebecca gave her around her face and nodded her head a fraction of a finger's width, but she could neither speak nor lower her gaze. The cold sweat under her arms held an odor of its own, the smell of sheer panic. She licked her lips with a dry tongue and swallowed. Her knees wobbled and she feared she would fall.

It was Barabbas who broke the spell. He spat, glared at her, and walked away, anger in his stiff stride and clenched fists.

Martha fainted.

When she woke, Rebecca stood above her fanning her with the edge of her cloak.

Martha blinked. She groaned and sat up. "I'm sorry."

"Why are you sorry?" Rebecca asked, helping her to her feet. "Did you faint on purpose? The sun is not that hot yet today. Are you with child, Martha?"

Martha felt the heat rise to her face. "No, mistress. I am an unmarried woman, and I have not known a man." Surely it was all right to lie in a situation such as this. Especially since her lack of virginity was involuntary.

"I thought you were a slave."

"My master loved only his wife. He did not take me as his concubine." A tear leaked from her eye, and Martha scrubbed it away.

Rebecca muttered something under her breath and scowled. "Come with me. I don't know why my son insists you will be my slave, but since he's the commander here, that's the way it must be. You would think he'd be more respectful of the one who gave him birth and fed him at her breast, but he thinks he can command me too. Children in my youth were much more respectful. My father would have flogged me if I spoke to my mother the way my son speaks to me."

"Yes, mistress."

"He'll learn I am not one to be treated so scornfully. That young man has lessons yet untaught. Do you not think that is so?"

Martha glanced sideways at her new owner. Was there any way to answer this without incurring Rebecca's wrath? "I...I."

"No, don't answer me. I'm talking to myself." Rebecca interrupted with a grin. "Old women are allowed to do that. Sometimes when I voice my anger aloud, the anger goes away. So I try to do that when no one is listening. I avoid a lot of arguments with my son—and with others—that way."

For the first time since she'd been captured, Martha laughed. "You are a wise woman, mistress."

"And stop calling me mistress. My name is Rebecca. And slave though you may be, we shall be friends too. We'll share the workload. I won't have someone doing the work that keeps me alive. When I don't work, the only thing I have to do is sleep. Too much sleep leads to death, you know."

"Yes, Rebecca, if you say it, it must be so. What do you wish me to do?"

"Let me tell you first what not to do. Do not go into the tent where the prisoners were placed. If Barabbas or one of the guards finds you there, it will mean your death."

"No, I don't plan to enter that tent. The men are Roman soldiers. I might go in there if they were my master—my former master—or Jews, to try to—to talk to them."

Rebecca narrowed her eyes and stared hard at Martha. "No, not even then. Even now, your life is worth nothing to my son. He does not think you are a Jew. I would not give him reason to be angry, my young friend. Come with me. We need to gather wood for this day's cooking. And tomorrow's, too, since the Sabbath is only a few hours away."

A cry sounded from a guard at the prisoners' tent, and several men, including Barabbas, ran to the door of the tent, leaving their breakfasts unguarded. As the dogs converged with growls on the deserted legs of lamb and bread, the men converged on the tent and angry voices mimicked the growls of the dogs.

Barabbas left the group and strode to his mother and Martha. With the back of his hand, he knocked Martha to the ground. "You let them go, you worthless whore."

Martha rolled away from his descending foot. "No. No! I swear I did not!"

Rebecca stepped between them. "Do not do this, my son. Are you now a murderer of women?"

"Step out of my way, mother. She may have you deceived, but she does not fool me. She lies. Who else in my camp would do this? Get out of my way before you also taste my ire." Veins stood out in Barabbas's neck as he shouted in his mother's face.

"You forget the law of Moses to honor your father and mother?" Rebecca's voice matched her son's, strident and loud enough to be heard in the next village.

Martha cowered on the ground, afraid to move, but when Barabbas's hand lifted to strike his mother, she sprang to her feet between them, this time receiving the blow from his doubled fist. Again she fell at his feet, and she beheld his eyes widen and jaw drop as darkness claimed her.

Marcus rode up to the walls of Caesarea at dawn.

"Who goes there?" The hail came from the top of the wall near the gate.

"Decanus Marcus Varitor of Jericho," Marcus shouted back, "with a wounded soldier. Open the gate."

The huge gate creaked open, and Marcus rode inside. "I need to find Centurion Julius Saturnius and the Greek physician Loukas," he said to the waiting soldier.

"I do not know the physician, but the centurion's home is not far. I'll get him if you will wait here."

"I'll follow you. He knows me well and won't mind if I wake him. I don't want to sit here and wait. This man needs help."

"As you wish, sir. Follow me." The soldier led the way at a trot, Marcus's horse following him.

When they reached the house, Marcus dismounted, struggling to keep the unconscious Brutus from falling. Once he was on his feet, he lowered the wounded man to the ground. "Stay with him, soldier. I'll return in a few moments."

Marcus whistled as he walked into the courtyard of the house Julius's father had purchased for him. An arched wooden gate covered with a red flowering vine opened to a marble slab path leading toward a large brick house. Two fountains, one on either side of the winding path, watered a variety of plants mostly foreign to Marcus. The inside of the walled courtyard sported several shades of green interspersed with red, yellow, blue, and pink flowers.

A servant opened the door and smiled. "Marcus! Welcome." The tallish dark-haired man stepped forward, hands outstretched.

Marcus grasped both the man's hands with his own. "Cyril—you're getting fat. Quinta must feed you well."

"Yes, and shaves me, too. Maybe you should find a wife. Come in. Julius is breaking his fast, and Miriam has her feet propped on his lap." Cyril led the way into the dining area.

Marcus couldn't help but admire the marble floor and heavy wooden low table.

Julius moved Miriam's feet aside and jumped to his feet. "Marcus! What are you doing here?

"I brought a soldier for Loukas to set a leg on. I think we're the only survivors of an attack by Barabbas. We were captured, but escaped thanks to someone who cut the ropes holding us."

"Loukas? I thought he was still in Jericho. I haven't seen him."

Marcus went still, a cold feeling beginning in his face and sinking to his stomach. "He—they—left Jericho before I did. Three weeks ago."

Julius and Cyril stared slack-jawed at Marcus as Quinta walked into the room. Her joyful cry and smile of greeting faded as the three men turned to her with ashen faces.

"What is it? What makes you so pale?"

With difficulty, Miriam stood, holding one hand on her distended middle. She walked to Quinta and pulled her close. "Loukas and Joanna and all their household left Jericho over three weeks ago."

Quinta's eyes widened, and she pushed back from Miriam. "No. They are not dead. No one would kill a physician. They cannot be dead. I would know. I would feel it in here." She tapped her chest as she turned to face the men.

Cyril strode to her side and grasped her arms. "Three weeks, Quinta. They could walk here in a week. They had wagons and horses."

Quinta shook her head in slow cadence. "No. No, not my mother and father. Not my friends Levi and Meskhanet. No."

Her shoulders began to shake, and Cyril held her while she sobbed. Tears rolled down his cheeks.

Marcus felt an odd jerky feeling begin in his chest, and he covered his face with his hands. He felt Julius's arms go around his shoulders, but he pulled away and stumbled out the door, sobs ripping his heart in two. "Ah, Meskhanet..." He leaned against the wall as his body shuddered with grief.

"Uh, sir? Decanus?"

Marcus straightened his shoulders but did not turn around.

Julius's voice sounded before Marcus could speak. "Yes, soldier?"

"Centurion Julius, sir, I need to know what to do with the injured man outside the gate, sir."

"Bring him into the house, soldier, then go find the company physician."

"Yes, sir." The sound of hobbed sandals receded then returned, accompanied by grunts of effort.

"This way, soldier."

Marcus slumped to the ground, his head in his hands.

"Marcus, come with me. I'll find you a room where you can be alone." Cyril's voice sounded rough, and his hand rested on Marcus's shoulder.

Marcus lifted his head. "I'll be all right, Cyril. It's just that I-I'm tired. No sleep for the past day or two. The news caught me by surprise."

"I know how you felt about Meskhanet, my friend. And Loukas and Joanna were dear to us all. I understand how you feel. Come with me."

Marcus stood. Cyril clapped him on the back and led him back into the house by another doorway. He suspected the room they entered must be well appointed, but he had no eye for beauty just then. His eyes felt like they were on fire. He sank to a couch, and Cyril sat beside him, silent.

Julius joined them a short time later, pushing his hands through his hair.

"Marcus, my friend, I think I know what you're going through. If it were Miriam..."

"Yes, I suspect you would feel even worse. I don't know if Meskhanet even knew that I cared for her, and we were not betrothed. I'm sorry. I didn't mean to fall to pieces and leave you holding… Oh, I'm even sorrier. I didn't warn you the injured man was Brutus." Marcus felt the corner of his mouth twitch.

"Of the men in your command to rescue, why under the One God's great heavens did you save that one?"

Marcus shook his head. "It would be a longer story than I can relate right now. Would you mind if I rested for a time?"

Cyril stood. "We'll leave you alone until dusk, then I'll wake you for some food. If you are hungry before then, just come out into the room we were in before."

Marcus lay back on the couch with his hands behind his head, staring at nothing. His chest hurt. *God, why? Why Meskhanet? Why Loukas and Joanna? Weren't they worthy of Your protection?*

The longer he lay there, the angrier he felt. He got up, gathered up his helmet, sword, and cloak. Cyril had left a skin of wine on a table by the lamp. He scooped it up and took a long pull of the honeyed wine and wiped his mouth on the back of his hand.

He strode quietly to the door and peered out. No one was around.

He walked to the stable and got the horse he and Brutus rode in on. When he rode out the gate, no one stopped him. No one seemed to notice.

Chapter 5

This time when Martha woke, it was Barabbas who stared down at her. He knelt by her side. "Why did you do that?" Curiosity vied with wonder in his tone.

Martha shrank back from him, quaking in fear.

"Be still and at peace, woman. I won't harm you. Why did you take the blow my mother earned?"

Meskhanet couldn't speak. The hair at the back of her head scraped at the neck of her cloak. Small mewling sounds of terror escaped her throat as she tried to escape his touch, pulling herself back, visions of Levi's severed hand with twitching fingers filling her mind's eye.

Rebecca pulled on his arm with both hands "Leave her alone. Can you not see she doesn't want you to touch her? Do you blame her? Your touch kills and maims."

"It's your fault, old woman. I would not have struck had you not angered me."

"Did I draw back your arm to strike? Did I make that decision for you? Fool! Do not blame your rage on me. You must bear your own sins, not stack them upon my shoulders."

Barabbas shrugged off her hands and jumped to his feet, fists clenched. "Take her then, old woman, and keep her…and yourself…out of my sight!" He tramped away and directed his shouts at the guard who had been at the door to the prisoners' tent.

Rebecca stood, hands on her hips, glaring after her son.

Martha rose to her feet. She stood behind Rebecca, still breathing in short gasps, and raised her hand to a tender cheek.

Rebecca turned to face her, eyes filling. "And you, child, you took the strike for me. I will never forget that."

Martha shook her head. "I could not let him kill you. I did it without thinking of anything other than that. You have been kind to me."

"Kill me? He would not kill me. I'm his mother. Even if I were not, he does not kill Jews unless they are traitors."

"I...I watched him kill a Jew. An old man who treated everyone with kindness and respect. He was not a traitor. His name was Levi." Martha's eyes spilled. "His only crime was in trying to protect me."

Rebecca's eyes widened. "He killed a Jew? He told me he does not kill Jews." She frowned and set her jaw. "I will have the truth of this from him." She turned and started toward Barabbas.

Martha grabbed Rebecca's arm, her heart pounding, her voice rising in timbre if not in volume. "No, no, mistress—Rebecca, you must not anger him again. Please, don't go over there now."

Barabbas had continued to berate the guard at the tent and had called other men to him. The men bound the guard and pulled him to a post. They pulled his cloak and tunic from his back, and Barabbas proceeded to use an ugly barbed scourge on the man, ripping the skin from his back as the man screamed in pain. The screams only seemed to spur Barabbas on, and he stopped only when his arm apparently grew too weary to wield the whip. The man by that time had passed out, his head hanging backwards and his mouth open. Blood flowed from the man's back in rivulets.

Martha ran to the edge of the camp and began to heave until nothing remained in her stomach but acid, and still it attempted to spew forth what no longer remained.

Rebecca rubbed her back until the vomiting ended. She gently wiped Martha's face with a wet rag and handed her a skin of cool water, but Martha's hands dangled limp at her side.

She hung her head, weakness making her knees wobble. "Sit...I need to sit."

Rebecca led her to a log and sat down by her.

Once the shaking stopped and her head cleared, Martha lifted her gaze to Rebecca's. "Is he a beast in man's clothing?" She remembered she spoke to the beast's mother. "Oh, I'm sorry, Rebecca, I...."

"Believe me, he did not use to be the man he is now. He was gentle when a child. A Roman soldier killed my husband, his father, right in front of him. That's when he began to change. I tried to turn him back, but I have failed." Rebecca dropped her head to her chest. "Maybe the love of a good woman could turn him back, but I have tried and cannot. My son is gone, replaced by a crazed animal."

Martha shook her head. It would take more than the love of a woman. It would take a miracle.

Rebecca stood. "We should get the wood. Sunset and the Sabbath are not far away."

Martha stood, her legs still shaking, and followed Rebecca. As they returned with firewood for the third time, the smell of stew cooking over the fire reminded her she hadn't eaten since breakfast, and breakfast hadn't stayed inside long enough to do her any good.

A growl emanated from her bowels, and Rebecca chuckled. "It won't be long now. Patience, child. It seems your stomach has settled."

Martha smiled a weak smile. "It seems. Perhaps I could eat a little when it's ready. It smells good."

"It does, but if we don't stack this woodpile higher, we will not have a fire tomorrow morning. Two more armloads. That should be enough." Rebecca wiped her hand across her forehead. "Then we'll need to take a donkey or mule to tow some big logs back."

"Did you do this alone before I came here?"

"Yes."

"Why is it that the camp commander's mother must do this?" Martha asked. "There are many other women here and strong men with nothing to do." She cast a glance at some men tossing sticks into a circle drawn in the dirt.

"I chose the work. I do not like to cook." Rebecca peered at Martha. "But perhaps you would rather cook?"

"I would rather remain at your side, Rebecca. The other women don't like me."

"They don't know you. When they get to know you, it will be better."

"Is one of them Barabbas's wife?"

"No. He has not taken a wife, although at one time he was betrothed. The woman who spoke to you by the fire, Nomah, was his betrothed."

"Why are they not betrothed still? Or married?"

"She wanted to, but Barabbas kept postponing their wedding. Her father asked him if he still wanted to marry her, and he said no. He divorced her, and there has been no other woman since then. At least, none that he wed." Rebecca clamped her jaw shut with a snap.

"Were the women that he didn't wed prostitutes, then?"

"Not until he was through with them."

"Were they Jewish women?"

"He says they were not." Rebecca turned her head away.

"Oh, no, you think that he will, he will...Rebecca, no. Please do not let him take me as his whore."

"What do you mean, 'he's gone'?" Julius stared at Cyril.

"I went into the room to see if Marcus wanted something to eat, and he and his gear were missing. I checked with the stable, and he left there on the horse he rode in on."

Julius lifted his hand to his forehead. "I can't believe he'd do this."

"You mean that he'd leave?"

"No, I mean that he would leave me with the care of Brutus." He laughed, but no humor sounded through the short bark.

Cyril smiled, but then his face lengthened with sorrow. "I thought he outgrew his irresponsibility. I wonder where he went this time."

"I don't know. And I have to report him. Sometimes the weight of duty is more unpleasant than one centurion would want to bear." Julius shook his head and turned toward the table where he composed letters and wrote reports. Not his favorite place. "Maybe he went back to Jerusalem to let Rufus know what happened."

"You could assume that. Then there would be no need to report him."

Footsteps interrupted the conversation.

The guard saluted. "Sir, Festus the physician wishes to speak to you."

Before Julius could respond, Festus walked in. "What in the name of Jupiter have you foisted on me, Centurion? That man is the most demanding and obnoxious soldier in the entire Roman Empire." The physician's raspy voice sounded from the entryway.

"Yes, I know, Festus. He's been a thorn in the side of many an officer."

"He wants to see the decanus who brought him in."

"I would like to see him, myself."

"What?"

"He's gone." Julius said. "He left this morning."

"Gone where? Back to his cohort?"

"I assume so. I'm not his centurion, and therefore he didn't ask my permission. Just tell Brutus that his decanus is no longer in Caesarea."

"I can tell him, but I do not think he will like the information."

Julius nodded. "You're probably right. I doubt the man has ever liked anything."

"He would accept this pronouncement from you. I don't think he will from me. He'll think I'm lying."

"I'll come with you. I want to ask him where Barabbas hides." Julius picked up his sword and helmet and turned to Cyril. "Tell Miriam I'll be back within the hour."

Cyril bowed his head. "Yes, sir."

Julius smiled to himself. Cyril, who had served Julius from the time they were small children, maintained the formal demeanor of a servant only in front of those not among their close friends.

They walked past the docks to the fortress housing the soldiers, a tall structure of rock, mortar, and logs with barracks lining the walls. Brutus was with other wounded and diseased soldiers in a large one-roomed structure across from the entrance to the fort. A breeze blew in from the west, lessening the usually strong odor of the city and of this fetid medical facility. The smell of decaying flesh and dying men depressed Julius, even more so now. These men were injured while under his command.

Julius removed his helmet and walked among the soldiers, stopping to say a word to each of the men. He went last to Brutus, knowing he would spend the most time there. Brutus lay in one corner. He gave orders for the others to be moved out of earshot.

He knelt by the cot and touched Brutus on the shoulder. The man twisted like an awakened snake and grabbed Julius's arm. When he saw who it was, he lay back on his cot and attempted a weak salute. "Centurion."

"Brutus."

"Where's Marcus?"

"He has gone. What do you want?" Julius gazed down on the soldier's pale skin and wondered if the man were as sick as he looked.

"Gone? Why?"

"He didn't tell me. I can only assume he went to try to find the rest of his regiment."

"I don't think so. He and I are the only ones who survived. He went down first. I was the last. I thought he was dead too, but they hauled both of us back to their camp."

"How did you escape?"

"Someone cut the ropes that bound us."

Julius felt his eyebrows rise. "Who?"

Brutus groaned through gritted teeth. "I don't know."

"Where was the camp?"

"I don't know. I was unconscious most of the time going to and leaving the camp."

"Surely you must remember something."

"Just that it was a large camp. I heard sheep."

"How many men were there?"

"The ones who attacked us, maybe fifty. Maybe more."

"How many were you?"

"Twenty-six." Brutus's eyes narrowed to slits and he spoke through gritted teeth. He began to shiver.

Julius wondered how long the man would stay conscious, and he hurried on. "What happened?"

"Th-three groups sp-spread out through c-canyon. Rockslides k-killed some."

Julius motioned to the physician. "Festus, Brutus needs blankets. He's shivering."

Was that gratitude he saw in Brutus's eyes? Impossible.

Festus brought blankets and felt the soldier's head. "He's fevering. You should come back later."

"I have just a few more questions. I'll be brief."

"You'll have to be. He's fading." Festus stood, hands on hips.

Julius nodded and turned back to Brutus. "What was it you wanted from Marcus?"

Brutus's teeth chattered and he stammered. "To tell him thank you. He saved my life. Didn't have to. Sorry I didn't give him respect." Brutus clutched Julius's arm. "Tell him."

"Tell him yourself, soldier. You won't die today. I'll be back to learn more from you later. For now, you need to sleep."

"Yes, sir."

Julius stood. Could it be the man might change from his perpetually angry and disrespectful attitude?

Festus bent over Brutus.

"Leave me alone, physician. Didn't you hear the centurion order me to sleep?" A trace of a growl accompanied Brutus's faint remonstration.

Julius shook his head as he strode away.

Chapter 6

Martha constantly shadowed Rebecca. Wherever Rebecca went, even to relieve herself, Martha followed. She didn't know whom she feared worse, the other women or the men—especially Barabbas. Her stomach felt tight all the time, and her gaze darted here and there, seeking any form of danger. Visions of torture and death filled her dreams, and she woke more than once panting as she tried to escape the night terrors pursuing her subconscious. It didn't help that Barabbas's gaze followed her so much of the time.

She lived in daily dread that someone would discover she was not the Hebrew Martha but the Egyptian Meskhanet. Three months in the camp had not diminished the fear. Not even Rebecca would protect her if they uncovered her secret identity. She must plan her escape from this camp, but she hoped to leave in such a way that blame would not fall on Rebecca. When she saw Barabbas strike his own mother, she knew the poor woman's life would be in danger if she were blamed for the escape.

The women went in turns to the nearest village for needed supplies and food to supplement the mutton and cheese. Perhaps when it came time for Rebecca to go Martha could stay behind, then she would make her escape while Rebecca was too far away to be blamed. Barabbas would blame someone though, anyone except himself. She shuddered.

"What ails you, child? Is the cloak not enough to keep you warm?" Rebecca glanced at her. "I could get a blanket for you."

"No, Rebecca, I'm warm enough. What do you wish me to do this day?"

"This day we will go to Sebasta for supplies."

No! Not this day. I am not ready. Still—she might not have another chance for weeks. "Shall I go with you, or do you wish me to stay and repair the men's clothing?" Rebecca's most hated chore, other than the cooking that she had exchanged for wood gathering.

She would probably welcome the opportunity to do something other than sew.

Rebecca hesitated. "If I leave you here, someone else must assume charge over you. Barabbas laid that responsibility on me, and he would not be happy if I left you with no one watching you." She cast a sideways glance at Martha and lowered her voice. "And you and I both know you would love to flee."

Martha winced. Was she so obvious? "How could I run away if everyone, even Barabbas, could see me at all times?"

"Who should I give charge over you? My son? You might not remain a virgin after I leave. No, I think you should stay with me."

Martha didn't know if she felt relief or angst at Rebecca's pronouncement. A little of both, she guessed. Any relief was short lived when Barabbas strode up to them. Martha's muscles tightened to a lyre string's tension.

"Martha will remain in camp while you go to Sebasta."

Rebecca scowled. "And will this virgin remain so while I am absent?"

Barabbas flushed. "That is none of your concern, woman."

"It is the concern of every Jew that a virgin remain so until her wedding day. Martha is not even betrothed. It would be a sin to deprive her husband of that gift."

Breathe, Martha reminded herself. She must not faint again.

Barabbas growled. "Be gone. Do not try my patience again, I warn you."

Rebecca's eyes misted. "Where has my son gone? The one I nursed, the one whose hurts I comforted? I long to see him again."

Barabbas shifted and flushed again. "Very well, Mother. I will respect her maidenhood. Just go and return in good order." He started to turn away, then engaged Rebecca's gaze again. "Ask while you are there if anyone has seen Romans in the area."

Rebecca nodded. As Barabbas walked away, she patted Martha's arm. "You should be safe, child."

Martha nodded, not trusting her voice.

Rebecca pulled her close. "Go with God, child," she whispered, tears in her eyes.

She knows. Tears filled Martha's own eyes and rolled down her cheeks. "And you also. Thank you, Mother."

Rebecca climbed aboard a wagon and clucked to the mules, glancing back at Martha one time. Martha waved and felt a tug on her heart. She would miss the old woman.

She turned to the pile of cloaks needing their rips and tears mended and sighed. Not her favorite task, either, but her hands were not gnarled and cracked with age like Rebecca's. She would give this last gift to the woman who had been her friend.

It took her most of the morning to complete the mending. She began the chore of gathering wood, keeping one eye on Barabbas. When they served the midday meal, she gorged herself with as much as she could force into her stomach. "The stew is so wonderful, Bellah. What did you spice it with?"

Bellah's look of suspicion changed to surprised pride. "Just a little salt and mint leaves. Here, have some more."

At last. Barabbas mounted his horse to lead a troop out of camp. He rode up to Nomah and spoke to her, staring hard at Martha. Nomah nodded and walked in her direction.

Martha dropped the load of wood on the pile and went for a donkey.

"What are you doing, slave?" Nomah grabbed Martha's arm and jerked her around to face her.

"I am gathering wood, mistress. We need the larger logs I cannot carry in my arms. Do you wish to accompany me?" She bowed her head in submission.

"I shall." Nomah mounted the donkey, a jenny with a sweet disposition. "Lead, slave."

Martha felt her heart sink. Now what could she do? Without changing her expression, she led the way into the woods and stopped by a dead snag. She stomped smaller branches off and wrapped the rope around the trunk.

"Mistress, do you mind walking now? The donkey will need all her strength to pull this one."

Nomah huffed and dismounted the animal.

Martha picked up the smaller branches to carry, looping the rope over her arm. Nomah picked up a few branches. The two women made their way in silence back to the camp.

Twice more they made their way to the woods and returned, still in silence.

"I have better things to do than follow you. But do not think I will not be watching." Nomah punctuated her warning with a fierce scowl.

Martha nodded. "As you wish." She hoped her voice conveyed respect rather than the excitement she felt. One more time she took the donkey out for a load and returned, hesitating for some time outside the camp before she reentered with the donkey following.

It happened as she thought. Nomah engaged herself in flirtation with a guard, casting only one negligent glance in her direction.

Her heart drumming so that she thought every man and woman in camp could hear, she again led the donkey into the woods.

Marcus peered between the branches, trying to locate the source of the sounds he had heard. When he saw the woman riding the donkey, he relaxed. One of the women from the sheep camp out after wood again, he supposed. Still, she rode toward Caesarea. Maybe after supplies instead, but why so late in the day? He shrugged and retreated farther into the cave.

He scratched his lengthening beard. How did the Hebrews stand the constant itching? Not only the beard, but this rough tunic. Next time he planned to take someone's clothing, he should plan to steal from someone wealthy enough to wear softer garments. The cloak that hung to his ankles tripped him more than once.

One more week should do it.

It must have been sheer luck that he'd found this cave so close to the camp. He'd pulled brush against the already indistinct opening, and he'd built his fire several cubits back from the entrance. Fingers of stone reached up as others reached down in this cave. Massive columns stood here and there, and fantastic toothy shapes of slippery rock adorned the walls and layered the floors.

He didn't know how far down or back it went. It was so large it could house a regiment. Several chambers were separated by holes sometimes large enough to walk through, and some so small only a mouse could crawl through. Fresh water ran through one chamber of the cave, flowing out of one large aperture and tumbling over and around huge rounded boulders before disappearing into another. Two small round holes in the high ceiling provided just enough light during the day to exercise by.

Marcus ventured out of his hiding place at night only long enough to hunt and allow the horse to graze. The rabbits were plentiful, and once he'd brought down a deer. He hadn't starved, but he'd lost weight. During the day, he practiced with his sword and bow and exercised.

Still, with time on his hands, boredom led him to explore the chambers. He found bones tucked into niches in the wall in one room and another opening into the cave there. The smell of death and spices lingered in the air. None of them looked recent, but it could be from Barabbas's camp. He peered with caution out the doorway, but no signs of life showed other than small birds chirping from the trees and hunting seeds and insects on the ground.

Another smaller room seemed to be the ancient lair of some predator. More bones, but smaller—probably rabbits and rodents.

Still another had charred wood remains from long-ago fires. More bones and a broken and blackened cooking pot attested to meals taken in this chamber. He wished the cave could tell him the stories of past residents. Could this be the cave where David cut a piece from Saul's cloak?

The week passed, and Marcus ventured out, leaving his sword and bow secreted in the cave, but strapped his knife to his waist under the tunic. A cloak hid his hair. He greased his beard with drippings from the venison, ground dirt under his fingernails, another dab of dirt on his forehead. A month without bathing and he could scarcely stand his own odor. The stick he'd practiced with helped him limp his way to Barabbas's camp.

He walked with apparent difficulty to the fire, earning stares from the people gathered around it. "Unghh," he grunted, pointing at the bread cooking on a rock in the fire. "Unghh?" He pointed at his mouth.

One of the women, yellowing bruises and a cut on her sullen face, handed him a loaf of bread. He grabbed it and ate it like an animal, eyes rolling as he looked at the gathering crowd.

Several people spoke, but he ignored them and reached his hand out again, begging for more food. One of the men grabbed his arm and said something to him, raising one hand. Marcus ducked and pulled back, quaking in what he hoped looked like abject terror.

An older woman said something to the man. The man growled a reply and shoved Marcus to the ground. He covered his head as though expecting blows. An argument ensued between the old woman and the man. No others spoke.

The argument ended with the woman walking away, but the man made no more move to harm him. He stood there with fists clenched, staring after the old woman. He turned and glared at the rest of the group, and the people quickly moved away. He pushed Marcus with his foot and demanded something.

Marcus pointed to his ears. "Unghh." The man pointed at him, then at the woodpile. Marcus nodded eagerly, stood, and used the stick to limp into the forest. He made several trips, carrying a load of wood under one arm. The apparent leader of the camp commanded the bruised woman, and she gave him more food—a piece of cheese, some grapes, and some watered wine.

The old woman returned, motioning him to follow her. She led him to a small wadi, pointed to him, then pointed to the water tugging on his cloak. Marcus made his eyes wide and shook his head. The woman scowled and tugged at his garment again, pulling the fabric away from his arm. She pointed at the stream, then she crossed her arms and scowled.

Marcus walked with many hesitations to the water's edge. He dropped his cloak there, but limped into the running water with his tunic on. The woman nodded and smiled, and then she strode back toward the camp. Marcus sank into the cool water with a smile.

The camp leader must be Barabbas. And would a man accept argument from any woman but his mother? Or a wife, but this woman had to be his mother, sort of a second in command.

As soon as he was certain and the right opportunity presented itself, he would act. Barabbas would never murder innocents again, and the death of Meskhanet would be avenged. If Marcus died in the prosecution or a result of the act, that would be even better. He had lost the men he commanded, the woman he loved, and Tsal. What was there left to live for?

Chapter 7

Meskhanet thought if she followed paths going west she would eventually reach the coast of the Great Sea. As long as the clouds didn't hide the stars, she could tell which direction she went. She couldn't stop, or they might catch her, but it was so dark. Could the donkey see well enough to keep them from falling over a cliff while they made their way over the steep and rocky paths?

The only thing she would have to do when she made it to the coast was find out which way, north or south, to go to Caesarea. Julius, Miriam, Cyril, and Quinta had gone there right after their wedding. If Loukas and the rest of his household lived, they probably searched for Levi and her for a while, but then they would have continued to Caesarea. Everyone she cared for would be there. If they were still alive. If their Yahweh had saved them. Tears blinded her, and a strangled sob escaped her tight throat.

The path became a steep decline, and she dismounted. She heard the cataract, but couldn't see it. The stone path grew slippery with moisture, and the donkey balked, pulling back against the rope. Meskhanet hesitated. Now what should she do? If she stopped, Barabbas could find her. If she went forward, she could slide into a waterfall.

That left only one option—climb the hill to her left. Get off this path until daylight could guide her. Backing up carefully, she edged her way to the fork she had just passed. The donkey seemed happier with that choice too. It went the wrong direction—south—but she could retrace her steps without too much difficulty. She led the donkey over some rocks off the path and hid the best she could behind a rock outcropping.

Voices woke her the next morning. Barabbas's voice overrode the others, louder and more belligerent. She leapt up to hold the donkey's muzzle and prayed the Jews' God would prevent the men from finding her. If she was discovered…no, she didn't want to think about how it would go for her if they saw her. She shivered.

A loud yell that turned into a scream of terror, man and horse, and she knew one of the men had made the slip she almost made last night. She hoped it had been Barabbas. But no, there was his voice again.

The donkey pawed the ground, wanting to call to the mules and horses she knew, but Meskhanet held her tight. "Sh, sweet jenny, we mustn't be found," she whispered. "Sh, sh."

"The donkey's tracks were slipping, you could see it. She and the jenny must have gone into the waterfall, just as Joash did."

That voice sounded loud and clear. *They must be close.* She shook so that the poor donkey's nose quivered under her hand.

"Maybe." That was Barabbas, his growl in place. "But maybe she followed this one. The other path is impassible until the rains stop. We will follow this path."

Their voices faded into the distance, and Meskhanet peeked from behind her outcropping. No one in sight. Still holding the jenny's nose, she followed the path back to the fork. She would have to find another way to Caesarea. If only she knew the country.

And if only she had something to eat. The full stomach of yesterday rumbled in hungry protest. She had been a server, not a hunter or gatherer, and she had no knowledge of what plants would be good to eat. No knife, no spear. All she had was the donkey. Hm—and the donkey's rope. Maybe she could snare something to eat. *Hah. If I only knew how to make a snare.*

A sharp stick, maybe. A sharp rock, if she could throw it straight. Or hope for a slow rabbit.

She found a faint trail leading west again. No recent footprints or hoof prints. She led the jenny down the path to a hidden place, then pulled a branch from a tree and went back to obliterate her trail, scattered sand, gravel, and weeds across the branch's scratchings. She might not know how to snare a rabbit, but she knew enough to hide traces of her passage.

She found a small spring and eagerly bent down to drink from the stream of water flowing out from between the rocks. The donkey dropped her head next to Meskhanet and snorted. The jenny thrust her mouth into the pond below the spring outlet and slurped the water up in eager gulps.

A stick snapped. Meskhanet lifted her head. *What was that?* The sound was not repeated, but her stomach tightened into a knot. She tied the donkey to a tree off the trail. The jenny stared forward along the path, both long ears pressed forward.

Meskhanet took off her sandals and crept toward the sound, dodging from one tree to the next, taking care not to snap a twig or mash a leaf. There—a flash of blue fabric! She pressed forward, still frightened but even more curious. Whoever it was acted as terrified as she.

There—a small campfire under a huge oak tree. But no one near it. A shriek rent the air, and the hair on the back of her head rose. She whirled.

"Meskhanet! Oh, Meskhanet, we thought you were dead." A figure ran out from behind a tree, arms outstretched, sobbing her name.

Joanna was scarcely recognizable. A red scar swept from temple to cheek to chin, and her hair—her beautiful long and mostly black hair—was now white, short, and sparse. Hollows outlined her cheekbones, and her eyes were red and watery.

When she threw her arms around Joanna, Meskhanet felt bones and very little flesh. "I thought you were dead, too. Barabbas took me captive after he...he killed Levi. Is...is Loukas...."

"Yes, he is alive, but only by the grace of the One God. The rest are gone or dead. The angel of death drew close to Loukas three times, once from his wounds and twice from fever. Come, come—he will be so happy to see you."

Meskhanet followed Joanna to a shelter made in a tight circle of cypress trees. Branches had been woven together to form a hut, and unless Joanna had led her there, Meskhanet would not have found it. She ducked her head to enter. Loukas lay on a pile of straw, his yellow skin drawn over his skull. Thin hands plucked at the blanket. His eyes followed a fly buzzing in the tent, but he didn't move his head.

"They must have thought he was dead. When they attacked, an arrow pierced his neck. I know he does not look well, but I assure you he is improving." Joanna's voice from behind her sounded more wishful than certain.

Meskhanet knelt at his side. Tears slid down her cheeks. He had been so strong, and now...

"Loukas," she murmured. "Loukas?"

His eyes turned toward hers. "Meskhanet? Is it truly Meskhanet?" His voice sounded raspy and weak. "Did you bring food?"

Marcus grinned. It felt so good to be clean again. He limped out of the water, just in case anyone was watching, and grabbed his cloak, then returned to the water and let the water run over the dark brown robe.

When he struggled back out of the water with the heavy garment, he grabbed the crutch and made his way to a snag where he hung the cloak. He sat on a nearby log and shivered in his wet tunic, even though the day had been warm. However, it was now cooling rapidly as the sun set.

He heard her steps behind him, but didn't react. He knew it was a woman or perhaps a child. But, since he pretended to be deaf, of course he wasn't supposed to hear it. He jumped when she touched his shoulder. The old woman had returned, bringing him a dried apple and some cheese.

He smiled broadly at her and grunted his thanks. She sat down beside him and began speaking to him.

Ah, Adonai, what a fool I was to pass on the chance to learn Aramaic. And then he remembered. He wasn't on speaking terms with God anymore. He frowned. Habits surely died hard.

The old woman tapped his arm and motioned to him to follow her. He grabbed his still-damp cloak and followed her back into the camp. She tugged his sleeve and pointed at a tent.

The man Marcus thought to be Barabbas strode up to them with what sounded like angry cursing. The woman said nothing back, but she scowled and snorted.

She tapped Marcus on the arm and pointed toward the fire. She walked to the edge of the flames and made motions of spreading something on the ground. He got the idea. He would sleep by the fire rather than in the men's tent. It might not be too long, though, until Barabbas trusted him enough to let him sleep there. And then….

He drifted off to sleep. The woman he had seen on the donkey wandered across his dream landscape of rocks and rivers and trees. From behind a tree, she waved to him and called "Come to me, Marcus. I need your help."

The dream jumbled into a sword fight with Barabbas, then back to the woman, who again called to him. Her face was hidden in shadows, but her voice sounded so familiar. The sword fight with Barabbas continued, but in a small clearing with a circle of cypress trees that hid a hut.

She called again, her voice urgent, and Marcus awoke with a start. He scratched his head.

The stars overhead indicated the night watches were only half gone. He yawned and pulled the cloak closer around his shoulders, but sleep would not return. His mind replayed the dream over and over, and his stomach felt tight.

He sighed. *All right, Adonai. I'm listening.*

Go retrieve your weapons and food. They need your help.

Go where, Adonai? Marcus listened, but the Voice did not return.

The sense of urgency increased. Marcus rose to his feet, tucked the crutch under his arm, and put on his still-damp cloak. He limped with the crutch toward the latrine. After he relieved himself he hobbled until he was out of sight of the sheep camp, then he trotted all the way back to the cave. Placing the crutch just inside the entrance, he lit a torch waiting in the same area. He strode to the chamber where he'd hidden the weapons and donned them under his cloak.

I don't know where to go, Adonai. I'll gather up weapons and food, but then what? He put out the torch, and after his eyes adjusted to the dark he crept back outside. He heard a soft whicker. To his surprise, the gelding he'd turned loose the day before walked toward him, ears pricked forward. Marcus chuckled and dug a dried apple from his pouch.

As soon as Marcus mounted, the gelding turned and trotted westward, ears pointed toward a call only he could hear. The horse stopped near a clearing that looked familiar to Marcus. He turned his head toward a rustling sound and saw a woman standing near a group of cypress.

"Sir?" She stepped forward. "I beg you, if you have any food to spare, would you mind sharing it? My husband and I don't eat a lot."

Marcus's jaw dropped. He dismounted. The woman moved a step back, and he realized with the long hair, beard, and strange clothing she wouldn't recognize him. "Joanna? It's me, Marcus."

Joanna gasped and ran forward, tears running down her face. "Oh, Marcus! I hope you can help us. We are so hungry. Meskhanet gave us her donkey, but we ate it and now there's nothing left."

Marcus turned back to the horse where he'd left his pouches and skins of water. "Here, you can have what I have. There's some dried meat, apples, salt, olive oil, and flour. There's even a little leavening, see? Where is Meskhanet?" His heart drummed a little faster.

Joanna shook her head, a bite of one of the apples filling her mouth, and motioned Marcus to follow her. He stepped into the dark hut. The smell of illness nearly overwhelmed him.

"Loukas, we are saved. See? Marcus is here. He brought food."

Loukas lay on a pallet with stained sheets. He rolled his head toward Marcus. "You have changed, my friend." He started to laugh, but a cough rattled his entire body. "I know you will say I have, too." He lifted himself to his elbow and extended a shaky hand to Marcus.

"What happened?"

"We were attacked. Everyone except Joanna and I were killed, and I'm sure they thought we also were dead. An arrow through my neck must have looked fatal. And Joanna…" He turned his gaze to his wife, and his eyes watered. "Joanna was raped repeatedly by Barabbas and his men. Then he cut her face and threw her against a tree, saying that no one would want this Greek whore ever again. But they didn't know the strength of my wife."

Joanna had been unpacking the food, and she began making unleavened bread with flour, oil, bread, salt, and water.

"I could hear everything," Loukas said. "But I couldn't move. The arrow traveled through the edge of my neck and into the edge of the wagon. When she woke, she came to me. She feared I was dead, but by the grace of the One God, the arrow had missed my arteries. She found a knife and cut the back of the arrow off. Working the other end out of my neck was a little painful."

Joanna chuckled. "A little?" She put the bread onto a flat rock set into the center of the fire.

Loukas sighed. "I'm weary, my friend. I am improving, but my body is still weak."

"One small question, and I'll let you rest. If I may. I thought Joanna said Meskhanet is here, but I don't see her."

"She left yesterday to look for help. I thought she guided you here. I guess not?" Loukas's face fell, and his eyes widened.

Joanna's eyes filled. "She didn't bring you? Then how did you find us? And where is she?"

CHAPTER 8

Meskhanet stumbled yet again on the steep slope, catching herself with a frightened gasp. Rain fell in a steady drizzle, and the moss covered rocky path had grown slippery. But she couldn't stop. Loukas had improved in the week while they ate the donkey, but now none remained.

Poor little jenny, she didn't deserve to become stew after her faithful service, but what else could they do? There hadn't been a lot of meat on the small animal, but the addition of meat to his diet had rallied Loukas.

Now she must reach Caesarea soon or risk the lives of both Loukas and Joanna. She knew Julius would help.

"O God of Loukas, please, I need to find help for them. Loukas would improve so much faster in a warm, dry building."

If only this path did not follow a cliff. She longed for flat ground where she could travel more than a few cubits in an hour. She didn't know which she feared worse, rain-loosened boulders falling from above or slipping over an edge to plunge to the rocks below. There was something about that gaping canyon below that sought to pull her down.

A skitter of rocks behind her sent her scurrying with less caution ahead, and she found herself at a dead end. A huge landslide blocked the path ahead. She turned, but a growing roar gave warning that the same thing was occurring behind her.

She sat down at the uphill side of the pathway and gave way to the frightened sobs she'd pent up for the past day.

The rain stopped. A hole in the clouds sent a stream of sunshine that warmed her, and Meskhanet lifted her head. The air she breathed held the sweetness that only a cleansing rain could bring. If this were to be her last day on this earth, she would at least appreciate these last smells and sights.

Above her head, deep shadows and glistening wet rocks made a stark contrast to the dull landscape shaded by thick clouds. Below the path, a few determined oaks pressed upward, scraggly imitations of their more privileged sister trees in the valley. Meskhanet looked upward again and back downward.

She feared falling, but to get out she'd have to climb. It was the only possibility. Forward and back, the landslides covered the slopes with loose rock and mud. From the edge of the path, she could see a drop of about fifteen cubits before the rocky slope moderated into a valley and stream. To remain where she was meant starvation and death. Tomorrow, then, she would climb as soon as the rocks above were dry.

She should pray to the Hebrew God since she walked in His land. She bowed low, face to the ground.

"O God of the Jews, mighty and powerful. I have nothing to offer You other than myself. Therefore, this I promise: I will serve you all my days if You will help me go forth in safety from this place to find help for Loukas and Joanna. If You wish, at the end of my quest, I will gladly sacrifice my life to You. I know I am not a worthy sacrifice, but I am poor and a lowly creature with nothing better to offer. Please accept me, O God of the Jews."

A soft peace settled on her, a sense of being loved—no, cherished. Warmth surrounded her, pulsating like a steady heartbeat. It was as though she nestled in her father or mother's lap, a feeling she had not had since a small child. Tears of joy rolled out of her eyes and splashed on the gravel beneath her head.

She didn't know how long she remained, eyes shut, face down, but when she opened her eyes, night had fallen. She pulled her cloak around her and slept as she hadn't slept in weeks, unafraid. That had not happened since Barabbas killed Levi.

She awoke when the sun rose. She heard voices. They weren't speaking Aramaic. It sounded like it might be Latin, a language she didn't understand. Roman soldiers? Where were they? She could see nothing, but the sounds came from above.

A face appeared above her. The man turned and shouted to his comrades, and a dozen faces peeked over the edge.

One of them shouted to her in badly accented Aramaic. "Woman— are you alive?"

She giggled. She stood and looked up at the soldiers. Was she alive? "Yes. Are you?"

The soldier laughed and said something to the other soldiers who also chuckled. "How long have you been trapped there?"

"Since yesterday."

"Do you have the strength to climb? Or should I send a soldier down to help you?"

"I have the strength, but I would appreciate a rope to keep me from falling."

The man said something to one of the others, and soon a rope trailed down the rocks. It landed about five feet above her. She climbed to a rock shelf close to the rope and tied it around her waist.

"O God of the Jews, please guide me up this slope. And please inspire these soldiers to be kind, not lusty." She began to climb again, feeling the security of the rope held taut above her.

When she stood at the top of the slope, she brushed the dirt and stickers from her cloak. "I give you thanks, sirs."

"Why were you on that trail in the rain, woman, and why alone?" The soldier who spoke Aramaic stood too close for her comfort.

She backed away a step. "I have friends who are starving and ill. I went for help."

"The names of your friends?"

"Loukas the physician of Jericho and his wife."

"Loukas the physician? Is he a friend of Centurion Julius of Caesarea?"

"Yes. You know Julius?"

"I know him. I am Centurion Domitius of Jerusalem."

Meskhanet stepped forward and grasped his sleeve. "Loukas is my master. Please, would you help him and his wife? I realize you must be here on a mission, but it would not take long just to leave him a little food, or perhaps take him to another physician who could help them. He and his wife are near starvation. I gave them my donkey for food and nursed them for a week. They are stronger now, but not strong enough to walk for help. Please?" Her words tumbled out in what she knew must sound like babbling.

Domitius scowled, but not fiercely. More as though he were thinking.

Please, God of the Jews.

"We are on patrol, but I can send a wagon and a couple of soldiers to help you. Have you seen any other soldiers?"

"Yes, but not what you want, I'm sure. When Loukas and Joanna were injured, I was taken captive by a band of brigands led by an evil man called Barabbas. Two or three weeks later, I saw my captors bring in two soldiers over the backs of horses. The soldiers were badly injured, I think. I was told they escaped, but I don't know where they went. I also escaped about a week ago. I found my master and his wife by chance while running from my captors."

"In return for helping your friends, would you show us where this band of brigands lives?"

"How many men do you have with you? These are maybe fifty or sixty vicious and strong men, and they would defend their home. I want them to be captured, but there is one in the camp who befriended me. She is the mother of Barabbas, but she is kind. I would not want her hurt."

"She is but a woman. We don't make war on women. However, if she gets in the way, I cannot guarantee she will live."

Meskhanet paused. Loukas and Joanna would live, but Rebecca might die. She had no doubt the old woman who befriended her would defend her son to the death. *God of the Jews, what should I do?* She sighed. She must save Loukas and Joanna.

"I agree," she said with a heavy heart.

Marcus gritted his teeth. Now that he knew Meskhanet was alive, he wanted with every fiber of his being to go find her. His duty was to capture or kill Barabbas. He would have to go back to the camp.

Meskhanet had left two days ago for Caesarea, and even though she travelled in the rain over a slow path, she still should have reached Caesarea by now. She would be safe, and she would be bringing back help for Loukas and Joanna. Just in case help were longer in coming, he'd left them with a deer.

As he rode back to his cave, he killed a rabbit. He'd have to have a reason to have left Barabbas's camp and returned. The rabbit might even put him in better favor with Barabbas.

Two hours later, he limped back into the brigand's camp carrying the skinned carcass in his free hand. He walked to the man he was sure was Barabbas, grinned, and handed it to him. "Ungh."

Barabbas's eyebrows rose as he took the rabbit and made a comment.

Foreign language or not, Marcus could understand sarcasm. Still he nodded and grinned.

Barabbas laughed and clapped Marcus on the shoulder. He handed his bow to Marcus and led him to the edge of the camp. He pointed to a tree and handed Marcus an arrow.

Hm, a test. Marcus lifted the bow and the arrow. He stared for a few moments at the weapons, fitted the arrow to the bow and clumsily dropped the arrow. Barabbas took the bow, picked up the arrow, and demonstrated how to stand and how to hold them. He handed them back.

Marcus lifted the bow again with the arrow. He acted as though he didn't have the strength to pull it back even by half, and he let the arrow fly. It not only fell short, but far to the left. Barabbas laughed again. He lifted Marcus's arm to feel the muscle, and Marcus let his muscle go slack. The man must not learn his strength. Barabbas pointed at the weapons and tree and handed him more arrows. When Barabbas strode back to the camp, Marcus fought the urge to sink an arrow into the man's back.

A week ago, Marcus probably would have given in to the desire to kill, but since he found out Meskhanet was alive the urge was no longer irresistible. He would instead attempt to capture the leader of this band of murderers and take him back to Jerusalem. How, he didn't know.

Marcus made a show of practicing, gradually improving aim and distance, regathering the arrows, and going again. Would Barabbas notice that the archery did not produce blisters? He remembered the first few weeks of his real initiation into use of the bow and arrow. The blisters rose, broke, and bled. Still Julius's father had pressed him to continue and didn't sympathize. Marcus had thought when he went whining to his parents he would no longer have to continue, but no. Senator Decimus Varitor had sent him back the following day to rejoin Julius in training. The memories brought a smile to Marcus's lips. He hoped his father would be proud of his second son when he brought Barabbas back. Or *if*.

He hobbled back to the campfire. He had scraped the callus on his finger so that it bled before he handed the bow back to Barabbas. Barabbas glanced at his hand and nodded satisfaction.

That night, Marcus slept in the tent of men. He allowed the snoring Barabbas to live. This time.

The next morning after he had eaten, Marcus approached Barabbas and pointed to the bow slung over the man's shoulder. Barabbas chuckled and handed him the weapons.

As Marcus limped with his crutch to the practice area he heard Barabbas talking with some other men, and again Marcus cursed the day he had refused lessons in Aramaic. Instead, he had chosen to go watch some Egyptian dancing girls. Had he known one certain Egyptian slave girl would capture his heart, he would have made certain he spoke a language she understood. He knew she spoke Aramaic and supposed she also spoke Greek, but he didn't know. They had never spoken.

A fact he hoped to rectify in the near future.

If he lived through this.

Maybe twenty of the men, including Barabbas, mounted donkeys or horses and rode away. Hunting? Thieving? Killing? He wished he knew.

It was late afternoon when the men returned, two dead oxen slung between four of the horses. A cheer rose up in the camp, and some of the women began to dig a pit. He walked to the women and made signs to indicate he would help dig. His mouth began to water at the thought of tomorrow's feast.

He grinned, and Barabbas's mother smiled back. Guilt smacked him when he thought about the reason for his grin—that her son would live free for not many more days.

He could smell the oxen roasting when he rose the next morning, and his stomach rumbled. Barabbas walked up to him, handed him the bow, and sent him out to practice again. This time, he would hit the tree. Perhaps the next hunting trip would have him along beside the brigand.

The shepherds had begun taking out their sheep when a cry sounded from the edge of the clearing. A woman ran toward Barabbas screaming. Men in Roman uniforms burst from the woods shouting, swords raised. The shepherds and huntsmen alike grabbed swords, spears, even poles and clubs.

Marcus stood, bow in hand, when a soldier rode toward him with his spear aimed at his unprotected chest. What a time to be without his armor! He threw down the bow and stood with empty hands stretched in front of himself. The soldier raised the spear, clearly intending to end his life. With a curse, Marcus threw himself aside.

"Stand off, soldier," he shouted in Latin as the spear pierced the edge of his sleeve.

The soldier whirled, drew his sword, and raised it to strike.

"Are you deaf, soldier? I am a Roman a decanus in Rome's army. And unarmed."

The man stopped, spit, and stared at Marcus with narrowed eyes. "Then you are a traitor. You are worse than they."

Chapter 9

Two soldiers and a wagon. It wasn't much, but Meskhanet was happy for the help. With Barabbas captured, she didn't feel so frightened of traveling. And with the wagon they could take Loukas to Caesarea.

It seemed like such a ridiculously short journey. One short day's travel and they were there. Why had it been so hard when she tried to go alone? Ah, yes, not knowing the way over the hill and to Caesarea. Too many wrong paths tried. And landslides.

They approached the open gate and went through unchallenged. It didn't take long to find Julius's house—this was a Roman city, and Julius was the lead centurion.

Loukas's back seemed straighter. Meskhanet ran to the house with only a cursory glance at the beauty of the courtyard.

Cyril stepped out the open doorway and grasped her arms. "Meskhanet! We thought you were dead." He pulled her by the hand into the house. "Quinta—come see who's here!"

Quinta came through the doorway and gave a small shriek as she ran to embrace her friend. Miriam followed her carrying a small bundle. Her smile of greeting was just as enthused, but she didn't run.

Meskhanet turned to her. "This is the new babe, isn't it? A son or a daughter?"

Miriam beamed. "A daughter. Is she not beautiful? We named her Milah." She pulled the soft blanket away from the sleeping infant's face and handed her to Meskhanet. The baby pursed her lips and stretched, then relaxed back into unperturbed sleep.

"Quinta, we have another surprise."

Quinta turned toward Cyril's voice and burst into tears as Loukas and Joanna walked in, Loukas clinging to Joanna's arm. She rushed to them and threw her arms around both, followed by a cry of dismay when Loukas fell to the floor. "Loukas—you are ill? You are so thin."

"Improving, my fervent daughter. I missed you too." Loukas laughed and held his hands up to Quinta and Cyril.

They lifted him to his feet and chattered like squirrels as they guided him through a doorway into a bedroom. Meskhanet followed them, staring at all the beauty around her. A polished cedar table stood beside the matched waist-high bed. Carved pomegranates and birds on vines wound around the posts and the edges of the bed and table. Ornate embroidered curtains hung from the ceiling and draped across the doors.

An opening through the ceiling allowed light into the hallway outside her room, and ivy and bougainvillea trailed vines down from the parapet around the opening. She could see on one side the edge of a long board visible in the floor below the parapet and a rope. What was that?

Cyril looked up at the women gathered around. "Would you women leave us for a few minutes? I'll help Loukas bathe and change into a clean tunic. Quinta, please send Miklos in with hot water." He pulled a cord releasing the curtain to cover the door.

He pulled the curtain back an hour later. Meskhanet peered in at the sleeping Loukas and her heart lurched. Cyril had not only bathed him but also trimmed his hair and beard to the short, neat style he'd worn before being injured. Except for his thin frame and face, he looked like the man she'd fallen in love with. Once more, her heart ached with longing for the man who would only ever love Joanna.

She would remain content just serving him.

Julius burst into the house and ran to Joanna and Meskhanet, hugging them both at the same time. "You *are* here. Miklos said my lost friends were here. Is Loukas here too? What about Marcus? Is he the one who found you and brought you to us?"

Joanna took his arm and pulled him to the bedroom door. "The robbers who attacked us almost killed both of us. I recovered faster. Loukas is much better, but it will be a few weeks before he is himself, I fear. And no, Marcus isn't here. He came to us one day and left food. He said then he had to go back to Barabbas's camp." She chuckled. "He looked so different we didn't know him. He had a scraggly beard—bright red and curly, if you can imagine—and long hair."

"Barabbas's camp? Why did he go there?" Julius asked.

"He didn't say. But he dressed like a Jew, and he looked like a Jew maybe from Galilee with his red beard."

Miriam entered the room with the baby and walked to Julius, wrapping her free arm around his waist.

"How did he find you, Joanna?" Julius turned to Miriam and kissed her hair, then he lifted Milah from her arms and kissed her head too.

Joanna lifted her hand to brush the infant's fingers. "Marcus said God told him to come to us, and then God led his horse."

"God led his horse? Huh—interesting. If he's in Barabbas's camp, he could be in danger. Maybe I'd better send a century after him."

Meskhanet cleared her throat. "If Marcus was in Barabbas's camp, I don't think he's there anymore. The two soldiers who came here with us could tell you more, but they captured all the men who were there. Or killed them."

"Did you see Marcus?"

"I don't remember seeing a man with a red beard. But I can't believe they would allow a Roman in their midst, other than as a prisoner."

He turned to Cyril. "Would you send Miklos after the two soldiers? I need to ask them a question or two."

"No need. They are in the kitchen having some of Quinta's honey cakes. I'll get them." Cyril left his place on the window seat and walked toward the kitchen. He reappeared with the two soldiers in tow, one tall and one short.

The soldiers came to attention when Julius stood.

"Relax, soldiers. Were you among the ones who took Barabbas captive?"

"Yes, sir."

"Did you see a Roman soldier anywhere around?"

The two exchanged glances.

"Not exactly, sir." The short one seemed to be the spokesman. "One man in the camp said he was a Roman. Scruffy looking. He had a red beard."

"Where is he?"

"He's walking to Jerusalem with the rest of the prisoners. If he lives to get there, I'd be surprised. We don't like men who join the enemy."

Meskhanet stood facing Julius and the soldiers with the open door into the house behind her. She heard a soft scraping sound. She whirled, but all she saw was one sandaled foot and the flash of a Roman cape as someone ran out of the house.

Marcus knew deep trouble when he saw it—or felt it. The spear jabbing into his back kept him going forward. Trickles of blood ran down his back.

"What do you want, soldier?" The centurion didn't seem to be in a good humor, brows drawn together and the frown lines pronounced between them.

"This one claims to be a Roman, Centurion Domitius."

"He doesn't look like a Roman to me. So, you, say something in Latin. For instance, your name."

Marcus looked up. "I am Decanus Marcus Varitor of Jericho."

Domitius's eyes widened. "Decanus Marcus? Were you not in charge of the soldiers sent out four months ago?"

"Yes, sir. We got trapped in a canyon. Some of the men were killed in rockslides, some in the battle with Barabbas and his men, and one soldier and I were captured."

Domitius glanced around at the prisoners and multiple bodies lying on the ground. "Where is the other soldier?"

"I took him to Caesarea."

"You took him to Caesarea. And yet here you are again. The company of brigands suits you then? Take him to his new friends, soldier."

"Yes, sir," the soldier grinned and added another prick with his spear to Marcus's back.

"Wait, sir, if you take me to the brigands, they will likely kill me." Marcus called after the centurion, but Domitius had turned his horse and rode at a trot toward a wagon at the edge of the clearing.

"Go, traitor. Join your friends or join your ancestors."

Marcus went.

Barabbas stood from where he sat in a circle with his men. He hurled a string of what Marcus assumed to be expletives at him and spat full in his face. The Roman guards nudged each other and laughed. They gathered the band of robbers and Marcus into a circle, and guards stood with spears pointed inward. He maintained as much distance from the other prisoners as he could, given the boundary of spears.

Marcus's stomach growled as aromas of cooking meat and onions rose in the morning air. He wagered the prisoners would not taste any of it. The women were made to cut up the ox and provide food to the soldiers, but none came his way.

They remained at the camp the first night. Even the women and children were herded into the circle. The following morning one of soldiers gave a command, apparently in Aramaic, because the male prisoners began moving south. The women, children, and old men stayed behind.

He caught a narrow-eyed glare from the old woman as he passed her, and he felt a twinge of guilt. She'd been kind to him when no one else had.

The slow, steady drizzle made travel difficult. Mud stuck to his sandals and made his feet feel heavier. And colder. Not enough to cup his hands and get much of a drink, but at least enough to keep him from asking for help from the soldiers. At the end of the day, they handed the prisoners a cooking pot and oats and pointed them toward the fire.

Gruel beat nothing, but Marcus surely did wish for a slice of that beef. When the thin porridge finished cooking, Marcus moved in to scoop up a share with a clay bowl. One of the brigands stood and moved between him and the pot. Three others joined him. Their meaning was unmistakable.

His stomach protested again, but he left. He walked to the soldiers' circle, but the threats there were more than cold stares and folded arms.

Marcus sat on a rock at a safe distance from the other prisoners. It didn't take much to know that he would not survive the walk to Jerusalem without food. Or water. Water hadn't been a problem this day, but the sky was clearing.

He shrugged. It wouldn't be the first time he went to sleep hungry. Maybe tomorrow he'd have a chance to talk to the centurion. Surely he could see Marcus was not a favorite of the robbers. At the least, the centurion should make sure he got food and water. Maybe tomorrow would be a better day. *Adonai, are You there? Do You see me?*

Rough hands awakened him as two soldiers bound his wrists and feet in chains, but his body felt weary. It didn't take long to drift off to sleep again.

He woke with his mouth as dry as a summer cistern. A soldier walked from one prisoner to the next with one water skin. The hands shackled in front made it easier to drink, but the soldier didn't allow more than a swallow or two for each.

The bonds were released from their feet, but the fetters on the wrists were left in place. Apparently they were to break their fast on what remained of the gruel, and the other prisoners still did not seem inclined to share with Marcus. Nor did the soldiers.

He walked up to one of the guards. "Please, allow me to speak one more time with the centurion. I can explain my presence with these robbers if he will just hear my story."

The guard lifted his spear to Marcus's chest. "You can tell your sad tale of woe to the tribune when we get to Jerusalem."

"Without food and water, I won't live to speak to him."

"Still sadder. Start walking, traitor."

He turned to follow the other prisoners. The soldiers were convinced he betrayed Rome. The centurion had no interest in listening. Even the One God did not seem to hear him.

Marcus fell—or was he pushed?—again. He thought he had spent more time on the ground than walking. This was the fourth day without food and little water. His knees wobbled as he rose once more. He had not one friend here. The soldiers thought he was a traitor, and the brigands knew he was. When the Romans dished out food, they gave it to one of the other prisoners to distribute. It didn't surprise him that the prisoners wouldn't give any to him.

Ironic. His plan failed to kill or capture Barabbas on his own after his men died. Not only had it failed, but now he was in as much trouble as Barabbas. More, in fact. His whole life he'd slid past all hardships, but neither his Senator father nor friends in command could help him out of this one.

One foot in front of the other. Just one more time, one foot and then the other. Lean forward a little and the feet moved more willingly. All he saw was the path and the person who preceded him. Aware of trees or rocks or people only when he bumped into them.

The sun dropped beyond the horizon before they stopped. Marcus lowered himself to the ground by a rock and laid his head back and shivered. He'd gone past hunger. All he wanted was a *metretes* of water and sleep. A mosquito landed on his arm, and he stared at it without moving. *Probably not enough there to fill you, blood sucker.* The insect must have agreed. It whined away.

Marcus felt himself sliding down the rock to a prone position, but it was more like watching someone in a dream. He felt nothing, saw nothing, thought nothing...except....

Meskhanet…

Chapter 10

"Who was that?" Meskhanet whirled when she heard the sound of running feet.

Julius trotted to the opening, but he shook his head. "Did anyone see who just ran out of here?"

One of the Romans who had brought his friends to Caesarea shrugged. "A soldier, sir, but not one I knew."

Cyril bowed his head. "Sir, I believe it might have been Brutus."

Julius stepped through the door. "Guard!"

One of the two soldiers who guarded their house trotted into the house. "Sir?"

"Was that Brutus who just left?"

"Yes, sir."

"Bring me Decanus Cassius," Julius said.

"Yes, sir." The guard trotted off at a brisk pace.

Julius turned. "Cyril, I need your help. I can't go with the men, but they'll need someone who can recognize Marcus. I don't want to send any of the women, Loukas is not strong enough, and that leaves you."

"Do I take your chariot and horses, sir?"

Julius laughed. "No. You'll be going on one of the infantry wagons. Sorry, Cyril."

"My limbs ache already. Those wagon seats could be used as implements of torture." Cyril's low mutter reached Meskhanet's ears.

"You could ride on one of the wooden saddles." Julius murmured his reply.

Cyril snorted.

The panting guard and Decanus Cassius strode into the house.

Meskhanet smiled as Cyril's face again became a mask of respect.

"Decanus, I want you to go after the century that took Barabbas captive. Take my servant here with you to identify a man who is probably among the prisoners. You—Jerusalem soldiers—come here. Meskhanet, too. Can you show the decanus where to find Barabbas's camp?" Julius walked to a clay tablet on a large table near a window. The tablet measured close to five square cubits.

She studied the drawing.

"Have you seen a map before?" asked Julius

She shook her head. "No, but I can see this must be an image of the land between here and Jerusalem. This is the Great Sea?" Meskhanet pointed to the smooth portion lining the left side.

"Yes, and this is Caesarea." Julius pointed to a small box shape next to the sea.

"We came down the mountain here, I think."

The soldiers both nodded.

Joanna had walked up beside her and followed Meskhanet's pointing finger. Her eyes lit up. "Ah, this is a wonder. Yes, the sea is here, Caesarea there, and this is where Loukas and I hid for so long." She touched lightly an area next to a curvy line.

Meskhanet followed another line south and tapped. "Here. This is their camp."

"Are you sure?" Cassius asked. "As I remember, a sheep camp is there. Nothing but sheep and shepherds with their families."

"And a lot of zealots ready to kill anyone who is not a Jew, Decanus. Even some who are Jews. Julius, do you remember Levi? Barabbas killed him when he tried to protect me."

"But then, you are not Hebrew, are you?" Cassius narrowed his eyes and studied her.

"No." Meskhanet dropped her gaze to the floor.

Julius's voice turned cold. "Does that make a difference to you, Decanus?"

Cassius flushed. "Uh, no, sir. I just wondered if that was why he killed someone who might protect her. Because he thought she wasn't a Jew, I mean. Although that does not excuse him, of course. He is a murderer, even if it were only Jews that he killed."

Julius paused, his eyes narrowed, and it was enough to set the decanus sweating. "You should choose your words and actions with wisdom, Cassius. If harm comes to my servant, Cyril, I will hold you personally responsible."

Cassius's Adam's apple bobbed. "Yes, sir."

"In addition, the soldier being treated as a prisoner by the century from Jerusalem is my life-long friend. You will free him if they allow, or conduct him in safety and good health to Jerusalem. Even if he remains a prisoner, he is a Roman citizen and entitled to a trial."

"Yes, sir."

"Upon the safe delivery of my friend Marcus to Jerusalem, you will return in haste and report to me. Are the orders clear, Cassius?"

"Yes, sir."

"Select a gentle mule and a wagon for my servant. He is not a soldier."

Cassius glanced at Cyril. "Yes, sir."

"Dismissed, Decanus."

"Yes, sir." Cassius saluted and left.

"Sir." One of the other soldiers stepped forward.

Julius turned his gaze to the two from Jerusalem. "You should accompany Cassius's contubernium."

"Yes, sir." The two men chorused their response, saluted, and marched out the door.

Cyril gave a dry chuckle. "At least you didn't go so far as to say I am no horseman, but he no doubt received your message. I suspect I will find a sway-backed nag of no less than twenty years awaiting me."

"You would prefer a spirited young stallion, perhaps? Because I have a hunch that would have awaited you had I said nothing."

Meskhanet couldn't help but appreciate the humor between the two friends, even though one was an employer and one an employee. Her master and mistress also treated their servants with honor and humor, but she knew this wasn't the typical way people treated their servants and slaves.

"My husband, you will come back to me safe, yes?" Quinta handed Cyril a leather-bound package and his heavy cloak, moisture in her eyes.

Cyril gathered her into his arms. "I will come back to you, my beautiful wife." He ran one hand down her waist-length pale hair.

Meskhanet suspected Cyril's eyes might be damp, too. She doubted he had been away from his bride for more than an hour since they married months before.

She knew Julius must feel torn. He was sending one of his two closest friends to rescue the other one. *God of the Jews, please hold his friends in safety.*

Sometime later, a nudge in his ribs moved Marcus to consciousness. He grunted and opened his eyes to darkness, but he lacked the energy to move away.

"Are you Marcus?" A low, gruff voice spoke in Latin.

"Mm."

A skin of water dripped water onto his lips, and he licked it eagerly, lifting a weak hand to hold the skin tight to his mouth.

"Water. Please, more water…."

Was that his voice, or had someone else spoken his thought? Or maybe it was only his thought, without spoken words. Meskhanet would know. Ask her. Ask her what? "Bring water, Meskhanet? Please?"

Another drop of water touched his lips. "More."

How did he come to be on the ground? Or was he on a horse? "Move, Tsal. Let's go."

Another drop of water. Two. He opened his mouth as more fell on his face and hands.

Rain?

He drifted in and out like waves on the sea. The next time he woke, someone held his head up. A morsel of something pressed into his mouth. He sucked the moisture from it, but he had no energy to chew. Or maybe he did. He swallowed. What was it? Sweet. Honey? "More."

Another glob of the sweet substance dropped into his waiting mouth. A little bread. Some watered wine. He sank into sleep again. He woke, this time to arms held beneath his knees and shoulders and the sound of a grunt as someone lifted him. He felt a horse's back between his legs as loud yells erupted from around them.

"What do you think you're doing with that prisoner, soldier? Who are you?"

"My name is Brutus. Why have you made a prisoner of my decanus?"

"He consorted with the enemy. And now it appears you are too."

"I am a soldier from Jericho. This man led us on an expedition to capture Barabbas. Both of us were taken captive and the rest of our troop killed. He saved my life."

"Come this way. You will explain to the centurion."

Brutus? What is he doing here? Marcus felt the jarring of the horse as it plodded. He clung to the horse's mane and tried to stay awake. "Water," he rasped as rain still dripped on his back.

No one responded.

Angry voices ranged somewhere nearby. Marcus struggled to understand.

"You woke me up for this? Take this dog out and scourge him, then tie him to his precious decanus."

"There is a troop following me."

"A troop? Why?"

"You have taken prisoner Marcus Varitor, son of a senator."

A long pause ensued, and Marcus drifted off to somewhere else. Somewhere with Meskhanet. Somewhere with soft, warm blankets and a gray haze. And Brutus?

His eyes popped open as strong arms lowered him to the ground. "Brutus? What are you doing here?"

"Someone had to stop that idiot centurion from killing you. Here—eat."

Marcus struggled to sit up and succeeded only after Brutus lifted him and propped pillows behind him. "Why am I so weak?"

Brutus shrugged. "Hunger, thirst, fever. The cut on your back festered. I cleaned it. "

"You saved my life?" Marcus struggled to comprehend.

"So I returned the favor. We're even."

Marcus stared in disbelief at his rescuer. "I must be dreaming."

"I have some trouble believing it too. Now use that flapping mouth to eat instead of talk. Sir." Brutus's continuous black brows dipped at the center.

With shaking hands, Marcus raised the bowl of broth to his lips and drained it. "Where are we?"

"On the way to Jerusalem. You're still a prisoner. So am I. But at least you'll live until you get there."

Marcus raised his hand and scratched the edge of his beard. "I don't understand. Why?"

"Why what?"

"Why are you here? I thought you were in Caesarea. Your leg…."

"I owed a debt. I pay my debts. My leg works fine." Brutus ran his hand up and down between his knee and his ankle. "Do you have to talk so much?"

Brutus jumped to his feet as a crunch of gravel signaled someone's approach. "Back away. The centurion promised us safe passage to Jerusalem."

"So I understand. I am Cyril, servant of Marcus's friend Julius. Julius sent these soldiers and me to find Marcus and assure his safety."

Brutus snorted. "You would have arrived too late."

Cyril turned away from Brutus and walked to where Marcus was propped. As Cyril knelt by his side, Marcus could see the moisture in his friend's eyes.

"Don't rain on me, Cyril. I'm healing fast. Thanks to Brutus and the One God who sent him."

"I tried to talk the centurion into loosing you, but he will not. He's angry that he has to give you special treatment and says you have slowed his march to Jerusalem."

"True. He might have had us there by now if not for me. I fell a lot."

Cyril scowled. "Domitius would have been happy to let you die. Julius would not have been pleased with him, and Julius's opinion carries some weight now as a centurion primus. I hear Tribune Rufus thinks highly of Julius too. Domitius might do well to back away from this course."

Marcus sighed. "He isn't swayed by who my father is. Why would he be impressed by a mere centurion?"

Cyril grunted.

"Did you bring a razor with you?" Marcus scratched his cheek.

"Of course." Cyril stood and walked into the darkness.

"Why didn't you tell me you wanted a shave? I would have done it." Brutus growled.

"You are not a servant. I'm grateful you saved my life." Marcus grinned. "It has not been so long since you would happily have shaved me a little close had I asked for one."

Brutus harrumphed. Was that a twitch at the corner of his mouth? The beginning of a grin from Brutus? Remarkable.

Cyril reentered the circle of light from the fire, and Brutus retreated to a rock on the far side of the ring.

As he finished the shave, Cyril scowled. "Your hair too? Your beard was full of vermin and I feel sure your hair will be. No wonder you itch. And your face is so thin I would not have recognized you if not for the color of the beard. Loukas told us you had grown a beard and that it rivaled the setting sun."

"Neither the soldiers nor the other prisoners felt like sharing, so I was without food or enough water. Yes, shave my head too. Anything to get rid of these fleas and lice. Did you bring some clean clothes?"

Cyril finished scraping the razor-sharp short knife across Marcus's skull and helped him into his soldier's garb. "Are you well enough to walk?"

Marcus gathered his shaking legs, tried to stand, then shook his head. "Not yet. Tomorrow, maybe."

Chapter 11

Meskhanet sighed. How did a new follower of the Jewish God begin? She supposed she'd have to find where they worshipped. Julius seemed nice, but he was a Roman. And a centurion. He might not want to help a slave. She approached Julius with trepidation and a voice so soft she wasn't sure he would hear. "Sir?"

Julius looked up from his desk. "Hello, Meskhanet. Were you looking for Miriam?"

"No, sir. I, ah, I made a promise to your God." Her face warmed.

"My God? You refer to the One God of Israel?"

"Yes. I—I promised to follow Him. He saved me, so I promised."

"Oh, I see. And tomorrow is the Sabbath, so you want to know what you should do?"

She nodded. "I don't know where the worshipers of the One God go. Is there a synagogue in Caesarea?"

Julius smiled. "Yes, but the Hebrews won't let us join them. Don't despair, though, several proselytes meet here. We're building a separate room on the synagogue where proselytes may go, but it isn't finished yet."

"I know so little about this God, but I need to learn. Loukas used to talk to me about Him, and I know he would still. But I think if I could go to a synagogue, that is what this God would want me to do."

"I think He would too."

Meskhanet brought a jar of water into the bedroom and set it by Loukas. "Do you need anything more, Master?" Her heart thumped, but she didn't think Loukas would notice.

Loukas lifted his hand and ran it through his hair. "I would like to get rid of some of this, young woman. Do you think you could cut it?"

"Yes, master."

"And Meskhanet—you saved our lives. I think you could stop calling me Master and try Loukas."

She felt the heat rising in her face. "I would rather not, Master. Forgive me, but it seems too…too disrespectful. When I was young, we did not call any man by name except a husband or brother."

Loukas opened his mouth as though to say something, then he dropped his gaze to his hands. "I understand. Call me by whatever you are comfortable with. One day, perhaps you will consider me a father."

"Perhaps, Master." She would rather call him husband, though that could not happen.

Joanna's voice sounded from behind her. "Good morning, Meskhanet. Did you see the rising sun? Was it not beautiful? It was not so long ago that I thought our remaining sunrises and sunsets would dwindle to none all too rapidly, and yet here we are enjoying yet another one with many more anticipated. Praise the One God and thanks to you, Meskhanet. You saved our lives."

Joanna placed her arms around Meskhanet in an affectionate embrace, bringing tears to her eyes. "He saved me to save you, Mistress. Your God sent help when I thought hope was gone. Now I need to learn more about Him. Would you teach me?"

"Of course we will, child." Loukas chuckled. "It seems we will have to buy another slave, Joanna. We need one to assist me when my work renders me unclean." He stood and made his way, slowly but without staggering, to the door. "I think it is time that I begin being a physician again."

"You forget, husband," Joanna said. "We have no coins to buy anything. Barabbas has our coins."

"Ah, but I am a physician. I shall just have to charge for my service to these Caesareans. Meanwhile, I'm sure Julius would be willing to provide us with the coins needed. It would not be long before we could pay him back."

Meskhanet felt a twinge of jealousy for Loukas's proposed new slave. Odd, she never felt jealous of Joanna. She loved Joanna as much as she did Loukas.

Meskhanet walked with Joanna to the docks in search of a new slave. The slave market brought forth unpleasant memories of her time there. After the capture of her city by Romans, most of the people had been made slaves.

Only twelve, she'd been humiliated at having to stand naked in front of so many eyes. Now her eyes would humiliate others as she stood in judgment of the flesh on sale. She had wished not to come, but Joanna asked her to help.

They would have been wise to bring Cyril and several soldiers, but Cyril was gone and Joanna didn't want to trouble Julius to order soldiers to come with them.

Did Loukas want a woman or a man? He said it didn't matter, and Joanna said they would know which one to pick because she had prayed. Meskhanet didn't understand. Why would the Jew's One God help them with a slave selection? She wished Loukas had felt well enough to accompany them.

Joanna walked past the strong men, the young women, a slight frown on her usually smiling face, her eyes on the ground. "I need your help, Meskhanet. I don't feel God's leading. No one of the slaves appeals to me. Do any attract your attention?"

"No, Mistress. Perhaps these aren't the only ones for sale."

"That could be the reason. Do you see one of the mangones? A slave seller should know if there are others." Joanna pulled her scarf across her face. "I don't like this place."

"There is one, Mistress. Over there, by that man on the platform."

Joanna lifted her gaze for a moment, and her face flamed.

Meskhanet sighed. "Follow me, Mistress." She walked toward the platform and avoided meeting the gazes of the men, both slave and free.

The man on the platform, like so many others, stood naked. Muscular, scarred, perhaps thirty years old. He'd just been sold, apparently, because the *mango* handed the man a tunic to cover himself.

"Sir," Meskhanet called to the *mango*. The man turned to her and his eyes slid over her like dirty oil. She frowned, her face hot. "Are these all the slaves you have?"

"What are you looking for, woman? A handsome young man, perhaps? Too bad this one isn't available. Now, we do have one other...."

"We seek an assistant for my husband," Joanna interrupted. "We want one who is neither a Jew nor a Jewish proselyte."

"None of these slaves for sale are Jews, madam." He descended from the platform and looked both of the women up and down. "Now, I could get a pretty coin for this one, but you with that scar, not so much—except women who want to buy an ugly slave so that her husband will not stray."

"Come, mistress, this man does not want to sell to us." Meskhanet tugged at Joanna's cloak.

Joanna pulled loose. Her eyes held sparks of fury. "I am the wife of Loukas the physician, friend to Centurion Julius. You will guard your tongue, or I will have my husband remove it."

Meskhanet gasped and pulled at Joanna's arm. "Mistress, please."

The mango's eyes glinted and he snapped his teeth. "Then let your husband come to see me. I do not negotiate with women. If I see you again, woman, it will be without your clothing and on an auction block."

"You are an insolent dog, mango. You will hear from my husband."

She whirled, but the slave monger grabbed her arm and twisted it, bringing her back with her nose a finger's width from his.

"Not if you do not see your husband again, woman," he hissed. He raised his free hand, and four men sprang out of nowhere.

Marcus opened his eyes as the sun rose in the red-blanketed east. *Hm. Rain could accompany us today.*

He stretched, sat up, and looked around. Cyril poked at last night's coals, blowing on them as he added small sticks. Brutus lay on his back, snoring loud from a gaping mouth.

Gingerly, Marcus stood. His knees wobbled a bit but held, and he walked to Cyril's side. "How long until breakfast?"

Cyril chuckled. "Same old Marcus. Ever on the watch for food. Not long, my friend. In fact, if you don't want to wait for me, get some for yourself. Cheese and grapes are in those leather pouches on the wagon bed."

"You've become insolent since getting emancipated. Julius should never have given you your freedom. You got your freedom, you become a proselyte of the One God, and you find yourself a bride from the wealthiest man in Jericho. You'll probably die richer than the emperor." Marcus walked to the log and dug through the food.

"Dying rich, dying poor. What does it matter? Does our Adonai look into a man's pouch on the last day he lives?" Cyril turned his back to the fire.

"Fresh apples. You didn't tell me you had these." Marcus bit into the apple and wiped away the juice running down his chin.

"I wanted you to eat food that would build your strength. Only you would select instead something sweet. But as long as you look for something sweet, there are honey cakes in there, too. Wrapped in grape leaves. And some raisins. Dried fish, bread, pomegranates, too. Why don't you just eat all of it?"

"I'll save a small bite or two for you. Fear not." Marcus wiped bread crumbs from his mouth.

Brutus walked up to them. "If there is not enough, I will get some from the soldiers."

"There's enough. Marcus excels in sarcasm." Cyril handed a loaf of bread and a pomegranate to Brutus.

Brutus grunted what might have been thanks and stalked back to a log to sit, scowling.

Marcus sighed and walked back to sit at Brutus's side. "Tell me, soldier, have you ever been happy?"

"Happy? What is there to be happy about? You may be better this morning, but both of us are still prisoners. You are accused of being a traitor; I'm accused of trying to help you escape. The best that could happen would be that the tribune will allow us to be gladiators and die in the stadium rather than on a cross." He crunched on the dry bread.

Marcus grinned. "That's the longest speech I ever heard you make."

Brutus grunted and broke a pomegranate open.

"Look at the sky, man. How's that for beauty? We are alive. There are friends here to vouch for us. We could be exonerated. And you saved my life, putting me in your debt. What more could you want? The One God is good."

"Which one? None of them have ever shown *me* any favor."

"Maybe you haven't tried the right one. I'm talking about the God of the Jews, Yahweh. He is the One God. None of the rest could show you any favors because they have stone hearts and wooden hands."

Brutus snorted. "I only rescued you because you saved my life. I pay my debts. That doesn't mean I have to listen to you preach." He rose and walked back to where Cyril stood.

"I need more. Give me some of the fish."

Cyril narrowed his eyes. "Get it yourself."

Brutus doubled his fists and stepped up close to Cyril. He raised one hand with obvious intent when Marcus barked, "Don't, soldier."

Brutus threw a glare over his shoulder, but subsided. He stalked over to the bags of food on the wagon, jerked out a dried fish, and began hitching the mules to the wagon as he crunched the fish, bones and all.

Marcus looked at Cyril and shrugged one shoulder.

They broke camp in silence, but the rest of the encampment was not so silent. The clanking of chains and harness, stomping feet and neighing from the horses, braying mules and donkeys, banging pots, and clinking armor from almost a hundred men filled the morning air. That coupled with the smells of the latrine and corral made Marcus glad they were moving.

The drizzle began as Marcus climbed onto the wagon seat. At least the seat wasn't wet when he sat, but no canvas covered the wagon—only the food in the back. The chill of cold moisture dripping down his neck made him wish he could crawl under the canvas. Oh, he could, but as a decanus and under Brutus's scornful eyes? No.

What was that proverb about pride going before a fall? Hmm. Marcus sighed. "Cyril, I'd like to get out of this rain. Any problem with me getting under that covering back there?" He jerked his thumb toward the back.

"You would be wise to do just that. I know you feel better than yesterday, but you are not completely well. I put plenty of blankets back there. You should be comfortable."

"Thanks, Cyril. I owe you much." Shivering, Marcus stepped into the back of the wagon, lifted the canvas, and surrounded himself with as many blankets as he could find. Within moments, he slept.

He couldn't have slept long when the wagon jerked to a stop and he awoke to the sounds of angry shouts. He would have ignored them, but one of the voices sounded like Cyril's. Lifting a corner of the canvas, he raised up on one elbow.

One of the soldiers had a spear aimed at Cyril's ribs, and Brutus and Julius's soldiers stood toe to toe with several of the troop from Jerusalem. It seemed as though all of the soldiers vied with one another over who could shout the loudest. Centurion Domitius approached, his horse throwing splatters of mud flying from his hooves.

Chapter 12

Julius paced from the table to the door and back again, his stomach feeling like knotted rope. "When did they leave? Joanna and Meskhanet should have been back hours ago."

"After we broke our fast this morning. They said they want to go early so they can be back in time for the midday meal." Quinta wrung her hands and stared at the sunset through an open window.

Loukas sat at the table, hands clenched. "I should have gone with them. They said they would return quickly."

"You could not have walked that far, Loukas. You are not yet strong enough. Then they went alone? Where was Miklos?" Julius asked.

"I do not know. They left a message on a wax tablet, but they did not say where Miklos was or why he did not accompany them."

Julius strode to the door. "Miklos!"

The short but broad Greek servant trotted up behind from the kitchen. "You called me, sir?"

Julius whirled. "Where were you when Joanna and Meskhanet left this morning?"

"I don't know. I found their message and gave it to Quinta when I came in from the garden."

Julius ran his hand through his hair. "Two women, alone in the slave market. One of them very attractive. Two, when the scar on Joanna's face fades. It's too easy to guess what has happened."

A sob sounded from Loukas. Quinta sat next to him, leaning on his shoulder and crying softly with him.

"Miklos, I want you to run as fast as you can to headquarters. I need the first available contubernium and decanus available. Tell them to meet me at the entrance to the slave market. I'll get my armor and meet them there."

"Yes, sir, I'll run faster than ever I have, I swear."

Julius strode to the bedroom where Miriam nursed Milah. "Joanna and Meskhanet went to the slave market this morning, and now they are missing. I'm going after them. I don't know when I'll be back, little wife."

Miriam nodded. "I feared that. Find them and bring them home, my love. I will miss you, but I know you won't rest until you've found them. Go with the One God."

He bent down to kiss the sweet lips that he loved so much, and she raised a hand to stroke his cheek as he kissed Milah's head.

"Come back to us soon, Julius. I will count the hours until you return with our friends."

Julius nodded, not trusting his voice. He stood, memorizing his wife and daughter's faces, hoping he would return successful this night. Not likely though. He swallowed and turned to the door.

Thirty slave masters. Julius lined them up on the dock and scowled in what he hoped would inspire the fear of Rome into the lot of them. He stalked to and fro in front of them, letting the tension build. Soldiers stood at the conjunction of the dock with the land.

"One or more of you are guilty of illegally seizing two women of my household. I'm certain more than one of you know who. If you do not care to identify the guilty one or ones, all of you will become prisoners of Rome. Those of you who are Romans will have a trial. The rest of you? It will not be so pleasant."

The mangos shifted from one foot to the other, scowling in defiance or eyebrows angling upward in worry. More and more of them glanced toward one man. Julius strode up to him, placing his nose a hand's breadth from the mango's. "You. It was you, you slime of a snail. What is your name?"

The man scowled and stepped backwards. "Stephanus."

"Stephanus, you are under arrest for illegally imprisoning a Roman citizen and stealing her slave. Take him away, Decanus. See that you get the information needed from him. Be thankful, Stephanus, that I will not do the questioning. Unless, that is, you refuse to give us what we want."

The man began to sweat despite the coolness of the evening. "Wait, sir. I did not know, sir. They were just two women, unaccompanied and insolent. Sir."

"Where are they?"

"On a ship bound for Rome. It left at midday, ah, sir."

"Decanus—take this man to the prison. The rest of these mangos may go free."

"But I'm a Roman! I bought my citizenship just a year ago."

"You will get your trial, Stephanus. But theft is not looked on lightly by the Roman courts."

Julius's hobnailed sandals resounded on the wooden planks as he marched to a Roman ship on the next dock. He wasn't sure what he wanted to do most, watch the mango hang on a cross or pull the man to pieces himself. He found the ship's captain directing the loaders. "When do you leave for Rome, captain?"

"Probably next week, Centurion. I await another ship from Alexandria with a shipment for Tiberius Caesar."

Julius grunted. "Do you know of any other ship leaving for Rome sooner?"

"No, sir, and I know all the captains here in Caesarea right now. The storms are too many and too severe to sail often in the winter. Shall I send word to you if I hear of one?"

"Yes. I'm Centurion Julius. All the Romans here know where I live."

Julius entered the house with slumped shoulders, wondering how he'd tell Loukas.

Miriam ran to him and threw her arms around him. "I'm glad you're back. I thought you would be gone from me for days or even months, but your face tells me the news is not good."

"It's not. They...."

He stopped as Decanus Cassius trotted into the house and saluted.

"Did you find Marcus, Decanus?"

"Yes, sir. He's being held prisoner, but alive. Brutus found him first, and he pulled him from death's grip, sir. However, we could not convince Centurion Domitius to release them. Both are now prisoners, but he allowed Brutus and your servant to tend him."

"Cassius, I want you to send a fresh soldier back to them on a fast horse, leaving this night with a message for Marcus and my servant. Tell them—tell them Loukas's wife and slave have been kidnapped and taken to Rome on a ship."

Cassius quirked an eyebrow.

"Loukas is a close friend to Marcus. And the slave kidnapped with Loukas's wife is Marcus's intended."

Julius heard a cough behind him. When he turned, he saw Loukas staring. "Or he'd like for her to be."

"What are you doing?" Marcus shouted to be heard above the soldiers' hurled insults. "Roman soldiers fighting Roman soldiers? What are you doing, men? Stop it, *now!*" It sounded like his father's booming voice rolling through his throat.

Another shout from Centurion Domitius, and the men lowered swords, spears, and shields and looked abashed.

One of the decani took a hesitant step toward Domitius. "We thought they allowed the traitor to escape, Centurion."

"Obviously, they did not, and he did not. Back to your posts. Did you leave the other prisoners without a guard?"

"No, Centurion. They are guarded. But even if they were not, they are chained."

"Never assume, Decanus."

"No, sir." The decanus saluted, turned, and marched the soldiers back to their posts.

The sound of pounding hooves brought everyone to attention. A soldier galloped into camp and saluted the centurion. "I have an urgent message from Caesarea for the Decanus Marcus and for Julius's servant Cyril."

Domitius snorted. "When did we begin allowing prisoners to receive messages?"

"This one is from Centurion Julius, sir."

"Very well, soldier. Deliver your message." Domitius nodded his head toward Marcus, and he sat his horse, not moving.

"Yes, sir." The soldier turned to Marcus. "Decanus Marcus, Centurion Julius said to inform you your friend Loukas's wife and her slave, your betrothed, have been kidnapped by slavers and are on their way to Rome aboard a ship."

Marcus felt the blood drain from his head. "What?"

Another soldier came running from behind the centurion. "Centurion Domitius, sir."

"Now what?" Domitius growled.

"Sir, one of the prisoners escaped."

"No, he's right here."

"No, sir, not that one. It's the one they call Barabbas."

Marcus groaned. *What can I do, Adonai? Barabbas will go after the one who led the Romans to the camp—Meskhanet.*

Domitius whirled his horse and raced back to the camp where the rest of the soldiers and prisoners were, the foot soldiers following at a run behind him.

Cyril lifted his head. "Marcus, I have to go back. Quinta will be beside herself."

"Wait," Marcus whispered.

Brutus rode up beside him. "Decanus, we have to get Barabbas."

Marcus called the remaining Caesarian soldiers to them. "Soldiers, they will need your help over there. Take your orders from Domitius."

"Julius told us to stay by you and make sure you get safely to Jerusalem."

"That was because he feared the others would try to kill me on the way. That is no longer a problem because the troop should be in Jerusalem by nightfall. Go help Domitius."

"Yes, sir."

"I won't go with them, Decanus." Brutus's brow furrowed.

"Good." Marcus grinned.

"What?"

"Cyril, how far can you walk?"

"What?"

"Let's get as many of the provisions as we can carry on our backs. Hurry."

Cyril's eyebrows shot up. "Ah."

"Why not on my horse?" Brutus asked.

"I wish we could, Brutus, but we need to move with stealth. Horses aren't easy to hide, and we don't have three fast horses that we can get away on. Cyril, somehow we need to make this wagon look like it has a driver."

"A forked branch, a rope, and a blanket. There's the branch, right there under that tree. Nice of it to drop the perfect branch off in such a convenient place."

Within moments, they had the stick tied in place with a blanket slung over it. Marcus slapped the mule's rump and sent it after the rest.

"Let's go. The rain will wipe out our passage, if we're careful."

"How do you know where to find Barabbas?" Brutus puffed as he climbed the rain-washed slope.

"Barabbas? I thought we were going after Joanna and Meskhanet." Cyril stopped, scowling.

"Sh. I hear voices." Marcus whispered, holding his hand up. He moved behind a cedar, peering through the branches. Brutus crouched behind a rock, and Cyril scurried to kneel behind Brutus.

On the path not far below, soldiers tramped along the path going back the way they came. Marcus breathed silent, slow, and even as the line of about forty men marched past.

Which meant that Domitius had split the men. Were these after Barabbas? Or had they discovered he also was missing? No, if they had discovered he was gone, there would probably have been fewer men in the bunch they just saw. They would have to split their men three ways, the majority to stay with the chained prisoners.

Marcus signaled to his companions, and they resumed climbing. At the top of the slope, they could see the rest of the men marching toward Jerusalem. He chuckled as he pointed to the mule-drawn wagon with the blanketed branch at the rear of the column.

"They haven't checked on us. We're still following dutifully behind them."

Cyril grinned.

Brutus blew a derisive breath through his nose. "Let's go. We have a long hike."

Marcus looked around. They could walk near the top of the ridge for a time, but what he wanted most was to spot Barabbas, then get off this too-visible mountaintop.

Marcus took a deep breath. "I want the two of you to be quiet and hold still for a time. Until we know where Barabbas is, we remain in danger. I know there are three of us, but I'm not my best yet. Brutus, you still favor your leg from when it was broken, and Cyril, you aren't a soldier. We have no weapons. Barabbas is a powerful and ruthless killer. And once the centurion discovers us missing, he'll be hunting for us too. We don't have any friends this side of Caesarea."

Brutus nodded. He sat on a rock and began scanning the countryside.

Cyril did the same. He caught his breath. "What was that?" He pointed toward another hill to the south of them, only about a mile away.

"What do you see?" Marcus asked, his gaze following Cyril's pointing finger.

"I don't know. A movement. Might have been an animal, I guess. Brown."

Marcus released held breath. "Barabbas wore a brown robe...dark brown, nearly black."

The three of them stared with squinted eyes.

Brutus raised his hand. "There."

A man moved out from behind a tree and stood facing the direction the soldiers had gone before. He shaded his eyes against the sun then started down the slope at a trot.

"Barabbas."

Chapter 13

Meskhanet woke with a headache and her mouth and hands bound. She groaned. Was this her constant fate? *O God of the Jews, I need your help one more time. I am sorry to bother You yet again.*

A sloshing noise and faint movement made her think they might be on a boat. She lifted her head and opened her eyes, wincing, and looked around. Ship, not boat. Sunlight streamed through an open door at the top, illuminating the hold where they were imprisoned.

Joanna sat beside her, trussed in a like manner. A bruise on one cheek made Meskhanet wonder if Joanna's head also hurt. Her large black eyes showed terror in the white rims around the dark centers. She rolled wide eyes to the right.

Meskhanet followed Joanna's gaze to where a huge, barrel-chested, rough-looking man stood, whip in one of the immense hands folded across his bare chest. He must have been five cubits tall. He grinned at Meskhanet when their gazes connected, revealing several missing teeth. Those remaining were coated with yellow grime. She shuddered and closed her eyes tight.

When she opened them again, she saw several prisoners chained by one foot to the sides of the hold. At least twenty men, some with heads resting on raised knees, some lying down. Women too, although not as many. One with a shaved head held her bound hands over her shaved skull. Another slept on the boards as soundly as though it were a feather mattress, snoring softly.

Were any of these others captured like they were? None but she and Joanna had gags, but all either had chains or ropes binding their feet.

Meskhanet heard the sound of many feet over her head, and the increased rocking of the vessel indicated they moved away from the dock. The rocking increased, and the man with the whip approached them. She cringed away from him, but he only touched her to remove her gag.

He took off Joanna's gag, too, then backed up a few steps and grinned again. "Hah." He pointed to their hands and shook his head, eyes sober.

She must have understood. "You cannot speak, can you?" she said in Greek.

He pointed to his mouth and shook his head then to his ears and nodded.

"I understand. You can hear, and you know what we're saying. Then did you know we should not be here, that we were taken prisoner? We are Roman citizens. These are illegal." She held up her bound hands.

The man's eyebrows peaked in the middle.

"Are you a slave?"

He nodded again.

"Are we to be slaves too?"

The giant shrugged.

One of the other prisoners cleared his throat. "I can answer that. Yes."

Meskhanet jerked her head toward him and regretted the sudden movement. She raised her hands to her head, willing the pounding to stop. When she lifted her eyes again, the man gazed at her. She recognized him.

Joanna must have too, because her face reddened. "You are the one we saw in the slave market."

"Yes, madam. I'm sorry you were taken. I should have warned you."

"At the risk of your life, I think."

The man heaved a sigh. "No, I'm too valuable to kill. They might make me wish I were dead, but the mongones would not kill me. Still, I should have done something. If I had, you could have run. My apologies to you."

"Who are you? I am Joanna, the wife of Loukas the Physician. This young woman is my adopted daughter, Meskhanet."

Meskhanet cut her gaze sharply to Joanna and raised an eyebrow. *Daughter?*

"My name is Appius. Our big, whip-bearing slave master here is Varrus." He smiled at the giant. "To my knowledge, he's never hit anyone. It's his size that intimidates, not his fierceness."

"Why are you here?" Joanna asked.

"I had the audacity to disagree with Tiberius Caesar. Unwise. Varrus used to be a gladiator, but he refused to fight. They give him a whip, but it might as well be a feather."

"Do you know where this ship goes?"

"They don't tell me, at least not on purpose. But I heard one of the sailors mention Rome."

Rome? Meskhanet's heart sank. Did the God of the Jews have any influence in Rome? So many evil things she'd heard about that city from friends in Jericho.

Joanna groaned. "My poor husband. Rome is a large city. I fear he'll never find me there."

Appius made a low noise in his throat. "Far truer than you know. My lady, these are hard words, but you must never expect to see your husband again. Where you are going, even if he finds you, he won't want you back."

Joanna's hand flew to her throat. "Why would he not? My husband loves me. He would look for me to the ends of the earth."

"Hope that he does not find you then, my lady. My guess is that the two of you are bound for the circus to be rewards for winning gladiators. Some are not gentle in their lovemaking. Some women return from the men's cells crippled, disfigured, or worse."

Joanna gasped. "They cannot do that to us. I am a Roman citizen."

"No." The moan burst from Meskhanet's throat before she could stop it.

Varrus dropped to his knees by her side and stroked her hair as though she were a child. Soft noises emanated from his mouth, and he shook his head vigorously.

"I think he's trying to say he won't let harm come to you. Is that it, Varrus?"

Varrus dipped his head.

"Varrus and I have been together a long time. Years, in fact. When I was a free man I hired him as a bodyguard."

"But he cannot speak. And if he is so gentle how could he be such a man?"

"He tried to defend me. They removed his tongue and made him a eunuch. He nearly died from infection." Appius lowered his eyes.

"How did you become a slave?"

"At the same time. I was indebted to the emperor and unable to pay. Several guards stepped up to take me to prison. That's when

Varrus tried to defend me. I showed them my muscles and offered to become a gladiator. They took the offer of myself and also took Varrus."

"Were you not purchased on the auction block, Appius? The mango there said when they handed you your tunic you had been bought." Joanna's face flushed.

"No, madam, I was not precisely sold, other than for breeding. They merely displayed me to advertise."

"What?" Joanna's eyes widened.

"They think to mate me with the strongest female slaves to breed more gladiators." Appius's tone dried like grass in an east wind as his gaze drifted over Meskhanet.

When he spotted Barabbas at the edge of the trees opposite where they stood, Marcus hissed at Cyril and Brutus to hide. Barabbas swung his body toward them. Marcus feared the man saw them, but without exposing himself again, he couldn't know. With slow deliberation, he lifted his head above the rocks. Maybe not. Barabbas had begun walking down the west slope of the hill he'd been on.

Marcus signaled to his companions. They eased their way behind the rocks to the trees, then stood and started their own trek to the west.

"We have to get him." Brutus jerked his chin in the direction of where they'd last seen Barabbas.

"Later. It's more important that we find Meskhanet and Joanna. Julius would not have sent that message just to inform. He intended Cyril and me to assist in their rescue. Once the women are safe, we'll continue the search for Barabbas."

"They are just women. Bringing Barabbas back alive or over the back of his horse would bring a monetary award and earn our own freedom."

Marcus gritted his teeth. Just women. "One of the women is the wife of a close friend. The other is the woman I wish to wed. Their wellbeing is worth more to me than ten thousand denarii or my freedom."

"I'm with Marcus. You can go after Barabbas on your own." Cyril narrowed his eyes and moved closer to Marcus.

Brutus stopped, glaring at the two men. "For two women you would forgo a reward which could buy many women?"

Marcus snorted. "I think you have never loved a woman, Brutus. Perhaps not even your mother."

Brutus doubled his fists. "My mother was a whore. She abandoned me on the streets of Rome in her quest for the next man in her life. She means nothing to me. I spit on women."

"So that means you will go after Barabbas alone?" Marcus asked.

Brutus glared at both of them, his gaze shifting back and forth under furrowed scowl lines. He snapped his teeth. "Not yet."

They trudged on, pushing aside branches and clambering over rocks. Marcus didn't want to travel on paths. Too easy to be caught by the army or Barabbas. Not that Barabbas would be traveling on the known paths, either. They really needed horses to move faster, but where could they find any? *Adonai*?

His question was answered the next day in a glade in the forest.

A small fire burned, and a man and woman sat on a log beside it. The looked up when Marcus and his companions approached, and a cry went up from the woman as she threw her arms around the man.

Marcus held his hands out, palms up. "We are unarmed, my friends. We mean you no harm."

Horses nickered from behind the couple. The man stood in front of his wife, a knife gleaming in his hand. He approached Marcus with menace in his crouched position.

Marcus sighed. "Brutus, try Aramaic. Tell them we're unarmed and will not harm them."

Brutus growled a few words which didn't ease the stranger's stance. The man tossed his knife from hand to hand, glancing between Brutus and Marcus with an eager expression on his face.

Marcus stepped forward and motioned Brutus to stay back. Again, he held his hands palm up. The stranger jumped in and sliced toward Marcus. He turned to the side, brought both hands down, grabbed the man's knife arm, and snapped it across his knee.

The man howled and pulled the arm to his middle. Rage snapped in his eyes. He picked up the knife from where it fell with his other hand and lunged. Marcus stepped to the side and brought clenched hands down on the man's neck. A crack, and the man dropped to the ground. The woman screamed and rushed to her fallen husband, babbling in a language Marcus couldn't understand. She turned him over, but his eyes stared at the sky and not at her. She screamed again and picked up the knife.

She jumped toward him but tripped over a branch. The knife twisted in her grip and plunged into her own chest. She fell face down across the man she accompanied.

Cyril stepped forward. "Why did they do that? I don't understand what just happened."

Marcus shook his head. "I don't know. It makes no sense to me either."

Brutus cleared his throat. "Maybe this is the reason."

They walked to where he stood at the edge of a ravine. Two Roman soldiers lay dead at Brutus's feet, three horses and a donkey hobbled behind them. Three dead horses and three more soldiers were at the bottom of the ravine. All were covered in flies, and the odor was enough to tell them they had been dead since at least a day or two before.

Cyril coughed and backed away.

A search of the camp revealed several bags of denarii. "One man and one woman defeated five Roman horsemen? Unlikely. I think we'd better leave. The man's companions could be back at any moment."

Marcus took weapons from the dead soldiers, placed one of the wooden saddles and a bridle on a bay mare, and leapt to its back. Cyril followed suit, but Brutus also bent to pick up the bags of coins, grunting under the weight.

"Leave them, Brutus. The horses don't need any extra weight. We have to travel fast. His friends will be after us. Now we have Barabbas, the soldiers, and a band of thieves after us. Let's go."

"One bag. Just one bag."

Cyril cleared his throat. "One bag each. Throw me one too, Brutus. Marcus, we might need money to buy the women's freedom."

"You could be right. I'll take one, too." Marcus slung his bag across his saddle. "Now, let's go." He set his heels in the mare's sides.

They galloped for a mile, hugging the horses' necks to avoid the branches, before they pulled their horses to a walk to let them breathe. Marcus glanced over his shoulders every few moments.

Cyril and Brutus also watched the woods and rocks around them, but no one seemed to be around to stop them.

Marcus pushed his horse to a trot, this time following a well-worn path. With luck, they would reach Caesarea tomorrow.

Chapter 14

Meskhanet, her back braced against a thick wooden column, crossed her arms over her knees and placed her head on her arms. She felt so tired, but sleep eluded her. Her stomach grew queasier with each toss of the ship on the waves. She feared she would lose what little gruel sloshed in her stomach.

Joanna seemed to be riding the storm with ease. She lay asleep beside Meskhanet.

Their oversized guardian even dozed near the front wall of the hold, prone on the floor with his head resting on his hands.

Meskhanet despaired. Her trembling hands knotted the fabric of her cloak in her grip. The *borasco* matched her mood as the storm tossed the ship like a small stick on the waves. The door at the front of the hold had been closed, and little light entered the hold through gaps and knotholes in the boards above, except when lightning lit the sky. Rain struck in constant splashes against the ship and dripped on sleeping occupants. How could they sleep with the water dripping on them in this ship that shook and rolled in the storm? Even if she and Joanna lived through this, they might wish they had perished instead.

"Are you awake?" Joanna touched Meskhanet's foot.

"Yes, mistress." Meskhanet lifted her head.

"Sh. You must call me 'Mother'." Joanna whispered.

"How will that help? We are destined for the circus. It will not matter who is the wife of a physician or the slave or daughter of that wife."

"It's our only chance, Meskhanet. We must place our trust in the One God to keep us in safety. I pray that we will be purchased together by a person who is honorable."

"Oh, Mistress, I wish I had your faith."

"Mother." Joanna reminded her as she brushed Meskhanet's cheek, wiping away the tear that fell.

"How can I force my lips to call you 'Mother' when my heart is still a slave? And how can I believe the God of the Jews will rescue us from the terror I see coming?" Her voice trembled.

The ship gave a violent shake, and a grinding noise against one side woke all the inhabitants. Pots of excrement and urine spilled their contents across the floor, and water began spewing through the boards. Cries of alarm sounded from the men and women alike.

Varrus jumped to his feet. He scrambled to loose one bound slave after another, wading through deepening water. Some of the men joined his efforts, including Appius. Some ran for the rope ladder leading to the deck, crowding against each other, pushing weaker ones behind, but soon all were on the deck, Varrus herding them like so many chicks.

The captain shouted orders to the sailors to take the slaves ashore. It seemed they had run aground next to an island. Several slaves and sailors had already jumped into the water. The boat canted alarmingly. They would have to jump. Or fall.

Meskhanet peered over the side. "Can you swim, Mis— Mother?"

Joanna stared at the water below, her eyes wide. "No."

"It's been many years, but I used to be able when I was a child. If you will hold onto my tunic, I'll pull you ashore. It's not far. Take off your cloak. It will only make you sink."

"But how will we stay warm?"

"We will worry about that later. Come, jump with me. Take a deep breath and hold it." She placed her arm around Joanna and jumped.

The water enclosed them like a cold serpent, dragging them down. Joanna threw her arms around Meskhanet's neck. Meskhanet kicked and pulled with her hands toward the surface, but couldn't rise.

Varrus appeared beside them. He grabbed the backs of their tunics and lifted them to the surface, moving them slowly toward the shore. He must have been able to touch the bottom. When a trough in the waves exposed his face, he would gasp a breath of air. It seemed to Meskhanet like an hour before they reached the edge of the island. She and Joanna clung shivering to each other on the sand.

Varrus dove back in and pulled two more women to shore. Did the rest make their way in safety to the island? Sailors and slaves alike gathered wood, but how would they start a fire in the rain?

Varrus found some dry grass beneath one of the trees and twirled a stick between his hands until smoke and then fire began to lick at the grass. Waiting hands thrust small sticks and more grass on the meager flames. It didn't take long before a roaring fire began to warm them.

Appius pointed toward the ship and said something. Varrus dove into the water again. He swam to the ship and climbed up the rails on the steeply sloped deck until he reached the ship's only small boat attached to the upper side. He released the craft, and it slid down the deck and splashed into the water. Meskhanet watched as the man threw one wet cloak after another into the small vessel.

Appius had also run to the edge of the water, and he pulled with strong stokes to where Varrus, now in the water again, struggled to pull the boat to shore. With Varrus holding one side, Appius pulled himself into the craft from other side. Freeing the oars from the bottom of the boat, he rowed toward the shore. Varrus swam beside it.

While the cloaks steamed from branches thrust into the sand, the survivors of the ship's wreck huddled around the welcome blaze.

"Varrus." Meskhanet touched the giant's elbow.

He turned his gaze to her with a question in his eyes.

"Thank you for saving my, um, mother and I."

He smiled widely and pulled her into a warm hug. When he released her he turned to Joanna and repeated the hug.

The women laughed and patted his arms. Someone cleared his throat behind them.

"Do you have no similar thanks for the one who directed him to help?" Appius asked.

As they trotted the horses toward Caesarea, Marcus finally felt like they made good time. They should be there tomorrow or maybe the next day. The forests were not so thick now, and soon they'd be able to use the main road.

"Marcus, wait. My horse is lame." Cyril slipped off his mount and lifted one fore hoof.

Marcus groaned and turned his horse around.

Cyril straightened. "Go on without me. This horse won't be able to travel any farther this day."

"Get on behind me. Brutus and I will alternate double riding with you."

"That won't happen. The Greek weakling will not ride at my back." Brutus sneered. "I would carry his coins, though."

Marcus narrowed his eyes and stared at Brutus until the soldier started to sweat.

Brutus swore and grumbled something under his breath. "As you wish, Decanus."

Marcus led at a walk. Cyril's limping horse only attempted to follow for a few steps, then neighed as the others left it behind.

Marcus began to recognize the country around him. They neared the sheep camp where Barabbas had hidden so well for so long. When they rounded a bend, he raised his hand and moved a finger to his lips. He slid off the horse and crept to the top of a small rocky rise. When he peered over the edge, the camp seemed empty of life. No sheep, no fire, no tents. He started to turn back to his companions when he caught a movement at the edge of his vision.

Slowly and deliberately, he swung his head back to gaze at the valley below. A man stood in the shade of a tree. "Barabbas," Marcus muttered.

He heard a woman's glad cry and saw the old woman he assumed to be Barabbas's mother hurry out from the other side of the clearing toward her son, arms held out.

He pulled his head down with the same care. No sudden movements—too easy to catch. He beckoned the others to come closer. "He beat us here."

Brutus exhaled through flared nostrils. "He must have run."

"How can a man run that distance?" Cyril twisted his mouth. "He must have found a horse, too."

"It's possible he could run that far, Cyril. He's young, strong, and practiced. A messenger can run for a full day, if he must. But I agree. He must have found a horse. Or a mule. Maybe he found the same camp we did."

As though to answer their question their horses neighed, and one responded from the clearing below.

Marcus groaned and smacked his forehead. "We won't surprise him this day. Cyril, you stay here. Brutus, follow me."

They mounted and descended into the valley at a gallop. Barabbas melted into the trees, and his mother's shoulders slumped. Brutus turned his horse to charge after him.

"Stop, Brutus. Stay with me." He dismounted, and he walked toward the woman.

Rage reddened her face, and she shouted something. She pulled a knife from her belt.

Marcus lifted his hands. "Brutus, tell her it was not me who betrayed them."

Brutus translated and scowled at the woman's lengthy response. "She says you made her son leave her. And she called us several insulting names. Shall I kill her?" He lifted his sword.

"No. Just tell her we mean no harm to her, but that she must come with us."

"With us? That's stupid…uh, that would slow us down, sir."

Marcus narrowed his eyes. "It could be foolish, Brutus, but it might save our lives instead. Would he attack us if we have his mother?"

Brutus grunted, scowling. Turning to the woman, he said something to her. When she raised the knife and started toward them, he lifted a sword. She dropped the knife, but her glare showered hatred on both of them.

When her hands were bound, they called to Cyril to join them.

"Now we'll all be riding double. The woman will have to ride in front of one of us. We can't trust her to ride behind. She's kind to people she likes, but I don't think she likes us much now."

Cyril lifted a cooking pot from the edge of where the camp's cooking fire had been. "They must have left this. We can use it. Provided, of course, that we find something to cook." He turned to the woman and switched to Aramaic. "Please, madam, we need food and so do you. Are there any meat or vegetables here?"

The woman frowned. "Why should I help you? You would have killed my son."

"No, we go to rescue two women, our friends, who are missing. We aren't after your son. Unless he tries to harm us. Then we would not have a choice."

"You're Greek, aren't you? And those two are Romans. Romans and Greeks are not friends of Jews."

"Two of us are proselytes. And the other one will follow the orders of his decanus."

"Proselytes?"

"Yes. We became proselytes over a year ago, at the same time."

"Huh. Proselytes." She stood to her feet and walked to a lean-to under a tree. Behind it, straw covered a hole in the ground. She reached into the hole with her bound hands and pulled a mutton haunch partway out when she lost her balance and fell headfirst.

Cyril lifted her out. "I'm sorry, madam. Let me." He brought out the mutton. "This will be wonderful. We haven't had much to eat the past two days."

"There are onions, lentils, and herbs in there, too."

"And raisins. Anything more?"

The old woman peered at him with narrowed eyes. "Are you planning to take all I have to live on?"

Cyril lifted a cloth bag of barley. "You're coming with us. You don't want to leave anything here for the rats and birds and ants to finish off, do you?"

"I don't wish to go with you. I want to stay here. My son will return one day, and he will expect me to be here."

"My companions will insist, I fear. I'm sorry, madam. The one called Marcus says you are our assurance that Barabbas will not attack us."

"You fool yourself." She bowed her head and swiped at her eyes. "My son bears little affection for his mother."

Chapter 15

When Meskhanet awoke, the rain had stopped and the fire had burned down to a few coals. She didn't want to leave the meager warmth of her cloak and the huddled closeness of other warm bodies, but soon Joanna would be cold too, even though now she slept. Meskhanet stood, shivering, and wrapped the cloak about her. She walked in the darkness to the stack of fire wood and gazed up into a sky lit by forty thousand stars.

God of the Jews, are You somewhere up there in all that beauty? Do you have any authority in this land, wherever we are? Loukas says you are Lord everywhere, but we are so lost. We are captives, bound to be slaves under terrifying circumstances. We need help. Please?

As she gathered sticks for the fire, wheezing gasps for breath came from somewhere nearby.

Meskhanet froze.

The faint sound came from the trees on the other side of the woodpile. She settled her load of wood as silently as she could on the ground, all but one stout stick. Placing each foot with intense caution, she eased her way closer.

The wheezing stopped then started again.

Meskhanet reached the edge of the trees and crept closer to the sound. There, on the other side of the bush, a small boy stood with mouth open, his eyes wide with terror. His gaze turned toward Meskhanet. A noose around his neck and a net tangled him. When he lifted upward on his toes he could breathe. When he relaxed, the twined fiber around his neck tightened, shutting off his breath.

She dropped the stick. What was this, some sort of animal trap? Meskhanet stepped closer and lifted the boy with one arm while she tore at the knots with the fingernails on her other hand, but the binding held. She tripped on the netting and fell, almost pulling the child with her. She rose and tugged downward on the rope above his head, but her weight didn't bring the branch lower by more than a hand.

What could she do? She had no knife to cut the rope. She raced back to where the others slept. Varrus had his back to a tree, his head on his chest. Soft snores blew through his lips.

She whispered in his ear and shook his shoulder. "Varrus, wake up."

The man blinked his eyes, yawned, and stood to his feet.

"Please, come with me. Hurry. I found a child over there in terrible trouble."

His eyebrows lifted in question, but he followed.

When they reached the boy, she feared they arrived too late. No sound came from his still open mouth. His head canted backwards, his eyes were shut.

Varrus jumped forward, lifting the knife at his belt. He sliced through the rope and began cutting the net away from the boy's arms and legs.

Meskhanet grabbed the boy and pounded his back. "Breathe. Breathe, child. God of the Jews, help him!"

The boy gasped and opened his eyes. At the sight of Varrus his eyes widened, and he opened his mouth wide and drew in a breath. Meskhanet stifled his scream with her hand. She sat down beside him and pulled him onto her lap and against her shoulder.

"Shh, little one, he just saved your life. Do not scream at him." She smiled and patted his back. His black hair tangled in curls above skin lighter than hers. He wore a white short linen tunic—well, white where it wasn't dirty—and a dark belt. The boy's sandals looked expensive. Where did this one come from? He surely did not look like an island native.

"Who are you?" the boy asked, his voice muffled against her cloak.

"We were on a ship, but the ship wrecked out there on the sea." She pointed toward the hulk of the ship visible in the growing light. "How did you get into this trap?"

"I followed a rabbit. I wanted it to be my friend."

"You followed a rabbit in the middle of the night? Weren't you afraid of larger bad animals? Where are your parents?" She brushed twigs and dirt from his tunic.

"No, I didn't think about big animals. And Papa—."

A voice sounded from behind her. "Here. What are you doing to my son?"

"Papa!" The boy jumped off Meskhanet's lap and ran to the broad-shouldered man who scowled, arms folded across an ample chest. "I got caught in a trap, Papa, and the big man and the woman saved me."

The man turned to Varrus, gleaming steel-gray hair curling in wet waves around his face. "Thank you for helping my son. Who are you?"

She thought he had to be a Roman, judging from his clothing. The fine linen tunic hung to his knees, and a cloak wrapped around him in a heavy swirl. A medallion pinned the cloak at shoulders, and even in this dim light it gleamed of gold.

Varrus turned to Meskhanet. "Mhh." He pointed to her and then to the Roman.

"My name is Meskhanet, and my friend is Varrus. He cannot speak. I found your son and could not rescue him, so I asked Varrus to come."

"Your ship?" He tilted his head toward the wreck.

Varrus and Meskhanet both nodded.

"Are you Roman?"

Again Varrus nodded.

"My m—," Meskhanet ducked her head and glanced at Varrus. "My mother and I were captured by evil men and put onto the ship. We were being taken to Rome as slaves when the ship ran aground."

The man narrowed his eyes. "Perhaps I can help. Come with me."

Varrus shook his head and tilted his head at the people now beginning to stir. One of the sailors looked toward them and pointed. Varrus made anxious noises and shooing motions with his hands.

"He wants you to leave. You and your son could be in danger from the captain of this ship."

"I don't think so, young woman." He raised his hand. Several armed men stepped out from behind several trees. "You see, I have a little help. My name is Senator Decimus Varitor."

Cyril walked to where Marcus stood with his back to the fire. "I think we could untie Rebecca's hands, Marcus. She's decided that since we are proselytes and not after her son, she likes us. Brutus could be a different story."

Marcus nodded. "It seems she hasn't connected me with the vagrant who came begging at their camp. I hope she doesn't. I thought when we first arrived and she raised her knife that she recognized me."

"I don't believe so. She thought we were after Barabbas. You and Brutus are just two Roman soldiers, and therefore a danger to her son." He knelt to where he'd placed the haunch of mutton on the rock and rubbed salt into it, then he skewered it on a stout green stick and began to roast the meat.

"Any way you can hurry that meat? We need to be on our way."

"Patience. An hour's rest will do the horses and us nothing but good." He lifted his chin toward the horses feeding on barley spread on a leather apron.

"Hmph. I can tell you've been married for a year. I can remember when you would have forgone eating for a week to see Quinta more quickly." Marcus paced in front of the fire.

Brutus glanced toward them from where he stood watch. "I agree with the decanus. We have to move on."

Cyril scowled. "You want your meat raw? Get it then. Get your share and go. You two can mount one horse. Rebecca and I will follow when our meat has cooked."

Brutus doubled his fists and marched with stiff steps toward Cyril. Cyril's eyes narrowed, and he put the meat on a rock and turned toward Brutus with clenched fists.

It could be a close match. Brutus was short, but broad and muscular. Cyril might be a servant with no training as a soldier, but he stood taller than Brutus by a hand, and his broad shoulders showed he was no stranger to physical activity. But, Brutus was born mean while Cyril's nature was gentle.

Marcus couldn't let them fight. It could leave them more vulnerable to an attack from Barabbas, and it would delay their travel to Caesarea. If they left within the hour, they should be there shortly after sundown.

"Stop it, both of you. We will wait for the meat to cook. But we should be ready to leave immediately after we eat." Marcus strode between them. "Brutus, back to your post."

Jaw clenching and unclenching rhythmically, Brutus glared at both he and Cyril for a moment before complying with the order.

Rebecca had watched the whole scene with narrowed eyes from the edge of the fire, and she flinched as Marcus approached her. He whirled his hand, trying to tell her to turn around, but her eyes just widened with fear. "Cyril, would you help me here? I want her to turn around so I can untie her hands."

Cyril relaxed his stance and turned back toward Marcus and Rebecca. He spoke a few words and Rebecca turned. Marcus loosed the ropes and stepped back. "There. You're free."

He smiled at her when she turned around. She looked into his eyes and started. Did she recognize him?

She shook her head and walked muttering toward Cyril where she asked him a question. He shrugged and shook his head, murmuring something back to her.

Marcus gritted his teeth. He needed to learn Aramaic. He trusted Cyril, but he needed to understand what she was saying when she said it. It could become crucial at some point, especially with Barabbas following them, and he had no doubt the brigand would follow them.

She began to walk toward the edge of the clearing, and Marcus stepped forward to stop her.

"Wait, Marcus, she just goes to relieve herself," Cyril said, chuckling. "This mutton could be cooked enough to eat soon. Maybe you could concentrate on readying the horses."

Marcus felt his face warm, and he stepped aside to allow Rebecca to pass.

"When did you begin giving the orders, Cyril? But you're right." Marcus strode toward the horses, then paused and turned to Cyril. "I need a favor from you, my friend. Would you teach me to speak Aramaic?"

Cyril laughed. "In one day? Probably not. And we'll be turning her loose when we get to Caesarea, won't we?"

"That's my plan. But if he presses us, we won't turn her loose until we board a ship for Rome." He grinned. "Or she might find she likes Miriam and Quinta and their families so much she won't want to leave. How could she resist cuddling the baby?"

Cyril laughed. "She might have to argue with Miriam's mother over grandmothering time."

"When are you going to produce a grandchild for Loukas and Joanna?"

"Soon, I hope. If we ever get back to Caesarea."

"Ah, then you agree we should mount up and go?"

"All right. The meat is still red, but if you so order...."

"I think I should have let Brutus have you," Marcus muttered. "You are the most insubordinate servant I've ever known." He turned back to the horses. The wooden Roman saddles weren't as comfortable as bareback, but they made it easier to attach items, like the bags of money. He wished they had a donkey or another horse to load the extra food and the bags, but they would have to carry it all on their backs.

Rebecca tugged on Cyril's sleeve. She chattered on for a few moments, pointing in the direction she had just come from.

Cyril nodded and turned to Marcus. "She says there is a horse in the woods. The animal showed up yesterday, nuzzling her for treats."

Marcus shook his head in disbelief. He followed the woman. There he was, the same bay gelding. It had to be the same one. The one he and Brutus rode away from the brigand's camp. The one that lived with him in the cave. The one he'd found waiting to take him to Loukas and Joanna. *He must be the One God's gelding.*

Chapter 16

A senator. Maybe a senator could help Joanna and her. If he would. Meskhanet felt a small hope rise in her heart.

Meskhanet knelt down at the boy's side and inspected the marks from the rope around his neck. "I'm glad you are well, little one."

"So am I." Decimus ruffled his son's hair. "This adventurous young man is my youngest, Septus. Our ship put into a cove in the lea of the island when the storm struck. We went ashore for a few moments and my son saw the rabbit. For someone so small, he moves remarkably fast."

"Where is your ship bound, Senator?" *Oh, please, say Caesarea.*

"We are on our way home. I wanted to take Septus with me on a journey to Egypt. We bought grain for my horses, did we not, Septus?" The Senator patted his son's back as the boy gazed at his father with wide eyes.

"I got an elephant too, didn't I, Papa?"

"Yes, an ivory elephant. Not quite as big as a real one."

"Show Mes-ki, um, Mes-kuh … How do you say it?"

"Meskhanet."

"Mes-ki-net. Show Mes-ki-net how big a real elephant is, Papa."

The senator grasped his son and tossed him over his head. "*This* big."

Septus giggled and threw his arms around his father's neck when back at the senator's eye level.

Decimus turned back to Meskhanet and Varrus. "Now, take me to your ship's captain."

The sailors who earlier had walked their way with threatening steps halted when the senator's soldier companions stepped into view. Now they stood in a respectful half-circle between the senator and the shore.

Meskhanet moved her gaze toward the sailors. She didn't want to take him past them to the captain. Her stomach tightened.

Varrus rumbled, put himself between Meskhanet and the sailors, and plowed forward. To a man, they moved aside. The soldiers followed Varrus.

The senator took his son's hand and Meskhanet's arm. "Shall we?"

Joanna rushed forward when they entered the camp. "Meskhanet! I have been so worried. No one knew where you were."

"I'm sorry, Mistress."

Decimus cast a sideways glance at Meskhanet. "Your daughter said you had been kidnapped."

Joanna cast a fearful look, first at Meskhanet and then at their captors. She lifted her head. "Yes, sir, we were."

"Are you Roman citizens?"

"Yes, sir. I am, and my...daughter will soon be."

Decimus cast his gaze between the two women. "Ladies, forgive me, but I believe I detect some deception in your speech. I am a senator, and I might help, but you must be truthful with me before I approach the captain."

"I'm telling you the truth, Senator. I have been a Roman citizen for twenty years. My husband, a physician, is in Caesarea, and I have no doubt but that he and his friend, the centurion primus there, are looking for us. It will not go well for the kidnappers when they are found."

"And Meskhanet?"

Joanna glanced down then raised her head and opened he mouth to speak.

Meskhanet interrupted. "I am her slave, Senator."

"But she will soon be my daughter. My husband and I will adopt her. She saved our lives at great risk to her own, and we love her. It's only right that we make her a part of our family."

One corner of the senator's mouth twitched up. "I see."

A man swaggered over to them, his chin jutted forward. "You wanted to see me?"

His broad forehead and large nostrils reminded Meskhanet of a bullock. The stains on his cloak had to have come from more than just the shipwreck. The man stank of too many weeks without bathing even after being dunked in the sea.

The senator's lidded eyes perused the man. "If you are the captain, yes."

"I am. What do you want?"

"Were you part of the scheme to kidnap these women?"

"They aren't kidnapped. They're slaves. Bound for the circus." The captain ran his tongue over his upper lip and studied Joanna and Meskhanet. "Makes me wish I was a gladiator, myself."

"They are Roman citizens, Captain, and were indeed kidnapped."

The captain sneered his reply. "Who told you that? The big man there?"

Decimus paused. He lifted his hand, and his men stretched into a line behind him.

The captain blanched and lifted a dirty sleeve to wipe his forehead.

"Captain, these women and the rest of the illegally gotten slaves shall be released into my custody. These two women will return with me to Rome. You and your men may remain here on this island until another ship comes by. If one comes by. It would not disappoint me if you spent the rest of your putrid lives here."

"Wait. We're Roman citizens too—or at least I am. You're sentencing me without a trial."

The captain's sailors began gathering behind him. They cast fearful glances to each other. Meskhanet suspected none of them wanted to fight the Romans.

"You did not answer my question, Captain. Were you a part of the scheme to take these women prisoners?"

"No, I wasn't. I was told they were slaves."

"You will tell me, then, who gave them over to you."

The color faded from the captain's face like a sunrise into the fog. "I can't do that."

"You can, and you will. Willingly or unwillingly is your choice." Decimus raised his hand again, and his men drew their swords. "Take him to the hold. How many of you others side with your captain?"

The sailors backed away, shaking their heads and murmuring.

"Who is the captain's first assistant?"

"I am, sir." A man strode forward, missing teeth turning "s's" into "th's."

"We cannot take all of you with us to Rome. There's not enough room onboard. I will send a ship back for you. Meanwhile, I assign you temporary captain with the care of not only your crew but also the rest of the ones held in slavery. If any come to harm before the ship returns for you, I will hold you responsible."

"Yes, sir. They will be fine, sir. But we are short on provisions, even if we are able to get them off the ship. How will I feed them?"

"There are people living on this island. I suggest you trade with them. And you have a sea full of fish." He scowled, and the man backed away. Decimus's voice boomed across the crowd. "Are there any others brought illegally into slavery?"

Meskhanet chuckled behind her hand—the senator's eyebrows shot upward as every one of the slaves stepped forward.

"I cannot believe this. Can it be?"

Varrus touched his shoulder. When the senator turned toward him, Varrus shook his head.

"Ah," Decimus said. "You know which were legally acquired and which were not?"

Varrus nodded.

"Were you?"

He nodded again.

"Show me then, which were kidnapped and which were legal."

Varrus stepped among the slaves and began selecting one after the other. He led them back with him and then touched also Joanna and Meskhanet.

The senator clapped Varrus on the back. "You shall also come with me"

Appius stepped forward. "Sir, if I may."

"Are you one of the slaves or one of the captain's men?" Decimus asked.

"One of the slaves, sir. My name is Appius, and Varrus and I have always stayed together. I like being a gladiator. I would likely starve or become a thief if freed on the streets in Rome."

One eyebrow lifted. "You wish to remain a slave."

"I wish to remain a gladiator."

"Do you know who you are bound to?"

Appius nodded.

"Then you should do as your owner wishes. As will the other slaves. I will hold them in Rome at my estate for their lawful owners once we arrive."

"What I mean, sir, is that I'd like to go with you. Surely you have room for one more. I could sleep with the sailors." His glance slid toward Meskhanet.

Marcus mounted the bay gelding and held his hand out for one of the coin bags. He balanced it across the horse's withers as Brutus mounted another of the horses with the remaining bags. Cyril, with Rebecca on behind him, kneed his horse into a brisk trot toward the north.

"Not that way, Cyril. I'd rather not take a main road. Remember, we're escapees too. We'll go west and then north. Once we reach the Plain of Sharon, we won't have much choice but to follow the road. If we save our horses' strength, we can run them once we get on the road should it become necessary. Most of the soldiers there should be from Caesarea, not Jerusalem."

Brutus snorted and smirked at Cyril.

Marcus grunted. How long would he have to stand between these two men? He hoped one or both of them would stay in Caesarea when he went on to find Meskhanet. And Joanna. Loukas would never forgive him if he brought back his beloved and left Joanna in captivity.

His beloved. Would she ever be, even if he freed her? He didn't want her to marry him because she felt grateful, if she did. But then, if he married her, perhaps love would come later. Maybe he should talk to Loukas.

Marcus patted the neck of his mount, marveling again at how many times the gelding had shown up when needed. The horse surely belonged to God. How else could it have led the way to Loukas and Joanna?

It was dusk, but Marcus and his companions could see the coastal road through the Plain of Sharon when Barabbas showed his face. He jumped his horse out in front of the bay from behind a rock. The gelding jerked his head up, but didn't rear or bolt.

"What is it you want, Barabbas?" Marcus asked, hoping the man understood Greek.

Barabbas swore. He pulled his sword and spoke with a heavy accent. "Release my mother. She doesn't belong with you."

"Do you see chains on her?"

Barabbas waved his sword in the air and directed an angry remark to Rebecca.

Rebecca shook her head and shouted back at him.

Cyril's eyebrows rose.

Barabbas and his mother continued railing at each other. For perhaps the thousandth time, Marcus wished he could speak their language.

Brutus growled and pointed. "Troops."

Barabbas jerked his horse around, looked toward the approaching regiment. He set his heels in his horse's side and sped back into the hills as the men approached.

"I hope we don't wish we'd followed him," Marcus said as he turned to face them.

"Who was that man?" The decanus leading the troop asked. "And who are you?"

"That was a robber and murderer named Barabbas. I am Decanus Marcus Varitor of Jericho."

The other decanus shrugged. "He's gone now, although I don't think he's robbed or murdered anyone in this area. His name isn't familiar. And you—why are you here?"

"I am a friend to Centurion Julius. The man with the woman behind him is Cyril, Centurion Julius's servant. The woman is a friend. This one is a man in my command, Brutus."

The decanus's eyebrows dipped and his eyes narrowed as he cast a sideways glance at Brutus. "I remember Brutus. Where are you bound?"

"To Caesarea. Who are you?"

"Decanus Gaius. Come with me. I'll escort you the rest of the way to Caesarea."

"Your presence is welcome, Gaius. Let's go."

Gaius stopped outside the gate to Caesarea. "This is as far as I go. We are on night patrol for the area between here and Joppa. A guard inside can show you where Centurion Julius lives."

"I know where he lives. Thank you, Decanus. And thank you for chasing off Barabbas." Marcus saluted.

"With two able soldiers and another man, you shouldn't have had any problem with him. Why did he approach you?"

"We're carrying some coins." Marcus patted the bags across the gelding's withers.

Gaius nodded, saluted, and left.

Cyril chuckled as they rode through the gate opened for them. "You are a master of minimal information, Marcus. Without lying, three times in less than an hour you have managed to convey an impression entirely opposite of the facts."

"The misinformation seemed necessary at the time, my friend."

They arrived in front of Julius's home and dismounted. Rebecca's eyes flew open wider than Marcus would have thought possible, and she babbled something to Cyril.

"Brutus, I'll take the coins inside; you take the horses to the stable and then come back here." Marcus ran his hand over the short stubble on his head.

Brutus muttered something, but handed the bags to Marcus and led the horses away.

Julius opened the door. "Ah, welcome. I'm glad to see you back, Cyril. Things have not run so well without you." Deep circles under his eyes hinted of little sleep and heavy worry. "What's in the bags?"

"I think it could have been intended as a legion's pay. We're not sure. We liberated it from some apparent thieves, and we found the bodies of several soldiers. We couldn't bring all of it, but brought what we could carry, and we can direct people back to the place where we found it. I doubt it's still there, though. There was no time to hide the remainder."

Quinta entered the room at a run and threw herself into Cyril's arms. Her waist-length blonde hair hung in wet tangles behind her. "Cyril! You're here! Praises be to the One God. Oh, if you had only been here. They would not have been taken if you had been with them. My husband, we must find them."

Loukas threw open the curtain hanging over the doorway to his bed chamber and marched up to Marcus. He clapped his hands to Marcus's shoulders. "Ah, Marcus, Cyril—I'm so glad you're here. We do need your help."

"That's why I'm here. I'm surprised you're still here and not on your way to Rome." Marcus began removing his sword and buckler.

"I will be tomorrow. We had to wait for a ship going in that direction."

Julius lifted his hand to Marcus's shoulder. "I prayed you would arrive before tomorrow morning, my friend. I cannot go, and Loukas should not go alone. Never become a centurion. Your life is no longer your own."

Chapter 17

Meskhanet walked to the senator's ship hand-in-hand with Septus who chattered about his ivory elephant, his home, his father's horses, his friends, and the myriad other things of interest to small boys. Meskhanet offered little in response. A smile or a nod seemed to be all the encouragement the child needed. Which was well, since her mind was not on the boy's commentary.

Joanna walked at Decimus's side, head bowed, just ahead of Meskhanet. She wondered what subdued her usually self-possessed mistress. This should be a happy time for her. She could be back with Loukas within a few weeks. Yet if Meskhanet were not mistaken, Joanna wept. The senator glanced down at her too, with the same concerned expression Meskhanet felt must be on her own face.

He led them down a flight of stairs and lifted the flap to a canvas enclosure against one side. "This will be your cabin, ladies. I'm sorry it is not larger, but this is not a ship for transporting people."

"You are kind, Senator. I appreciate your help more than I can say." Joanna touched his arm.

Decimus placed his hand over hers. "Dear lady, anything you need, you have only to ask. I am at your service."

"Me, too. Mes-ki-net may even play with my elephant." Septus beamed.

Meskhanet knelt and hugged him. "Septus, you own my heart. Will you wed me?"

Septus blushed. "I'm too little. But someday I'll be big." He stood on his toes. "I'll be as big as my Papa. Then we can marry, can't we, Papa?"

"Well—."

"Oh, but then I will be old, little one. You will want a young wife."

"Julia might be jealous," Decimus said, winking at Meskhanet.

Septus stood for a moment in thought. "May I have two wives, Papa?"

The senator chuckled. "No, son. At least not at the same time."

"And our religion does not encourage divorce, Septus." Joanna said.

As soon as they were alone, Meskhanet took Joanna's hand. "What is it that makes your face so sad, Mistress? What may I do to help?"

Joanna met her eyes. "I worry for Loukas. I know him. He is taking the blame and beside himself with worry. It was my fault, not his. I should have listened to you, but I acted with arrogance. Both of us are here because of me. I was foolish. Will you forgive me?"

Meskhanet shook her head. "There is nothing to forgive. It was not your fault. That wicked mongo did wrong, not you. Who would know he would do something so evil? We should be back in Caesarea in a few weeks. And if I know Loukas, he is searching for you now."

"Yes, but in his search and in our return, will our ships pass each other? Should I remain in Rome until he arrives? Shall I return to Caesarea and hope he waits there for me? Tell me what to do."

Meskhanet lowered her gaze to her hands. "I do not know, Mistress. In everything else, you have prayed. Perhaps you could start there."

"We are so far from home, Child. I do not know where to go to pray." Joanna looked out of the porthole of the small canvas room they'd been given.

Meskhanet shook her head. There was so much to learn about the Jew's God. "Oh. We cannot pray to the Jewish God on a Roman ship, then."

Joanna lifted her hand. "No, it's not that. There is no place quiet to go. How can I hear His voice in all this noise?"

"He speaks to you? You have heard Him?" Meskhanet gazed in awe at her mistress. "Are you a priestess?"

She shook her head. "No. There are no priestesses in the Jewish religion, and if there were, they would not be among those who converted to our faith. Only descendants of one of their patriarchs, Levi, can be a priest."

"What has He said to you before? How did you know it was the Jewish God? Did you see Him?" Curiosity made Meskhanet's heart leap.

Joanna laughed. "No. He hasn't appeared to me. Except…perhaps, once, I saw His Son."

"He has a Son?"

"You might have seen Him, too, but you probably wouldn't have noticed Him."

Meskhanet's hand flew to her chest. "I? I saw Him? Where? When? What does He look like?"

"There were so many people at Quinta's wedding. He was there. He spoke to some of the people there. He looks like so many of the other Hebrews—a narrow nose, skin almost as dark as yours, dark hair, dark eyes…it was His eyes that captured my attention."

"Oh, I remember. He held Leah's baby." Her voice dropped to a reverential hush. "I saw Him. He spoke to me, and His eyes—they looked into my heart."

"Yes. That was Him."

"If that is what the God of the Jews is like, I'm glad I promised to follow Him. And God spoke to you?"

"Not exactly. Not a voice. Just sometimes a knowing *this* is what I should do. Or *that way* is where I should go."

"Like what you said in the slave market? That He didn't show you which slave to choose?"

"Yes. When I chose you, it was at His leading."

"But how did you *know*?" Meskhanet had to find out.

"I felt pulled to you, as though a thick soft rope drew my heart toward yours. I have never doubted since that you belonged in our household."

"I remember when you chose me. You were the only one who looked at my eyes. Everyone else looked on my nakedness. I was happy when you bought me." Meskhanet felt the heat rise in her cheeks.

"Meskhanet, you answered my question."

"What question?"

"The one about where could I go to hear His voice."

"I did? How did I answer your question?"

"You reminded me His voice is quiet in my ears but loud in my heart."

Marcus ran for the side of the boat for the third time since boarding an hour before. He'd rather ride a Roman saddle for ten thousand miles than climb aboard a ship for ten. He'd as soon be mortally wounded as die of sea sickness. It didn't help that Cyril and Loukas chuckled and Brutus glowered at his agony. Rebecca looked puzzled, and she winced as she brushed back wind-blown gray hair from her face.

Loukas held his hand out and touched hers. He murmured something to her, and she showed him a raw sore on her wrist. He left them and returned with an ointment that he spread on the sore.

Brutus glared at Rebecca, too. A lot. He had voiced his objections to Marcus. "Why does that woman accompany us? She's not young. Or pretty, either."

"She wouldn't stay at Julius's. You know that. She'd be gone the day after we left and probably tell Barabbas where we went. She will be no trouble for the two short weeks we'll be on this ship."

Two weeks, maybe more if there were bad storms. He would die of this illness before then. How could he be responsible for these men as well as rescue their friends if he were dead? And he did sincerely wish he were dead.

"Want something to eat, Marcus? The ship's cook made some mutton stew I know you'd like." Cyril waved a clay bowl under his nose with congealed grease floating on the surface. "Mm. Doesn't it smell good?"

Marcus turned away. There couldn't be anything left in his stomach, but he headed for the rail again anyway. The dry heaves left him shaking like a forty-day drinking spree and as limp as a hank of wet hair.

Marcus felt an arm slip around his shoulders. He raised his head and Loukas wiped his mouth with a rag.

"I know you feel sick now, but the nausea will pass. In a day or two, you'll feel like your old self."

"I feel like my old self now. Maybe a hundred years or so old." He put his elbows on the rail and leaned his head on them. "The same thing happened when I came from Rome to Israel."

"And you didn't die then, did you?"

"No, and I realize I won't die this time, but that doesn't make me feel any better now." He raised his head and opened his eyes.

Sand. He must have sand in his eyes.

Two days later, he began to eat again. Bread and watered wine. He couldn't quite stomach the stew the cook served day after day. Not yet.

The borascos didn't help, but given the season the storms could be with them for the entire voyage. There wasn't much he could do about that. Spring was close but not near enough for his liking. It appeared there was not much he could do about anything. He paced the deck, slept, ate, and paced again.

Cyril walked up behind him with another bowl of stew. Marcus could smell it. Ugh. "Remind me, why did we have to bring you? And is there a good reason why I shouldn't throw you and that stew overboard?"

"Because my wife insisted Loukas would need my help. You too. And maybe she wanted to be sure you actually returned. You might decide it's not necessary to go back to Caesarea if you have Meskhanet with you in Rome. Come to think of it, I think Julius might have been of the same mind. And in your weakened condition, I doubt you could throw a mouse overboard. I'm safe." Cyril scooped a bite of stew into his mouth.

Marcus fought his rising gorge. "Where's Brutus?"

"Probably in the galley berating the cook. Last I heard, he'd been able to irritate everyone but the captain at least once, and it's mealtime, so it's the cook's turn."

"And why not the captain?"

"Captain Octavius is non-irritable. Even the borascos do not shake him. Must be why he's a captain. He ignores Brutus, which really annoys the man."

"I thought maybe he might be beginning to respect authority. He does obey me, now, but sometimes I feel like it's almost as much as he can stand. I've never known any soldier who questioned authority so much as he does. At the same time, he did save my life at the risk to his own career, and he's been loyal."

"Yes. I'm grateful he saved your scruffy hide too. Badly as it needed washing, your hide is as important to me as Julius's." He cleaned up the last bite and dumped the remaining liquid into the sea.

"And yet you bring that glop and wave it under my nose. I'm ready to jump overboard myself just to get away from the smell. Except that you already put some into the water, so now even that will smell of this evil concoction."

"It fills the hole in the belly, and that's about all I can say for it. But someone here has to have enough strength to complete the assignment. Maybe we'll find decent food in Rome."

"That's still some time off. Too much, if the winds don't stop blowing the wrong way. I hope I live that long. Walk with me?" Marcus waved his hand in front of them and walked toward the stern. "Where's Loukas?"

"Resting, I think. He said something about some sleep this afternoon."

"Is he sick?" Marcus stopped and looked at Cyril.

"No, although he's still not as strong as I'd like to see. I wonder whose ship that is?" He pointed at a ship deliberately pulling up on the bow.

Marcus felt the blood drain from his face. "The only ones who would stop a Roman ship would be a Roman garrison ship or pirates. And that's not a Roman ship. Hurry, go get Brutus. Send him to me, and then you go below with Loukas."

"And why would that be? I do know how to fight. Remember? I used to practice with you and Julius when we were young."

"Yes, but there's a difference between wooden swords and steel. Quinta would never let me back into the house if I allowed you to get yourself killed."

Cyril trotted toward the stairway to the galley, shouting for Brutus. He nearly collided with Loukas coming up the steps.

Brutus must have understood the urgency in Cyril's tone, because the man arrived at Marcus's side before the shouting started. He drew his sword and stood with Marcus, close to the other men gathering on the deck, all of them armed.

Despite what he told Cyril, his friend Julius's servant and Loukas had both joined them. No time to send them back now.

The two ships closed. Men lined up behind Marcus, and more men lined the rails of the other ship. Marcus could feel his heart pounding. His muscles tensed. He stood ready for battle.

Chapter 18

Meskhanet quivered when the ferocity of yet another borasco shook their ship. She didn't know if she'd rather go up on deck where the winds buffeted anyone brave or foolhardy enough to be there, or if she'd rather be here in this small and narrow tent-cabin wondering if the ship's walls would fall in on them. She heard Joanna's soft voice even above the storm.

Joanna's head was turned toward the one porthole, now boarded to shut out all but the least amount of light and rivulets of water. "O Adonai, please don't let this ship fail, please. We're so frightened. Where will we be safe, Adonai? We cry to You from the depths of our hearts, from the bowels of this storm-battered vessel. Where is Your compassion and Your strong arm? Where is Your mastery of the sea and land? We are small, smaller than the smallest insect in Your sight. You lift your hand, and the winds listen. You speak, and the sun begins to shine. You have the ability to rescue us or destroy us. We pray Your indulgence on our fears and ask You to forgive our lagging faith. We trust in You and You alone to guide us to safety."

Meskhanet's fears ebbed while Joanna spoke. "You pray so beautifully, Mistress. Surely the God of the Jews will hear you."

"He doesn't hear because of beautiful prayers, Daughter. He hears when the words come from the heart."

Meskhanet pondered that question for a moment. "How could a person speak to the Jewish God if not from the heart?"

"That is the perfect question. Perhaps those who pray to be heard by others within hearing should think on that one."

Meskhanet fell silent. There seemed to be so much she didn't know. There were priests of other gods in Egypt who spoke as though they wished to be heard by people too. Could it be that some priests would also only give lip service to the God of the Jews? Why would they do that?

As the storm began to subside, voices and other noises reassured Meskhanet all was well. She and Joanna peered out the flap that served as their door.

"There are the senator and Septus." Meskhanet pointed toward the bow. "All seems calm now."

Joanna smiled. "Except Septus. He seems just as excited as usual. His father is so patient with him. I haven't seen him once get angry, have you?"

"Not with Septus, but after watching his actions with the other captain, I wouldn't want him angry with me." Meskhanet lifted her gaze to the deck.

"Who is angry, ladies?" Appius appeared and leaned, arms folded, against the wall next to their doorway. "Zeus, maybe? Or Neptune? Whichever one, the god seemed wrathful, as though he wished to shake the ship apart." He ran a hand down Meskhanet's hair, free of her usual scarf, and pulled his fingers through a handful.

Meskhanet jerked away and pushed at his hand, fear widening her eyes. The man's chest and legs lacked covering, and his eyes glowed with desire.

Joanna stepped between them. "I do not believe in Zeus or Neptune, Appius. They are made of wood or stone and cannot create a storm. And keep your hands off Meskhanet."

He pushed Joanna aside and took another step toward Meskhanet. "Perhaps she will become a gladiator's woman. Would you like that, beautiful Meskhanet?"

Meskhanet backed away. "No. Don't touch me."

"Oh, come now, sweet child. Would you not like to be my woman? The woman of the undefeated gladiator, Appius?"

Meskhanet drew a breath and backed as far away as the room would allow. The walls of the room closed in on her as the muscular Appius stalked her.

Joanna grabbed his arm. "Either you leave or I will call the senator."

Appius whirled on her. "Who do you think you are? You are a slave like me. And I have a right to the woman of my choice. Or women." His gaze raked her too.

"Ask the senator, gladiator. I doubt Meskhanet will be on your list. Or I."

Oh, be careful, Mistress, he has the look of a jackal about to leap. Meskhanet shivered and felt her mouth go dry.

"And why not? She also is a slave." A light dawned in his eyes, and he nodded. "Ah, he wants Meskhanet for himself."

"No, that's not it. Leave, Appius. Not every man thinks only of lust and fighting. We do not want your company." Joanna inserted herself again between them.

Meskhanet stepped closer to her mistress, but did she do it for protection of herself or her mistress? Fear pushed rational thought from her mind. A grunt sounded from the doorway, and every muscle in her body shrieked with tension.

Varrus, scowling, grasped the gladiator's upper arms and lifted him out of the room.

"Varrus! Put me down. What do you think you're doing?"

Meskhanet relaxed a bit. Varrus would protect her even against Appius, his friend?

Varrus dropped him, his brows still furrowed. He stepped into the room, his bulky presence blocking the gladiator's access to the women in their narrow cabin.

"Varrus, you are *my* friend, are you not? I wouldn't hurt her, my friend. I only want her to carry my son. Would that not be a good thing?"

I would rather carry a spider's son!

Varrus crossed his arms and spread his feet.

A cold voice stopped all action. "What goes here?"

Appius turned toward the sound. "Ah, Senator. It is good to see you. May the gods bestow their benedictions upon you this day. Nothing of import is happening here. As you know, a gladiator is given his choice of women amongst the slaves. I choose these women." His head lifted and he licked his lips as he perused them again.

Meskhanet cringed. Was she a meal he would consume and then throw away the bones?

"You do not get your choice of free women, gladiator. These two are free." Decimus stepped into the doorway.

Meskhanet exhaled. She hadn't realized she held her breath until now. Her teeth unclenched, the skin on her forehead relaxed, and her shoulders returned to their natural position.

Appius bowed with a smirk. "As you wish, Senator. Come, Varrus." Appius grasped his former employee's arm and tugged.

Varrus shook his arm free with a scowl. "O."

Meskhanet liked that. Varrus told his former master no. *Did You send this large protector to us, God of the Jews?*

Appius frowned. "Come, Varrus."

Varrus shook his head and stood in the entryway. "'O."

Decimus laughed. "I believe Varrus has declared his new allegiance. Give up, Appius."

Marcus jumped the rail onto the other ship, sword slashing toward the nearest of the pirates. "Die, fool!"

Brutus followed, short sword in one hand and knife in the other. "For Rome!"

Behind him and before him, shouts of rage coupled with screams of pain rang in Marcus's ears. Blood and sweat splashed into his eyes, and he couldn't tell if it were his or someone else's.

Time seemed to pass in slow motion as one slash followed another and one scream drowned out the one before. When would it end? Marcus's muscles burned and his throat scraped out one battle cry, and another, and another. His sword grew slippery and he tossed it to his left hand as he drew a dagger and pursued the next enemy.

An eternity or a moment later, Marcus wiped perspiration from his face and looked around him. The bleeding and dead lay supine on the red deck.

Cyril stood at his side, his eyes glazed. Brutus leaned back on the rail, grinning.

Loukas—where was Loukas? Marcus scanned around the deck. "Where is our noble physician?"

Cyril turned toward him, tears filling his eyes. "There." He pointed to a body behind him with a nearly severed arm, lifeblood pumping out of it with decreasing energy. He dropped to his knees.

Marcus knelt beside him and gently turned his friend over. "Loukas, can you hear me?"

Loukas opened his eyes wide. "Tell Joanna…I…love…."

"No, Loukas, stay." Marcus pulled his belt off and wrapped it around his friend's upper arm, but Loukas's eyes fixed and a long sigh expelled his remaining breath.

Cyril's ragged sob behind him nearly undid him. He couldn't weep, not in front of Brutus. He rested his head on his knee. "El Shaddai, please take this saint to Your bosom. I loved him like a brother. My heart aches because he will no longer be here to counsel me, but You will never find a more faithful friend to stand next to You."

He stood and nodded to Cyril. "Help me, would you?" Cyril took Loukas's legs, and together they lifted their friend's body over the rail. Marcus saluted and Cyril watched in solemn silence as Loukas's lean frame sank slowly beneath the waves.

Marcus turned back. Rebecca approached them, tears running down wrinkled cheeks. Even she had come to love the physician in the short time she'd known him.

Marcus straightened his shoulders and inhaled. "Let's clean off the deck, men. Rome has gained a new ship."

"Do you mind if I lie down instead, Marcus?" Cyril's voice sounded shaky and weak.

Marcus took a close look at him for the first time since the battle ceased. Cyril's face lacked color, and his left arm leaked blood in a steady stream.

"Why did you not say something, man?" Marcus stepped closer and caught his friend as he slid to the deck.

"Help me, Brutus. We'll take him to my tent." He raised his voice to address other men throwing bodies overboard. "Put some planks across the rails to our ship."

An hour later, they had Cyril's arm bandaged and Brutus left to continue the cleanup activities. Marcus lifted Cyril's head and gave him a drink of honeyed wine.

"It seems our roles have been reversed, my friend." Cyril's speech sounded a little faint. "It feels strange to lie in bed while someone serves me. I'm sorry."

Marcus grinned. "It will cost you once you have healed. Double meals for a month at least."

Cyril grunted. "You will be so round it would take two horses to carry you. Four to pull a chariot. And a team of mules to carry your food alone. Your centurion would never approve."

"My centurion I hope thinks me dead. I'm an escapee, remember? Hmm, there could be another problem. You'd probably be in a small amount of trouble too, unless I told them I kidnapped you. That could cost you yet another month of preparing my meals."

"A cost I might not live to pay if you don't allow me to rest." Cyril's eyes closed.

"Understood. But before I go, take another drink. You leaked a lot of liquid out there." Marcus lifted Cyril's head and put a cup to his lips.

Marcus found Rebecca hovering outside the door wringing her hands. She chattered to him and pointed at Cyril. He led her back into the canvas room.

"Cyril, what is she saying?"

Cyril opened his eyes and asked her a question.

She nodded and chattered, pointing first to him and then Marcus.

"She wants to help take care of me. She says you are a man, and this is woman's work."

Marcus chuckled. "Well, sometimes maybe. It's fine with me." He nodded to Rebecca and strode out onto the deck.

The captain of their ship walked with a sailor's rolling gait up to Marcus. The breeze blew strands of graying hair across a weathered forehead. "You handled yourselves well, you and your friends. Had it not been for you, our ship might have been lost. I'm sorry for the death of the physician. We could have used his services, especially now with so many wounded men. I understand you and he were close friends too. You have my sympathy."

"We were, and thank you. I will sorely miss him."

"We need someone to captain the pirates' ship to Rome. Would you do that?"

"Captain Octavius, I'm flattered, but I know nothing about ships. Don't you have a second in command you could assign that job?"

"He was killed in the fight. I can give you half the sailors. I'd give you the most capable and reliable ones, of course. All you would have to do is follow us. I will put a large lantern on the stern. You wouldn't need a navigator." One bare muscular arm reached out and grasped his. "Please. I know of no others onboard who can command."

Marcus pursed his lips. *Adonai, I need some help now.* "Let me think about this for a time, Captain. Would you give me an hour?"

"Certainly, Decanus." Octavius saluted and strode to the foredeck.

Marcus strode to the side and crawled from one vessel to the other on the planks tied to and extending from one ship's rail to the other. "Brutus."

"Sir." Brutus swished a bucket full of sea water across a red stain.

"I've been asked to captain this ship to Rome. I want you, Cyril, and Rebecca to come with me." He turned to recross the makeshift bridge.

"He's a servant. She's a woman." Brutus used a grimy hand to wipe a trace of gore from his cheek, leaving more behind than he removed.

"What?" Marcus turned to face him.

"Julius's servant and the woman. They do not need to go with us. He's wounded and would be of no use." Brutus shrugged his shoulders as though trying to rid himself of unwanted burdens.

"His name is *Cyril* and hers is *Rebecca.* She's taking care of him. He's a friend I've known since childhood. He will stay with us, and so will she." Marcus gritted his teeth and fought back an angrier retort. There were times when he wondered why he brought this curmudgeon with them. "Get Loukas's medicine chest."

Chapter 19

Meskhanet pulled her cloak over her head. Was it morning already? No, not possible.

"Come, child. It's time you were up." Joanna's cheerful voice only made Meskhanet want to burrow deeper. "It's beautiful out today. I can see land, and the captain says it's Italy. We'll sail between Italy and Sicily, then up the Italian coast to Rome. He says with fair winds we'll be there in just a few days. I haven't seen Rome before. Come with me. I want you to see the horizon."

She groaned, but pushed one edge of her cloak back. "You are a harsh taskmistress. Could you not sleep just a moment longer?" In obedience only, Meskhanet lifted her reluctant body off the pallet. She'd seen land before. She stepped on deck and pulled her cloak closer. The morning still held a chill, even with the taste of spring in the breeze. The taste of spring? Wait. Was that not the smell of…of green? Did green have a smell? And yet, she smelled something other than the sea and fish. "Do you smell that, Mistress?"

Joanna inhaled deeply. "Yes."

Varrus, ever their shadow since the episode with Appius, breathed in noisily. He smiled wide enough to expose all his missing teeth and inhaled again.

Appius glowered from where he stood next to the prow.

"Mes-ki-net!" Septus ran to her and threw his arms around her legs.

She bent down and lifted the child. "Shalom, Septus."

"What's a sha-lom?"

"It means 'peace.' How do you say 'peace' in Latin, little one?"

"*Pax*." He squirmed, and she put him down. He ran to his father. "Papa, I know a new word. Sha-lom, Papa."

Decimus laughed as he swung the child up onto his broad shoulders. "Shalom, Septus. Did Joanna tell you the new word?"

Joanna shook her head. "It was not I this time, Senator."

"No, it was Mes-ki-net. She knows a whole other language, Papa. She told me yesterday. She says it's Ar-i-may-ic. Do you know that language?"

"Only a few words, son."

"I'm learning lots of words. If I spoke in Ar-i-may-ic, I would call you 'Abba.' Do you know that one?"

"I do now. *Pax*, ladies." He made a small bow toward them.

Meskhanet and Joanna smiled at each other and then at the senator. At nearly the same moment, they both said, "Shalom, Senator."

"Ah, do I see land? Look, Septus, do you see the bit of cloud and the darker form beneath it?" He pointed west, and the boy's gaze followed his hand.

"Yes. Does that mean we're almost home?"

"It will be a few days, but not many. Most of our trip is behind us."

"Is Mes-ki-net coming to our house?"

"Yes. And Joanna, too. Would you like that?"

"Yes. They can stay and live with us forever, right Papa?" Septus wriggled again and Decimus set him on his feet.

"It would be agreeable to me too, Septus, but I think they have other plans." The senator lifted his gaze to Joanna's.

"Yes, Septus. I have a husband who wants me to come home to him."

"You could divorce him." Septus's eyebrows lifted in earnest question as he looked into her eyes. "Then you could marry Papa and be my new mama and Mes-ki-net could be my sister."

"My religion forbids me to divorce my husband, little man. And I love him. I would not want to divorce him even if I could." She slid her gaze from the child to the man.

Decimus's eyes darkened, but his mouth smiled. "Of course."

Meskhanet noted what passed between them. The firmness in her mistress's voice was meant for the senator.

"Do you not already have a mama, Septus?" Meskhanet knelt next to the child.

"No. She went away when I was born."

"My wife died in childbirth," Decimus said. "We are alone, Septus and I. I have three other sons, but they have grown and gone. All are in the service of Tiberius Caesar. Two are soldiers, one is a scribe."

"I'm sorry, Senator. Not just for the loss of your wife, but also that it must be difficult raising a child without his mother." Joanna touched his arm lightly then turned to gaze again at the nearing coast. "Will we dock at all before Rome, Senator?"

He cleared his throat. "Ah, yes. Yes we will. At Rhegium. But only long enough to load provisions."

"May we go ashore, Meskhanet and I?" Joanna looked up at their protector. "With Varrus?"

"Of course. If you will allow, Septus and I might go with you."

"We would be honored, Senator."

"Mistress, would it be all right if I remained on the ship? I would rather rest for a time."

Appius strolled toward them. "Did I hear you might go ashore, Senator?

Meskhanet jumped and moved closer to Varrus.

"Yes, but I think you will remain aboard, Appius." Decimus cast a narrowed glance his way.

"Of course, sir. I expected that. But perhaps you should allow Meskhanet to stay on the ship, sir. You know she is also a slave. I would guard her with my life."

Meskhanet shrank back as Varrus stepped forward.

Appius raised his hands, palm up. "Be at ease, Varrus, I mean her no harm. I have changed my mind. I no longer desire her. She is not my choice anymore."

Varrus grunted, nodded.

"If she does not go ashore, sir, then I will stay onboard." Joanna placed her arm around Meskhanet. "We will give her manumission papers as soon as my husband finds me in Rome, and she will no longer be a slave. And we will then adopt her." She glared at Appius.

Decimus raised an eyebrow. "Meskhanet is a grown woman. Would not the manumission be sufficient?"

"Yes, she is nearly seventeen. But my husband and I have a marriage in mind for her."

Meskhanet felt her mouth fall open and clamped it shut. "For me, Mistress? But I do not wish to marry. I want only to stay with you and Loukas." Fear rose in her heart. *Please, Adonai, do not let them send me away from them.*

Joanna turned to her. "There is a young man who looks at you with such longing, Meskhanet. He is a proselyte, and one we both approve. Do you know who I mean?"

Meskhanet shook her head. "No, Mistress. Please, I do not wish to marry, and I do not want to be free. Please, keep me as your slave." She fell on her knees before Joanna and placed her forehead on Joanna's feet.

"I don't care if we are short of men. One man will stand watch at night. You, Brutus, will stand first watch." Marcus strode to and fro in front of the men, hoping he looked more commanding than he felt.

One of the sailors laughed. "Should such a bulky man walk the rails?"

"He might over-balance the ship, Captain."

"Or break the figurehead. Such an impressive god should be given more respect."

Laughter rippled amongst the men, and Brutus clenched his fists and glowered. He took a step closer to one of the sailors.

"Relax, Brutus. They mean you no disrespect." Marcus laid a restraining hand on Brutus's arm and spoke in a voice to be heard by only him.

"They mock me." The muscles in his jaw clenched and unclenched.

"They would do the same to any other. Leave it alone and climb up to the box." He squeezed the man's arm and pointed upward.

Brutus began climbing the rope ladder to the bridge in the fading light, grumbling.

One laughing sailor grabbed the ladder and began shaking it. Marcus stepped forward and pulled the man back. "Is that something you want him to do next time you climb the ladder? Or would you want him to fall on you?"

The sailor shook off his hand. "You are not a real captain. You have no authority over me."

His sneer touched off a fire in Marcus's stomach. He lost control of the deliberate calm demeanor he had affected and backhanded the man, sending him sprawling to the deck. He whirled toward the rest of the men. "Do any of the rest of you wish to challenge the authority your captain handed me?"

The sailors murmured among themselves, scowling. The man he'd knocked to the deck stood to his feet, wiping away the blood from a split lip.

"This one will wash the decks tonight. If the ship is not clean when I rise tomorrow morning, he will do the same tomorrow night." Marcus swung away and stomped his way to the bow.

"Tell me how this boat works," he growled to the sailor manning the steerage. "And make it simple. I'm not a sailor."

With much waving of hands and many foreign terms, the sailor explained the masts, sails, rudder, and other parts and uses of the ship.

When the man finished, Marcus wondered if his aching head would whirl off his shoulders. How would he retain even a small portion of all the information? "The only thing I ask of you is that you keep us following behind that ship. If you have difficulty with that, let me know." He started to leave then turned back. "If we should lose sight of that lantern, do you know how to get us to Rome?"

"Aye, captain."

"Good. You are in charge of this wheel, and you will be my second in command. Is there anyone else onboard who knows how to steer this ship?"

"Yes. Crispus—the one you just assigned the job of cleaning the ship."

Marcus grimaced. Not the best one to have angry with him. "And your name?"

The sailor grinned. "My name is Crispus, also."

"Confusing."

"We don't have any problem with it, sir. We call him One, and I am Two."

"All right. That satisfies me." Marcus strode toward his cabin beneath the raised deck. Time to check on Cyril. And perhaps get some sleep.

"How do you feel now, my friend?" He started to lift Cyril's head to give him another drink, but Cyril pushed him back and lifted himself to a sitting position.

"I can do it myself. You've almost flooded me, between you and Rebecca. Good thing there's a pot under this bed."

"Oh, this is great news. I'm a captain, but I'm reduced to emptying chamber pots. This will make me the butt of every joke from bow to stern and port to starboard."

"Rebecca already did it." Cyril sipped from the cup and reached for some grapes. "What's a starboard?"

"The starboard is the right side of the ship. The bow is the front, the stern is the back, and the port is left. The new ship's mate taught me more terms than I'll ever remember." Marcus knelt to remove his sandals.

Cyril nodded. "Tomorrow I'll be able to take care of myself. And Rebecca and I will take over the cook's duties. I'm not sure we could do any worse than he if we tried. Let him trim the sails, whatever that means."

"I'm not sure he could do that. I understand he has only one arm." He looked thoughtful. "Although that just means to lower the sails, I think. Maybe he could do that." Marcus removed his cloak, hanging it on a nail pounded into the doorframe.

Cyril grunted. "That's probably why they assigned him to the galley. It wasn't because of his culinary abilities. *That* I am convinced of."

"It fills the stomach. Isn't much worse than the cooks in the century. But then, you work for the centurion primus. You probably have access to victuals primus." He swiped his hand across a shelf to rid it of a dead fly. He wiped his hands on an almost equally dirty rag. "Ugh. Did this pirate ever clean anything?"

"I don't think so. It's dirty, and it smells like many things died tortured deaths in here."

"Oh, a tortured death smells worse than a normal death?"

"You would know that better than I. I've never tortured anything. I'm a simple servant. You, on the other hand…."

A banging on the door interrupted them. Marcus groaned. "Now what?" He opened the door.

Two stood there with One right behind him. "Captain, we have a question."

"So do I. Who is steering the ship?"

"For a few moments, one of the other sailors holds the helm," Two said. "If One is cleaning all night, who will take over from me at the end of the second watch?"

One smirked, his arms crossed. He leaned against the deck wall.

Marcus narrowed his eyes. "Are any storms expected tonight?"

"No, Captain. Everything appears calm."

"I will come up to the helm before your shift ends, you will show me what to do, and One will continue cleaning until morning dawns. He will take the wheel at that time."

One straightened. "But Captain, I can't work without sleep."

"You will this time. Let us hope there will not be another."

Chapter 20

As they walked the streets of Rhegium, Meskhanet remained silent, responding only when Septus paused long enough in his questions that she could tell he wanted an answer. She had much to think about.

Freedom? She had tasted freedom when she escaped Barabbas's camp, and if that was it, she didn't want it. Fear had been her constant companion. Fear of being caught, fear of reprisal, fear of being alone. The sense of safety she felt with her master and mistress seemed her only security. What would she do without them? She didn't want to find out. She would choose slavery over freedom.

Marriage. Joanna said someone wished marriage to her. No, that could not be possible. She would have noticed anyone wanting to marry her. Had Joanna claimed she had an admirer to discourage Appius? But what if that were not the reason? What if they wanted her to marry someone they knew?

Marriage would mean moving into a husband's home, away from Loukas and Joanna. She might never see them again. And no one would treat her as well as they did. She did not want a husband if she could not have Loukas, and she could not have him.

Could a husband tell she was not a virgin? If he could, he would divorce her. That would bring shame on Loukas and Joanna. No, no husband for her.

Appius. He made her feel so uneasy. At first he pursued her, and then he said she no longer interested him. Why? Did her face become ugly? Or maybe he found out somehow she wasn't a virgin. But how? She had told no one about that Roman swine. Not even Joanna. So why did Appius now find her unattractive?

So many questions, but no one she could ask for the answers.

"Meskhanet?"

"Yes, Mistress?"

Joanna laughed. "I wondered if perhaps you were walking in your sleep. I asked you a question three times."

Heat rose in Meskhanet's cheeks. "I'm sorry, Mistress. My mind was fascinated by—about how interesting this city is."

The senator chuckled. "Indeed. Such goods in the marketplace are awe-inspiring."

She flushed again. They were in the midst of several stalls of men's cloaks, togas, and tunics. "Your question, Mistress?"

"The senator offered to lend us enough to provide a second set of clothing until Loukas arrives. We have winter clothing, but it is spring. And our tunics have developed holes."

"What colors would you like for your stola? Here you find blue, and over there red. It could be considered pretentious to wear purple, and I don't advise that. It generates too many curious questions. You will need an interior tunic and a palla, too. Both of you may have them, but you, Joanna, must have one. How are your sandals?"

Joanna shook her head. "Sandals would be too much. We are simple people, and a tunic and a stola apiece will be sufficient."

"Madam, please be reasonable. You should not go out in the stola alone on days when it is chilly, and your cloaks are worn. You would draw unwelcome attention to yourselves if you go outside my property dressed as slaves or foreigners rather than as Roman citizens. Or at least you, madam. Since Meskhanet is not yet free, she might not need a palla, but she also should at least wear a cloak with no holes."

"Mes-ki-net needs a pretty stola too, Papa. Please?" Septus pulled at his father's toga.

"You see? Even my son agrees," Decimus said, chuckling.

Joanna smiled. "Yes, but Septus does not have to concern himself with a husband who will have to pay what I owe."

"I need nothing, Mistress." Meskhanet's ears warmed. "See, Septus, the bird in the tree over there? Does he not sing a sweet song? His feathers are brown, but he needs nothing except his song to make him beautiful."

The senator shook his head. "In that case, I will to pay for it myself, and you will not repay me. I do not want others in my household or on the streets to mutter about you behind their hands. It would shame me, even if it does not shame you. I insist you must accept my hospitality, including respectable clothing."

"Decimus, you place me in a difficult position. I do not wish to be so deeply obligated to you." Joanna stared at the ground with a small scowl and red face.

"Joanna, I am a senator. The people in my household are expected to dress well."

"Even your slaves, Senator? We would be willing to reside in the slave quarters. When we were kidnapped, they intended us to be slaves. And I know we'd rather be in the slaves' quarters in your house than at the circus." She glanced at Meskhanet.

Meskhanet hoped the gratitude she felt expressed itself in her nod.

The senator pinched his mouth with his fingers. "Madam, how can I convince you? Will you not allow me some small pride? May I not expend these small coins to help you? You worry about spending more than your husband wants you to. I worry that people will think I treat my guests poorly. May we strike a bargain?"

"That would depend on the bargain, sir. I have pride as well. Some would say too much pride. I will not do anything dishonest or dishonorable, I will not worship any God but Yahweh, and I will not allow Meskhanet to be misused in any manner."

"Oh, Joanna, you mistake me entirely." His normally soft bass voice boomed loud enough to make passersby turn their heads. "I would not misuse you, or Meskhanet, either. Please, dear lady, let me buy you enough to salvage my pride. You, in return, will serve as my hostess. Only until your husband's arrival, of course."

Meskhanet could see Joanna staring at their worn sandals and clothing. *No, Mistress, do not accept this!* They would be too deeply in debt to this man. All the fine clothing would cost Loukas too much, and she didn't think he had anything to spend on them. When Barabbas attacked them, he took all they had. And what if Loukas didn't find them? How would he know where to look? Thousands of people lived in Rome. If he had even discovered they were being taken to Rome.

And if Loukas didn't find them…

Despite what she had said and thought before, Meskhanet felt her spirits lifted by the way the pretty pale blue palla looked on her new tunic. Ignoring their protests, the senator had purchased two interior tunics, stolas, and pallas, a pair of sandals for Meskhanet, and two for Joanna. She and Joanna had flatly rejected the offer for the public bath, but when they returned to the ship, a basin of water apiece had accomplished the same purpose.

When they returned to the deck, Decimus's eyes lit with an admiring gaze as they approached him. "Dear ladies, you give my heart pleasure. How elegant you look. No one would mistake you for slaves now."

"Mes-ki-net, you are so pretty!" Septus clapped his hands. "Joanna, too."

Meskhanet gazed in pride at her mistress. The scar Joanna bore from Barabbas's attack had faded to a thin line, scarcely visible, and she did look elegant. "You look like a queen, Mistress."

Joanna blushed. "I am no queen. Anyone would look wonderful in this. Such a deep red it is. How do they make such colors?"

"I do not know, madam, but I am so grateful they do. For however short a time you may be my hostess, you will provide my house with a grace missing for too many years."

"Your beauty would grace the emperor's palace." Appius had moved up behind the senator and smiled as his gaze scanned Meskhanet and Joanna. Varrus standing beside him smiled and nodded.

Meskhanet moved behind a scowling Joanna.

Varrus took a step back. "Uh?" He held his hands to his face and smiled, then pointed at her and her mistress.

Meskhanet smiled at Varrus. "Thank you."

"Excuse us, Senator. We will go back to our tent, away from too many eyes. We are made uncomfortable by so much attention." She slid her eyes in Appius's direction. "Come, Daughter."

Meskhanet followed her to their canvas cabin, happy to be away from Appius's stare. What had happened with Varrus while they were off the ship? Had Appius convinced his large friend that his intentions were just? Appius had been his friend before the giant decided to be her and Joanna's protector. Perhaps Varrus's loyalties to Appius ran deeper. His mind was as uncomplicated as a child's, and a child's loyalties ran deep.

Joanna pulled the palla and then the stola off, folded them, and placed them in a chest Decimus had also purchased. "Give me yours, too, Meskhanet. I'll keep them in here until we are safely in the senator's household. While we are on this ship, our old holey cloaks will do."

Meskhanet sighed as she pulled her tunic over her head. She had never had anything colorful to wear before, and she was reluctant to part with it. Even so, she was happy to put the new garments away just so Appius would stop staring.

Two more days of sailing under warm spring skies and soft breezes brought them to Pozzuoli where some of the merchant ship's goods were sold, then on to the mouth of the Tiber River and Ostia. The busy seaports had so many ships coming and going Meskhanet could not see the end of them. Where did they all come from? She thought Caesarea had many, but this many seemed unbelievable.

"Captain, why do the ships anchor here so far from shore? Why do we not go to the docks?" Meskhanet's impatience to reach shore must have shown in her words, because the portly old captain chuckled, his bushy eyebrows quivering. With his silver hair and grandfatherly air, he seemed like such a kind man.

"The water in the river is too shallow for our deep hulls, Meskhanet. A barge will come out to us and begin taking grain ashore within the hour. I believe the senator plans to go ashore on the first boat. Are your lovely pallas packed? You might want to wear one. What a grand entrance into Rome you would make!"

"Joanna says we will not wear them until we reach the senator's villa." Meskhanet looked toward their canvas home, wishing it would be acceptable to her mistress to wear them now.

"A pity. Such beautiful women should wear that which brings them admiration."

Meskhanet's face heated, and she dropped her gaze to her feet. "My mistress is most beautiful, Captain. But she does not wish undue attention."

"Undue? Not at all. Especially you, Child. Your perfect face, alluring dark eyes, flaming lips, and curvaceous form will cause every man to turn around and follow you. If I were younger..." His tongue darted out to touch his lips. "Ah, the sons we would make."

Did she just think of him as grandfatherly? "Captain, you should not say such things. I must go. It has been pleasant to travel on your ship. Goodbye." In her confusion, she turned and bumped into the steering oar. Holding her hand to her face, she went looking for Joanna. She hoped her face wouldn't turn purple on that side.

Appius stopped her. "Did you hurt yourself? Let me look." He pulled her hand away. Before she knew what he intended, he leaned in and kissed her cheek then moved quickly to her mouth.

She backed away, scrubbing at her lips. "You had no right to do that." She looked around, but neither Varrus, Joanna, nor the senator was in sight.

She turned to escape his attentions, but he grabbed her again and pulled her around. "You are a most beautiful woman. Your thighs were made for bearing, and you will bear my sons, Meskhanet, have no doubt." He dropped his lips to hers again and pulled her tight to himself.

"No! Leave me alone. Captain, stop him!" She shouted at the top of her lungs and pushed him away. Everyone but the captain seemed to be on the other side of the ship.

The captain made no move to stop Appius. He stared wide-eyed and slack-jawed, rubbing his hands on his tunic.

Appius stepped slowly toward her. His eyes narrowed to glowing slits, and a predatory smile exposed his teeth. "Mine," he said in a hoarse whisper as he grasped her arm and forced her toward her canvas cabin.

No! God of the Jews, please, not again!

Chapter 21

Land. The joy of putting both feet on a non-moving surface brought laughter to his lips. Marcus never thought he'd ever be so happy to give up a position of leadership than when he handed the helm over to a captain who actually knew how to sail. It had taken Octavius a couple of days to find another captain he found acceptable in Rhegium. Oh, the agony of seeing the land and not being able to disembark. And Meskhanet still ahead of them, a prisoner on a slave ship.

Now they rode north to Rome on horseback. Even the knowledge they would all have saddle sores before they arrived couldn't dim his joy of being on solid ground. He hummed a marching song punctuated by the jar of each hoof landing on the bricks of the road. Brutus and Cyril had ceased quarreling, at least for the moment. Rebecca, as usual, remained quiet.

The air smelled fresh from the previous night's rain, the blue sky promised they could take their cloaks off by midmorning, and trees bloomed everywhere. Birds sang from every bush and tree. Travelers they met on the road waved a friendly greeting. Everyone seemed cheered by the spring sights, smells, and sounds. *Ah, Adonai, such beauty You provide. Thank You.*

Cyril broke into Marcus's reverie. "How long do we have to bounce on these saddles?"

Marcus turned around to look at his friend following behind him. "I'm sorry, my friend. I realize you aren't used to this type of riding. However, considering what Joanna and Meskhanet might be going through, we can't go at a leisurely pace. Most of the distance will be covered at a trot, with breathers for the horses and us at intervals. The letter we carry from Julius will get us fresh horses along the way, so one day of trotting most of the time won't hurt our mounts. It's about a week's travel from here."

Cyril groaned. "Why didn't we stay on the ship?"

"If the ship could have sailed straight to Rome, it would have been an advantage to stay on it. Sailing time is negligible, maybe four or five days. But by the time we'd stop for the captain to take on supplies, disgorge and take on passengers and/or soldiers in two more ports, then find a barge to take us from Ostio to Rome, we'd be ahead to ride by a couple of days. I was beginning to feel trapped on that ship too. Weren't you?"

"No, but I am rubbed raw by this saddle. Couldn't we have gotten a chariot?"

"There weren't any available. Give thanks. You could have been running the entire distance."

"I don't think so. I might have run the first hundred cubits or so. After that I'd probably be tripping over my tongue. Now, convince me that either of you could run any farther."

"Huh. I could do it." Brutus, riding at Marcus's side, threw a disparaging glance over his shoulder.

"Let me propose something then." Cyril's eyes were narrow and steamy. "Let's give the horses a break. We'll run as far as we can, leading the horses. We'll see who can run the farthest."

"For what?" Brutus stopped his big gray gelding.

"What do you mean, 'for what'?"

"What will you wager?"

"Nothing. I only want to see if your feet are as active as your mouth." Cyril pulled his chestnut mare to a halt beside Brutus.

Marcus sighed and dismounted. "If you want to do this, we will do it without coins or anything else other than sweat. Let's go." He began trotting along the road, leading his mare, another chestnut with a white blaze.

Muttering to himself Brutus followed, and Cyril trailed him. The horses seemed confused and resisted being led at a trot. Their eyes showed white at the apexes, but as Marcus's horse began to follow more willingly, the other two also did.

Even Rebecca dismounted, her eyes alight. Did she begin to understand them, or was she just happy to get out of the saddle? She trotted next to Cyril, her small gray gelding following without objection.

Still, their progress was less than notable, and all of them panted heavily in a mile. Marcus stopped, placed his hands on his knees, and gasped for breath. "It is time we started training again," he wheezed once he could talk. "We have been too long on the ship."

Brutus nodded and mounted. Cyril clambered back onto his saddle without a word.

Marcus gathered his reins and mounted. "Don't think we have quit doing this. It started as a wager, but we will do this two or three times a day or more until we are back in fighting form. It will give the horses a break and give us strength we need. You had a better idea than you thought, Cyril."

"I should learn to hold my tongue." Cyril wiped his red, sweating brow.

Brutus grunted and turned his horse toward Rome.

Marcus grinned. A good idea in more than one way. Keeping the two of them from trouncing each other might be easier if they were too tired to fight.

On the third night, the rain started and their progress slowed. The horses didn't like the rain blowing in their face and blew noisy protests. Marcus didn't enjoy the rain either, and he suspected the other three didn't like it any better than he. The cold water ran down his neck and soaked his tunic.

He heaved a sigh. "We need to find shelter. Either of you see anywhere out of the wet?" He glanced around, peering through slitted eyes under a sheltering hand.

"Would that work?" Cyril pointed toward a rock outcropping from the mountain on their right.

"It might. Let's check it." Marcus dismounted and led his horse toward the hillside.

Brutus reached the outcropping just as a dribbling of gravel came over the top.

"Jump back, man, jump!"

Brutus jumped at amazing speed for a man his size, and rocks bounced around him. One a hand's breadth in diameter glanced off his shoulder, and he grunted as he made it out of the path of a few boulders and several smaller rocks. A grumbling noise above them settled it. The three men ran for the road to where Rebecca held their tied horses. Better riding in the rain than buried under mud and rocks.

Before Appius could tug Meskhanet out of sight, someone heard her cries for help. Varrus reached out his great hands and pulled Appius away. Not only pulled him away…he carried Appius to the edge of the ship and dropped him over the rail. The gladiator's shout of alarm was cut short by a splash.

"Help me," he cried. After some choking sounds, he called again. "Can't swim. Help!"

Varrus peered over the side. He peeled off his cloak and jumped overboard.

Meskhanet ran around to the other side of the cabin where a barge had pulled next to the ship.

"Oh, there you are, child. The senator…."

"Mistress, Senator, please come! Appius and Varrus are in the water. I'm afraid they will both drown." She turned and led them at a run.

"Captain!" The senator's booming voice seemed to echo from every ship in the harbor. "Send a boat to the other side of the ship."

The captain shouted the orders he should have been giving earlier.

Meskhanet leaned over the rail. Varrus must have managed to rescue Appius, because the two of them clung to the anchor chain. "A boat is coming for you. Hold on."

Varrus grinned at her. Appius scowled.

She took a deep breath. Had the God of the Jews provided a rescue for her again? Why did she continually get into these difficulties? She must stay closer to Joanna. And the senator. She began to think he might be trustworthy.

But, she thought the captain had been worthy of trust, too. What man could be trusted? Maybe none. It would be wiser not to place trust in any man. Except perhaps Loukas.

The carriage ride along the river and through Rome took her breath away. The river…so wide and powerful. Steep, rocky sides prevented ships from approaching too close to the edge. Large homes lined the roads as they approached the city, but the closer they got to the city the smaller many of the homes became.

Her first sight of the senator's villa dropped her mouth wide open. Julius's home in comparison seemed a hovel. Pillars marched across the front in a glistening marble row. The shaded portico held several couches, one occupied by a colorfully clad man and a thin, pale woman. Ivy clung to the columns in ethereal white and green wisps. A smiling man and a woman, slaves or servants, greeted them, and Meskhanet noted they all had clean white tunics. The woman wore a peach-colored palla, and the man a tan cloak. They both seemed happy to see their master.

The tall thin man rose from the couch he laid on, both hands spread in welcome. "Decimus, so good to see you home again. We despaired over your decision to sail in the winter, but it seems you have outwitted the gods again. Or perhaps you are one of the favorites who may escape Neptune's grasp."

"Perseus." The senator's greeting nod seemed curt. He carried Septus, sound asleep on his shoulder, and he didn't extend his free hand to return the grasp offered. "Have you nothing better to do with your time than occupy my house?"

Meskhanet thought the man's oily expression treacherous. Perseus's smile looked more like a wolf showing its teeth. "Senator, I'm offended. Did your own wife not say I was welcome?"

"My wife has been gone almost five years. Perhaps that welcome expired with your sister."

Perseus shrugged. "As you wish." He made a mocking bow, eyes glinting. "I'm sure we will see each other again, Decimus. Soon." He sauntered toward a chariot with two matched white mares hitched to it.

Meskhanet watched Decimus staring after Perseus, his eyes narrowed. He shook his shoulders, inspiring a murmur from the still-sleeping Septus. He turned his attention back to his guests. "Ladies, I apologize. Please, come with me. I'm eager to show you my home. And your home for as long as you need it."

Two muscular, dark-skinned male slaves stood next to the wagon and lifted first Joanna and then Meskhanet down. The slaves' disdain for their travel-worn and patched cloaks and tunics registered in the slaves' eyes, but they bowed to the senator's guests as though they were royalty. Meskhanet had to wonder if the senator trained them himself.

"Would your guests prefer a private bath or the public bath, Senator?"

Meskhanet felt the heat crawl up her cheeks. Yes, they probably smelled that strong.

"We prefer private baths, sirs." Joanna handed her cloak to one of the slaves without a trace of embarrassment. "As soon as the senator has assigned us a room, please bring two baths. The chest at the back of the wagon should go to our room as well."

Meskhanet gazed at her mistress with admiration. Joanna looked like a queen with her chin high, but her smile was gracious and kind.

The senator quirked an eyebrow. "Put them into the east corner room, Quintus."

"Ah, sir, the lady Portia…"

Decimus coughed. "Yes. Well. Put them in the west corner instead."

"Yes, Senator."

"Would you like to see my home, ladies?"

Joanna glanced at the vanishing back of the slaves who carried the chest. "I think we would prefer to bathe, first, Senator. I hope we won't be a burden to you while we're here. This lady, Portia? Will our presence be an embarrassment to you? She might misunderstand."

His face reddened. "It is not what you think, Joanna."

"Please, Decimus, you have been more than kind to us. You have accepted us almost as members of your family. It is not our desire to cause awkward scenes. Please, just allow us to bathe and don clean clothing."

He bowed his head to her. "As you wish, dear ladies. Normally we eat at day's end. I hope you will join us."

"Of course. It will be our pleasure."

The senator escorted them to the second floor and a spacious room with the largest bed Meskhanet had ever seen.

When Joanna closed the door, she turned to Meskhanet. "Look at this room! Have you ever seen a house so luxurious?" She swooped to the balcony and threw back thin silk curtains. The corner room looked west over a courtyard and a stable to the Tiber River and north to a temple on a wooded hill.

Meskhanet joined her. She caught her breath. The river sparkled in the afternoon sunlight like thousands of precious stones. A flowering tree on the north side provided a sweet perfume. Soft laughter and children's voices floated on the breeze.

"So beautiful, Mistress. I have never seen anything so beautiful."

"Now, Meskhanet. You must choose. Either you call me Joanna, or you call me Mother. Otherwise, the slaves and visitors here will not treat you with respect. You are a beautiful young woman, and the men visiting the senator will only see you as a plaything to use as they wish. You must hold your head high. Do not follow anyone's orders, other than the senator's and my own. Instead, give them a haughty stare. Most will follow my lead, but you must remember. Do not act like a slave."

"It will be difficult, Mistress, but I will try."

Chapter 22

Marcus scowled. Three days of riding in the rain produced short tempers and sullen attitudes, especially when the shortest-tempered of the lot had a sore shoulder. Marcus ordered silence, because no one could speak without an angry response from the others. That included himself. Rebecca was no problem. She seldom said anything anyway, other than to Cyril.

The dried mutton they carried had dampened until the smell forced them to throw it away. Bread molded. Dried fruit fared better but didn't fill the stomach for long. Result? Three hungry, wet, ill-tempered men who would almost be willing to eat each other. One soggy, silent woman. At least they weren't thirsty.

"Dismount. We're running."

"I'm not." Cyril said through gritted teeth. "Mud and sharp rocks in my sandals."

He had a point. Marcus shrugged. "As you will. You are not under my command." He set off at a trot, limping from a previous rock in his own sandal. But he was a soldier, and soldiers did not complain about bruises and blisters.

Brutus's horse stumbled in the mud, and he turned around with a fist raised, but he hesitated. Instead of striking, he stroked the horse's nose.

Marcus snorted. The man would not have withheld the blow for anything but a horse.

They had to find food and shelter before they killed each other. One meal at an inn in Pozzouli had been enough to dry and warm them for only an hour, and the full stomach had lasted about four hours. Tomorrow, though, they should reach Rome.

A cottage came into view perhaps a quarter mile off the main road. Maybe they'd be willing to share their homes and some food for one night. He had to try.

He stopped. "Wait here." He mounted his horse and rode to the small villa.

A man appeared at the door. "Hold. What do you want?" He was almost as bulky as Brutus but older. His voice quavered as he spoke.

"A dry place to sleep and a meal. We can pay." Marcus shivered as another drop or two of cold water ran down his back.

"This is no inn. And we have no extra room. Ten children here."

"Is there an inn close?"

"New one three miles north. Try that."

"Thank you." Marcus turned away and remounted the horse. *Why am I thanking him for turning us away?* He shook his head. He must be more tired than he thought.

Wordlessly, his companions followed him, their horses as weary as they. Their mud-encased hooves dragged the ground and their heads hung low as they slugged on.

When the inn came into view, even the horses picked up their ears. One of them neighed. There must be at least one other horse at the inn. Marcus breathed a sigh of relief. Warm food and rest were only minutes away.

They dismounted, tied the horses to a post in front of the door. They walked into the lamp-lit great room. Water dripped off them and made muddy puddles on the stone floor. Something smelled good enough to eat. Marcus gazed around the sparsely occupied room. A few men and women sat on benches, talking with each other or staring at the newcomers.

A man in a dirty once-white tunic limped in their direction followed by a bedraggled girl. The thin waif was maybe ten years old, dark hair hanging in stringy tangles to her waist, an obvious bruise on one cheek.

Rebecca's eyes filled with moisture, and she reached a hand to touch the girl's face. At first the child drew back, but Rebecca's obvious compassion softened her narrowed eyes. She flashed a tired smile at the old woman and patted her hand.

The innkeeper rubbed his hands together. "What can we do for you, sirs? A room? A meal? A wench?"

"First, a meal. Then a room. Do you have a stable for horses with food for them? Maybe oats? They are as tired and hungry as we are."

The innkeeper turned his head. "Boy!"

A youngster who could have been the girl's twin ran up to him. "Take care of these men's horses. Oats, and towel them down."

"Yes, Master." The boy bowed and hurried out the door.

Brutus gazed at the girl.

Marcus stepped in front of him. "No," he whispered. "She is a child."

Brutus grunted. "Looks old enough to me."

The inn master bowed again. "Come, sit over here. The girl will bring you some hot stew."

The girl nodded, turned, and with dragging steps disappeared through an open door. Faint wisps of smoke or steam wafted through the opening, and Marcus assumed it had to be the culina.

He sat on the bench, waving the other two men to follow suit. Brutus sat across from him, Cyril next to him.

When the bowls of stew arrived, the three men shoveled the stew in hurried spoonsful. Rebecca ate more slowly.

"More," Brutus told the girl. "And beer."

Nodding, she picked up the bowls and returned with them filled again. In a moment more, she brought a tray with the ale in a tall jug and four clay mugs.

"Want some?" Brutus asked her, wiping his arm across his mouth.

"No," she said, the first and only word she spoke.

Rebecca snickered, earning Brutus's narrowed eyes.

Marcus struggled not to laugh. It would only anger Brutus, and he didn't need another argument. "We need sleep, Brutus. We will have only one room, and I will not allow you to bring that child in there."

Brutus drew his already connecting brows to tight furrows between his eyes. "I begin to wish I hadn't saved you."

"I accept that. But I'm glad you did. And I'm glad you came with us." A small half-truth. He hoped the One God wouldn't hold it against him.

Brutus growled, but the furrows decreased a little.

"Innkeeper!" Marcus held up his hand to wave the man to their table. He stood, and Cyril rose wearily to his feet. Brutus followed suit.

"We want a room. If you have any, we want a room with no others already in it."

"You have coins?"

"Yes." Marcus pulled four denarii from the bag at his belt and handed it to the man.

"Follow me." He grabbed two lamps from a table and led the way up two flights of stairs and to a room about halfway down a lengthy hall smelling of sweat and urine. "This is it, the only room left that doesn't already have occupants. You can break your fast any time within a couple of hours after sunrise."

The room didn't have a bed, but it was dry. That was more than what they'd had for three days. A half-dozen bare wooden pallets stood stacked against the wall. They each selected one, threw their cloaks on them, and within minutes snores told Marcus the other two men at least were asleep, if not Rebecca. It didn't take him long to join them.

Meskhanet followed Joanna down the stairs. A soft gasp escaped the female servant whose eyes had previously held distain even while they bowed. She must hold her chin up. Keeping her eyes lowered would be a hard habit to break. There were few whose gaze she had met as equals and none who were subservient to her, but she remembered Joanna's warning.

"Ah, ladies, what a splendid sight you are. You make the blossoms on the trees fade from view." The senator held both hands to them. As they reached the bottom steps, they wrapped their hands around his elbows. "Aphrodite and Venus could not vie with you."

"And they're pretty, too, Papa." Septus skipped up to them and took Meskhanet's hand, his dark eyes sparkling.

His papa chuckled. "As pretty as goddesses, son."

Joanna shook her head. "We believe in only One God, Decimus. Please do not compare us to what we believe to be false deities."

"My apologies, madam. I meant to compliment, not offend."

"I am not offended, sir, but I can't seem to resist correction. Poor Meskhanet usually receives my frustrated mothering, but today it is you. Perhaps I should apologize too." Joanna smiled at him and turned a fond glance on Meskhanet. "I am eager to officially adopt Meskhanet so she will be my daughter indeed."

Meskhanet blushed and smiled. "I am humbled and eager as well, Mother."

The senator grinned. "You learn quickly, Meskhanet." He lowered his voice. "You must learn quickly. Otherwise, this city will devour you. Be very careful. One so beautiful is in constant danger, but if you hold your head high the danger will be less."

"That is what Mother tells me, sir. I will be cautious."

"If either of you wish to go out into the city, tell me. I will arrange an escort for you. Do not go alone, or even the two of you. Not without an escort." He barked a laugh. "Even if you were not prime targets on your own, there are a few who might wish to harm me, and they would not hesitate to hurt you or Septus to injure me."

"Why, Senator?" Joanna raised an eyebrow as they strolled toward a spacious dining hall.

"Why do they want to harm me, or why would they hurt you to injure me?" Decimus turned her serious question into a teasing joke with a twitch of his lips.

"Yes." Her eyes twinkled back at him. "I want to know both."

"I'll protect them, Papa. I have a sword."

"I'm sure you would, Septus." Meskhanet smiled at him and took his hand.

Decimus waved at a luxurious pillowed couch next to a broad and long inlaid mosaic table. "Ladies." He bowed them to their seats.

Meskhanet let her gaze wander around the room. Tapestries with rich metallic embroidery glistened in the sunlight by the high open windows. A gentle breeze blew the soft linen curtains in gentle curves, exposing a beautiful red and gold sunset behind flowering trees. The day's rain had washed the dust from the air, and the air itself seemed to sparkle. She wondered what the flowering trees and shrubs were and promised herself to find out. Perhaps the senator knew. The marble tile on the floor shown in polished white glory; not a trace of dust marred the surface.

He sat across from them. "A senator always has enemies. It goes with the position. And why would two lovely ladies be in danger? I think that goes without saying. It is the same anywhere, is it not? Were you not kidnapped in Caesarea? I'm sorry, my friends, even with your heads held high, it is obvious you are not from Rome. Even with your black hair and eyes, your features would give you away."

"Yes, I suppose. You would think there would be another place as safe as Jericho."

Meskhanet's gaze dropped to the table. She hadn't told her mistress Jericho was also not safe.

"Tomorrow, ladies, I will take you on a tour of Rome. I look forward to showing you how beautiful our city can be. Later, I will have to attend the senate, but my morning is free."

"Senator, we cannot go with you tomorrow. The sunset begins our Sabbath, and we spend the day remembering our God and all He has done. Perhaps the day following. Which reminds me, do you know of a synagogue near here?"

The senator raised his eyes. "Portia, how nice that you would join us. Come and meet our guests."

The emaciated woman Meskhanet had seen earlier entered the room. Her haunted grey eyes, light blonde hair, and silent steps made Meskhanet wonder if she were a ghost. The white tunic and stola emphasized her paleness.

She hesitated before she reached the table, almost as though she feared contamination from these foreigners.

"Portia, this is Joanna and her soon-to-be daughter, Meskhanet. They had the misfortune to be in a shipwreck, and we brought them home with us. Joanna's husband should soon arrive on a ship to claim her."

Joanna lifted an arm toward the girl, her hand palm up. "I'm happy to meet you, Portia."

Portia drew back, her arms clasped around herself.

"This is my daughter-in-law Portia, the wife of my oldest son, Vitus. Vitus is absent from us at this time, gone to Germania. He is a centurion there. Are you hungry, Portia?"

She shook her head, turned, and exited the room.

Septus lifted a spoon. "She doesn't like to eat, but I do." He shoveled bites of a fruit pudding into his mouth.

Meskhanet smiled at his enthusiasm, but then turned her gaze back to the departing Portia.

Decimus watched as she left, then turned back, sighed, and shook his head. "She is a sad thing."

"What is wrong with her, Senator? Is she ill?"

"Ill of mind. She has been like this for a year. She lost a baby, a boy, not long after Vitus left for Germania. She doesn't like to eat. She goes nowhere. She never smiles. She sits and stares out the window from their room."

Joanna gazed toward the sea and sighed. "I wish…"

"So do I, Mistress. Mother." Meskhanet corrected herself before Joanna had a chance.

"What?" The senator's eyebrows lifted.

"That my husband were here. Perhaps when he arrives, he might be able to help her. He is a physician."

"I remember. But we have had physicians come, and they have not been able to bring her back to herself."

"My husband is more talented than any physician I've heard of, except One. That One is the Son of the One God who can heal anything. But my husband is second only to the One God's Son in healing ability."

Chapter 23

As they rode into Rome, Marcus gazed at the familiar streets and buildings—paved street, brick and stone buildings, marble porticos. The rains had washed the streets free of dust, and the temples of the gods gleamed in the morning sun.

They had one more in their company this morning. Rebecca had managed to convince Cyril to buy the girl. Marcus had protested, but his only real objection was that she would need protection from Brutus. Rebecca had assigned herself to the child, and Marcus didn't think she would allow the soldier within ten cubits of the girl.

He shifted in his saddle so his companions could hear him. "Our first stop will be the circus. If that's where they were taken, and if their ship didn't get delayed by a storm, and if the slave master is forthcoming with information, we could be on a ship going home by nightfall. That would take a miracle. I don't expect any slave master to be so willing."

"That's why we brought the coins, is it not? Have you given any thought to how you are going to tell Joanna about Loukas?" Cyril's mouth turned down, and his eyes moistened.

Marcus's eyes stung. "No. I know no easy way. I might as well stab her in the heart."

Brutus raised his eyebrows.

"No, Brutus, that's only a metaphor. I meant this news will almost kill her. She will be devastated. I don't expect you to understand. I don't think you've ever loved anyone."

"My Bellia."

"She would be a mare, right?"

"Yes."

"All right. I don't know how to tell Joanna her husband is dead, one she loves even more than you love your horse." That had to be about as close as Brutus would come to appreciating how someone could feel.

In fact, he was not sure he wanted to find them just for that reason. Yes, he wanted to remove Joanna and Meskhanet from the grasp of slavers, but he didn't want to have to tell them about Loukas. What could he say or do to soften such a fierce blow?

He dismounted in front of the Circus Maximus and entered through one of the hundreds of arched doors. He hoped he wouldn't have to walk the circumference of this structure. At twelve hundred cubits long, it could take him the rest of the morning, and the gruel he ate when they broke their fast lasted about as long as it took to ride the distance from the inn to Rome, only an hour or so ago.

"Hello—you there, soldier. What are you doing here? The games aren't until tomorrow." A mite of a man, bald and aged, hurried toward him.

"I need to talk to the lanista. Where is he?"

"He is not available and won't be until tomorrow morning, early. He is busy training fighters."

"There might have been two women brought here for the gladiators within the past two or three weeks. I have come to take them home. They were kidnapped."

The little man wheezed a laugh. "Kidnapped or not, you might not want them back."

"Allow me be the judge of that. Lead me to them."

"They are in the kitchen. Follow me." He trotted off, Marcus following at a fast stride.

When they entered through another arched opening into a smoky room, a heavyset woman greeted his guide with hands on hips. "Antonius, you promised more geese. Where are they?"

"Coming, Leah. This man wants to see our newest slave women. He says they were not slaves but were kidnapped."

"So? I was too." She sneered her answer, hands propped on her hips.

Marcus narrowed his gaze. "Worse could happen, woman. Bring the new slaves out. Now."

Leah snorted, turned, and waddled out through another door.

Marcus felt his heart beating in his temples. Any moment now.

Leah returned with two young women in tow. One, a blonde, sported a black eye; the other, with auburn hair almost the same color as his, had one swollen arm in a sling. Both wore sullen expressions and wouldn't meet his eyes.

Marcus shook his head. "These are not the ones I seek. Have you had any other recent additions to your slaves here?"

"No."

"Would any be in a different location?"

"No. Now go away and let us get our work done. We have a meal to prepare." Leah turned her back on him and began pulling feathers from a headless goose.

Marcus felt his heart sink to his sandals. What could he do if Meskhanet and Joanna had been in a shipwreck? Or caught by pirates?

He exited the room and trudged back toward the entrance. A huge man trotted toward him flapping a short whip in the air and making strange noises. Marcus scowled and waved the man away. There was no need to be chased from the enclosure.

He knew his shoulders slumped, and he deliberately straightened his posture before he walked through the arch. He mounted his horse and took in the expectant expressions of his companions. "They're not here. Let's try the docks."

The information received at the docks produced so many leads it would take at least week to check them all. One ship had been filled with slaves, all taken to the slave market a week before. That one alone could take months to pursue. Almost all landings had a slave or two. One even involved his father, but both slaves were male and were going to the circus. For which he breathed a silent prayer of thanksgiving.

He heaved a sigh. They would have to find lodging. "Cyril, we need a place to stay while we are here. The barracks are out—they don't take women or children. See if you can find a small house. One that won't use any more coins than necessary."

"We would have free rooms in your father's house, would we not?"

"No."

"No? Why? He would charge you rent?" Cyril's eyebrows punctuated his questions.

"The last time I saw my father, he informed me I should not expect a welcome at his home until...well, even drunk, I could hear the steel in his voice. Which, I might add, could be heard at the far end of the city."

"So you were drunk. You are sober now. In fact, I haven't seen you in that condition for more than a year."

"His reasons involve more than one of my occasional overindulgences. And let's just drop this conversation now. I repeat, please find us a place to stay for however long it takes to find our friends. Take Rebecca and the child. Brutus and I will begin tracing the first of these bits of information and meet you back here at the eleventh hour."

Meskhanet raised her head and blinked her eyes. Still dark. A sound had awakened her. Joanna? No, soft even breathing revealed her mistress asleep on the other side of the bed. What was it? There it was again—a soft thump. She rose to her feet and padded to one of the windows, standing to one side with the curtains softly billowing around her.

A torch below her lit a woman's path. Meskhanet couldn't tell who it was. A slave perhaps, because the person went from one tree to another apparently looking for something. The woman pulled a bench over, producing another bumping noise as the marble-topped seat connected with hard-packed dirt. Another sound began to accompany the woman's progress, a breathy keening.

Someone stepped out of a shadow and gestured to the woman. She stopped keening and stood facing the other figure. Larger than the woman. A man? Yes. The other said something in a deeper voice, and the woman shook her head. Again, and she nodded. She turned and pointed up toward Meskhanet.

She stepped back enough that they couldn't possibly see her, if they had even been able to before. The trouble was that she could not see them, either. After a time with no sound she ventured another glance. Nothing. No torch, no persons, not even any further noises. She shrugged and returned to her blankets, but sleep had fled.

When daylight arrived, Joanna stretched and smiled.

"Why do you smile, Mistress?"

"'Mother,' remember. We have been here a week, Meskhanet. Loukas might even now be in the city searching for us. I have no fear that he will find us. I know he will." She stretched again. "I vary between being despondent and exhilarated."

Meskhanet laughed. "I hope you are right. Do you think he will have any others with him? Cyril? Julius? Surely he would not travel alone. He was still so weak when we left."

"Or Marcus. Or maybe even Julius's other Greek servant at Caesarea. What was his name?"

"Miklos. Who is Marcus?"

Joanna turned to her, eyes widening. "Who is Marcus? Do you not remember Marcus?"

"No, Mother. Who is he?"

"Think back to Jericho. I know that seems so long ago. When Julius came to visit, he often had a friend, Marcus, with him." She shook her head. "Marcus stared at you with such fixation. I cannot believe you did not notice him."

Meskhanet shrugged. "Men stare. It is an occupation most of them share." She lowered her gaze to the floor. "Loukas does not stare. Other men should learn from him."

"Yes, true. He is a remarkable man. The best of men. And I miss having him here beside me. But soon…soon." She smiled again. "I'm hungry. Shall we go break our fast?"

When they descended, Decimus met them again at the bottom of the stairway. "Such a beautiful sight to greet my eyes in the morning. Thank you for gracing my home, dear ladies."

A movement caught Meskhanet's attention. She turned her head and looked upward to see the ghostly Portia staring at them. The woman's eyes narrowed, and she turned her back to float away, into her room.

"Why does she not like us, Senator?" Meskhanet's gaze returned to the man in front of them.

"Who, Meskhanet?"

"Portia."

"She doesn't like me, either." Septus scowled. "I don't know why."

Decimus led the way toward the triclinium. "She hasn't expressed much interest in anyone since her babe's death. Has she said something to you? Perhaps you mistake her melancholy for dislike."

Meskhanet shrugged. "I think perhaps it is more, sir. Although of course I cannot be certain."

Joanna looked at her with some surprise mirrored in wide eyes and cocked eyebrow.

Meskhanet resolved to tell her later, and she shook her head slightly.

Joanna nodded and shifted her gaze back to the senator. "Are visitors allowed to listen to the senate proceedings, Decimus?"

The senator pinched his lips between thumb and fingers and scowled slightly. "Joanna, you might not want to be there. You follow the God of the Hebrews, and you said once you would not attend the worship of any other god. The senate begins with a sacrifice to one of our gods, often Jupiter."

"Oh. Yes, you're right. We will find another source of entertainment."

"Perhaps you would like to see a chariot race at the Circus Maximus? Or a theater production? Or would you enjoy watching Appius fight? I understand he will battle another gladiator next week. With any luck at all, he will be vanquished."

"Me too?" Septus bounced up and down on his toes. "I want to watch Appius fight."

Joanna laughed and knelt in front of him. "Much as I would like to see Appius with a few bruises, I would not like to watch even him be injured or die." She rose to her feet and touched the scar on her face. "I have seen enough blood to last me the rest of my life."

Meskhanet cringed and stroked Joanna's arm. "I hope you will never see anything like that again. I feared you and Loukas must have died in Barabbas's attack. The happiest day I have known was the day I found you both alive."

"And perhaps my happiest day, too. You kept us from starving."

The senator cleared his throat. "What happened, ladies? This sounds like a warm and pleasing story."

Joanna turned to the senator with tears running down her cheeks. "One day I might tell you more, Decimus, but please don't ask me now. The events are still too painful to talk about."

She took a deep breath and expelled it. "Perhaps the races? That sounds exciting and not so bloody."

"Not usually, although it has happened. Sometimes a racer or a horse will fall during the race and be hurt, but it is not typical. I hoped this would be your choice. Some of my children will be racing tomorrow."

Joanna's brows rose. "Your children?"

Decimus chuckled. "I am fond of my horses. Especially the colts and fillies. They seem like members of my own family."

"Does that mean they are my brothers and sisters, Papa? May I go watch them, too?"

Chapter 24

This Marcus lifted one hand and ran it through his hair. Slave owners didn't want to bring their newly purchased slaves out for viewing. He'd used several silver denarii in bribes, and even one gold aureus slipped to a servant to view a new slave from a distance. Too far to see their facial features. Still—the female slave didn't resemble Joanna or Meskhanet. Tall, ruddy, and robust didn't describe either of them.

He'd written a list on a piece of parchment, and he gazed at the next name on the list. Perseus Caecilius. Why did that name sound unpleasantly familiar? He scowled and rubbed his forehead, but it didn't help. Nothing came to mind.

They trotted their horses through the city to the street where Perseus lived. Not exactly one of the prime estates in Rome, but not the worst, either. Clean. Marcus strode to the door. A woman in a thin tunic greeted him. A silken palla looped across one shoulder and draped loosely around her hips. Glossy black hair hung straight to her waist. Kohl outlined her already large dark eyes, and she lowered long lashes at his gaze. No blush rose to her cheeks, though, as she scanned him from head to toe.

"Is Perseus here?" He hoped his discomfiture didn't show.

A smile lifted full lips. "You prefer to see Perseus?" Her voice, throaty and slow, sent chills up his spine.

"Uh. Yes, I believe so. But first tell me, are you the slave he purchased last week?" He shifted from one foot to the other.

Her eyes narrowed. "And why would you assume I am a slave?"

Marcus felt his ears heat. "You are not?"

She laughed, a low, husky sound that belonged in a brothel. "Why, soldier, I believe you are blushing. Won't you come into this humble house? And bring your compatriot. It could be worth your while."

He cleared his throat. "You've not answered my questions."

"Perseus is…occupied, but he should be available soon. And I am not a slave."

Marcus stepped through the door. "Do you have any recently purchased slaves here? The barge master informed me at the dock Perseus purchased a female slave and brought her to this house."

"She is pretty, but I can give you more pleasure, soldier. I have more experience, and my trainer was none other than the emperor, himself."

"She might be one who should not be here, Mistress. We seek two women kidnapped in Caesarea. She could be one of them."

"I would be happy to be rid of her. She is the one with Perseus now." She smiled and lowered and lifted her lashes again, her gaze direct and provocative. "We could…entertain each other while we wait. Come, let Aula help you pass the time."

Marcus set his jaw against the thoughts that threatened to overcome him. "I do not wish to wait, Aula. You must interrupt them and bring the new slave before me now. Otherwise, I will be forced to take both you and Perseus as prisoners, under arrest for kidnapping a Roman citizen."

Aula stomped her foot. "You are no man. No *man* would turn me down. Perhaps you would prefer Perseus, instead." She snorted. "I will get them."

She returned within moments. "They will be here like that." She snapped her fingers.

Ah, that *Perseus.* The thin man who swaggered into the room was the brother of his stepmother, Sila. He owned several brothels, wealthy but not accepted among most other wealthy denizens of Rome. His father's wife, younger than Marcus, had been paraded before the available patricians in Rome and literally sold to the highest bidder by her own brother. She had been a tall beauty, taller than his father, and incredibly shy and embarrassed by her brother's activities supposedly on her behalf. Perseus had constantly told her he did it for her benefit, and she believed him.

When Sila's marriage to a senator did not bring Perseus the acceptance he apparently wanted, he threatened to expose her as one of the prostitutes in his employ—a lie that too many would believe. Marcus's father had bought him off with a price Perseus couldn't resist: Senator Decimus had recommended to the emperor to promote Perseus to patrician status and ensured his entry into the elite society with a sizeable donation to Tiberius's coffers.

His father's decision had been the source of a heated argument between them, and Marcus had become persona non grata in his father's house.

Marcus shook his shoulders. Not a memory he wanted occupying his mind.

"So, Perseus, we meet again. I wish I could say 'well met,' but we both know I'd be lying. I'm seeking two women from Caesarea who were kidnapped and taken to Rome as slaves."

"Ah, Marcus, it's almost a distinct pleasure to see you again. A pity I cannot help you. This sweet girl has been a slave since her birth." He turned to the young woman beside him and placed a finger beneath her chin to raise her rosy-cheeked face to view. "She is still a virgin. Her first experience is for sale, if you're interested." He moved to lift the girl's tunic, but Marcus shook his head.

She couldn't have been more than thirteen or fourteen years old. Marcus steamed and gritted his teeth. The man's oily voice grated like a rough blade against his ears. What Perseus sold was legal, but Marcus wished he could stop him.

"She is not either of the ones I seek." He turned to leave before he could change his mind. If he bought the girl, though…He turned back to Perseus. "Would you sell her to me? I don't mean for a night, I mean forever?"

Perseus laughed. "I don't think you have that much money, Marcus. Your father, perhaps, but you are a second son."

Marcus gritted his teeth and nodded with a scowl. He probably could purchase this poor girl, given that they still had most of the three bags of coins, but then he might not have enough to purchase the women they did seek. "Goodbye, Perseus."

Brutus grunted and leered at Aula. "You should have taken your time with *that* one, Decanus."

"I did not wish to dally with her. I spoke to her employer. This is another dead end. The slave he bought was not either of the women we seek. Let's do something different for a time, Brutus. How would you like to see some breathtaking beauties?"

Brutus's eyebrows did a surprised dance and his eyes lit. He nodded.

An hour later found them watching a herd of mares and their foals. One of the most prevalent reasons spring was his favorite time of year. The new foals gamboled, chasing each other and kicking their heels high. Even Brutus grinned. They leaned on the fence, pointing out this colt or that filly.

Marcus glanced up. Uh-oh, his father's chariot. Time to leave. It appeared he escorted two patrician ladies to observe his beloved foals.

Enough. They needed to get back to their search. At least the respite had begun to melt the tension in his neck and shoulders.

Meskhanet laughed. The senator had regaled them with one story after another of his precious equine 'family,' and both she and Joanna alternately giggled at the foals' antics or gasped at the achievements of the horses.

"Come into the stable with me. I'll show you my favorite stallion, the sire of many of the war horses I told you of and not a few chariot racers. Despite their size, they are fast. The first were imported from Asia. I kept the best for breeding, most after proving their bravery and ability in battles. They have yet to disappoint me." Decimus led them to a stall where a tall, white-maned black stallion leaned his neck over the door.

The senator ran his hand down the steed's soft nose. "Ah, Regillus, my son. Have you had your exercise yet today? No? We must tell Naso to take you outside. You can watch your harem and your children. Would you like that?" The stallion threw his head up and down, and they laughed.

"He understood you, Decimus." Joanna held a withered apple out, and Regillus lipped it delicately from her hand. "Is he your only breeding stallion?"

"No. Each of my sons has one, proving them in either battle or speed."

Meskhanet wandered back outside to watch the foals, much more interesting than the stallion or mares either. To her delight, a colt came up to her and nuzzled her hand. She cooed to the small one, stroking his neck and back and laughing as he took her tunic in his teeth and pulled, jumping back as she flapped her hand at him.

"So you like the little ones, do you?"

Meskhanet jumped to the side, but not quickly enough to avoid Appius. He clapped one hand over her mouth as his other arm swung around, pinning her arms to her side.

Another man laughed. "This one is a beauty, Appius. Just remember you promised her to me after you get a brat off her."

She kicked him, invoking a yelp and another laugh as they bound her mouth with a piece of cloth and her arms with rope. The other man helped him get her on the horse and handed Appius the reins. He galloped away with Meskhanet held in front of him.

He chuckled and kissed her neck. "We will have such fun, my sweet. You will see. I will treat you with gentleness—unless you fight me, that is. This time, Varrus will not disturb us. He won't even know you are there."

Joanna looked around. "Where did Meskhanet go?"

Decimus raised an eyebrow. "I thought she was right here. Maybe she went back outside to see the foals again."

Joanna trotted toward the door, her stomach tightening as a burly man entered.

"Ah, Naso, there you are. Did you see a young woman outside?" The senator strode toward them.

"Yes. She asked where to find the latrine. I pointed the way, and she went that direction." Naso slid his eyes toward Joanna.

Why didn't her stomach relax at his words? And why did her anxiety increase when Naso looked at her? "I'm going to look for her."

"Naso, take Regillus out to the corral. He wants to watch his wives. I'll come with you, Joanna." Decimus strode to the door and held it for her while Naso went after the stallion.

They walked toward the latrine, and Joanna's anxiety built. "Meskhanet! Are you here?" The silence screamed its message in her ears. "No. Please, Adonai, no!"

Decimus paced around the compound. "Here—tracks. Two horses. Two men stood here for a time. They must have been watching, but I would think we would have seen them if they'd been here when we arrived."

"I saw two soldiers over on this side of the pasture as we arrived, but I thought they left."

"Maybe they returned. Or one did." Decimus looked at some other prints in the dust. He began following one set of footprints leading toward the barn. "Naso!"

No answer, other than a nicker from inside the structure. The stallion appeared at the open door, his ears and eyes intent on the mares. His nostrils flared, and he trotted with determination in his gait toward the mares' enclosure.

Decimus began talking to the stallion, walking slowly toward him. The horse reared, flailing his hooves in the air. "Easy, my prince.

Easy." The Senator walked to the horse's head and stroked his neck. Decimus took a grip on the halter. "Come with me, my beloved. Come." He led the reluctant and blowing steed toward his corral, a high sturdy enclosure of poles and posts.

"Joanna," he said in the same singsong tone of voice. "Open the gate, slow and easy, then move away. Easy, big one, here we go. See, I'm taking you to where you can see your wives."

The sound of running hooves drew Joanna's attention. Naso galloped away on a mare. Regillus jerked his head up, but his training must have been thorough. He followed the senator's firm lead into the corral. He shifted his attention to the field full of mares and neighed at them. Decimus shut the gate.

Joanna and Decimus raced to the chariot and clambered aboard. Decimus snapped a whip in the air above the team's heads, and they flew after the disappearing form of Naso. Too late. The man disappeared behind some buildings, and by the time they reached them, he was gone.

When they returned to the villa, Joanna restrained her hysteria by a thin margin.

Decimus pulled her into his arms and held her while she sobbed. He patted her back and kissed her hair, murmuring reassurances.

Septus ran up to them. "Where is Mes-ki-net? Where is she?"

Decimus knelt in front of him. "We don't know yet, son, but we will soon. I sent an entire century in search of her."

"How did you lose her? Did she run away?"

"No. Someone took her. With help from Naso." The senator's brows furrowed.

"That big man at the stable?"

"Yes."

"But why? He doesn't even know Mes-ki-net."

"That's a good question, little man. I think if we knew why, we might be able to find out who took her and where to find her."

Chapter 25

Marcus sat his horse and greeted Cyril's arrival with a raised hand. Rebecca and the child weren't with him. Good news, maybe. "Did you find a place for us to live?"

"Yes. Not bad, either. Not like Julius's house or your father's, but it will do us just fine until we are ready to return to Caesarea. We don't even have to sleep in the same room."

"Lead us there, my friend. I'm weary and hungry. Remember, you owe me many, many meals."

Cyril chuckled. "I fear it will have to be me. Rebecca and Dinah have gone to the marketplace to buy food."

"Dinah? That's the girl's name? Then she's not Roman?"

"No, Hebrew."

"Ah. That explains a lot. Like how Rebecca could communicate with her."

"Yes. And why she pleaded so desperately for me to buy the girl. It seems she's ten years old, an orphan, and the boy at the inn is indeed her twin. Dinah's been begging me to go back and buy him, too." Cyril shook his head. "I told her it was unlikely. That we might need all we have left to purchase our friends Joanna and Meskhanet."

"I understand. It was all I could do to stop myself from buying another young woman. She's about thirteen or fourteen and her first, uh, experience is for sale. The girl is more than we can afford too, because I asked and her owner just laughed at me. I didn't want to reveal just how much we have because he would spread the word. I know the man, and I know I can trust him only as long as I can see, hear, and touch him."

They dismounted in front of a house near the south edge of the city. From the outside, it didn't look like much. A few generations previous, it might have been considered somewhat luxurious, but now weeds and vines and bushes and trees nearly hid the entire rock and mortar building.

The inside looked better. Perhaps the previous residents had cared more for the living quarters than how it looked to the public. The main room's inlaid rock floor had chips in a few places, but not bad.

Windows had no glass, but the shutters looked adequate to protect against storms. A circular table in the center of the room looked to be made of oak, and the benches around it matched the wood. Couches against the walls were in good shape, wood with plump pillows.

The culina sported a large stove and plenty of cookware. Wooden shelves next to the wall held dishes, spoons, and knives. Good. Not too much to purchase.

"Wait until you see the bedrooms. They're large enough to house a family. I think we'll put Rebecca and Dinah in one, and you, Brutus, and I may each have our own." Cyril threw back the woolen curtains hanging over one doorway.

Marcus nodded his approval. "You did well, Cyril. Did it take all the coins we had left?"

"No. I leased it for a week with options to continue the lease until we don't need it. The owner said he wasn't in a hurry. I told him we were. He seemed sympathetic, so I told him why we are here. He knows of a woman who just bought two slaves at the market, not sure whether male or female, but I found out where she lives."

"We'll go check after we eat. Speaking of which, shouldn't our companions be back?"

"I think they might already be here. I saw food peeking out of the pantry. Rebecca said something about cleaning out a place for the horses."

Brutus raised his eyebrows and led the way back to the kitchen and through the door leading from there to a corral and stable. "Huh. Good. They can get out of the weather."

Rebecca and Dinah appeared in the opening to the stable. Rebecca waved a trident and disappeared back inside. Marcus puzzled over what she would do with it and strode to the building. She reappeared with a scoop of moldering straw and manure on the tines.

Brutus grunted from behind him. Marcus turned around. Brutus's eyes held surprise and something more…respect?

"Brutus, get the horses and put them in the pen. I think they would enjoy being free of their saddles for an hour or two. And Cyril, how fast can you get us something to eat? I think Rebecca and Dinah are busy."

"Even if they weren't, Rebecca doesn't like to cook. Dinah? It's a little early to know, but the way she follows Rebecca around, she might not either. You could be stuck with my cooking."

"All right. I've sampled yours before and didn't die. But make it quick. I would like to see the woman who bought the slaves before the sun goes down."

"So would I. The longer it goes that we don't find them, the more anxious I get."

"My stomach has been tied in so many knots it would take a ship's captain to count them. Brutus and I visited my father's stable today, and watching the foals kicking up their heels helped for a time. Before we met back up with you, though, the knots returned." Marcus set his jaw. "We've got to find them."

"Your father...."

He scowled. "Let's not start that argument again."

Cyril shrugged. "I don't want to leave any chance of finding them off our list."

"Make it last on our list. I'd rather not see him, but as a last effort, perhaps. And I'm confident he'd rather not see me either."

"No one else is listening. Tell me why." Cyril placed his hand on Marcus's shoulder.

Marcus shrugged it off. "It wouldn't change anything."

Cyril turned to take a pot from the shelf. "I don't know who is more stubborn, you or your father."

Marcus grunted and walked out the door. He wasn't stubborn. Cowardly, maybe, but not stubborn. If his father found out he was in town, the senator's roar would petrify a pride of lions.

Meskhanet shivered. Her tunic had been enough while the sun was in the sky, but now the stars were her only light, and her tunic insufficient to keep warm. She was afraid to move around. The senator had been right. This city was no place for one lone woman, especially at night.

It had taken almost the whole distance to the circus to loosen the ropes on her hands, but then she had easily slipped out of Appius's grasp, leaving him holding only her palla, her beautiful new palla, but the loss couldn't be helped. She ran between two buildings the horse couldn't get into, then turned on one street after another until she lost him.

And herself. She had no idea where she was, but loud drunken voices made her wonder if she were close to a tavern.

She didn't speak Latin, although almost everyone in the world spoke Greek. They would be able to understand her. But she feared talking to anyone. Especially the men, but even the women. Would they help her or give her to a man to save themselves? *God of the Jews, where are You?*

The river…she could hear the sound of moving water. If she could get to the river, maybe she could find the senator's home from there. She stood as close as she could to the wall and peered out from behind the building. She gazed from one building to another, trying to see into the shadows. No sounds came from the street.

Then the sound of hobnail sandals disturbed the night, and she slipped behind a pile of decaying vegetables with a hand over her nose to block the smell. A rat scurried away from the garbage, and she squatted low, hoping to be invisible.

If only her tunic weren't so white. Anyone could see her, but she could see nothing. When the sound of soldiers faded, she stood. Caution demanded she stay in the shadows, working her way south along the walls and looking for anything familiar. Wait…what if the senator's villa lay to the north? What direction had she been going? Confusion and exhaustion made her head whirl. She slumped down between two walls and wept.

She must have slept. She felt stiff, and she shivered…cold, so cold. Where was she? Daylight began to light the buildings, and she squinted, hoping to see something, anything she recognized.

At least now she knew which way was east. Maybe she could watch for women going to the market or after water. Yes, that's what she should do. She pushed herself further into the crevice in the walls and watched the piece of street she could see, shivering constantly.

Voices! Better yet, female voices.

Three figures came into view, and Meskhanet slipped out of her hiding place, still shaking. "Please, can you help me?"

The girls stopped and stared at her. They glanced at each other and nodded. One of them stepped forward and said something in Latin. Meskhanet shook her head and shivered, her arms wrapped around herself. Again, she spoke in Greek. "I'm lost. I need help."

The one who stepped forward held out her cloak, wrapped it around Meskhanet, and indicated she should follow them.

She did, wondering where they led her. She hoped it would be somewhere warm and with food. Her stomach growled, and the others tittered. One rubbed her own stomach. Meskhanet smiled, feeling a small heat in her cheeks.

She felt safer with them than she had alone, and after a walk the cloak had warmed her. She handed it back to the girl who had lent it to her, smiling. "Thank you."

She remembered Septus's word he taught her and spoke it to the girls. "Pax." It probably didn't make much sense to the young women, because they giggled again. But it was the only word she knew, and they seemed to understand.

The girls were younger than she. The youngest might not even have reached womanhood, the oldest maybe as much as fourteen. Probably not slaves or servants, judging by their carefree attitudes. But why didn't they know Greek?

She hesitated when they walked up to a small villa. She knew her tunic was dirty. They looked at her questioningly and motioned for her to follow. She indicated her tunic, pointed to a splotch of mud on the hem, felt her face grow warm again.

They looked at each other. One of them grabbed one of her hands, one the other hand, and the third motioned her to follow, opening the door wide.

Several girls inside the room came rushing up to them, and Meskhanet felt a moment of panic. They chattered incessantly with the three she came in with until one of them, tall and thin, turned to her.

"What is your name? Where are you from, and why were you on the street?" The tall one giggled as one of the other girls asked her a question. "And why are you dressed in only a tunic when it is so chilly?"

Finally, one who could speak Greek. "I am Meskhanet, a…a guest of Senator Decimus. And I…I got lost last night when I, ah, went for a walk. My c-cloak fell off. And I-I couldn't find it." The friendly faces surrounding her began to close as the tall one translated.

She hung her head. After a long silence, she shook her head and sighed. "I lied. Except for being a guest of Senator Decimus and my name. I was abducted by a man yesterday, and I was able to escape him. But then I was lost and frightened and alone. I was so grateful when you came by. I'm sorry I lied. Please forgive me."

Again, Tall One translated. Their faces softened. The youngest, perhaps about five years old, came up and patted her arm and said something. She pointed to herself. "Bianca."

The tall girl tapped her chest. "Bellisima." The rest similarly indicated their names.

"We are orphans," Bellisima said. "Adopted by a woman who was also an orphan. Her life was not pleasant, but when she earned her way to freedom and wealth, she vowed to help other girls. Some of us were victims of cruel masters, but most, like you, were on the street. Frightened, alone, and cold. Each morning, very early, three or four of us will take a walk, like this morning. Many times, we find other young girls. Now we are here."

Meskhanet clapped her hands. "I'm an orphan, too, but my mistress says she and my master will adopt me. As soon as he gets here from Caesarea. Where is the woman who adopted you?" She glanced around. The furnishings were plain, but the house was warm, and she smelled something good cooking.

"She is not often here. There are two servants who teach us to cook, clean, and wash. And how to be ladylike and how to please a husband. Many times when the mother comes, she brings a man who will choose one girl to be his wife. Then we don't see her any more. It's a sad and happy time."

"Don't you go to her wedding?"

"Oh, no. Only the mother and friends of hers and the man, I suppose." Bellisima shrugged.

How odd, that they would not attend a sister's wedding! "Why do you never see them again? Would your sisters not want to come back and visit?"

Bellisima told the others what she said, and they looked at each other and shrugged again.

"No, they haven't; none of them. Are you hungry?"

"Yes, but I have to go back to the senator's villa. My mistress worries about me. Do any of you know where he lives?"

"Perhaps our mother does. We will ask her next time she comes to visit."

"Do you know when that will be?"

Chapter 26

Marcus picked up the reins and mounted, heading back toward their home. Another empty lead, and darkness would soon overtake them. He'd lost count of the number of homes they'd visited, but only one location remained. He lifted his gaze to Cyril's. "The slave market is next. I'm sure that will mean expanding our search beyond the walls of Rome."

"Or you could ask your father to help. He has wide influence." Cyril stopped his horse, a scowl on his face and a set to his jaw. "It's time, Marcus. Time to swallow your pride."

Marcus's glare matched Cyril's as he turned to face him. Brutus loosened his sword in its scabbard. Silence surrounded the three men. Marcus swallowed and blew out a long breath from pursed lips. "Very well. But not tonight. Tomorrow, then, after we break our fast."

"Now." Cyril turned his horse and plodded toward the river. "You can come with me or not, but I'm going to see the senator."

"You are the most insubordinate servant I've ever seen, Cyril. Fine, then, but I hope you're prepared for the roaring we'll hear. You can plug your ears, but sons are not allowed to do that."

Darkness had fallen, but the villa had torches lighting the outside and candles and lamps throughout the house lighting every room. Apprehension brought beads of sweat to Marcus's face, even with the coolness of the evening. They left Brutus holding the horses as they walked past the portico and into the house.

"Marcus!" One of the female slaves ran to meet them and stopped close enough that he could feel the heat from her slim form. "Oh, Marcus, I have missed you so. I'm glad you returned. Tonight, after you visit with your father, perhaps you—."

"Celia, this is my friend Cyril. Please take us to my father." He'd forgotten about Celia completely. Another problem he'd have to address, but not now.

Cyril grinned, and Marcus heard an amused grunt from behind him. Celia led the way into the triclinium with an enticing sway, and he could feel his ears burning.

Decimus stood, his eyebrows and the edges of his lips raised, but before he could speak, a woman ran from behind him.

Marcus's jaw dropped. Joanna! What was she doing here? *Meskhanet—shouldn't she be with Joanna?*

She threw her arms around him, then Cyril. "Marcus, Cyril! Oh, I am so grateful you are here! I knew you had to come soon, but I didn't know how to let you know where we would be. You have come in time to help us find Meskhanet. Or did she find you and then lead you to us? Did Loukas stay in Caesarea?"

"You know my son?" The senator's eyebrows threatened his hairline.

"Marcus is your son? Why didn't you tell me? Oh…you wouldn't have known I wanted to know. Forgive me. Yes, Marcus is a good friend. He and Julius came to us in Jericho and…no, that's a story for another time. Where is Loukas?"

Marcus sat on a bench and motioned to her to be seated. He opened his mouth, but tears blinded him, and a sob choked his words. She looked from him to Cyril and back. He heard a strangled sound from Cyril's direction and realized his friend had similar problems. He reached for her hand.

She jumped to her feet. "Oh, no." She breathed the words. "No, don't tell me Loukas…he can't be…I would have known. I don't believe it. You're mistaken."

Cyril placed his hands on her shoulders. "We were with him, Joanna." He grasped her hands. "Pirates." He released his hold on her, choked, dropped to the bench, and slid his head into his hands, elbows on his knees.

Marcus rose to stand beside her and took a deep breath. "He said to tell you he loved you."

A small boy ran up to her, his face screwed up in sympathy, and threw his arms around her legs. "Don't cry, Joanna, please don't cry."

Joanna's face had turned a stark white, and she stared wide-eyed at them. "Loukas, no, not my Loukas. She fell to the floor in a faint.

Marcus dropped to his knees and lifted her head and shoulders.

"Celia!" The senator roared. "Prepare the lady Joanna's bed." He walked to the side of the table where Joanna lay against Marcus. "Help me, Son."

They lifted Joanna, and Decimus carried her up the staircase and to her bed. He blew out the lamp. "Stay with her, Celia, and call me when she wakes."

The three men walked back down the stairs followed by the still crying child. "Papa, is Joanna sick? Did these men hurt her? Why did she cry? Why did she fall asleep?"

"No, Septus, no one has hurt her. She found out someone she loved has died. Now, please, do not ask any more questions for a time. We will talk before you go to your bed."

Papa? This little boy is my brother? Marcus shook his head. His father's latest offspring. Where was Sila?

The senator clapped Marcus on the back. "Well met, my son. I didn't know you knew Joanna. Last I knew of you, you were still in Jericho. Although Perseus did tell me at the senate yesterday that he'd seen you. I wondered if he lied." His eyes narrowed. "And I wondered what you were doing here if he did not lie, and if you would come to see me."

Now it comes. "And so I did. It appears we should have come here first. Cyril said we should, and it is my fault we did not."

His father quirked an eyebrow, but he didn't explode. What was this?

"Is this my brother, then?" He managed a smile at Septus. "Pax, little brother."

Septus grinned, his tears forgotten. "You're my brother Marcus?" He raised his right hand.

Marcus returned his salute. "Yes. We'll talk another time, little brother, but let me talk with Father now. Is that all right with you?"

A thousand questions burned in Septus's eyes, but he glanced at his father then back to Marcus. "All right."

"How has our beautiful stallion done in battle?"

Marcus felt his eyes dampen again. "He was better than any horse we ever raised. He died taking the blow of a sword meant for me. I'm sorry, Father."

Decimus bowed his head. When he raised it again, Marcus could see he wept. "This is a sorrowful day, Marcus. I grieve with Joanna over her husband and now over the loss of Tsal. But I rejoice that you are alive and returned to me. I heard disturbing word from

Jerusalem that your contubernium had been exterminated by a Jewish murderer's band."

Marcus hoped he hid his sense of shock. His father still did not look angry. But he still had more to tell him. "Father, I have a confession to make. I am probably sought for arrest in Jerusalem. It's a long story. The shortened version is that Barabbas did kill my men, all but one other and me. I grew a beard and infiltrated the murderer's camp hoping to kill or capture him, but then a century from Jerusalem captured all the men in the camp. Including me."

"You must have felt great relief with this Barabbas captured. You were freed, of course, as soon as they discovered you were not one of them."

Marcus shook his head. "They accused me of being a traitor. It's too long a story for now, but the short version is that I escaped to go to Julius's home in Caesarea when I heard Joanna and Meskhanet had been kidnapped. Now I see you must have rescued Joanna, but where is her slave, Meskhanet?"

His father blew out a breath between pursed lips and scowled. "That, too, is a long story."

The door opened, and a beautiful woman walked in with a man who looked familiar to Meskhanet. Oh, yes…the one the senator had angry words with the day they arrived at the villa. Petrus? Perseus? Something like that. He didn't seem to recognize her. Good. She kept her eyes on the floor. Maybe they wouldn't notice her. All her new friends seemed to be chattering to the woman at the same time.

Please, oh please, don't let the girls mention that I'm a guest of the senator.

But no, they had. He cut his eyes sharply to her and said something in Latin. When she didn't answer, he spoke in Greek. "What is your name?"

"My name is Meskhanet, sir. I am not a member of this household." She kept her gaze on the floor.

"You are a guest of one of the senators?" He brushed at one of his thin eyebrows.

"Yes."

"What are you doing here?" His sharp questions felt like daggers, creating first one nick and then another.

"I became lost last evening. These young women found me and brought me in here to warm myself." Her heart slammed against her ribcage. *No, don't ask me anymore!*

"Which senator?"

She gulped. "Decimus. I'm sure his household must be out looking for me."

Perseus laughed. "Perfect."

He turned to the beautiful lady. "I choose this one," he said, pointing to Meskhanet.

"She is new, Perseus, and obviously not an orphan from the street. Until I have talked to her, maybe you should select another." The woman looked at Meskhanet, her eyes reflecting tense concern.

"She is the one I want."

"I do not know her. She could be entirely unsuited. She might not even be a virgin. For all I know, she may, ah, be already married." The woman shifted from one foot to the other and pointed to the tall girl. "Now, Bellisima, I know she would be suited…"

"Nevertheless, this is the one I will take. I will pay double."

"Double?"

Chills ran up Meskhanet's spine. "Madam, I fear there has been a mistake. I am betrothed. I cannot marry another. I am only in this place because I wandered from my dwelling and became lost. Bellisima and her friends—sisters— helped me. But I cannot stay here, and I cannot go with this man."

Perseus walked up to her, his eyes lit with something unholy. "Betrothal is a small matter, woman. You are not wed. You will come with me. Do not make me angry. These new friends of yours could suffer if you refuse."

Bellisima's eyes widened. "Mother, surely this man is not one to give Meskhanet to. She speaks the truth. She is only here because we found her searching for her home, shivering with cold."

Perseus's palm struck the girl's face. "Do you allow such insolence from your charges, Aula?" He raised his hand to strike again, and Aula stepped between them.

Bellisima's hands flew to her cheeks, and her eyes filled. He reached for her again, this time with a doubled fist.

"No, do not hurt her!" Meskhanet pulled her new friend away and stood between them.

"Then you will come with me. Without further argument. Aula? Here is your…bride price." He handed her a bag of coins without a glance in the woman's direction.

Aula looked in the bag. "You said double."

Perseus turned to her, eyes narrowing, his multi-ringed hand rising to backhand her.

"No, no! I did not mean it." The woman flinched away from him, covering her face.

Meskhanet's heart thumped so hard she thought surely all could hear. What could she do? She wouldn't be the reason this man harmed her new friends. Or this woman either. *God of the Jews, what should I do?*

A sense of peace and knowing filled her heart. "Don't hurt them. I will go with you. The God of the Jews will go with me."

Perseus started, both eyebrows jumping to his low hairline and his eyes widening. "The God of the Jews? What contact do you have with Him? I heard nothing." He smirked and rolled his eyes in mock fear.

Meskhanet tapped her chest. "He speaks in here. And He said He will be with me, that I should not be afraid."

A low growl emanated from his throat. "Come with us, then. Aula, you too." As they exited from the villa, Meskhanet heard the low sound of a fearful keening.

"You do not intend to marry me, do you?"

Perseus laughed, a humorless sound. "No. But if my brother-in-law cares anything about you, little beauty, you will yet see your betrothed without harm to your lovely body. If Decimus does not, I have use for you. Either way, I will get my coins back with interest."

Meskhanet shuddered. Had there ever been a smile with less friendliness or a gaze so cold? His black eyes reflected no light. He should have been handsome, but the perfection of his features instead made him appear sinister.

They stepped onto a chariot. When Perseus snapped the whip over their backs, two matched white mares moved forward as one. They rode in silence to a brick villa. "You are home, Aula."

"Will you not come in with your new woman, Perseus?" Aula had not lost her fear. Even in the descending dusk Meskhanet could see Aula's large brown eyes rimmed with white, and her voice shook as she stepped out of the chariot.

"No. I will take her to another house."

"Yours?"

"Where I take her is of no concern to you."

"Oh—no, of course not. She belongs to you now. I did not mean to imply…."

"Good night, Aula." The whip stung the horses' backs, and the chariot jumped forward.

Should she jump off again? Meskhanet eyed their surroundings. They would soon leave the city. There were fewer buildings to hide behind and none to squeeze between. Yet the sense of peace that pervaded her earlier had remained. She would stay on the chariot with this man she knew had evil plans for her.

They arrived at a country villa off the main roads. Perseus snapped an order to a thin man who ran to meet the chariot. Perseus grabbed her arm as though he expected her to run, but she walked beside him with the serenity of one following an angel as the thin slave took the horses to a stable.

He took her into the house and locked her in a room with an impossibly high window. The furnishings were sparse—a straw-covered pallet, a lamp, and a basin. Meskhanet looked around her for a skin of water to quench her thirst.

Before long, Perseus entered the room, a grim smile in place. "I sent word to your friend, the senator. Do you think he loves you enough to pay the ransom to get you back? You had better pray to your Jewish God he will."

Meskhanet should have been frightened, but peace filled her. She shrugged. "If he does not, and I do not think he will, I suppose you will have to kill me."

He snorted. "No, I will not kill you. But I would sell your virginity to the highest bidder."

She shook her head. "It is too late for that. I lied about being betrothed and I am not a virgin. I am but a slave. You might get thirty pieces of silver for me, but that is all I am worth."

Chapter 27

Marcus scowled at the floor, glanced at Cyril and Brutus, then looked up at his father. "What happened to Meskhanet?"

His father's lips tightened to a thin line. "My stableman assisted someone in her abduction. He escaped, but soldiers found him about a half hour ago. I don't think it will be long before we know who else was involved and why."

"I realize you probably have people looking for her, but perhaps we could join the search."

"There is one entire century searching the city. I suggest we wait to find out what my former stableman will reveal."

As though he had been summoned, a soldier trotted through the door. His gaze landed on Marcus, and he started. "Have you already had a report, Senator?"

"No. This is my son. What have you, soldier?"

The soldier saluted. "The prisoner says a gladiator paid him to help capture the young woman. He didn't say the gladiator's name, sir."

"He probably will before morning, correct?" Decimus narrowed his gaze at the soldier.

The man colored. "Ah, I think not, sir. Your stable man died. I'm not sure why, because no one had begun to be rough on him. He blurted out the information about the gladiator. His face went white, then red, then he screamed and died." A trace of scorn crossed his face. "It appears he died of fear."

Marcus's father grunted. "A gladiator." He pursed his lips.

Marcus laid his hand on his father's arm. "A gladiator? Then we will visit the circus. Care to come with us, Father?"

"Let's check on Joanna first. If she's awake, we'll let her know what we know and where we're going. She and I may know who has her."

"You do?" Marcus followed his father and Cyril up the stair.

"One of the people shipwrecked with Joanna was a gladiator. He developed an obsession for Meskhanet. Twice that I know of he tried to rape her, and both times another slave stopped him—a very large man called Varrus."

When they topped the staircase, Joanna stepped out of her bedroom. Her gaze met Marcus's, and tears filled her eyes again. He walked to her, wrapped her in his arms, and held her tight while sobs racked her body. At length, she pushed back.

"There is another problem, Marcus," she said. "Meskhanet...."

"I know. Father told me. We have a lead on where she is."

"Where?"

"At the circus." Marcus glanced at his father.

Her eyes widened. "Appius."

"That is my opinion, too." Decimus turned to descend to the ground floor. "We're going after him."

Marcus followed him, Cyril's footsteps close behind.

Marcus glanced back and saw Joanna in the doorway to her bedroom, wringing her hands.

"Father, shouldn't someone stay with Joanna?" Marcus pitched his voice low.

Decimus turned. "Yes, you're right. Cyril, would you?"

Cyril opened his mouth then clamped it shut. He nodded. "I know. I'm the least trained to fight. I'll stay, but please bring Meskhanet back safely and soon."

"We'll bring her." Marcus grit his teeth. *Adonai, please lead us to the one I love. And protect her from evil, even if she never loves me.* He donned his cloak and followed the others out the door. *If I had listened to Cyril, we would have been here in time to save her. Forgive this stubborn man, Lord.*

They found Brutus near a patch of bushes and grass with the horses. Marcus paused only to explain where they were going. His father mounted Cyril's horse, and the other Roman soldier, Brutus, and Marcus their own mounts. They galloped through the dark streets to the circus a few short blocks away.

They tied their horses to the posts and ran into the circus. A very tall, imposing slave stopped them at the door.

"Varrus, well met." The senator slapped the slave's arm.

Varrus broke into a wide, gap-toothed grin and patted Decimus's shoulder. "Ungh."

"We seek Appius. Do you know where he is?"

He pointed toward the barracks and led them in that direction, his long legs forcing Marcus to trot to keep up.

Didn't his father say this Varrus had been a friend of Appius? This was one giant he wouldn't enjoy fighting...but for Meskhanet? Yes, he would. Marcus took a long look at the big man and shook his head. He'd probably lose.

They reached the arched door into the barracks, and Decimus touched Varrus on the elbow. "We might have to take Appius prisoner. We think he kidnapped Meskhanet. Have you seen her?"

Varrus shook his head, and his eyebrows lifted in the middle. He turned, lit a torch, and preceded them into a long hallway with cells along each side. Some were locked, some not. Varrus took them to one that was not.

Marcus, his father, and Brutus walked into the cell. Appius sat at the edge of his pallet, his head in his hands. Marcus's fingers itched to close around the gladiator's throat.

"Where is she?" The senator shook Appius's shoulder.

Appius fell back on the pallet and raised his hand to shade his eyes against the torch. "Who's there? What do you want?" His words slurred, and the empty beer jug at his side completed the story.

"You're drunk."

Appius belched and grinned. "You could be right."

"Where is Meskhanet?" Marcus stepped forward, his sword lifted.

Appius peered at him. "Who're you?"

"Not important. Where is Meskhanet? I won't ask you again." Marcus slit a piece of cloth from one shoulder of the gladiator's woolen tunic.

"She's gone. Ran away. Didn't even say goodbye." He hiccupped. "I thought she liked me. Oh, sure, she acts shy, but she likes me. She wants to be a gladiator's woman. That's me." He snorted a laugh. "A gladiator, that is. Not a gladiator's woman." He giggled, choking when he hiccupped again.

Marcus turned away, disgust roiling his stomach.

His father waved the Roman soldier forward. "Take this man back to your garrison and sober him up. Find out where the girl got away from him. Then imprison him. If he ever walks free again, the man who sets him loose will suffer."

He turned to the tall slave. "Varrus, my friend, would you like to change jobs? I think you should be our women's protector. Introduce me to your owner."

Varrus nodded, but hesitated, looking after Appius.

"I'm sorry, Varrus. I know he was your friend, but he did something bad. He would have hurt Meskhanet. In fact, she may have been hurt. His days as a free-roaming gladiator are over." Decimus patted the man's arm.

Varrus scowled at Appius's disappearing form, then he led them back farther into the barracks. He took them to a lamp-lit doorway at the end of the corridor.

A man looked up as they walked in. "Ah, Senator, good to see you."

"Caldius. Does this man belong to you?"

"Yes. Has he done something wrong?" Caldius frowned at Varrus.

"No. Two women friends of mine are fond of him, and he would make the perfect bodyguard for them."

Marcus nodded his head. If only Varrus had been with them at the stables….

Caldius laughed. "I think you might be making a mistake, sir. He wouldn't swat a mosquito if it were biting him."

"He might surprise you. He has twice saved one of these women from being raped. His strength and size alone would deter most with evil intentions."

"I was unaware of that. Huh. Very well, senator. Thirty sesterces will be sufficient, then."

"And a horse," Marcus said. "Large enough to carry our friend here." He nodded toward Varrus. "I'll pay for it."

The ludus master laughed. "Not here. Maybe not anywhere."

Meskhanet stared through the window to the stars beyond. The one lamp in the room did not shed enough light to blot the stars from her view. Although the room was large, she felt as though she were in prison. She shook her head at the absurdity and chuckled.

You are so big, God of the Jews, how can I hope to relate to You? Joanna says You hung those stars in place. Loukas says You are everywhere.

Am I only the God of the Jews?

Where did that Voice come from? She crouched in a corner, shut her eyes tight, and covered her ears.

The Voice didn't soften. *Will you allow me to be the God of Meskhanet?*

Her eyes flew open, and she dropped her hands. "Where are You?" She could see nothing. "What do You mean?"

Silence.

Her God? She had promised she would follow only Him, but that only meant she belonged to Him. He was the God of the Jews. She was not a Jew. How then could He belong to her? What right had she to ask Him to be her God? And yet, did He ask her permission, her agreement?

If so, then, "Yes, God. I want You to be my God. My Adonai." Tears leaked from her eyes. "I belong to You. I want You to be my God, too."

How could she feel His smile? And yet she did.

"Thank You, my God." She lay on the straw-covered pallet and fell asleep almost immediately.

Joanna paced back and forth in front of the window in her bedroom.

"How can he be dead, Adonai? How would I not feel my heart dying in my chest if my beloved passed from this life? He kissed me before I left and told me to hurry back. I want to go back to that day. If I had known, I wouldn't have left him."

Back and forth again.

She put her head in her hands. "It's my fault. If I had not gone so impatiently to the slave market…if I hadn't gotten so impatient with that mongo, he wouldn't have been angry enough to imprison us. Adonai, if only I could go back and change what happened."

She stared out the window.

"And now Meskhanet. My fault also. I should have paid attention to her, not that stallion who cares for nothing but his mares."

Tears ran down her face, but she didn't care.

"Adonai, will everyone I love be endangered? Please, Adonai, keep Meskhanet in the shadow of Your wings. And Marcus and Cyril and Decimus. I am weak and powerless, but You know everything everywhere, and You are powerful."

She lay down on the bed and wept. She still wept when Celia entered the room.

"Mistress, a man at the door insists he must see the senator, but I do not know where he is."

Joanna lifted herself heavily. "They are looking for Meskhanet, and they probably went to the circus."

Celia left, but shortly she returned. "Mistress, please help me. He wants to stay and wait for the senator, but I'm afraid to allow it."

Joanna sighed. She understood being afraid. "Go get the male servants to come to the front of the villa. The bigger the men, the better. Run as fast as you know how. I will go talk to the man."

Joanna threw her old dark cloak around the white tunic. She didn't feel like wearing the happy colored stolas and cloak Decimus had purchased for her.

She descended the stairs feeling like an old woman, slow and holding onto the ornamental rail at the side.

She reached the bottom and opened the door as two stablemen rounded the corner of the villa. She could understand why Celia didn't want to allow the man to wait in the house. Wide eyes in a gaunt face stared in at her then glanced at the two stablemen and the additional servants arriving one after the other. The skeletal man held his cane more like a defensive weapon. It resembled him somehow, knotted and twisted from one end to the other. A scar gripped one side of his face, pulling his mouth into a permanent grimace.

Thinking of the scar that decorated her own face, she greeted him with kindness. "Sir, the senator is not here now. I'm not sure how long until he will return. You might come back tomorrow."

A voice as thin as the man emanated from him as he quivered in gray-faced fear. "I am ordered to wait for him if he is not here. If you send me away without delivering the message, my master will beat me."

"You may give the message to me. I promise the senator will receive it."

His voice raised an octave and shook. "He said I must give it to no one but Senator Decimus."

"It is late. I cannot allow you to wait in the house, but perhaps on the portico. I will send blankets out to you."

Joanna motioned to one of the stablemen. "You will stay here with this man as he waits for the master."

The stableman bowed. "Yes, mistress."

The other man also dipped his head, but he backed away when she stepped toward him.

Another servant shut the door behind her as she reentered the villa. "Celia," she called to the shy slave again approaching her.

"Yes, mistress." Celia hurried to her.

"Get enough blankets for two men and take them to the stableman and the messenger on the portico. And thank you for being so quick to get the others."

"Yes, Mistress, and I do appreciate your help, too. I didn't know what to do, because he would not leave."

"He said his master would beat him if he didn't deliver his message to your master. He was frightened too, you see."

Celia blushed. "I didn't think of that. It's just that he looks so...."

"Yes." Joanna touched the scar on her face. "Sometimes scars can make a person look alarming."

Celia ducked her head. "Yes, mistress. But I do not see yours any more. I see you. I will go find blankets for the men."

Chapter 28

Marcus led the way at a slow trot back to his father's villa. Varrus didn't seem to have any trouble keeping up, nor did he act winded.

They arrived to find two men sleeping on the portico. One of them jumped up and saluted the senator. The other rose with jerks and starts, as though his joints did not work as they should.

"Sir, this man has a message for you. The mistress asked me to stay with him until you arrived."

"Thank you, Servius. Take Varrus here in to the mistress." Decimus turned to the other and started as the man lifted his face. "What is it you have for me, man?"

Marcus had to admit the stranger could make a corpse shiver. Varrus rumbled as he ducked through the door after Servius.

The man lifted his arm and handed a rolled piece of parchment to Decimus.

"Bring a torch, Marcus."

Marcus took a torch from one of the many sconces on the villa and brought it to his father's side. He lifted it over Decimus's shoulder so he could read the missive.

"'I have Meskhanet. Such a lovely slave would do well in my houses, don't you think? And she will, unless you buy her back from me. Twenty aurei. ~ Perseus.'"

The senator's reddening cheeks made Marcus wonder if his father would explode.

"That stinking pig. That diseased donkey. That conceited, arrogant son of a bloated fish. Death for him should be deliberate and agonizing. If there ever was a man I'd give my last aureus to watch being tortured until his death, Perseus is that one."

The messenger blanched and stepped backwards several steps until he fell off the portico. He picked himself up from the ground, stumbled to his horse tethered nearby, and galloped away.

Marcus leapt on his mount and galloped after him, followed by his father, Brutus, and Cyril. The man's horse was fresh and fast and carrying a man who weighed as much as a ghost. They couldn't catch him.

Marcus stopped his blowing horse and turned to face his companions. "What now, Father? Any ideas on how we can find Perseus?"

"The missive didn't say. I doubt he will confront us publically, unless it is to tease us with further demands. He's clever. It would be a safe wager that he doesn't have her at his home. But fear not, he will contact us again."

"I wish he would contact us personally. I'd like to question him as to where he's taken my…our friend."

His father narrowed his eyes at Marcus. "Your what?"

"Uh, not just mine. *Our* friend."

"Loukas said he and Joanna wanted to adopt Meskhanet, so that would make her my wife's sister," Cyril said, setting his jaw. "I think that means I should have first rights to interrogate him."

"He's my brother-in-law, and I'm Marcus's father, and I believe that gives me the superior right. In addition, you are a servant. Perseus is a Roman citizen and a patrician. Meskhanet belongs to Joanna, and Joanna is my guest. We have the right to sue him, but all he would have to pay us is the price of a slave, and I fear she would be ill-used before he returned her. If I had caught him stealing her at night from my home, I could have killed him with no repercussions."

"Yes, Father, I still remember the twelve tables. I had to memorize the laws too. All right, I understand we can't legally torture him, but what do we do now?" Marcus twisted in his saddle to peer into the darkness.

"We wait. With knots in our chests, perhaps, but that's all we can do. At least until morning. I'll put out word of a reward for anyone who can lead us to him or to her. For now, we'll return to the villa."

With a heavy heart, Marcus followed his father and companions back home. Poor Meskhanet. He could imagine how frightened she must be. There was nothing they could do but wait. But after Meskhanet had been returned to them in safety, nothing would stop him from going after Perseus. Nothing.

He sent Brutus to take the horses to the stable and trudged up the steps onto the portico. Joanna and Varrus met them at the door to the villa. Her eyes looked red and puffy. It didn't surprise him. How could a woman lose a husband without a part of her own heart dying? Would the mourning ever cease? He thought about how he felt when he thought Barabbas had killed Meskhanet, and the joy he felt when he heard she lived.

Cyril slid his arm around Joanna's shoulders, and she turned to sob against his chest. Cyril's eyes also showed moisture, and he felt his own eyes fill. To his surprise, his father, too, wiped tears away as he laid one hand on her shoulder.

A wraith-like woman floated into the room from the peristylium. She viewed the group with narrowed eyes. "Touching," she murmured, her lips twisting. Still—loud enough to be heard by all present. "Such grieving was never shared with me when my son died."

"Portia, you know our sorrow matches yours. You pull away and will not let us comfort you. Come over here—we will join in mourning together. You have lost a child; I lost a grandchild. Joanna has lost a husband."

Portia narrowed her eyes and glared down her nose at them, then she turned to ascend the stairway and disappear from view.

"Who was that, Father?"

"Portia, your brother Vitus's wife. She's been a little demented since their baby died. She spends most of her time in their room and refuses to communicate with us. Not even Septus seems to be able to reach through her grief." Decimus rubbed his forehead. "I'm tired, and I suspect the same is true for all of you. I suggest we try to get some sleep while we can. It won't be long until the sun rises."

Meskhanet opened her eyes and saw a crimson sky through the high window. Oh, if only the window were larger or closer. She loved the beauty of a sky with the multiple colors of sunrises and sunsets. And rainbows. Her heart always lifted whenever she saw such splendor. This morning, her joy in the hues she saw were heightened by the joy she'd encountered the night before when she'd asked God to be her own God.

She stretched her toes to a point, lifted her hands to reach as far over her head as they would go, and twisted right and left.

The sound of the bar lifting came from the door, and she rose from the pallet. Perseus's cold smile greeted her as he slithered closer. She smiled at the thought of a snake with Perseus's face, and he started.

"Shalom, Perseus."

"Why would you wish me peace, slave girl?"

"Why would I not?"

He scowled. "You are my prisoner. You will not earn your freedom by currying my favor."

She chuckled. "You are not the reason for my smiles, sir. My God is."

"Unless I mistake your looks and name, you are Egyptian. To which of those gods so far inferior to the gods of Rome do you refer?"

"I agree the Egyptian gods are inferior. But then, so too are the gods of Rome. The God of gods is my God. The great God, Yahweh."

Perseus snorted. "I do not wish to argue theology with an ignorant slave woman."

"Nor I." Meskhanet hoped she could contain the laughter pushing at her throat.

Perseus's eyes widened. "What?"

"I would not want to argue theology, not even with an intelligent slave."

Perseus stepped closer, his hand upraised, but he apparently thought better of that action and lowered his hand without striking.

Where did this courage come from? *Adonai, am I being fearless or foolish?*

"I sent a message to the senator telling him I have his precious slave. Next I will see him at the Forum, but I do not know how long that will be. He might not go there today or even tomorrow. He might think I will send him another message, but I won't." He smiled a reptilian smile.

Meskhanet could almost hear him hiss, but instead of quaking in fear, she wanted to giggle. She looked down at her feet and thought about the dirt between her toes, but that only increased her amusement.

Her stomach began to contract, and she could hold it no longer. She laughed until tears ran down her face. She clenched her arms over her abdomen. She dropped to the pallet, snorting and giggling uncontrollably. She looked up at Perseus's contorting face, which sent her off again.

His face—so comical! His mouth worked, his eyes squinted, his nose twitched. "You are a sorceress, aren't you? Well, you won't put any spells on me." He left the room huffing.

When she could stop laughing, the hiccups began. Which only made her chuckle again. *Adonai, what is happening? I should be frightened. I should be hungry. The hiccups should irritate me, not inspire more amusement. Instead, I overflow with laughter—and hiccups. I am so full of joy I cannot control myself. Does this happen to everyone who makes You their own God?*

Perhaps she should focus on a way to escape this prison. But where would she go if she got out? It was a few miles to Rome, and the few houses she'd seen on their way to this villa held no guarantee of friendliness toward her, an Egyptian slave woman.

Adonai? Should I try to find a way out? Should I stay? My life is in Your hands.

She hoped His hands did not resemble those of any of the idols she had seen. A vision of cupped hands entered her head. She sat safely enclosed in those hands, much like a small bird had rested in her hold once when she had been a child. She had climbed a nearby tree and placed the small bird back with its nest mates while the parents swooped over her head making frantic cries.

A sweet memory. Did God mean He had her in His hands and would return her to her friends? She chuckled. She felt His smile again.

A knock sounded at the door and a rubbing sound as the bar lifted. The emaciated man who had taken the chariot horses entered the room with a tray loaded with a bowl of soup, a loaf of flatbread, and a skin of something liquid. She stood and walked toward him, intending to take the tray. The man's eyes widened, and he stepped back, almost tripping over a cloak too long for him.

"Do not fear. I cannot harm you."

The man said something back to her in Latin, his voice quivering. She shook her head. She must ask Loukas to teach her Latin when he arrived from Caesarea.

She motioned to a small table, and the man set the tray on it then scurried out of the room. The bar scraped into place on the other side of the door.

This had to be the first time any man had ever been afraid of *her*. She snickered again.

Food. She hoped it tasted better than it looked. Congealed grease with a few onions and something else green she couldn't identify. She shrugged and pulled the stopper from the skin. She raised it to her nose. Wine. Or maybe watered wine. She took a sip. Acceptable. She hoped it didn't make her any giddier than she had already been.

She started to lift a spoonful from the unappetizing bowl to her lips and shuddered. It smelled like rotten meat. She couldn't eat this. She put the spoon back in the bowl and took another sip of the watered wine and crunched on the dry bread.

Although she didn't feel all that hungry now, she knew that time would come. *Adonai, I hope my rescuers will come before long.*

Chapter 29

Marcus rolled over on the soft bed, wondering if Meskhanet had slept in a cold dark dungeon somewhere. He hadn't slept, but at least his bed was soft and warm. He swung his legs off the side of the waist-high bed and slid off, landing quietly on the balls of his feet. Daylight streamed through the window. Morning had come with a menacing red sky.

He donned his sandals and tunic and descended the staircase. Varrus stood behind Joanna, scrubbing his hands together and occasionally patting her back. She sat alone in the dining area, shoulders slumped and head in her hands. She wept almost silently, a whimper revealing her sorrow. Marcus walked to her and sat beside her.

She jumped. "Oh, it's you, Marcus. I didn't hear you."

"Yes, it's me. Did you sleep?"

"A little. I tried to pray, but I find I'm angry at God. And I'm so tired my head will not hold still. I feel as though I've had too much wine." She raked a hand through her tangled hair, strands of snowy white far outnumbering the black.

Strange. He didn't remember her having any white hair before. "Angry? I can understand that. I've felt furious, myself. Angry when I thought Meskhanet was dead, furious when the two of you were kidnapped. It's hard to pray when you're irate because the One God hasn't done things as you think He should." He lifted his hand to her shoulder.

"I want Loukas back, and even though I know it's impossible, I still want it. And then I'm cross with myself for being so foolish that morning we were kidnapped. And I'm livid that Meskhanet is missing." She leaned her forehead into his shoulder. "Loukas thought of you as a son, you know. He wanted Meskhanet to marry you."

"I loved him too, Joanna. Loukas was the finest physician I've known, and his friendship sustained me more than once."

Footsteps sounded, and Decimus appeared at the doorway followed by his small shadow, Septus, who clutched a carved elephant under his arm. Deep shadows under his father's eyes revealed how little he had slept, too.

"Good morning, Father, Brother."

Septus left his father and climbed into Marcus's lap. One thumb slipped into his mouth, and he leaned his head on his big brother's chest.

Marcus's mouth dropped for an instant. He smiled and touched his cheek to Septus's tousled head as he wrapped one arm around the boy. "That is a fine elephant you have, Little Brother," he murmured.

Septus extricated his thumb for enough time to speak. "Papa bought it for me in Al-ex-an-dree-uh. His name is Pharaoh."

"An elegant name."

"Yes." Septus closed his eyes and snuggled closer.

"I think you have been accepted." One corner of their father's mouth lifted, but the smile failed to reach his tired eyes. "I'm going to the Forum this morning. That's the most likely place to see Perseus. I don't know if I'll be home until the evening meal, but I plan to return by then."

"Go with God, Decimus. And thank you." Joanna turned to him. "We owe you so much. I have nothing with which repay you."

"It is nothing, Joanna. I have enough and to spare. And my dislike of Perseus spurs me as well. That he would kidnap an innocent young woman just to hurt me and gain more coins is enough to start a fire in my heart. He does not need more lucre. He does this to injure me."

"What is his grudge against you, Father?" Marcus shifted the sleeping child from his lap to Joanna's. He stood and accompanied his father to the atrium.

"Celia, ask Servius bring my chariot to the front."

"Yes, Senator. As you wish." She bowed and departed.

He turned to Marcus. "The man sold me his own sister at a rather high price, I might add. I know you disapproved at the time, but you didn't know the whole story. Had I not purchased her, she would have gone to the Consul Fufius. He would have used her and returned her to her brother, and she would have been condemned to a life of prostitution. Yes, she was beautiful, but she was also kind."

"Did you come to love her? Or did you just desire a virgin?" His face heated, and he could have cut out his own tongue. "I'm sorry, Father. That was the reaction of a sixteen-year-old, and unfitting of one who supposedly had matured since then. Please, forget I asked that."

Instead, his father laughed. "Yes, it did sound a little like the son I used to argue with so much. But yes, I did come to love her. She was so sweet-natured and trusting it was impossible not to love her, and it was even possible to forget she was a sister to Perseus. Yet she continued to love her brother, despite his evil intentions for her." He shook his head.

"What happened to her?" Marcus mounted his horse and turned back to face his father.

"Thank you, Servius." His father's face clouded as he stepped into the chariot. "She died in childbirth."

"Oh. I am sorry, Father. Forgive me. I judged her—and you—with all the grace of a striking sword."

"Septus is much like her. Open, trusting, loves everyone." The senator gave him a quick grin. "Even you."

When they tethered their horses in front of the Forum, Perseus stood, hands on hips, arrogant and smiling. "Well, well. The senator and his son, well met. You have hurried to seek me, then. How wise of you. Do you have the, ah, purchase price for one precious item with you?"

Marcus fought the urge to reach for his sword. Later.

"Precious item? Are you joking? Why would I pay twenty aurei for a slave? A slave not even mine?" The senator snorted.

Marcus gritted his teeth. He knew his father had to barter, but he wanted to just hand over the money and free his love.

Perseus hissed. "I know better, Decimus. This young beauty is just what you want to replace my sister."

No, that could not be true. He glanced at his father.

"I'm getting old, Perseus. Even a seventeen-year-old could not warm me enough to make me pay so much. I could go to the slave market and find one for less. Prettier, too. I go for the light-haired Germans these days. I saw one at the market last week that made my mouth water, but I was in a hurry and she was gone before I got back. Now, one like that I would pay maybe an aureus for."

Marcus breathed a quiet breath between clenched teeth. *Remember, he's only bartering.*

"Enough. I'll try to find one for you, if you would pay so much. The pretty Egyptian can go to my brothels." Perseus's eyes narrowed, and he smiled with all the charm of a hungry wolf.

Meskhanet accepted the bowl of weak gruel from the thin man again, and again he flinched when she accepted it from his stretched out hands. "Wait." She took a step closer to him, holding one hand out, palm up.

The man backed away, his eyes widening. He shook his head, hands in front of his face. When he hit the wall, he slid down and pulled his knees up to his chin and covered his head, shaking. "Non, non, non."

Meskhanet knelt in front of him, soundless. She placed the bowl in front of him and waited.

He stopped whimpering and slowly lowered his hands from his eyes.

She pushed the bowl toward him, spoon on his side of the dish. She nodded. "Eat," she said in Greek. Maybe he would understand that.

He shook his head and rolled his eyes toward the still open door. He jumped to his feet and bolted through, and she heard the bar drop in place behind him.

Why did he fear her? He wasn't a large man, but she was still smaller than he.

Meskhanet sighed and shook her head. She pulled the bowl back and tasted the gruel. It pleased her mouth and stomach. Maybe her hunger made it taste good. At least the food didn't stink this time.

A white-footed mouse ventured into the room from a hole in the corner. Its nose twitched, gaze fixed on her.

"Are you hungry?" Meskhanet broke off a small piece from her flatbread and tossed it toward the mouse. It skittered back into the hole. She smiled and sat like a stone, still and quiet.

The nose appeared again, and the mouse ventured in short spurts toward the bread. When it reached the crumb, a quick scurry took it back to the edge of its hole where it munched the bread and watched Meskhanet.

She chuckled, but the mouse stayed where it was, washing its whiskers. "Bold little fellow, aren't you? I think I shall call you Soldier."

She tossed another piece, and this time the mouse hurried to pick it up and ate the bit where it landed. She could hear the crunching.

Meskhanet spent the rest of the morning teasing the mouse closer and closer. It began taking the scraps back into the hole, but it came back again and again until the bread was gone. It took the last piece from her outstretched hand.

A noise outside the window startled her—a crack, like a branch breaking. The not-so-bold-now mouse ran back into its hole. She laughed and brushed the remaining crumbs from her lap. "Should I change your name?" she asked as the rodent ventured nose and eyes out from its hiding place.

She still couldn't wipe the smile from her face. Laughter bubbled up, as it had for no reason at all the past day. *Adonai, would that I had asked You to be my God many years ago!*

She lowered herself to her pallet and lay on it, smiling at the ceiling, the window, the mouse, even the door. She examined the walls with her gaze, giggling over one pattern of cracks reminding her of a rabbit. Her eyes closed, and she slept. And dreamed.

She floated over rocky and grassy mountains, wide and narrow rivers, and verdant forests. Behold, there on a path below her! The Man she had seen at the wedding of Quinta and Cyril, the One Joanna said might be the Son of God, walked along a path below her. He looked up at her, and the sun shining on his face made it glow. He smiled at her, and she floated down to walk next to Him.

He told her many things about His Father, of His love for others and for her. He told her He and His Father would be with her always. They continued through a flowered field and sat down on a boulder next to a small waterfall in a deep canyon. As He spoke to her, he faded from view, but she knew He stayed beside her. His voice faded from spoken aloud to a whisper in her heart. Meskhanet could still feel the warmth of His hand on her shoulder, and she could hear His loving voice.

Then the wind began to blow, rain poured down, and thunder and lightning surrounded her. She should be afraid, but His voice sustained her. The lightning revealed a place to hide from the storm, a cozy cave with a warm fire burning. She ran into the cave and warmed herself at the fire.

A large, hook-beaked bird the size of a horse swooped through the storm, spied her, and dove, talons outstretched. Before it could grasp her with its sharp claws, a strong gust of wind blew the bird away. In peace, she lay down beside the fire and stared into the flames.

An ominous growl sounded from the woods in front of the cave, then a roar that echoed off the walls of the canyon. A lion charged from behind a tree, fangs dripping blood, but it slipped on a wet rock and fell into a deep pit. In her dream, she smiled and held her hands up to the Lord.

She woke with her hands in the air. "Lord, it's pleasant to know Your hand has been there through my storms. I remember when You saved me on the trail and from the hand of Appius. I will try to remember You are there when storms assail me."

Chapter 30

Marcus fought the urge to tell his father to pay what Perseus asked for Meskhanet. She was worth the twenty aurei and more. And it would be worth it to know she didn't sleep another night in who knew what type of squalor and fear.

Perseus clenched his fists and stomped a well-clad foot. "Still, if she is not your slave, she is the property of another guest, am I not correct?"

"Yes. But my guest could buy several slaves for what you're asking. Be reasonable—if you know how." The senator curled a lip at Perseus.

"Perhaps we should ask your guest." He glanced at Marcus.

"My son is not my guest. He is an heir, and my house is his."

"Why does he not speak up? He visited my house looking for a missing slave. Maybe this is the one he sought. *Is* she, Marcus?" He turned his focus on Marcus, his black eyes narrowed.

Marcus blew on his nails and brushed them against his tunic. "How would I know? I haven't seen this slave you say is in your possession. Bring her forth, and I might know."

"Describe her." Perseus slid his gaze between the senator and Marcus.

Marcus shrugged. "Black eyes, black hair, short, and youngish."

"That's the description of mine as well."

Marcus kept his grin inside. Tormenting Perseus had become fun.

His father gave him a wink when Perseus's gaze left the senator to glare at Marcus.

"You know that's not adequate. That description fits most of the young women in Rome. What's her nationality? What was she wearing?" Perseus's voice rose in pitch and volume with each question.

"When last I saw her, she wore a simple brown tunic such as slaves in Israel wear."

Perseus whirled on Decimus. "And yours?"

"A white tunic, and I don't remember what color her palla or cloak was. I do not know her nationality. Why do you want all this information? Bring her to us, and we shall see if she is one either of us seeks or if she is worthy of purchase." Decimus turned as if to leave.

"Wait." Perseus's shoulders slumped, and he scowled. "I'll bring her. Where?"

"To my home, of course." The senator turned again. "Do not delay. I grow impatient with you and wish to have this disagreeable business finished."

"I should kill her. I will before accepting a paltry thirty sesterces for her."

Marcus's stomach froze. He turned back to Perseus, and his father's hand on his wrist was all that kept him from drawing his knife and attacking the smaller man. Heat returned to his body in a rush. With his left hand he tried to brush away his father's grip, but it stayed. Sanity returned slowly. He shook his head to clear it.

"Ah, you do not wish her killed. An interesting reaction for a worthless slave, I think." Perseus smirked. "I'll bring her to your house this evening, and we shall bargain then."

The senator nodded and tipped his head toward Marcus's horse and his chariot.

Marcus followed him. Once trotting back toward Decimus's estate, Marcus spoke. "I'm sorry, Father. That was stupid of me."

"Yes." His father answered through tight lips. "That describes your actions well. I thought you had outgrown your temper, but it appears to have resurfaced. It also seems you might have feelings for this young woman. Am I correct?"

Heat rose in his cheeks. Marcus cleared his throat. "Yes, Father. I don't think my affections are known to her, and they probably are not returned, at least not yet. But I hold hopes that will change."

"I would hope *not*. She is a slave. You are a Varitor. Your affection is misplaced."

Marcus pulled his horse alongside his father's and held his father's gaze. "Yet if she would have me, I would gladly change my name and lose every trace of inheritance I might receive from your estate."

His father's silence could indicate disapproval or that he thought over this declaration.

Decimus pinched his lips with his free hand. "What makes her so appealing to you?"

Marcus could have fallen off his horse with surprise. Yet again, his father hadn't roared his disapproval. He thought about the question for a few moments. "She's pretty—you probably noticed that—but she doesn't seem to know it. She serves with hands and feet and heart, yet she's not without spirit. She was the one who waited on Loukaṣ when, as a physician, he would become ceremonially unclean and no one else could touch him. She saved their lives at great risk to her own. And she has an inner purity I've seldom seen in any woman."

Decimus nodded and dropped his gaze. "We'll speak of this more later."

They rode up to the house, and Servius strode forward to take their horses.

Joanna appeared at the door. "Any word of Meskhanet?"

"Yes. Perseus will bring her here this evening. And I know this will be difficult for you, but we must give him the impression she is just another slave." He turned to Marcus. "That includes you, my son. We will brush off your reaction today as a piece of rash temper. I want you to continue to act as though you are easily angered, but try to direct your temper to something other than his treatment of Meskhanet."

Marcus's ears heated. "Yes, sir."

The door opened, and Perseus charged in with a fierce scowl aimed at Meskhanet. "Come with me. And stop smiling that way."

Meskhanet hid her mouth behind her hand and stood. "Forgive me. I meant no disrespect, sir. I had a pleasant dream." A dream to carry her through what this evil man had planned for her, perhaps.

"Can you write?" He led at a fast walk to a wagon.

"Only in Aramaic." She trotted to keep up with him.

"Stupid woman. How will anyone read what you write?"

"My mistress can read it."

Perseus stopped and turned to her. "Is the senator also your master?"

Adonai, how do I answer? "I serve him too." There. That was not a lie. Exactly.

"Your mistress is the woman who rode in the wagon with you and the senator?"

"Yes." She couldn't help it; her mouth tilted upward again.

He slapped her. "I told you to stop smiling, slave."

She raised her hand to her cheek and lowered her eyes.

Perseus climbed into the wagon and frowned as she pulled herself up to the seat beside him. He handed her a piece of parchment, a quill, and a jar of ink. "Write what I tell you."

He slapped the horses' rumps with the reins.

"How am I to write in this bouncing wagon?"

Marcus took his father's wagon through the streets of Rome to the house Cyril had rented for them. Rebecca trotted out of the house to meet him, chattering. He slapped his forehead. Why hadn't he brought Cyril? More to the point, why hadn't he learned Aramaic yet?

He dismounted, and he stood listening to the woman's excited speech. She waved her arms, pointed into the house, and tugged at his arm. He followed her. She pointed at the girl and chattered at an alarming rate.

Dinah looked up from her pallet where she sat holding a small gray furry something on her lap. The thing rumbled as she stroked it. "Please, may I keep it?"

Marcus scratched his head. "What is it?"

"I do not know, but it is friendly." She lifted the thing and held it up to Marcus.

After a moment's hesitation, he took it. It licked his fingers with a raspy tongue and rumbled louder. He held it up for a closer view. "It looks like a young cat. I've seen one or two, but they're usually wild. Where did you get it?"

"Here. Under a bush outside. More are there, very small like this. May I keep it?"

"All right, but you have to care for it. What does it eat?"

"Meat. Milk. Gruel. Bread."

"Hmm. Imagine that. Why is Rebecca so excited?" He handed the kitten back to Dinah.

"She thinks it is a lion and it will grow big to eat us." She smiled, revealing dimples. Amazing what a bath did for the child. Hair that had been dingy and tangled now gleamed as it hung to her waist in soft brown waves. A clean tunic, even patched, made this child look like a princess.

"Tell her it will only get about this big." He held his hands not quite a cubit apart. After she had translated to Rebecca, he began gathering their things. "Tell her we have a different place to live. We're moving our things to my father's house."

"May I keep two little lions?"

"Why two?"

"One for me, one for my brother, David."

Marcus grunted. "What if we do not see your brother again? I don't think we will have enough to buy him too."

Her chin dropped, and her brown eyes filled. "You won't buy my brother? Why?"

He scooped his hand through his hair. If she cried, it would be his undoing. "It takes money, and we might not have enough."

"Maybe?" Tears dripped off a quivering chin. "Please?"

"All right. Maybe. But maybe not. If we have enough coins left after today, all right?" *Adonai, why am I such a soft touch with children and women? I'm not this way with the men. Help me, Adonai. I'm sinking!*

"Get your belongings onto the horses." He tried so hard to sound gruff, but the scamp just grinned at him. He lifted the chest that had belonged to Loukas and put it in the back of the wagon.

Rebecca even grinned. Was there no one who believed him tough?

As they made their way back through the streets to his father's luxurious home, Marcus puzzled over his father's treatment of his friends. One who used to meet with Father's endorsement was Julius, but Cyril had been a slave and beneath his gaze. Now he seemed willing to part with a healthy ransom for a slave not his own nor even one he seemed attracted to. Something strange was happening with his once-severe father.

Decimus met them on the portico. He clapped his hands, summoning Celia. "Take this woman and child to the baths. Then give them new clothing. They may have a room together next to Joanna's."

"Yes, sir." Celia bowed her head, but when she lifted her chin her gaze sought Marcus.

The longing in her eyes reminded him he had to talk to her. Not now—soon, though. Very soon.

Rebecca and Dinah followed Celia with eyes wide and mouths gaping, each of them clutching a kitten.

Marcus grinned and glanced at his father.

He pinched his lips and shrugged, and one side of his mouth tilted up. "You choose most unusual friends, Son."

Septus burst into the room. "Papa, Papa! Did you see the baby lions? May I have one? The girl says there are more where this came from. Please?" He tugged on his father's toga.

He chuckled. "Baby lions? Who told you they were baby lions?"

Septus stopped, eyes wide. "They aren't? That girl told me they were."

"What girl? The one who just came in with the old woman?"

"Yes. Did she lie to me?" Septus propped his hands on his hips and scowled toward the door Dinah had disappeared through.

Marcus covered his mouth to hide a smile.

"I think maybe she teased you. Do you remember the animal on the ship that caught rats and mice?" The senator flipped a wink at Marcus.

"Yes. The cat. You said they were like the lion's little brothers."

"That's right. These are infant cats instead of lions." Decimus ruffled his son's hair.

"May I have an infant cat?"

"I don't mind, but your brother will have to get it for you." He raised his gaze to Marcus. "Would you find a little cat for your little brother?"

"I would. Would my little brother like to come with me to search for it?" Marcus held out his hand. "You may ride with me."

"He has his own horse. Have Servius bring yours and his around. Don't be too long. I expect Perseus will be here before long. With Meskhanet, I hope."

Chapter 31

As Marcus and Septus rode back into the yard, Marcus carried two kittens. Septus had one. How could Marcus explain the presence of these small creatures to his father? But he couldn't leave them there. They would starve. He'd found the mother cat behind the bush, dead.

Cyril met him at the door, one eyebrow cocked. "Kittens?"

Marcus twisted his mouth into a grin. "Yes, I know. Not exactly what you would expect me to bring home, is it?"

"No, but you're a surprising man. You'd better let me have them though. The senator awaits you inside." Cyril held out his hands to receive the squirming bundles.

Marcus's heart thumped. "Is Meskhanet here?"

Cyril shook his head. "Come with me, Septus. We'll find these little ones some food."

Marcus fought to keep his shoulders straight as he marched into the atrium.

Perseus stood before the senator, a triumphant smirk on his lips.

Marcus's father stared at a piece of parchment, but he shrugged his shoulders. "I don't read this language."

"Try your concubine."

"And who exactly would that be?"

"The slave girl's mistress."

"Ah, you must mean Joanna. She is not anyone's concubine. She is a guest in my house, a widow, and you will not insult her." Decimus dropped his voice to a flat imperative.

Marcus recognized that tone. It had often preceded removal of some privilege after another of his rash behaviors. Or a blow that would knock him across the room. If he had wanted to warn Perseus, he would do it now. If he had wanted.

"The slave said her mistress knew how to read it." Apparently Perseus already knew that tone. His voice almost sounded whiny.

"Celia!" The senator's voice boomed off the walls. In an instant, she came running. "Ask Joanna to attend us." Celia ran up the stairs just as Joanna began descending. Joanna nodded to her and continued her graceful way to Marcus's side. If it weren't for the dark circles under her eyes, he wouldn't know the stress she endured.

"Joanna, we are in need of your help. I'm told you can read this." He handed her the note.

Joanna's eyes swam, but her voice was level. "It says if we do not pay an aureus for Meskhanet, she will die this night."

He dropped the price—take it, Father! Marcus wanted to shake him, but he gritted his teeth and maintained his silence. He shifted his glance from Perseus to his father. He hoped his thoughts didn't show on his face.

Decimus pinched his lips, scowled at Perseus, and exhaled noisily. "Done. However, you will not be paid until the girl is here."

"Very well, but you will sign a paper saying you purchased her from me. I do not want to be arrested as I leave." Perseus rocked back on his heels, smiling in triumph.

"I will hand it to you as you present her to us undamaged, or the deal is off."

"I will have her back here within the hour." He left the house.

Marcus released the breath he didn't realize he held. "Father, I will pay the coin."

Joanna laid her hand on Marcus's arm. She smiled up into his eyes. "One hour."

She turned her head toward Decimus. "There is a bit more to the note than what I read aloud. She also said not to give Perseus anything. She said she would be happy to die now."

Meskhanet couldn't move. A rope bound her hands and feet to a bench in the brothel's atrium, and a rag covered her mouth. When Aula walked into the room, her eyebrows raised. She spoke in Latin, but Meskhanet shook her head. Did the woman remember her?

She walked to Meskhanet and pulled the rag loose. "What are you doing here?" she asked, this time in Greek.

"Perseus brought me." She rubbed her face against her shoulder trying to get her hair out of her mouth.

"Why are you tied up like this?" Aula sat on the bench beside Meskhanet.

"A girl said something to him, and he bound me. I could not understand what they said, but he sounded angry."

"He is often angry." She smiled. "Shall we remove the ropes?"

"I would very much appreciate that, Aula." Meskhanet lifted her hands.

Aula started and looked more closely at her and then began untying the knots. "Ah, yes, you are the girl who is a guest of Senator Decimus. Why did Perseus bring you here?"

"He didn't say. He holds me for a hoped ransom, but I do not think he will get what he wants. He also said he will kill me if he does not get what he wants. I do not expect to live to see the sun rise."

Aula stared at her as she knelt and loosed the last knot on the ropes around Meskhanet's legs. "Aren't you frightened?"

She shook her head. "No, not anymore."

Aula stood. "Come with me." She led the way through a red bead curtain through a thick wooden door to a courtyard with several stout wooden doors. She opened the biggest door and peered left and right, then motioned Meskhanet through. They walked to yet another door, Aula again checking both ways. She led Meskhanet up a stairway to the roof.

"If you go to the next building—see, over that parapet—and down the stairway on the other side, you will be in a stable. There you will find my horse and my donkey. Take the horse and ride like the wind to your friend's home. Have one of the senator's men bring her back to me. I suspect most of them know where the House of Aula is."

Meskhanet dropped to her knees. "Mistress, I am in your debt. I know of no way I can repay you, but I will pray for you."

A frown brushed Aula's forehead and she made a flipping motion with one hand. "Just keeping one girl from Perseus's ire is reward enough." Her brown eyes liquefied. "But tell me, how is it that he does not frighten you?"

"My God, Yahweh, is with me. I think that if Perseus killed me, I would go to heaven and walk with His Son one day. While I was captive, He spoke to me with reassuring words while Perseus held me for ransom. His Son came to me in a dream and walked with me through many trials." *O God, my God, tell me what to say to reveal You to her.*

"Your God must be different from those in our land. I would like to know more about Him, but you must not stay. Perseus could be back at any time."

Meskhanet stood and grasped Aula's hands. "Yahweh, please come to this woman and show Yourself to her." She leaned forward and kissed Aula's cheek before she made her way across the roofs and down into the stable.

Aula walked with slow steps back to the entry room for her brothel. The place wasn't really hers; it belonged to Perseus, but men associated it with her. She knew how to attract men. She knew how to make them wild with desire and how to run a business. What she didn't know was how to find this God of peace this girl talked about. Was there a temple for Him here anywhere?

Somehow, she had to find out more about Him, this Yahweh. The young woman thought she would die, yet she showed no fear. Her face reflected only peace. Her eyes glowed with happiness. Happiness. What made her so happy?

Aula felt happy when each new girl came in from the streets to her other house. She shivered when she thought of how cold she used to feel on the streets. Even life in a brothel, pretending to enjoy the attentions of a smelly, rough man, seemed better than the hunger and cold of the street.

She did try to find husbands for the girls, and sometimes she succeeded. But sometimes when the girls became too old for marriage, she brought them here. At least she could monitor the clients and assure that the girls were not treated so roughly they died. On the streets, that assurance could not be found.

Still, how nice it would be to find happiness that lasted. Perhaps she would visit Meskhanet one day and ask.

Aula walked through the arch into the entryway. Perseus paced there.

"Pax, Perseus." Peace…where could *she* find peace?

He strode up to her and gripped her. "Where is she?"

She flinched. "You're hurting me. Which one is it you want?"

He pinched the flesh on her arms. "You know which one. The one I brought here this morning."

"I don't know. She must have gone." Aula tried to pull away, but he gripped her tighter.

"Who turned her loose? You?" He shoved her into the wall. "That woman is worth money to me."

Aula picked herself up off the floor. "She must have worked herself loose. You know I would never turn a girl away who might work here."

He backhanded her, and she fell again. "Be careful Perseus. You know no one will want a woman who is scarred." She pressed two fingers to a cut on her lip.

"Where is she?" Perseus's face had turned to a deep red. He lifted her to her feet and raised his hand again. *"Where is she?"*

Aula lifted her hands to cover her face. "I don't know. All I know is she's gone."

He threw her to the floor. She screamed once. He kicked her in the belly, stealing her breath. Another hard sandaled foot connected with her head, and darkness descended.

Marcus sat on one of the couches on the portico. An hour had passed. Soon it would be two. Where were they? He stood and walked to the street, looked both ways. A couple of carts, a few strollers, a woman on horseback.

Wait.

That woman….

His heart skipped a beat. She rode closer. "Meskhanet," he breathed. He turned back toward the house as Joanna ran past him.

"Meskhanet!" Joanna stopped at the end of the driveway, waving, and waited for her there.

Cyril and Decimus strode out to join them. Cyril helped her down from the horse.

"Mek-ki-net! You're home!" Septus galloped up to her and threw one arm around her legs. The other hand cluched a wide-eyed kitten no doubt wanting to run away from all this noise and activity.

She laughed and knelt in front of the boy. "Shalom, Septus. What is this?" She stroked the still struggling animal, and it calmed.

Did she see Marcus? She hadn't cast a glance in his direction.

Septus held the creature out to her. "You want one? We have extras. It's a little brother to a lion."

"Oh, he is so sweet. Look at this." She held the kitten to her face, where it proceeded to lick her cheek and purr.

Marcus never thought he would envy an animal before.

She stood, still holding the cat. "Cyril, you found us. Did Loukas come with you?"

Marcus knew his face must reflect the same expression as the suddenly dampened countenances around him. The kitten had begun sucking and kneading Meskhanet's tunic. Its purr rang loud in his ears.

She looked from one to the other of them. The color drained from her face, and Marcus felt the realization hit her like a fist to his own stomach when tears filled her eyes and slid down her cheeks. "What happened?"

Marcus sent Brutus and Servius back with the horse Meskhanet rode. Meskhanet's grieving seemed as deep as Joanna's, and both women had retired to their bedchamber to weep together. Marcus longed to hold Meskhanet when she wept, but thus far she did not even seem to recognize him. She had not so much as cast one look in his direction as she greeted everyone else.

Now his heart felt doubly heavy. What if she would not consent to his troth? Maybe it would be best if he just forgot this notion. *Huh. As though I could.*

He sat in front of the house on a couch, morose. A movement in the bushes at the end of the driveway caught his eye. Instinctively, he froze. Without turning his head, he kept his eyes trained on the furtive passage of a brown cloak.

Chapter 32

Meskhanet wiped her eyes and blew her nose on a clean rag. "Oh, Mistress, I am so sorry and so sad. Loukas was the finest man in the world."

Joanna moved her arm around Meskhanet's shoulders. "I know you loved him too, Meskhanet. Everyone did. He had no enemies."

"I hope our Adonai took him to heaven. He was one who loved Yahweh so much, one who suffered with each person who felt pain. If anyone deserved to live forever, Loukas did."

Joanna's eyes widened. "*Our* Adonai? Meskhanet, something has changed, hasn't it?"

Meskhanet nodded, and a small smile played on her lips. "He showed me He is also my God, not just the God of the Jews or the God of Joanna and Loukas."

Joanna stood and grasped her shoulders. "I prayed so much for you while you were gone. I prayed He would protect you and give you peace. We—Decimus, Marcus, Cyril, and I—feared Perseus would harm you. He is an evil man."

Meskhanet's smile broadened. "He wanted to, especially when I couldn't stop laughing. Adonai had just come to me moments before, and everything Perseus did seemed funny. I think he decided I had lost my mind because I laughed so hard."

"You weren't frightened?"

"No. Not at any time. Perhaps I *was* demented. I should have been frightened. I made friends with a mouse. I tried to make friends with the man who brought me food, but he seemed terrified of me. I think Perseus must have warned him I was demented." Meskhanet chuckled. She shook her head. "The poor man was horribly disfigured by a scar on his face and so thin you could blow him over. I don't think I've ever seen a man so afraid."

"Ah, we saw the same man here. He seemed frightened of us too, but more frightened of his master. He wouldn't leave until he delivered Perseus's message to the senator." Joanna pulled her stola over her shoulder. "Shall we return to the men, daughter?"

Marcus would wager the man making his way through the bushes was Perseus. He couldn't believe the weasel would give up so easily. Yet…would Perseus wear brown? The man loved the red and deep blue togas. He'd probably wear tunics with purple stripes and purple togas if he didn't fear being assassinated by senators and equestrians in Rome.

The man moved toward the back of the villa, the top of his head visible over the top of the bushes. Marcus stood, stretched, and yawned, turning casually toward the man as though admiring the flowering shrubberies.

The brown cloak stopped.

Marcus strolled to that side of the portico, scratching his back with both hands. The man's head disappeared. The sneak wanted to get to the courtyard. Fine. He would meet him there. Marcus turned and walked into the house. Decimus and Cyril stood talking in the Atrium.

"We have a visitor, Father. I think we might want to greet him. He was sneaking toward the back of the house."

Decimus scowled. "Perseus?"

Marcus hesitated. "I don't know. Perseus would be the most logical suspect, but can you imagine him wearing brown? This one almost escaped my view because he blended with the bushes."

The senator pinched his lips. "No."

Marcus frowned. "Are you sure that gladiator is still in prison?"

Decimus shook his head. "No." He strode to the wall where several short swords hung and picked up two, holding one out. "Cyril?"

"Yes, I'll take one too. I may not be an expert, but I know where the sharp parts are."

Marcus chuckled. Leave it to Cyril to make a joke even now.

Meskhanet and Joanna descended the staircase.

Decimus met them at the bottom. "Ladies, I want you to stay inside. Where is Varrus?"

Joanna's eyes widened. "I sent him to his quarters to sleep. He stayed awake all night to guard us."

His brow furrowed. "Cyril, go wake him, please. Where is Septus?"

"I think he took a kitten out to play in the peristylium or the stable." Meskhanet's eyes widened. "Is he in danger?" She started for the open garden area, but Marcus grasped her arm.

"No. You stay here with Joanna, please." He turned to his father. "I'll get him." He trotted through the hallway toward the courtyard, Decimus behind him.

He found Septus dangling a strip of cloth in front of a bounding gray kitten by the peristylium fountain. Marcus knelt beside him. "Septus, I want you to take the little lion in to show Meskhanet what it has learned to do."

Septus's eyes lit. "She will like that." He picked up the kitten and ran into the house.

Portia stood at the outer edge of the peristylium with her back toward them.

"Portia, come here, please." The senator voice made it a command.

Portia turned toward them. Her head lifted, and her eyes narrowed. "I am neither your servant nor your slave." Nevertheless, she glided toward them. "What do you wish?"

Decimus lowered his voice. "Quickly, go into the house. Stay with Joanna and Meskhanet. Someone has been seen sneaking around the house in this direction. You could be in danger."

Portia's lip curled. "How nice that you are so concerned for me, but I will not associate with those women. You may have invited the plebeians into your home, but that doesn't mean they are suddenly patricians."

Marcus could see the muscles in his father's jaws working. *Uh-oh.* He backed away a step, ready for the roar.

Decimus cleared his throat and paused. "Think what you will, daughter-in-law. I personally will be happy to see your husband's return. It might mean you will no longer...*grace* our home. I suggest you retire to your quarters."

He twitched his head at Marcus, and they continued to the end of the stone walkway, swords ready. Methodically, they had checked each place that could hide a grown man. They proceeded through the courtyard to the stables. Still nothing.

Marcus breathed a sigh of relief. "It must have been a thief discouraged by the number of men here."

Decimus shrugged. "I don't believe we've seen the last of Perseus. He might have sent someone to kidnap Meskhanet again. It's easy to check on Appius, but he is probably still in prison. Even if he is not, he will have lost his freedom to roam. Nevertheless, I'll send Servius to confirm it."

They walked together back into the atrium.

Decimus raised his hand to rub his mouth. "Joanna, I think we must waste no more time. You must emancipate and adopt Meskhanet today."

"I agree. What do we do?" Joanna stood.

"If she were older, you could just say that you free her in front of us, but she's not the required thirty years old by quite a bit. We'll have to go before a court. This is a day when they hold such petitions. We should go now. With luck, we can complete both manumission and adoption at the same time."

Servius strode into the house with Brutus behind. Servius bowed his head. Brutus saluted.

Meskhanet's eyes widened and she turned away from the newcomers.

Marcus puzzled over her reaction. Did she try to hide from Servius? Or Brutus? Why?

"Senator, Decanus. We took the horse back. I wanted to tell you what we learned." Servius glanced back at Brutus. "After we delivered the horse, Brutus wanted to go inside, so we did." He flushed and exchanged another look with Brutus. "A group of women stood in the entryway in a circle. Another woman lay on the floor bloody and bruised. If she hadn't worn a stola, we wouldn't have known she was even female."

Meskhanet gasped and turned back toward Servius. "No!"

"Yes, mistress. The woman had been beaten. One of the others said she saw Perseus riding away. We helped them take her to her bed. I don't know if she will live or not."

"He killed her." Meskhanet moaned and her eyes closed. "She helped me escape, and he killed her."

She swayed. Marcus strode to her, ready to catch her if she fainted.

Decimus laid a hand on her shoulder. "I'll send my physician after her. But before anything more can happen to you, let's ensure you are freed and adopted."

Brutus stared at Meskhanet, a frown drawing puzzled brows together.

Marcus's gaze slid back and forth between them.

Meskhanet sat on a bench beside Aula's bed and watched her uneven breathings. The senator had brought her to his own home to be attended by his physician. Could Decimus a man who might be trusted, like Loukas?

And this poor woman. Perseus hurt Aula because the woman helped her. "Adonai—what happens next? I know You have walked with me through the storms. It would be nice to walk with You sometimes with fair weather, too. The woman who helped me, Aula—I don't know if You know her—I know she is a prostitute, but she has kind places in her heart. I think she would like to know You, but she is so badly hurt. I don't know how to help her know You. Do You also care for her?"

Talk to her.

"But Adonai—she is not awake."

Talk to her. I want her to know Me too.

Meskhanet gazed at the unconscious woman. "Aula, I know you are asleep, but the God of the Jews, Yahweh, told me to talk to you. I know you're not a Jew, but neither am I. I'm Egyptian. Yet He has become my God. He saved me from harm several times, and He cares about me. He cares about you too."

What could she say that would convince Aula? Meskhanet bowed her head for a moment, listening. "Aula, Yahweh will walk with you through this storm if you will trust Him. He wants you to follow Him. He will show you the way."

Aula's features softened, as though tension left her. She breathed a quiet sigh, and her breathing became regular and relaxed.

Meskhanet smiled. Perhaps this kind woman would recover. Better, maybe this kind woman would discover a kind God.

Meskhanet stood and walked through the doorway into the peristylium. The sunshine through the leaves on the trees warmed her arms and face. She hadn't realized she had been chilly. She rubbed her arms and walked to the edge of the courtyard where no shade stretched to hide the sun.

A low noise like someone clearing their throats sounded behind her, and she turned. The Roman soldier who had been with the others earlier stood across the courtyard. He must have just come out of the house. "Yes?"

The soldier cleared his throat again. "Hello, Meskhanet. Do you remember me?"

"Remember you? You have been around here the past two days."

"I mean from Jericho. I was a friend of Loukas. Also of Cyril and Julius and Joanna. And I'm the senator's son. My name is Marcus." He dropped his gaze to the rock path and scuffed his feet.

Meskhanet felt the blood drain from her face. "Oh." Marcus. This must be the one Joanna said wanted to marry her. What should she say? She didn't want to ever marry anyone. No man had ever seemed trustworthy except Loukas. "Yes, I think I remember you."

"Father sent me to tell you dinner is ready."

He sent his son and not Celia? Odd. There she was, behind him. Looking at him with tears in her eyes.

"May I escort you to the triclinium?" He stepped forward a hesitant step.

She shook her head. "No need. It's only a few steps."

Red suffused his face, and he bowed. "As you wish." He stepped off the path, and she passed him with her gaze lowered and muscles ready to jump should he make the slightest move. Celia had disappeared. Maybe into the culina to begin bringing food to the table.

She could hear his footsteps behind her, and she fought the urge to run. Her heart thundered with fear. Surely a friend of Joanna wouldn't accost her here. She forced her steps to a measured cadence and held her breath until they passed through the door into the dining area where the others sat around the large table.

Septus jumped to his feet and ran toward her. Meskhanet extended her arms to receive him, but he ran past her.

"Marcus! Look, Mes-ki-net, this is my big brother." He held out his hand to her as Marcus picked him up and swung Septus up on his shoulders as he walked toward the table.

Meskhanet dropped her arms and managed a weak smile at the boy. "That's nice, Septus." Did she have a choice? She walked beside them, but at an arm's distance away.

"You can hug him, too, Mes-ki-net."

"No, I don't think so. It would not be proper, little one." Meskhanet's face heated.

"But why? You hug me all the time. I hug you and I hug him." Septus threw his arms around Marcus's head and covered his eyes..

"Wait, little brother, how am I supposed to see?" Marcus held his hands in front of himself as though blind.

Septus giggled. "Mes-ki-net can lead you. Hold his hand, Mes-ki-net."

Marcus swung his arm in her direction. "Help me, Mes-ki-net."

Her face couldn't feel any hotter. *Adonai, what should I do?* She hesitated. Reluctantly, she lifted her hand to his wrist and led them the rest of the way to the table.

She sat beside Joanna, and Marcus moved Septus from his shoulders to Meskhanet's side. He walked to his father's side and dropped to the bench beside him. Marcus smiled at Septus and then at her.

Joanna placed her arm around Meskhanet's stiff shoulders and squeezed. In a voice so soft it didn't carry over the voices of the rest, she said, "Cyril says he and Marcus traveled to Rome to rescue us. Julius found out we had been abducted and where we were bound, and he requested their help."

Meskhanet nodded.

"Marcus has become a fugitive because of it. He was accused of joining Barabbas's band of thieves when he disguised himself and entered their sheep camp with the intent of killing or capturing the brigand. A century from Jerusalem raided the camp, taking Marcus captive with the rest. He escaped from the century and boarded a ship for Rome with Cyril and Brutus and…and Loukas." Joanna's hand moved in a circular motion on Meskhanet's back.

Meskhanet's brows rose and her glance involuntarily moved to Marcus and caught him watching her. She frowned and dropped her gaze to her hands. She wasn't sure she wanted to hear the answer to this question, but she had to know. "Why did they concern themselves?"

Joanna's eye's misted. "Julius couldn't come, and Loukas intended to come after us by himself. Marcus and Cyril loved Loukas enough to risk a tribunal. And he loves us, too, you and me. You as a woman, me as a friend. He is a worthy man, Meskhanet."

"I do not love him, Mother. I do not love any man. I don't want to marry," Meskhanet whispered. She knew she sounded like a pouty child, and she sighed. "There is another who loves him." She tilted her chin only a bit, but Joanna raised her gaze to where Celia stood behind Marcus.

Chapter 33

Marcus woke with an aching head. Meskhanet's last look at him had frozen his heart, and he drank more wine than he had in a long time. It didn't warm him any, and His father had sent him to bed—which also hadn't happened since his impetuous youth.

Oh, I'd wager that made a wonderful impression on Meskhanet. And You, Adonai. At least I think You will eventually forgive me for this stupidity. I'm not sure Meskhanet will.

He dunked his head into the basin of water on the table in his room. The cool liquid cleared his head and eased the ache. He rubbed his fingers through his hair vigorously.

He walked out of his room, through the peristylium, and out to the courtyard. Fresh air. And into the stable—ugh, not so fresh. A kitten ran across his path, and he almost tripped over it. Another. This one with Dinah in pursuit. He caught her arms. "Whoa, Dinah. Where are you going?"

She chattered excitedly, pointing at the kittens. She pulled her arms free and ran off.

I still need to learn Aramaic. He grinned. She knew he didn't understand. Had it been important she would have slowed her speech and spoken Latin. He shook his head as he strode to his horse. He led the bay gelding out of the stall and picked up the currying equipment.

Rebecca ran into the stable. She tugged on the sleeve of his garment and spoke rapidly, pointing with the long spoon she held in one hand and gesturing wildly with the other.

"Dinah!" He shouted. Judging from Rebecca's expression and excitement, this could be important.

The girl peeked out from a stall.

"I need an interpreter, please."

Dinah walked out cuddling a kitten. "Yes, Master?"

"Not master—I'm Marcus, remember? Tell me why Rebecca is so excited."

Rebecca repeated her babbling.

Dinah turned to Marcus. "She says there is a woman here she knows. One named Martha."

Marcus shook his head. "I don't know of anyone named Martha."

Rebecca grabbed his arm and tugged him toward the door.

He nodded and followed.

Meskhanet stood at the entry to the peristylium, staring in their direction, Varrus like a huge shadow behind her. Rebecca dropped her spoon and ran to Meskhanet. They embraced with enthusiasm and tears, both of them chattering in that unintelligible Aramaic.

Martha?

"Dinah, can you follow what they're saying?"

"Only a little. Not when they both talk at once. But Rebecca calls her Martha and is happy she's alive. The one called Martha asks what Rebecca's doing in Rome."

Marcus strolled in their direction, and Meskhanet stopped talking and started blushing.

"Martha?" he asked, one eyebrow rising.

Meskhanet's chin lifted. "I chose that name so Barabbas would not dishonor me. When he thought me a virgin Jewess, he exercised greater restraint."

Both his eyebrow jumped. "When were you in Barabbas's camp?"

"A few weeks before he was captured by the Romans."

"Ah. Did you perchance witness two captives being taken into a tent? And were you responsible for their release?" Marcus grinned.

Meskhanet tilted her head. "I did see the captives, but I thought they escaped. No, I didn't release them. The whole camp watched me much too close for me to be able to release anyone. How did you know about them?"

"I was one. Brutus was the other. Who else would have set us free?"

Meskhanet stared into the heaven, a light scowl crossing her brow. Her gaze dropped to Rebecca, and she spoke a few sentences in Aramaic.

Rebecca reddened and nodded. She murmured a few sentences back.

Meskhanet hugged her and looked at Marcus over the older woman's shoulder. "Rebecca did it. She doesn't like her son's love of torturing. Tell me, how did Barabbas's mother come to be in Rome, here at your father's house?"

"We brought her with us." It was his turn to flush. "For protection."

Meskhanet patted Rebecca's back, released her, and laughed. "Protection?"

What a delightful sound—I don't believe I've ever heard her laugh before. He smiled. "Her son escaped from the Roman soldiers. We brought his mother with us because we didn't think he would attack if she were along. At that time, I was still weakened by an injury and fever. Brutus favored a leg that had been broken earlier at Barabbas's hands. Cyril isn't a soldier. The three of us together didn't add up to one whole man, and Barabbas is a strong and able fighter. We had to get to Caesarea quickly to catch a ship before winter storms closed the sea."

Meskhanet cocked her head. "But why did you bring her to Rome?"

Marcus shifted from one foot to the other and dropped his gaze to the ground. Actually to one set of golden brown toes peeking out from under a white tunic. *What was the question? Oh, yes.* "To Rome. Yes. Well, Cyril had become fond of her. So had I. Then too, I feared if we left her in Caesarea, Barabbas might have gone after the weaker ones in Julius's household."

Rebecca looked up at Marcus. "Barabbas?"

Marcus moved his gaze to Rebecca, then back to Meskhanet. "Would you please translate what we said to her? She doesn't understand Greek." Heat rose to his face again. "And I don't understand Aramaic."

Her eyes widened. "All the time you spent in Jericho, and you didn't learn Aramaic?"

He shook his head.

She turned to Rebecca and translated.

Rebecca smiled and patted his cheek, chattering. She turned back to Meskhanet and pointed at Marcus, talking nonstop.

Meskhanet laughed again.

"What did she say?" He wiped the sweat from his neck.

She turned back to him, her large, dark brown—black?—eyes sparkling. "She says I must teach you to speak the language the One God speaks."

He knew there must be a good and logical reason he brought Rebecca along. He smiled "And will you?"

"I owe Rebecca much. This I will do. For her only." A small frown brushed across her perfectly arched brows and disappeared. At the same time one corner of her mouth twitched.

"Of course." He bowed his head. His heart began to thaw. Or melt. "Shall we break our fast?" He waved Dinah and Rebecca forward and proceeded by Meskhanet's side, his pulse beating like the hoof beats of a hundred galloping horses.

He heard a gasp. Portia stood at the entrance to the house, her eyes narrow with condemnation. "You bring the dirt from the stables into the house?"

Marcus grimaced. Meskhanet and Rebecca might not understand Latin, but they surely understood sarcasm.

Dinah stopped and backed up, her eyes on the floor. Rebecca's eyes snapped. Meskhanet's narrowed and her chin lifted.

Marcus took Dinah's hand. "Ignore her." He met Portia's gaze. "There are many kinds of dirt, sister-in-law. Move aside under your own power, or I will move you."

Portia stepped backward. She grasped her blue stola and pulled it and her tunic aside as though to avoid contamination, staring down her nose.

Rebecca shook her head, grasped Dinah's other hand, and pulled back.

His father stood at the entrance to the triclinium. "Celia, provide this woman and the child with proper attire and a basin of water. When they have washed and changed clothing, bring them in to break their fast. They are also our guests. When you have finished, take Portia's food to her room. She will dine there."

Marcus's eyes widened. What had happened with his father? Something had changed him, but what?

Joanna yawned and pushed her toes and her arms to their most extended reaches. The Sabbath. They could join the other Jews in Rome at the synagogue. This would be a day of praise. Meskhanet was back, unharmed, and now officially her daughter. A now-familiar ache squeezed her heart. This was also a day for knowing her beloved Loukas would be gone from her for the rest of her life.

Still—even with the pain—a day to give thanks. She walked barefoot to the balcony and pulled the curtains. From the corner of her eye she caught a shadow darting into the stable. She froze and stared into the darkness of the stable doorway.

Meskhanet stepped to her side. "Good morning, Mother."

"Shh. Look—in the stable doorway. Do you see something there?" Joanna's whisper was followed by the hiss of an arrow flying past them, missing Meskhanet's head by a finger's width.

Meskhanet screamed.

Joanna jerked her away from the opening. "Varrus!"

Her shout had been unneeded. The slave had bounded into the room. The arrow still quivered from where it stuck in the wall. Varrus snatched the arrow and vaulted over the parapet to the courtyard below, landing with a grace astounding given his bulk.

Another scream came from the stable. A child's scream, high and frightened. A man backed from the stable holding Dinah. Varrus plodded after them, but made no move to capture him. He maintained a distance of about four cubits.

Adonai, please, don't let him hurt Dinah!

Meskhanet dashed out the door and down the stairs. Joanna followed at a run. "Wait! Don't go out there!"

Marcus poked a tousled head from his bedroom then chased them through the hallway. "Stop!" He caught Meskhanet and stepped in front of her, blocking her path.

Decimus threw out his arms and caught Joanna. "Where are you going?"

"Someone shot an arrow at us, and now he has Dinah. Let me go!" Joanna pulled against Decimus's grip.

"Stay here. Marcus—the swords!"

Unnecessary command. He already had them and tossed one to his father as they ran for the courtyard.

Varrus had the man holding Dinah cornered. The attacker turned his head toward Meskhanet.

"Barabbas!"

Barabbas threw the child aside and drew a knife. He threw it at Meskhanet, but Rebecca threw herself in front of the young woman.

The knife buried itself in Rebecca's shoulder. The woman dropped to the ground, howling in pain.

Varrus shook Barabbas in an angry grip a cubit above the ground, shouting dire unintelligible threats in his face.

Joanna moved to Rebecca. She pulled the knife from the woman's arm and wrapped her hand around the wound. "Someone bring some clean rags and wine, quick!"

Joanna glanced up and watched Decimus run to Dinah who sprawled in a still heap next to the wall where Barabbas threw her. Varrus tucked the vainly struggling brigand under his arm and hurried to their side. "Ungh?" He pointed at Dinah, now folded limp against the senator's shoulder as he carried her to Joanna. "Ungh?"

A swelling on the back of Dinah's head bled, but Joanna reckoned Rebecca's knife wound to be more important. "Decimus, we need some wine."

"I think that has been taken care of, my dear."

Cyril had appeared carrying cloths, a basin, and wine. He set the basin beside Joanna, holding out the wine to her.

The red from the wine blended with the red blood, and Joanna quickly wound a long cloth around the cut. She held Rebecca's wounded arm up and moved her other hand to her arm. "Hold it up, Rebecca, and it will stop bleeding faster."

Barabbas had stopped struggling, staring at her. "Mother? I'm sorry, Ima. Forgive me. I meant to kill Martha. She betrayed us. It's her fault." He raised his eyes to Portia, who had just arrived on the scene.

"You, woman, tell them I came after the traitor," he said, switching from Aramaic to Greek.

Portia's eyes widened as Decimus turned toward her with eyes narrowed and a face so red Joanna feared he could suffer apoplexy.

"You know this man, Portia?" His voice dropped to a deadly quiet growl.

"No!"

"Yes, she does. She gave me a place to hide while I awaited the chance to get Martha."

Decimus lifted his free hand and slapped Portia.

Portia stepped back, raising one hand to her cheek, eyes wide. "You struck me."

"If you were not a woman and my son's wife, I would kill you. Get out of my sight. To your room, preferably for the rest of the day. I fear what I might do if you do not."

Joanna stood and took the awakening Dinah from Decimus's arm. She cooed to the child and knelt again by the basin, glaring at Portia's rapidly retreating form.

The senator turned to Barabbas, still held by Varrus, and pulled his sword. "This man deserves to die."

"He does, Father, but not by our hands. I have to take him back to Jerusalem." Marcus laid his hand on his father's arm.

Meskhanet dropped to the ground next to Joanna, stroking Dinah's cheek. Joanna glanced at her. *Good—Dinah doesn't look quite so dazed.*

Decimus turned to Marcus. "To Jerusalem? No, I forbid it. You could be arrested."

"Yes, I could. But if I bring in Barabbas, they might just demote me back to a soldier. I know I am guilty of at least of desertion and escaping. But I don't want this charge to follow me for the rest of my life. And I don't want Julius or Cyril to suffer for aiding in my escape."

Joanna glanced toward the stable. "Oh, no."

Brutus staggered into view. Blood covered the front of his tunic. His knees folded, and he collapsed.

Joanna kissed Dinah's forehead. "Stay here with Meskhanet." She picked up the basin and cloths. "Cyril—more wine and rags!"

Decimus followed her to the soldier's side and then ran into the stable. "Servius, where are you?"

Oh, no, Adonai, not another one. Joanna pulled back Brutus's tunic to expose an arrowhead protruding from his right shoulder.

Cyril ran to her with wine and pieces of fabric.

"Can you help me? Do you have a knife?" At Cyril's nod, she indicated the shaft in Brutus's back. "Cut the arrow close to the skin. Then I might need you to help pull it from this side."

Marcus ran up to them.

"Marcus, Son, I need your help." Decimus's voice sounded strained.

Adonai—how could one man do so much damage? Joanna shook her head and returned to her effort with the arrowhead. "Pour some wine on the cloth and press it against the wound in back. We need to stop the bleeding."

Marcus and Decimus carried the hefty Servius and laid him beside Brutus, grunting with the effort. Meskhanet stepped up to them. "Let me help. I used to give Loukas aid in treating his patients too."

"Here...help me pull this arrow first." Joanna lifted an arm and used her wrist to push her tangled hair back from her face.

Meskhanet wrapped two strips of cloths around the base of the arrowhead, giving one set of ends to Joanna and kept one for herself.

"One, two, three, *pull!*" The arrow came free with a sucking sound, and fresh blood flowed.

Brutus screamed through gritted teeth.

Joanna wrapped more cloths around his shoulder and chest and tied them above the wound. She wiped the blood on her hands on a rag. "Now, let's see how we can help Servius."

"Is he hurt badly?" Decimus pushed the hair back from his servant's gray face.

No blood that she could see. Joanna put her head against his chest. His breathing seemed normal, and she could hear his heartbeat. She pulled his eyelids up. His pupils shrank against the bright light. She ran her hands through his thick hair and found the lump she sought. "No, I think he'll be all right. He's been knocked out, but the skull doesn't feel broken."

As though to confirm her diagnosis, Servius groaned and lifted a hand to the lump.

She let her breath go and nodded. "Shall we take our patients inside?"

She heard the sound of crying and looked up to see Septus carrying a kitten. "Can you fix my infant cat, Joanna? Or Mes-ki-net? Please, can one of you fix him too?"

Meskhanet lifted the limp kitten from Septus's hands. "He's warm, and his heart is beating." She turned it over. "Barabbas must have stepped on it. Or kicked it."

Joanna peered in its ears. "No blood."

"What's this?" Meskhanet pushed the fur back from a string around the cat's neck.

Joanna lifted a knife and cut the string. The kitten sucked in air and coughed. She cocked an eyebrow at Septus. "Do you know why he had this string around his neck?"

Septus scuffed his bare toes in the dirt. "I wanted to lead him. You know, like a horse."

Chapter 34

Marcus and his father carried Brutus into the same room as Aula. Aula, still unconscious, and Brutus, also unconscious and disabled, couldn't get into much trouble in their present conditions. Having them in the same room would make caring for them easier.

Meskhanet followed them in. Despite Brutus's unconscious state, Marcus noted she still eyed Brutus askance and kept her distance. She knelt by Aula and brushed the woman's hair back from her face with a tender touch.

Marcus cleared his throat. "May I ask what your connection is with this, uh, woman?" He'd almost said prostitute. Not the way to get on her good side.

Meskhanet glanced up at him. "Perseus took me to Aula's house, tied me up, and left me. She found me, untied me, and told me to take her horse. I did. He must have found out she released me. But that doesn't sound like reason enough to kill her."

Marcus heaved a sigh. "My father and Perseus have been enemies for a long time. Father offered a ransom for you, and Aula setting you free prevented Perseus's receipt of that coin from him. But he probably saw this as his perfect chance to humiliate Father. My wager is that Perseus would have spread the word that either he had bedded you or used you in his brothels. Or both. It wasn't that Aula let you go, it was that she stopped him from revenging himself on my father."

Meskhanet dropped her gaze back to Aula. "She has two sides, you know. Yes, she's a harlot, but she also mothers girls she rescues from the street. She has a great heart."

Marcus thought back to the day he met Aula. "I met her only once. You know her better." Meskhanet's description of the woman certainly didn't fit with what he remembered. But it probably didn't matter. Aula was dying. He'd heard the death rattle before. Should he tell Meskhanet? No, she would just be distressed that much longer.

"She knows about our Adonai."

"What?" Marcus dropped his gaze to hers with a start. "You are one of us?"

She smiled. "Yes. And I told Aula about Him."

"Meskhanet, you are a wonder." He helped her to her feet, his gaze fastened to hers.

Celia appeared at the door. "Breakfast is ready, Marcus. And Mistress."

Marcus started. "Thank you, Celia."

She probably hadn't heard, because she had whirled and run when she saw them together. He would have to talk to her. Later.

"May I escort you to breakfast?" He held out his hand.

Meskhanet hesitated, and then she placed her hand lightly on his arm.

What was this? When Marcus lifted her to her feet, Meskhanet had felt a curious thumping in her chest. For a moment, she had been unable to breathe. An illness, perhaps? Her face had flushed, too. Whatever it was, it had passed. She shrugged and walked with Marcus into the triclinium. He bowed slightly when he left her at Joanna's side. He joined his father on the opposite side of the table.

Meskhanet dropped to the bench beside Joanna. "Mother, do you remember when I told you about the villa full of young women? I worry what will happen to them. Aula fed and clothed them, but she cannot do that now. I do not wish to operate a brothel, and I do not know how to help them. Have you any thoughts?"

Joanna stared out the window, a thinking scowl on her forehead. "No. I don't know anything we can do. We don't have any coins. We are dependent on others too. We have no home to invite them into. I wish we did. They might be servants, but at least they would have a safe home."

A knot began to form in Meskhanet's stomach. "What will happen to them?"

"For now, they have a home, clothing, and food. Perhaps Aula will feel better soon." Joanna sounded doubtful of her own words.

Marcus cleared his throat. "I don't know if it would help, but we have some coins left. We will need some to return to Caesarea, but other than that…"

"My brother! Remember my brother, Marcus." The usually quiet Dinah piped through Marcus's offer.

"Oh, yes, and we'll need to keep enough to buy her brother from the innkeeper, too." He reached a hand over and ruffled her hair.

Dinah yelped and lifted a hand to her scalp.

Marcus put an arm around her thin shoulders and hugged her. "I'm sorry. I forgot about your bump."

"You have a brother, Dinah?" Meskhanet lifted her last piece of flatbread to her mouth.

"Yes. We were both slaves for an innkeeper on the south side of Rome. Rebecca made Marcus buy me, but my brother is still there. The innkeeper is mean."

The senator started chuckling. He burst into loud laughter, holding his sides.

His laughter was infectious, and even though Meskhanet could not imagine what he laughed about, she began laughing, too. Everyone but Marcus laughed.

His eyebrows lifted. "What?"

His father wiped the tears from his face. "Last time I saw you, my son, you would spend your precious coin only on yourself. Lavishly spend on yourself, but not a quadrans for anyone else. Now you have purchased one little girl, offered to give me the funds to buy Meskhanet at twenty aurei, brought home forty kittens for the children, and now you want to purchase another child and give the rest to an orphans' home."

Marcus grinned, then he laughed with him. "I guess I have changed a little. But Father, talking of changes, what happened to your famous temper?"

The room went silent. Meskhanet's eyes fastened on the senator's face. His smile had disappeared along with most of the color in his cheeks.

He shook his head. "I…I can't tell you. It's a story too awful to say." He ran his hands through thick hair that curled much like Marcus's and looked around. "No, perhaps I should. Dinah and Septus, please go out to play with the kittens."

He waited until their footsteps could no longer be heard, cleared his throat, and dropped his voice to a level that required them to lean in to hear him. "Septus was only two years old. I thank the gods he does not remember. He'd been difficult that day, I suspect because he had teeth coming in. Septus threw some food at me. I shouted at him to stop. He screamed with every ounce of voice he could muster, 'No!' His favorite word. He threw his plate at me, and it shattered on the table. Pieces of the pottery struck me, but I was not hurt." The senator took a deep, shaky breath, and his face paled even further to a pasty gray. "I had a knife in my hand to cut pieces of meat for him."

Marcus reached a hand out to place it on his father's shaking shoulders. "You must have missed, Papa. He's fine. And he's a good boy. You've done well raising him."

Joanna stood and walked around the table to where Decimus sat. "You do not need to flog yourself. It's in the past, and we can't change what has been done. What you learned from it is far more important. Now your love for him shines through and reflects in his eyes." She stroked his back.

"You don't understand." His father's voice sounded ragged. "I didn't miss. The knife missed his heart and lungs, but not by far. The glancing blow bounced off his ribs. I thought I had killed him. There was so much blood"

Marcus pulled his hand away and sucked in his breath, stunned.

His father focused on his trembling hands. "I picked up Septus and carried him to my room. I washed his wound in wine and wrapped it in strips of white cloth from a tunic. It soaked up the blood fast, so I wound more around it. When he slept, I ran to clean up the blood in the triclinium.

He took a deep breath and let it out with a shaky groan. "I learned. I will never lose my temper like that again. All I have to do is remember." He lifted a watery gaze to Marcus and the others. "This is the first time I talked about this to anyone. You are the only ones who know. I treated him myself. It's been my unbearable secret until now."

Joanna, who had snatched her hand from his shoulder when he said he had struck the child, returned her hand to his shoulder for a brief pat. "You sinned, Decimus, but you repented and grew from your mistake. Septus has forgiven you. How can we do otherwise?"

"It took me a year to earn his trust again. A year. The look of fear in his eyes whenever I approached him or if I picked up a knife…My own son was terrified of me. I can't get rid of this ugly wrong. It haunts my sleep." The senator held his hands splayed on the table and stared at them again.

Meskhanet leaned across the table and covered his hands with hers. "There is One who can take away your sin."

Marcus started. Who could forgive something like this? He leaned away from his father, remembering the sometimes harsh punishments his father inflicted.

Joanna nodded. "There is One, the Most High God, Yahweh. He can rid you of this sin."

"How?" Decimus asked. "I have been to the other gods' temples, and still I have night terrors."

"Come with us to Sabbath services at the synagogue tomorrow. Or come back with us to Jerusalem. The priests can offer sacrifices to Yahweh to atone for sins. And you could join with us as we learn more about Him. Joanna, Cyril, Marcus, and I are all proselytes." She drew her hands back.

The senator's back straightened and his eyes widened. He turned to Marcus. "You?"

Marcus could feel his cheeks heating. "Yes. For close to two years now."

"Why? Why would you turn from the gods you always knew?" His father's voice rose.

"As you said, the Roman gods could do nothing. I saw One called Jesus being baptized in the Jordan River and heard a thundering voice from the heavens saying Jesus was His Son. And I witnessed Yahweh's power when he healed Julius in front of our eyes." Marcus lifted his chin. He would not back down, not even if Decimus disowned him.

"Julius. Legate Gaius's son?"

"Yes. Gaius was there, too."

Decimus raised his hand to purse his lips. "Well. So *that's* what happed to him. You couldn't help but notice the change in Gaius. Hmm. Tomorrow's Sabbath service—what time?" The senator shook his head. "If that man can change, anyone can. What do I have to lose?" Decimus clapped Marcus on the back.

Joanna's eyes lit. "At the third hour, Senator."

Marcus trudged up the stairs to where he knew Celia cleaned that morning. He found her in his chambers slumped in a chair by the arched door to the balcony. He walked toward her and spoke in a gentle voice. "Celia."

She jumped to her feet with a soft yelp. She turned, and joy lit her eyes. "Marcus!" She ran to him and threw her arms around his neck, raising her lips to his. "I knew you would come to me," she whispered.

A sharp gasp came from behind him. Marcus pushed Celia back and turned. *Meskhanet.* He groaned. "This is not what it appears to be."

"It is not my concern, sir. The senator sent me to tell you that Perseus approaches." Meskhanet lowered her eyes and walked toward her room.

Marcus groaned again and hit his head with the heel of his hand. He turned around to Celia.

Celia stepped back. "You do not care for me anymore. You love *her.*"

"I cannot deny it. I'm sorry. I hoped to let you know with greater gentleness than this." He grimaced. "I have to go. Perseus...."

She backed another step, tears rolling down her cheeks. "Go. There are other men. You are not the only one in the world. Servius would be happy to have me."

"Servius is a good man." Marcus turned and ran from the room.

He trotted down the broad staircase, meeting his father at the bottom. They stood, swords ready, at the door.

Perseus walked in without an invitation, a tall young woman at his side. "Here she is."

Marcus and his father looked at each other.

"Who do you think you are trying to fool?" Decimus grated his response through clenched teeth.

Perseus widened his eyes. "This is not the one you sought?"

"Don't act the innocent with me, Perseus. You know she is not. We know, too, that you beat a woman so badly she might die because she released Meskhanet."

Meskhanet's voiced sounded from behind them. "You are evil, Perseus. May you crawl back into the rotten scum that nourished you, you stinking spawn of the gutter. May the worms of your corruption destroy you."

Perseus blanched and stepped back. His eyes rolled back, and he grasped the door. "No. No. No!" He slumped to the floor, clutching his belly.

Marcus grasped Meskhanet's arm and taking the elbow of the girl Perseus had brought with them, pulled them back. "Get behind me, quickly."

Perseus spewed forth the contents of his stomach, writhing.

Decimus's fierce scowl had become wide-eyed amazement. "What happened?"

"He believed Meskhanet. Should we send for a physician or haul him out onto the street?" Marcus couldn't find any sympathy in his heart for the man.

"I won't waste a single quadrans on him."

Perseus coughed violently, clutched his throat, and then lay still.

Servius strode up next to them and wrinkled his nose at the man lying in his own vomit. "Is he dead? What happened to him?"

"I don't know, Servius. I really don't know." Decimus shook his head. "He still breathes. I suspect he'll recover, unfortunately. Take him out to the street and prop him on a wall, a building, or a tree. Or drop him in a gutter. I don't care."

Chapter 35

Marcus watched Servius drag Perseus out the door and shook his head in wonder. Meskhanet, a sorcerous? The young woman behind him released a long shaky breath, and he turned to face her. "Are you Perseus's slave?"

"No, sir. He came to our house and demanded that I come with him. He had been there before with our mother. I think she might have been a business associate of his. He came to us before and took another girl away with him."

"And who are you? Where do you live? Who are your parents, that we might return you to them?"

"Bellisima?" Meskhanet stepped from behind him.

"Meskhanet?" The girl turned to Marcus. "This is the woman Perseus took away before."

Bellisima held her hands out, and Meskhanet grasped them.

Joanna stepped from behind the door. "Did that snake Perseus bring you, young woman? Where is he?"

Bellisima glanced at Meskhanet. "He became ill."

Marcus nodded.

Joanna's eyes widened. "You did not put him in with Aula, did you?"

"No. He's out in the street. I don't think he'll be back." Decimus cast his glance from the young woman to the other. "How do you know each other?"

Meskhanet turned to him. "This is Bellisima, Senator. She's one of the young women from the house I told you of."

Marcus watched her eyes fill. She had such a tender heart.

She turned back to her friend. "Perseus assaulted Aula—your mother. She is here. I don't know if she will recover."

Bellisima's eye's widened. "No, don't tell me that—not our mother. She is so kind. Why would he do that? Where is she?"

"Come with me." Meskhanet touched her arm and led her through the hall.

Marcus followed. Aula might already be deceased, and he'd like to be around if Meskhanet wanted a shoulder to cry on.

Meskhanet glanced over her shoulder. Why did Marcus follow them?

When they entered the doorway to the room, she started. Brutus lay on his bed, hard black eyes staring through her. She stopped. She couldn't go into that room with *him* there staring at her. "Marcus, Brutus is awake. Please, would you take him to another room?"

Marcus raised his eyebrows and then frowned. He stepped between Brutus and her. "I am here. He will not hurt you." He turned to the injured man lying on the pallet and said something to him in Latin.

Brutus growled something unintelligible. Would he tell Marcus what had happened? She shivered.

Marcus turned around to face her. "Don't worry, Meskhanet. I'll guard your back."

She hesitated, then grasped Bellisima's hand and led her to Aula's side. Meskhanet knelt and gently pulled a strand of hair away from Aula's face, careful not to touch her blackened and misshaped cheek. To her surprise, Aula opened her one good eye a narrow slit.

Aula blinked and focused her gaze on Bellisima. "B'lisss."

"Yes, Mother." Tears rolled down Bellisima's cheek and dripped on the blanket.

"Yoursss. All. Box underrr…bed. Share…sssissstersss."

"I will, Mother." Bellisima reached for her and stroked an unbruised portion of Aula's arm. "I'll take care of my sisters."

Aula closed her eye and opened it again, this time to focus on Meskhanet. "Yahhhwehh."

Meskhanet nodded. "Yes, Yahweh. He is the One God. You know him?"

Aula's eyes shut, and a faint smile crossed her lips.

Meskhanet couldn't see Aula's chest rise. Was she gone? No, her mouth opened, and she gasped for air. Once, twice, and no more. Meskhanet's cheeks felt wet. She leaned down and kissed the woman's forehead. When she rose, Bellisima bent and also kissed Aula. She turned to Meskhanet, and the two young women clung to each other as quiet sobs shook them.

Meskhanet felt a touch on her shoulder and whirled to find Joanna standing there, the senator behind her. Meskhanet released a gasp and threw her arms around Joanna. "Two precious ones gone." She gulped and tried to control her tears. "No more, please, Yahweh."

Bellisima patted her arm. "Meskhanet, would you come with me? Please? I do not know the way."

"The way?" Meskhanet wiped at her eyes with the heel of her hand.

"To the home of Aula. I have to tell the others who live there, and I should look under her bed. She must have hidden a few coins for us. I hope there will also be enough for her funeral."

Bellisima sniffled, and Joanna handed her a rag. "You will need some men to go with you."

Marcus cleared his throat and glanced at his father. "I could go with them. And I think Father might be willing too."

Meskhanet glanced up at him, then to Joanna. "Would you come, too, Mother?" Joanna would assure Marcus's good conduct.

Joanna nodded. "Of course."

Decimus placed one hand on Meskhanet's arm and the other on Bellisima's. "We will go with you. No one will harm you or prevent you from retrieving what Aula saved for you. I'll tell Celia to prepare her for a funeral, and I'll get a wagon for us. By the time we return, all should be in readiness."

Joanna turned her gaze to Decimus. "Where can we bury her?"

The senator's eyebrows lifted. "Bury? Oh, no. We don't bury. We cremate."

Meskhanet turned to him, her own brows high. "Cremate? Does that not mean you burn them? That sounds so cruel."

Bellisima touched her arm. "She cannot feel pain now. She was a Roman citizen; it would be what she would want."

Meskhanet paused. "Yes, I suppose that is true."

Marcus ran his hand across his face. "I think we had better go now to the broth…to Aula's house. It occurs to me Perseus might also look there for anything she might have hidden away from him."

Marcus had to smile to himself. Here they were, a prominent senator, a soldier, two expensively-dressed women, and one woman in humbler attire, all trooping into a well-known brothel.

Odd. A smile teased at the corner of Joanna's mouth, too.

His father looked grim. He pushed the door open, not bothering to knock. A woman whirled, her eyes wide. When she saw the two men, her painted lips rose in a seductive smile, kohl-lined eyes inviting. "Welcome, Senator. Would you and your handsome friend like some companionship?"

Her smile froze into a grimace when the three women followed them.

Marcus cleared his throat to avoid the chuckle rising in his throat.

His father shot him a look demanding good behavior. "Pax. We brought someone with a message to your house. You may want to gather all the women here. Without any companions."

The curvaceous blonde dropped her act. "It could take a few moments."

"Make the moments short, young woman. I don't care to linger here. And before you leave to collect the others, direct us to Aula's room."

"Yes sir. It's the first room on your right from the peristylium." She bowed her head then turned and hurried from the room.

His father turned to the rest. "Marcus, Joanna, Meskhanet—find Aula's box. Bellisima and I will wait here for Aula's women."

"Yes, sir." Marcus fought the urge to salute, remembering when his father had demanded it.

Meskhanet led them through an arched entrance into the enclosed courtyard. She walked to the door and tugged, but it didn't open.

Marcus stepped up behind her. "May I try?"

She stepped aside, and he pulled. The door didn't budge. Marcus exchanged glances with Meskhanet. "Would you mind summoning my father?"

Meskhanet nodded.

Decimus strode into the peristylium and pounded on the wooden panel. His thunderous voice echoed off every wall. "This is Senator Decimus Varitor. Open this door, or we will break it down. If we have to do that, I can guarantee it will not go well for you."

Silence.

"We need a battering ram, Marcus."

"I'll have to get a few more men, too. If you want to stand guard, I'll go after Cyril and Servius and a ram."

The girl who had been in the entryway laid a hand on Marcus's arm. "Wait, sir, don't destroy the door. There's another entrance."

"Another entrance?"

"Yes. Aula would sometimes need to rescue one of us if a man got too rough, so she made sure each room also had a door to the roof that could not be locked."

Marcus flushed. Of course they would have a second entry.

The young woman led the way across the courtyard and up a stairway. "My name is Varga. I am second only to Aula. I have been here nearly as long as she." She walked to a trap door marked with *I* and pointed to a rope handle.

Marcus pulled the door up. A wooden ladder extended to the floor below.

"Young woman—Varga. Are the others assembled?" The senator took Varga's arm, and they walked back to the stairway.

Marcus descended to Aula's room, sword loosened from its scabbard. A high window and the opening above provided the only light. "It appears to be safe," he called up the ladder to Meskhanet. He looked around the room for a lamp.

Meskhanet lifted the bar and opened the door to the peristylium.

Ah, light. Marcus turned to the outsized bed. Looking under it wouldn't be easy. Heavy-looking wood framed it, and a covering of soft fur indicated perhaps Aula had been well off—unless the furnishings belonged to the house. Did Aula own the house? Or did Perseus?

Dropping to the floor, Marcus crawled around the two exposed sides of the bed. No obvious breaks where an opening might exist. He sat back on his heels and scratched his head. Rising to his feet, he took hold of one edge next to the wall. He grunted with effort as he slid it a finger's width, two, then three, the boards in the bed protesting as they scraped the concrete floor.

Meskhanet put her face next to the wall. "I don't see anything but more wood. And I don't think Aula could have moved this." She pulled the straw mattress, wool blankets, and the soft fur covering back. "There."

He laughed, wiping the sweat from his face. "Couldn't you have found the opening before I moved this elephant?"

She smiled! He had made her smile. A grin warmed his face as he knelt and put his shoulder to the frame. The bed protested just as loudly returning to its place next to the wall. He stood back to his feet.

Meskhanet lifted the panel and gasped. "Look at this!"

A goatskin bag lay open, gold coins and silver spilling from its mouth.

A cry sounded from outside the room, and Marcus whirled. He saw no one in the doorway, so he stepped to the entrance. More wails emanated from the front hall. They must know about Aula now. He turned back to Meskhanet.

Meskhanet lowered the lid to the stash and pulled the bedding back, smoothing it quickly. "Do you think anyone saw it? We should close the door."

"I don't think anyone saw us, but you're right. We should have shut the door. We need to take the box with us. I don't know if Perseus owns this brothel, but if he does he'll keep the coins for himself." Marcus glanced back toward the main hall. "Truly, I wouldn't be surprised if he'd keep them for himself whether he owns this place or not."

"Yes. These must be separate earnings. Where would she get such an amount?"

"Years ago, there was a rumor that the emperor had a favorite consort, a very young woman. I heard when he was tired of her, he gave her a parting gift. It appears Aula might have been that consort." He pulled the heavy door closed behind him. "Let's pack the coins."

Chapter 36

Marcus gave a gentle slap of the reins to the horses' backs, and the wagon moved forward. They had left Bellisima at her home. What a heavy day. Aula's death, informing the women at the brothel, and accompanying Bellisima while she told the other girls. So much sorrow weighed him down, and these were not the heaviest things on his mind. His father sat beside him, the ladies behind. Marcus heaved a sigh. "Father, I have to find a ship going to Caesarea. You have one. Is it here or out?"

"It's here, and it is scheduled to leave tomorrow, but I wish you would wait. What good can going back there now do?" A scowl darkened the senator's face.

"Tribune Rufus gave me an assignment when I left Jerusalem to bring Barabbas to justice. I haven't completed my task yet. Can't you understand? It's not something I want to do; it's something I have to do."

"But what of the charge of treason? Do you really think Rufus will dismiss it just because you bring Barabbas in? Especially after you escaped his centurion and took a detour to Rome? If he has a choice between his popularity and your life, you won't stand a chance." His father paused, and his deep voice took on a note of pleading. "Please, Son. It would kill me to see you crucified."

Marcus shook his head, his heart heavy. "I'm sorry; I must go. It's my duty. If you stay here, you won't have to see."

"What about your duty to me? What do you think I will do while you are gone? Do you think I am so uncaring that I will not think of you because you are out of sight?" Decimus sat stiff, fisted hands on his lap.

Marcus's eyes swam. "No, Father, I don't think that. Forgive me. But I still must go."

Silence stretched to an uncomfortable tautness. When his father spoke, resignation washed through his voice. "Then I will go with you. Perhaps I may have some influence on Rufus's decision. And if not, at least you will not face this alone."

Marcus breathed a heavy sigh. "What will you do with Septus? You can't allow him to see it."

"I know. And yet I cannot leave him here with Portia. He will have to come. If it happens you are sentenced to…." He exhaled through pursed lips. "I will make arrangements to keep him from being there, somehow." His father's shoulders sagged.

Their voices had been low, Marcus hoped too low for Joanna and Meskhanet to have heard. They had been carrying on their own conversation behind them.

Marcus sighed again. "Father, there is one more task I need to complete before I leave. There is a boy, Dinah's brother. Rebecca and Dinah have pleaded with me daily to go get him because he is with an abusive master. I told them if we had money left after we freed Meskhanet, we would also buy him."

His father laughed, but there was no humor in it. "What do you propose I do with all these charges you would leave me? You can imagine what would happen to them if Portia were unrestrained."

"The two children—Dinah and David—could come with us. Rebecca, too, since she seems to have become Dinah's adoptive mother. When we get to Israel, we could let them go where they wish or stay with Julius." Marcus cast a glance toward the back of their wagon. "I don't know what Joanna and Meskhanet will want to do."

They pulled the wagon into the villa's driveway. Servius arrived by the time they helped Meskhanet and Joanna from the wagon to the ground.

The senator turned to the servant. "Servius, would you take these beauties back to the stable and give them some grain?"

"Yes, sir." Servius patted the two bays' necks.

Marcus followed his father and the two women onto the portico, but let them proceed to the atrium without him. He stopped short and stared at the villa. *Adonai, I wish I could stay here. I love this house, this city, and my father. Are You sure I must go back?*

He shook his head. He knew the answer without asking. He could hear his father's voice and the murmurs of the women, the rise and fall of questions and answers. He took a deep breath and walked forward.

Joanna turned to him. "We will go with you."

Marcus narrowed his eyes. "Only as far as Caesarea. I don't want you to go with me to Jerusalem."

Meskhanet stepped to him and touched his arm. "All the way."

He brushed her hand away. "No." He turned and walked down the hall and into the room where Brutus lay.

The big man opened bleary eyes. He lifted one hand and dropped it as though it were too heavy.

"Brutus, you feeling feverish?" Marcus reached down a hand, touched the soldier's forehead, and answered his own question. "Yes, I think so."

"Willow bark." Joanna's voice came from behind him. "Any idea where we can find some?"

"Yes. I remember some willows along the road just before we rode into Rome. I can get some at the same time that I go after the boy." Marcus rubbed a hand through his hair.

"The boy?" Joanna raised her eyebrows at him.

"Dinah's brother." Marcus stepped to the entry and looked toward the stables. She'd probably be there with the kittens. And where Dinah was, Rebecca wouldn't be far away.

"Oh, yes. Dinah told me about him. Her twin, correct?" Joanna walked to his side, and they strolled together to the stable. "Are you going to take her along with you to the inn?"

"I'm not sure that would be a good idea. The innkeeper might decide to steal her back. Rebecca, maybe." Marcus smiled grimly down at Joanna. "She's not young and pretty."

Her lips thinned. "This is not a safe city for the young and female, is it?"

Marcus smiled. Purchasing the boy had been surprisingly easy. David had sprained an ankle a few days before, and taking care of horses and running and fetching otherwise for the innkeeper wasn't happening as fast as the owner had come to expect. The boy hopped on one foot with many grimaces, and the horses got excited when someone jumped around in front of them. Add to that the innkeeper's decrease in business lately, and the man was happy to be rid of the boy and his appetite.

Rebecca rode behind David and chattered with the boy.

Aramaic. Not exactly a musical language, like Latin or Greek. Still... Marcus sighed. Maybe on the ship. Although—What good would Aramaic do him if he were put to death?

They neared the Liri River and the patch of willows he'd noticed before. He'd have to get the bark himself. Rebecca didn't have a knife, and David couldn't hop through the mud to the willows and back. Marcus left them holding the horses and used his sword to chop several stocks. He tied the willows to the back of his horse and just had time to mount before David set his heels in his horse's sides, leading off at a gallop.

It wasn't a problem for Marcus, but Rebecca yelped. He shouted at the boy to stop.

David stopped his horse and turned him. "I want to see Dinah. Can we not hurry?"

"Do you know how to find your way to my father's home? No? Then wait. We will not discomfort Rebecca to grant that request."

David and Rebecca came back to him, and Marcus led at a slow trot, much easier on the woman. As they drew closer to his father's villa, he laughed. Dinah must have been watching for them. She charged toward them screaming David's name.

Marcus held up his hand. "Stop, Dinah—you're alarming the horses!"

Too late. Rebecca and David both spilled onto the brick roadway, and their horse galloped away. Marcus set his heels in his mount's side and quickly caught the animal. When he returned to the old woman and the boy, David held his ankle and cried, rocking back and forth. Rebecca sat at his side, patting his back and crooning in that cursed Aramaic. Marcus dismounted and knelt by them.

Dinah stood next to her brother with tears streaming. She repeated a phrase over and over in what Marcus could only assume was Aramaic for "I'm sorry." She wrung her hands and hovered over David.

Marcus dismounted. "Here—hold the horses, please, Dinah. Rebecca, help her lead them back to the stables. I'll carry David."

The boy didn't weigh much. He'd quit crying and lay stiff and still against Marcus's shoulder. He wondered if Celia had remade the bed where Aula had laid. He walked into the house and met his father in the atrium.

Decimus smiled and shook his head. "Now what? Maybe I should convert my home to a hospital."

Marcus grinned back. "I hope not. Is Joanna or Meskhanet around? He had a sprained ankle. He sprained it at the inn while he was working, and just now he fell off the horse. Dinah spooked them with a little too enthusiastic a welcome. I hope the boy's ankle isn't broken now."

Marcus carried the boy into the bedroom.

Brutus opened his eyes. "Who's that?"

"Dinah's brother, David. The boy who took care of our horses at the inn."

Brutus glared at the boy, and David clutched Marcus's neck. Or maybe Brutus wasn't really glaring, but even his casual glances looked antagonistic to most people.

Marcus patted David's back. "Don't worry. He won't hurt you, will you, Brutus?" Marcus narrowed his eyes at Brutus, hoping the soldier understood his words as a command.

"No, sir." Brutus shut his eyes.

Decimus strode into the room behind Marcus, followed by Joanna and Meskhanet.

Joanna knelt by David's side and murmured something. The boy nodded, and she began feeling his dusty ankle, accompanied by pained yelps through gritted teeth.

Marcus muttered. "I really have to learn Aramaic. Meskhanet, while we are on the ship, will you teach me?"

Meskhanet laughed. "In such a short time you think you can learn?"

Joanna looked up at them. "How can we go now? There are patients here to care for. Perhaps I should stay here."

"No," Decimus said. "Portia cannot be trusted. Varrus might stay, but she could have him sent back to the circus along with you. There would be no one here to vouch for you or protect you."

Marcus sighed. "That means I go alone. Or rather with Barabbas."

"No, that means we all go, including Brutus and the boy. And Dinah and Rebecca."

Septus trotted into the room. "And me too, Papa."

His father ruffled his hair. "And you too, Septus."

"And the little brothers of the lions?"

"No, I think not. I do not think Portia would harm them. Servius will feed them, and by the time we return perhaps they will be feeding themselves on mice."

"Please, Papa? Just one?" Septus grasped his father's hand and stared at him with wide eyes. "Please?"

Decimus harrumphed, scowled, and lifted his hand to his lips.

"Please, Papa, please? I will take care of him." His long lashes batted once, twice over moist eyes, and his father's mouth began to twitch at the edges.

Marcus laughed. He wished he'd had the little scamp to teach him this art while he was growing up.

Joanna began to chuckle, then Meskhanet giggled behind those lovely, slender, golden fingers.

Marcus could watch those graceful appendages all day.

Decimus threw up his hands and joined in the laughter. "I'm outnumbered. Very well, you may take one."

Septus raised one small fist in triumph and cheered. "Thank you, Papa," he shouted over his shoulder as he ran out the door. "I have to go tell Dinah."

Meskhanet heaved a sigh. One task remained before she could pack their belongings in the chest for the trip back to Caesarea. She would help Bellisima bury her mother. But someone would have to go with her. She would not walk or ride anywhere in Rome alone again. Not even since this was her last night here.

She paced back and forth in the peristylium. Who, though? Who would go with her? Decimus or Marcus or Servius? Decimus had left to take care of some business at the senate, Servius worried over one of the horses who seemed to have picked up a stone. Marcus then, although the idea of him accompanying her tied her stomach in knots—or was it in excitement?

Meskhanet walked with hesitant steps toward Marcus's door and lifted a reluctant fist to knock. She dropped her hand. She couldn't. What would he think? That she pursued him? No, she couldn't allow that.

Yet, she could not forsake Bellisima, not with the sorrow that weighed her. She turned and entered the room where Joanna bent over Brutus, changing the dressing on his shoulder and back. Black scabs had formed on both sides, but the redness around the wounds seemed to be retreating. Meskhanet nodded. Joanna had treated them well.

She became aware of Brutus's stares, and she backed away. "Leave me alone, you evil man."

Joanna looked up at her, startled, then turned her gaze to Brutus, her eyes narrowing. "What are you doing, Brutus?"

The brows across his forehead crumpled into a scowl. "Nothing."

She turned to Meskhanet and raised an eyebrow.

Meskhanet shook her head, an uncomfortable heat rising from her throat to her cheeks.

Joanna nodded almost imperceptibly. "What is it you need, Meskhanet?"

"I wish to help Bellisima grieve. Her mother is dead. Aula was her adopted mother, as were several other girls and young women who live in her house. I cannot go alone, but Decimus is away, and Servius is treating a horse with a stone in its hoof." She lifted her gaze to the hallway to Marcus's room.

Joanna nodded. "One moment, daughter." She finished tying off Brutus's bandage and stood to her feet.

She led the way out into the hallway, but instead of stopping at Marcus's door she continued into the peristylium. "Now, my dear, please tell me what it is that Brutus does that frightens and angers you."

Meskhanet's face flamed, and she dropped her eyes to her feet. "He...while we were in Jericho...." She stopped, unable to go on, her breath caught in her throat. "Forgive me, Mistress. I cannot say it."

"I'm not your mistress, child," Joanna said, her voice soft but firm. "I'm your mother, and I love you. Did he rape you?"

Meskhanet covered her face with her hands and began to cry.

Joanna pulled her close. "Why didn't you tell me?"

"I was an Egyptian slave. He was a soldier in the Roman army. I was afraid." Meskhanet scrubbed the heels of her hands across her eyes.

Joanna's eyes narrowed as her gaze burned the door to the room where Brutus lay. "I will kill him. To think I have bandaged and cared for that scum. When I tell Marcus…."

"No, please! You must not tell him!" Meskhanet grasped Joanna's arms. "Or anyone, ever. Please, Mother. And if you kill him, they will crucify you. I could not bear that."

Joanna stood with arms held stiff at her sides for several moments, her jaw set and nostrils flared as she continued to glare down the hallway. Finally, she met Meskhanet's eyes again. "Very well, child. For you. But I will no longer treat his wound. For all I care, his arm may blacken and fall off."

The door to Marcus's room opened, and he gazed in surprise at the two women.

Joanna drew in an audible breath. "Marcus, we have a favor to ask. Would you please take us to Bellisima's house? We wish to help her and the others there grieve."

Marcus glanced back into his room, sighed, and nodded. "Of course."

Chapter 37

Marcus stared at the ship and gulped. He dreaded getting on that shifting, swaying monster. How long would it take to get his sea legs this time? He broke his fast with a crust of bread, unwilling to trust his stomach to hold more once onboard the ship.

They were all there. Barabbas in chains, his mother patting his arm and chattering, only earning his scowl. Meskhanet, Father, Cyril, Joanna, Dinah, David, Brutus, Septus…and three kittens? How had the little beggar managed that?

Cyril and the children were the only ones smiling. He knew his friend looked forward to seeing his bride again. He'd only had one letter from her. The children looked on this trip as an adventure. Marcus wished he could agree.

He didn't know what Brutus had done this time, but Joanna gave a stony-faced refusal to treat him anymore. Had the man said something that offended her? Marcus snorted. It wouldn't surprise him. The man thought more about fornication than food.

Meskhanet's face showed signs of weeping. Such a tender heart. She scarcely knew Aula and Bellisima, yet she still cried for them this morning.

Marcus helped each of them into the boat that would carry them to the anchored ship. He wished he could stay behind, but no amount of procrastination would change his destiny. He gritted his teeth and clambered in after the others. The rocking boat was bad enough, but the rolling roiled his innards. He climbed the rope ladder from the boat to the ship behind everyone else and then made sure Barabbas was securely chained in the bottom of the vessel before he joined his father topside.

They'd been under way for an hour when Cyril strode up beside him and grinned. "Should I give you something to eat now or wait until you are rid of what you've already eaten?"

"Just as full of sympathy as ever, aren't you?" Marcus swallowed. "Why did you have to mention food?"

"I'm trying to pay my debts. Remember? I owe you a month of meals. Sumptuous mutton stew, a leg of lamb, honey cakes…." Cyril laughed as Marcus bent over the rail and discharged his breakfast.

Clammy sweat dampened his face, hands, and body. Marcus groaned. "I'm so glad you're my friend. Who knows what sort of torture you would devise if you were my enemy?" He used one of the rags he tucked into his belt to wipe his face.

His father stared at the two of them. "Are you sick, Son? There is a physician on the ship."

"No, Father. It's not a sickness a physician can cure. The sea is the source of my illness. Compounded by the wounds of a supposed friend."

His father clapped a hand over his eyes. "The shame of it may kill me. The son of a senator of Rome disgorging over the side of said senator's ship." Not a glimmer lit his eyes, but one edge of his lips twitched.

Marcus moaned and rested his head on the cool rail. "Leave me alone, both of you. I wish to die in peace."

Joanna and Meskhanet joined them, Septus and the twins following with their kittens.

Must even Meskhanet witness his weakness? Maybe he should just jump overboard and let the sharks end his misery.

Meskhanet lifted her chin to take in a deep breath of the light sea breeze. What a difference between the close and usually fetid smell of a city. She hadn't realized how much she missed the clean smell of the open ocean. How pleasant it would be to live where decaying vegetables and human and animal wastes didn't foul the air.

However, as she and Joanna approached the three men standing at the side of the ship, the clean smell turned fusty. Poor Marcus. His skin resembled the mortar used to hold bricks together. The only colors on his face were his straight rusty eyebrows and long sandy lashes rimming red eyes.

She had a startling urge to rub the back of the man who bent in such misery over the barrier. She turned to Joanna. "Do you have a potion to relieve sea sickness, Mother?"

Joanna pursed her lips and gazed at the distant horizon. "Perhaps in Loukas's medicine chest. Something tickles the edge of my mind, if I could just remember. Loukas mentioned something once, years ago—an herb or plant that relieves nausea. I'll look in the chest."

She turned and ran into Brutus, almost losing her balance. He put out a hand to prevent her fall, and she batted it away. She hissed at him and said, "Don't touch me. I'd rather fall."

Brutus raised a threatening hand, but Decimus caught the man's sore arm and pulled it up behind his back. "Do not consider striking her, soldier. I could easily break this arm." The senator lifted Brutus's wrist even further.

Brutus howled.

Joanna smirked.

Meskhanet's stomach relaxed. The man would not hurt them with Decimus, Cyril, and Marcus around. Well—perhaps not Marcus, at least not until he bested the sea.

Marcus lifted his pale face from the rail. His voice sounded tired. "Brutus, go to your bunk. These women are under our protection, and you are not to harm them. Do you understand?"

"Yes, sir," Brutus said through clenched teeth.

Meskhanet smiled to herself. Perhaps even before Marcus could conquer his seasickness.

Decimus released him, and Brutus retreated to the men's tent.

Meskhanet gazed at Marcus. Even ill, he exerted authority over Brutus. And Adonai had protected her recently when all seemed hopeless, when no one had been around to save her.

Joanna walked to Marcus with a smile of triumph. "Drink this."

"What?" Marcus took the cup. He sniffed and jerked the cup away from his face. "What is this?"

"Ginger root tea. Loukas left instructions for many cures. He wrote that this one worked for nausea."

"It smells terrible." Marcus started to hand the cup back to Joanna.

Decimus made a sound in his throat. "Stop arguing and drink it."

Marcus hesitated. Taking a deep breath, he drank the whole thing in a couple of gulps and prayed it would not come back up.

Caesarea. There it lay, ahead of them by not more than a mile. Marcus heaved a sigh. Dry land that didn't sway and jolt and lift and drop. Even though it brought him a step closer to probable imprisonment and possible death, the thought of solid earth beneath his feet brought a surge of delight to his heart. Or perhaps it was instead his stomach that leapt for joy. In addition, Meskhanet had taught him a lot of Aramaic and in the process they had become close. Or at least closer. He chuckled, earning a raised eyebrow from his father.

"What amuses you, Son? I confess I could use a piece of your humor. I see nothing but trouble ahead." Decimus gazed at the landing ahead, a faint scowl darkening his face.

Marcus patted his back. "Father, don't worry. It won't help anything. Be happy for this moment. Right now, I'm pleased to just get off this ship. Cyril is joyful because he'll soon see his bride. Meskhanet, Joanna, and Rebecca look cheerful too. Maybe they look forward to seeing Quinta and Miriam and Miriam's baby. The children are happy because—well, because they're children and they're on an adventure. Brutus?" Marcus sighed. "I'm not sure Brutus knows how to be happy, except with horses."

"Brutus is good with horses? It's hard to imagine him having the patience to work with the animals. Or anything else." Decimus pulled at his lip and studied Brutus, standing at the stern of the ship.

"Surprising but true. You'd think they were his babies. He sings to them, brushes them as though their skins were tender, and makes sure they are dry and fed before he cares for himself. Amazing. You cannot trust him around a woman alone, age ten to fifty, but I would trust him to take perfect care of any horse in my possession. Not that I have any in my possession."

The crew had begun tossing ropes to another crew on the dock. Any moment now Marcus would be standing on solid ground. The only one more eager than He was Cyril.

There—moored! Marcus followed Cyril to the planks stretched from the boat to the dock. He touched Cyril's shoulder. "My friend, I have a favor to ask. As soon as you reach home, would you send a wagon back for us?"

"I will. And I think I will see if I can still run as far and fast as I used to. It won't be long, I promise you." Cyril set off at a brisk trot, leaving Marcus chuckling.

The problem with finally getting used to the rocking motion of the ship was that now solid ground rocked. Marcus thought back to the first time that happened. He had been sure Caesarea must be having an earthquake. Another chuckle escaped his throat.

Meskhanet, who had exited the ship just behind him, gave him a curious glance. "You find Caesarea amusing?"

Marcus grinned down at the lovely young woman by his side. All those Aramaic lessons onboard the ship had helped. She had finally relaxed around him. "I am amused at your brother-in-law. Do you think he might be eager to see Quinta?"

She laughed. "I think that is so. But will he remember that he left all of us at the pier?"

How he loved to hear her laugh—like water bubbling in a brook. He stared down into those dark eyes and lost his heart in them once again. Her eyes met his with a twinkle and something more.

Decimus cleared his throat. "It seems Cyril must have come across Julius first. Here he comes."

Marcus glanced in the direction of his father's gaze.

A chariot raced toward them. Julius pulled the horses to a prancing halt. He jumped from the chariot and ran to Marcus, wrapping him in an exuberant hug. "Ah, my friend, you are back. It's so good to see you. And you, Senator. And ladies." He scanned the group. "Where is Loukas? Still onboard retrieving his precious…" He stopped abruptly when Marcus and the rest lost their smiles.

Joanna and Meskhanet' eyes filled with moisture, and they held tight to each other's hands.

"Oh, no," Julius breathed, and tears filled his eyes. "Not Loukas."

Marcus nodded, wet rivulets on his cheeks again. "Pirates."

Julius circled Meskhanet and Joanna with his arms. "I'm heartbroken with you, dear friends. Come, we'll go to my home."

Marcus cleared his throat. "We're waiting for Cyril to send a wagon. We have a few people and belongings to transport."

"Of course." Julius glanced up. "Who is that?"

Marcus followed his gaze to the man descending the plank in chains followed by one of his father's crew. "Barabbas."

"And who is Barabbas? Oh, wait. I remember. The man you sought who got you into such trouble. How did he come to be with you?"

"He followed Meskhanet to Rome. He decided she was the source of his trouble and that he would kill her." Without thinking, Marcus slid a protective arm around her shoulders.

Meskhanet cringed at his touch.

Marcus pulled his hand away. "Forgive me. I find myself wanting to protect you."

"I do not need protection at this moment." Meskhanet slid apprehensive glances at Barabbas and Brutus.

"Not at this moment. But if you do, I hope you will call me."

"But soon you may also be in chains. Shall I call you then?" She clipped her words and pressed her lips into a thin line.

Marcus flinched. How could he protect her if he became a prisoner?

"In chains?" Julius raised an eyebrow. "Why should he become a prisoner?"

"Your Roman compatriots call him a traitor because he infiltrated Barabbas camp. The soldiers found him there with them." She spat her answer at Julius as though he were at fault.

Julius watched her with widening eyes. "What happened to our sweet demure Meskhanet? Yes, I knew about Marcus's imprisonment, but I have hopes we can clear him of all charges."

"You do? How?" Marcus's heart beat a little faster. He spoke to Julius, but his eyes sought Meskhanet. She didn't want him to become a prisoner.

Chapter 38

Marcus approached the tall bay horse in the darkness of the corral. The animal pricked his ears forward and nickered. "Hello, God's Gelding. Do you remember me?"

The horse trotted to him and nudged his arm. Marcus chuckled. "You do." He pulled a withered apricot from the bag at his waist. The gelding took the fruit with soft lips.

"Would you carry me one last time, my four-footed friend? Then I fear I must tell you goodbye for the last time, along with all my other friends. Will you miss me? Will they?" Marcus stroked the horse's muzzle. "Will Meskhanet?"

Despite Julius's hopeful words to his father and friends, Marcus doubted that the delivery of Barabbas to the jail would be sufficient for Rufus to dismiss all charges against him. He had lost his troops in an obvious trap. Then, instead of returning to Jerusalem to admit his failure, he had apparently joined the enemy. Add to that escaping the centurion who had made him a prisoner. He was a fugitive, and if any of that century saw and recognized him, they could kill him without fear of reprisal. All they would have to say is that he tried to escape again.

"If I take any of my friends or my father with me, they would fight for me and could be killed or also imprisoned. I have to leave without them. Just take Barabbas, no others. You understand, don't you, God's Gelding?" He leaned his head on the bay's neck.

He slid the bridle over the horse's head and reached for the saddle resting on the fence.

Meskhanet opened her eyes and froze. She had heard something. There it was again. A metal against metal sound. Outside the window. She walked barefooted to the arched opening and eased her way forward to peek around one edge. Someone led a horse—no, two horses—on the street. One horse carried a man. Too dark to discern anything other than that, but they didn't seem to represent any kind of danger. Once the horses had clopped and clanked their way past the house, she slipped back into bed and back to sleep.

She and Joanna walked into the dining area the next morning. It seemed everyone but Marcus had beat them awake and to the table. The twins giggled over Milah's efforts to crawl. Septus demonstrated his ivory elephant to Julius. Decimus laughed with Miriam over something, and Quinta and Cyril murmured to each other at the edge of a bench. Rebecca chattered first with Quinta and then Miriam or anyone else whose ear hadn't been bent to another. And kittens, kittens everywhere.

Meskhanet glanced around the room and peered into the hallway to a set of bedrooms. No sign of Marcus. Where was he? Perhaps at the stables checking on the horse he called God's Gelding? Maybe he still slept.

Joanna voiced Meskhanet's question. "Julius, where is Marcus this morning?"

"I haven't seen him. It's early. Let the poor man rest. From what Cyril tells me, ships treat our poor decanus badly. He is probably tired." Julius stood, dropping a kiss on Miriam's loose black waves. "I have to go. I'll be back early this day to ready myself to leave tomorrow." He tossed a wave at the rest of them and disappeared out the door.

"I will be going with them," Decimus said. "Of that probably none of you had a doubt. Miriam, would you allow us to leave the children with you?"

"Of course, Senator. We will care for them as our own."

Meskhanet glanced up at him when he snorted.

He chuckled. "I don't suppose the fact that both Dinah and David are slaves would change that, either. Julius always did treat his slaves as friends. And look where it got him. Cyril is as disrespectful a servant as I have seen in all my almost fifty years." He frowned with mock fierceness. "His lax attitude rubbed off on Joanna, too, I see. Quinta and Meskhanet end up as beloved daughters. I don't know what to say about this generation."

Joanna smiled. "Jealous?"

Decimus laughed and shook his head. He slapped both hands flat on the table. "Well, the lot of you may think Marcus should sleep all the day, but I for one think my son has slept long enough." He rose from the bench and strode down a hall, returning shortly with a scowl on his blanched face. "He's not in his room. And it does not appear his bed was slept in."

Meskhanet and the rest of the adults stopped talking and stared at him.

Miriam's soft voice eased the tension. "He has a favorite horse. He probably went to groom it."

Meskhanet's voice caught in her throat. "I fear I know where he has gone." She swallowed. "I think he left for Jerusalem."

Decimus's eyebrows lifted and then dropped into a thundercloud scowl. "What?"

"A noise woke me last night. I looked out the window and saw a man leading two horses, one of them carrying another man. I heard a clanking sound. It could have been Barabbas's chains."

Meskhanet's throat felt dry. He left because he didn't want them there—maybe especially her.

Marcus pulled the horses to a stop in the shade of oak trees by a stream. "We'll stop to give the horses rest and food, but it will not be a long stop. Dismount, but do not sit or lie down."

Barabbas glared at him. "Are you strong enough to make me?"

Marcus heaved a sigh and rolled his eyes. "I don't have to be. It doesn't matter if I bring you in alive or dead. If I kill you now, you won't even stink before I get you to Jerusalem."

"What does it matter? You kill me, I die now and quick. You take me to Jerusalem, I die a long and painful death on a cross. If you were in my place, what would you do?" Barabbas leaned forward in the saddle.

Marcus felt a sympathetic jolt to his heart, but he frowned at the man. "Maybe I should just cut off an ear or a nose or a hand or a foot. Something that won't kill you, just make your existence miserable."

Barabbas hesitated, then swung his leg over the horse's back.

Once he was on the ground, Marcus also dismounted. "I have a hard time feeling much pity for you, Barabbas. You're a murderer even of your own countrymen, and you tried to kill my beloved. Don't think you can convince me to set you free. It won't happen." Marcus pulled off his helmet and ran his hand through his hair.

He'd gotten used to being without the helmet, and now it rubbed sore places on his head. He'd left it at Julius's home when he'd gone in disguise after Barabbas months ago, but for this trip he had decided he should wear it. It identified him as a Roman soldier and a decanus.

He placed some grain in his helmet and fed each of the horses. They mounted and rode on again at a ground-eating trot.

"I'm going with you." Meskhanet had changed into a plain brown tunic and cloak and led a white-footed bay mare out to where the others gathered.

"No. I told you, this trip could be dangerous and unpleasant. I don't understand why you want to go." Decimus scowled from the back of his mount.

"If you leave me behind, I will follow you by myself. I don't know why I need to go, but I've learned to listen for Adonai's leading, and when He says 'Go,' I go." She jumped to the back of the horse and swung one leg over its rump.

"I am too." Joanna walked from the barn leading a dark chestnut mare. "I cannot let my daughter go alone, and Marcus is like a son to me."

Meskhanet's heart warmed. Could a woman ask for a better mother?

Brutus growled. "Women," he said with a snort.

Cyril tossed him a narrow-eyed look. "For once I agree with you."

"Do we have enough food for two more horses and people?" Decimus glanced at the big black mule with the thick pack on his back.

"Yes. I know my mother-in-law. And somehow, I expected we would also have Meskhanet with us." Cyril sighed. "Let's get moving."

Meskhanet laughed. She knew her mother, too. Joanna would have packed enough food for at least a contuberium.

Rebecca ran from the house, a bag over her shoulder.

"Oh, no. No, Rebecca, you cannot come with us." Julius waved her back.

"He is my son. I know Barabbas has done harm, but still he is my son." Her eyes flooded with tears. "I swear I will not set him free."

Meskhanet glanced at Julius. Would he allow Rebecca also?

Julius sighed. "All right. Get the chestnut gelding with the white face in the stable."

"Ungh!" Varrus patted his chest with one hand and pointed at the women with the other.

"I don't have a horse big enough for you, Varrus."

The man shook his head and pointed at his feet.

"Don't worry, Julius; Varrus will have no trouble keeping up with us." Decimus said.

Septus, Dinah, and David trotted toward them carrying kittens. Meskhanet chuckled.

"Us too, Papa?" Septus walked up to his father and patted his leg. "Please?"

"No. This is not a trip for children." Decimus bent to touch his son's face. "No. Go back into the house. Miriam will need your help with Milah, you know, since her Papa will be gone."

Ah, good strategy.

Septus looked back toward the house, a mournful look on his face. "Oh. I suppose she will miss her papa too."

"Yes. Now go inside, Son." Decimus gave his son a small push, and Septus trotted off, Dinah and David and the cats in his wake. Decimus stared after them until they disappeared.

Rebecca returned riding the gelding, and the seven of them rode out the gate and south along the road, Varrus jogging easily beside them.

Julius fumed. If Marcus hadn't been his closest friend, he would have let him suffer the consequences on his own. What had gotten into the man? Didn't Marcus realize he would need the testimony of the centurion who sent him to Rome? Rufus wouldn't look kindly on a man who apparently deserted.

So many people accompanying him. Would he be able to get there on time? On his own, he would have pushed his mount to the limits of its endurance, possibly finding someone who would trade horses along the way.

Now, it would take a miracle to reach Jerusalem in time. *Are You listening, Adonai? Do you have a miracle or two You would grant us?*

Julius hadn't told Marcus about the visit from Decanus Domitius.

The walls of Jerusalem had always enthralled Marcus. The white marble blocks and plating on the temple shone in the rising sun, and Marcus could feel his weary heart stir. He'd had no sleep for two days, his face felt like cacti, and his eyelids scraped against dry orbs. He squeezed his eyes shut, hoping to induce a bit of moisture to wet them. Then he didn't want to open them again. He slumped forward, but jerked upright at the sound of a derisive snort from Barabbas behind him.

The crossroad from Bethany lay in front of them. Hoof beats from many horses and footfalls of marching soldiers pounded from the other road, along with the rattle of armor and leather. Marcus pulled their horses off the road to let the troop pass.

The officer in the lead pulled his troop to a halt.

"Well, if it isn't the escaped decanus. Would that I could say we were well met, Marcus."

Marcus squinted his eyes. "Centurion Domitius. Hail." He raised his arm in greeting.

"No longer Centurion Domitius since I lost two prisoners a few months ago," Domitius said through clenched teeth. "Who is this with you?" He pointed his chin at Barabbas.

"You don't recognize him? It's Barabbas. He's my prisoner." Marcus shifted in his saddle to gaze at the man behind him.

Domitius laughed, but no lightness lifted the sound to humor. "Your *friend* Barabbas, you mean. What did you intend to do, set him free to murder a few citizens in Jerusalem?"

"I'm taking him to Tribune Rufus." Marcus cleared the gravel from his dusty throat.

"Wrong. *I'm* taking *both of you* to Rufus." He waved some men forward. "Put this man in chains."

Marcus felt the fire rise in his muscles. "You can't do that. I'm a Roman citizen. I'm entitled to a trial."

"I didn't say you wouldn't get a trial. But the tribune doesn't look lightly on traitors." Domitius smirked. "I might get my commission back when I bring in the prisoners who escaped before."

"I'm not a traitor." Marcus fought the urge to draw his sword.

"I didn't believe you when you told me before, and I don't believe you now." He jerked his hand forward, and three men rode their horses up to Marcus. One snatched both sets of reins from his hands. Two more soldiers wrapped chains around his wrists and bound them to his chest.

His heart sank to the soles of his sandals. *Adonai....*

Barabbas laughed. "See how it feels, traitor?"

"I am no traitor. I am a loyal Roman soldier. At least I have never knifed any of my countrymen in the back. I don't fit in your swamp." Marcus spat his anger at the only one safe to revile.

"What were you doing in my camp? Making friends with your enemies. I didn't recognize you until today, but now that your beard is growing out...so nice to see you found your voice and your hearing has improved." Barabbas curled his lip and laughed again. "You will hang on a cross beside me, traitor."

Chapter 39

Pray for Marcus.

Meskhanet looked around, startled. Where had those words come from? The rest of her companions rode forward as though they heard nothing. The voice had sounded above the clops of horses' hooves, the rattle of Julius's saddle, and the chirping of the birds in the trees. Why hadn't they heard?

Adonai, did You speak?

Nothing. But she knew.

"Wait," she called.

Julius, in the lead, held up his hand. "What is it, Meskhanet?"

"Our Adonai says, 'Pray for Marcus.'"

Decimus jerked his head toward her, the color from his cheeks vanishing.

Julius nodded, his expression serious. He pulled his horse back to Meskhanet's and dismounted. The rest followed his action.

Julius clapped a hand on Decimus's shoulder. "Do you want to join us in prayer to the One God?"

Decimus's voice shook. "I would pray to any god who could save my son."

Joanna turned to him and laid her hand on his arm. "There is only one God able to do that, my friend." She bowed her head.

Others lowered their heads or raised their hands. Meskhanet dropped to her knees, placed her forehead on the leaf-strewn earth, and gave her attention wholly to the One God of Israel.

Marcus stood in chains before Rufus. Dust covered every part of Marcus's body, caked across his shoulders and chest. Rivulets of mud swam down his arms, and he felt sure his face must be similarly marred. Domitius had made sure his prisoners looked their worst. Marcus and Barabbas had walked the remaining distance to Jerusalem behind the column of horses and men.

Rufus raised an impatient gaze to the men. "What is this, Domitius?"

Domitius saluted. "I retrieved the prisoners who escaped me last winter, Tribune. The former decanus Marcus and the murderer Barabbas."

"I don't recall removing Marcus's commission." Rufus set his quill on the table. "Barabbas should be taken to the prison now."

Two guards led Barabbas away.

Domitius flushed. "I assumed when you were told Marcus was a traitor you would have taken it from him."

"I'd like to hear why you think he's a traitor," Rufus said.

"He led three contubernia into the Samaritan hills, and all were killed but him. Later we found him in Barabbas's camp, dressed as one of them, carrying a weapon, obviously friends with the whole lot of thieves and killers." Domitius glared at Marcus. "The two of them escaped together, even after we allowed another soldier and another man to wait on him."

"And why did you allow people to wait on him? Perhaps these others released him and Barabbas."

"One of them, the soldier, had been part of his contubernium. The other was a friend's servant. There were a few other soldiers too, from Caesarea, but they didn't defect like Marcus did." Domitius shifted from one foot to the other.

"Why were soldiers from Caesarea there? And you didn't answer my question about allowing anyone to wait on him." Rufus leaned forward, his lips thinning.

Domitius shifted again. "Uh, Centurion Julius sent the soldiers, and he sent his servant. I don't know why he sent them. We allowed the soldier and Julius's servant to attend Marcus because he was wounded."

"Wounded? I tire of asking for details you should know to give, Decanus."

"One of the soldiers, ah, prodded him with his spear, sir. When he thought Marcus was one of the band of brigands, sir. He resisted arrest."

Marcus smiled to himself, tired as he was. Seeing Domitius squirm felt good.

Rufus turned to Marcus. "Step forward, prisoner."

Uh-oh. Being called a "prisoner" instead of by name does not bode well for me. He stepped forward, chains rattling. "Yes, sir."

"Domitius, how do you charge this prisoner?" Rufus addressed the decanus, but kept his eyes on Marcus.

"I charge him with desertion, betrayal, and escape, sir."

"And what is it you believe should be his reward?" Rufus slid his glance to Domitius and back to Marcus.

"Crucifixion, of course." An air of triumph puffed through Domitius's voice.

"Marcus, what do you have to say for yourself?" Rufus leaned back and cast a narrowed stare into Marcus's eyes.

"Sir, may I tell the whole story, or should I just answer yes and no questions?" Marcus held his breath.

"The whole story. And you tire me just keeping my neck arched to look up at you. Sit there on that bench."

Marcus sat with a grateful sigh. He raised manacled hands to brush sweaty locks away from his eyes.

Julius rose to his feet, his eyes wet. "Brutus, you and I need to ride fast. Decimus, I would take you, but I fear your testimony would not be accepted because you are his father. And I would like for you, Varrus, and Cyril to stay with the women. If you would, sir?"

Decimus's jaw clenched, muscles working at the edges of his cheeks. He jerked a nod. "I understand."

Brutus murmured into his mount's ear and jumped into the saddle.

Julius mounted, too, and both men moved their horses toward Jerusalem at a gallop.

They still had twenty miles to go. They wouldn't be able to run their steeds the whole distance. They would have to vary between running and walking to allow the horses to blow. He hoped they'd find some flowing water.

Julius pulled his gelding back to an easy trot. Thus far, he didn't seem to be breathing too hard, but the sweat on the horse's neck gave evidence it had run far enough.

Brutus stopped his mare and dismounted.

Julius stopped and pulled around. "What's wrong?"

"Resting my horse. She's working too hard." Brutus stroked the mare's nose, and her eyelids drooped in contentment.

Julius reminded himself that Marcus would need Brutus's testimony. He asked his Adonai for patience. He gritted his teeth and counted the rocks on the road. And he could restrain himself no longer. "We have to proceed toward Jerusalem now. Marcus may be marching toward Golgotha as we rest our horses. Let's go."

Brutus gave him a narrowed glance, but he mounted. Julius led at a rapid trot.

Still ten miles to go. Julius's stomach tied into a thousand knots, but he pulled his horse to a walk. If the horses gave out, they would not get there in time. His heart knew it. The urgency tightening his bowels grew worse with every step too slow.

Marcus finished his story. The manacles on his wrists had bitten into his skin every time he emphasized a point, reminding him over and over not to talk with his hands.

Tribune Marcius Rufus sat with lips pursed. "Do you have anyone who can corroborate this account, Decanus?"

"The man you just ordered into prison, Barabbas. I brought him in as you ordered."

Domitius jumped to his feet. "He lies. *I* brought Barabbas in, along with this traitor."

Rufus turned to the two soldiers standing by the door. "Bring the prisoner Barabbas. And an interpreter."

"He speaks Greek, sir," Marcus said. "Poorly, but he does."

"Nevertheless," Rufus said, his eyes narrowing. "An interpreter too."

First rule: don't speak unless addressed. His stomach clenched.

One guard brought the interpreter, a tall, scholarly Greek who looked down his nose at the tribune. Domitius ushered Barabbas back into the room. Barabbas cast almost a conspiratorial glance at Domitius. Barabbas squared his shoulders as he stood in front of Rufus.

"Tell him we want to know if he knows this man." Rufus pointed his chin toward Marcus but maintained a narrowed stare at Barabbas.

Barabbas's eyes glinted with an unholy glee at the interpreter's words. He spat some words back.

Marcus felt the blood drain from his face. He was reasonably sure the man had just declared their undying friendship. The interpreter confirmed it. Domitius smirked.

Rufus stood, his face a volcano about to erupt. "Marcus Varitor shall go to trial before Pontius Pilate. Today, if he is available."

Julius pulled his gelding around, gritting his teeth. "Now what?"

"She limped." Brutus lifted the mare's front right hoof and peered at it. He walked to the side of the road and picked up a dry branch. He picked up her hoof again and scraped, then brushed it with his hand. He stood and patted her shoulder.

"Is she all right?"

"A rock." Brutus picked up the reins and mounted. "It's out."

"Let's go then." Julius led off at a brisk trot. He could see the walls of the city. It wasn't far now. He leaned forward in the saddle, and his horse began to canter. He turned his head far enough to make sure Brutus kept pace and nodded in approval as the mare drew up alongside.

Cold sweat trickled from Marcus's face, his back, his chest. Pilate must be in a sour mood. The scowl on his face didn't forecast good news. He'd listened to Marcus's version of what had happened, then Domitius's and Barabbas's, the scowl only deepening. The beauty of the glistening marble and flowering bushes on Pilate's portico did nothing to lessen Marcus's anxiety.

It didn't help that they'd interrupted Pilate's entertainment. And his dinner. Marcus wished he knew if the scowl was directed at himself or at Rufus, but he feared the worst.

Adonai, I need your help. I'm willing to die for my country or for You, but I am reluctant to die for nothing.

Pilate coughed, deep and phlegmy. He rubbed his throat. "Are there any other witnesses?"

"No, Procurator." Domitius's voice held a triumphant ring. He glanced at Barabbas.

"Take this defector out of my sight, then. Scourge him. Then crucify him." Pilate stood and marched back into his villa.

Marcus's heart stopped. *Adonai, let me not disgrace You. Help me, Adonai. I am afraid.*

Domitius strode to Barabbas and loosed his chains. "You are free to go. Just try to resist the urge to kill from now on."

"I only kill traitors." Barabbas slid a glare at Marcus and laughed. "Unless you kill them for me."

Rufus's eyes widened and he stared at Barabbas. *"You* consider Marcus a traitor?"

Marcus stared at Domitius, then Rufus. Now would they understand?

Barabbas laughed again. "You have had all you will get from me, Romans." He shook his arms, lifted his head, and walked free into the streets of Jerusalem.

"It matters not what Barabbas thinks," Domitius muttered. He spoke louder to the guards. "Take this man to the fortress. I'll wield the scourge myself."

Julius strode into Rufus's quarters. "We need to speak to the Tribune immediately."

"He has gone to the praetorium, sir," the young guard said, saluting.

"When will he return?"

"I do not know, sir. They went to see Procurator Pilate. Along with two prisoners, Decanus Domitius, and several guards."

"Prisoners? Was one of the prisoners a Roman?" Julius's throat tightened.

"Yes, sir."

"How long ago?"

"A couple of hours, Centurion."

Julius whirled and ran down the stairs to where Brutus held the horses.

Marcus lifted his head. Was that Julius? And Brutus? He only caught a glimpse as two horsemen galloped past. No, it could not be. Domitius ordered him to remove his tunic. Marcus gritted his teeth and heaved a sigh as he pulled the one-piece garment over his head. He straightened his shoulders and walked to the post.

The guards pulled his hands to the opposite side of the post and chained them together. He could hear Domitius muttering to someone else, probably the tribune.

Adonai…

Julius dismounted and ran inside Pilate's house. "Is the procurator available, and is Rufus with him?"

A tall servant looked down a very long nose at him. "How important is this? My master has been disturbed enough this day."

"A man's life is at stake." Julius shuddered as he thought just how literal that statement might be.

"Whose?" The servant spoke in a voice filled with disdain and frost.

Julius narrowed his eyes. "If you don't lead me to the procurator and the tribune, it could be yours."

The arrogant domestic blanched. "Rufus left, but I'll ask my master if he will see you. However, I doubt he will consent."

Julius stewed as he waited for the man's return, pacing to and fro. Rufus had gone. He had to see Rufus as well as Pilate.

The servant returned, a frown dashing across stony features. "My master will see you. Follow me."

A moment later, they strode into a large bedchamber. A woman reclined on a couch, Pilate standing near her head. A bowl of fresh fruit sat on a table next to the couch, and the woman took a bite of melon.

Julius saluted.

"What is it, Centurion?" Pilate clipped the words.

"Sir, forgive me for intruding on you. I have ridden hard to try to stop an injustice. I hoped to find Rufus here with you so that I could tell you both at once. He was not in his quarters."

"Tell us what? What injustice?"

"A decanus, sir, and my friend, Marcus Varitor. He is accused of being a traitor because his actions were misinterpreted by Decanus Domitius."

Pilate's eyes narrowed. "Tell me more, Centurion."

Chapter 40

Marcus quivered. The weight of the crossbeam on his raw and bleeding shoulders caused him to stumble more than once on his procession through the city and outside the gates. So far he hadn't cried out in pain, but how much more could he stand? A scream hid just behind his tightly clenched teeth.

If only he had died beneath the scourge. His torn back burned with every breeze that brushed it.

Domitius marched at his side, if you could call it marching. Marcus could go no faster than an aging desert turtle. He could see emotions coursing over the man's face, but why? What was done was done. Did the decanus hold regrets? Unlikely. *But if he did, would h stop this farce before they pound the nails through my wrists?*

It didn't matter. The pain could be no worse than the agony in his back and shoulders. He raised his head, but his eyes wouldn't focus. Someone screamed. He moaned as he fell to the ground, consumed with a deep weariness he couldn't overcome.

Meskhanet had pushed her friends and their animals to the edge of their endurance. They must get to Jerusalem before....

Before what?

She didn't know. But she knew they must hurry. Almost there.

And then she saw the procession on the road. A man with a shredded and bleeding back carrying a thick board. He raised his head, and she screamed.

Decimus dismounted and ran to the head of the procession. "Stop! What are you doing?"

An officer dismounted and saluted him. "Pax, sir. We are transporting this prisoner to the place where he will be crucified."

"That man is my son. What are the charges against him? Has he had a trial? He is a Roman citizen."

"I'm sorry, sir. He was tried by the procurator and convicted of treason."

Meskhanet scowled. He could not be guilty. They were wrong.

Decimus roared at the shaking decanus. "Treason? That's preposterous. He brought the prisoner Barabbas back to Jerusalem all the way from Rome. Following the orders of his tribune. How is that treason? I am Senator Decimus Veritor, and that man is my son."

The man backed away. "I wasn't there, Senator. I'm only following orders."

"Go no further. I shall return. Take that crossbar off his shoulders and find him some shade and water." Decimus walked to Marcus. "Son, I will end this travesty. I'll be back."

"Papa?" Marcus squinted his eyes and raised his gaze. "You're here?"

"Meskhanet. She made us hurry. She said it was urgent. I didn't argue. I'll be back within the hour." Decimus ran to his horse and galloped toward the city.

"Meskhanet?" Marcus tried to make sense of the words he heard.

She knelt at his side, tears streaming down her face and dripping on his bleeding shoulders.

He winced but rejoiced with each drop of salty liquid. "You're crying." His voice rasped, and he coughed.

She took the edge of her cloak, spat on it, and began to brush his face, wiping the sweat and dirt from his eyes. "Marcus, I'm so sorry. Please don't die, Marcus."

Joanna brought a skin of water and poured it into the cup she carried. "Lift his head, Meskhanet."

"I fear I will hurt him, Mother. He has skin torn from his neck, too."

"He needs water. Just lift carefully."

A centurion marched up to them. "Women, what are you doing? This man is a prisoner, convicted of treason and bound for the cross."

Marcus raised one hand and grasped Meskhanet's as she lifted the cup to his lips. He held it even after the watered wine was gone. Some of the cool liquid escaped to run from his mouth into the stubble on his face.

Cyril cleared his throat, drawing the officer's attention. "Sir, we believe there has been a mistake. This man's father, the Senator Decimus Varitor, has gone to Pilate to attempt to correct the error."

"This soldier is Senator Decimus Varitor's son?"

Marcus watched the color drain from the centurion's face.

Hoofbeats pounded nearby as the world faded away.

Julius jumped from his horse and ran to the centurion. He handed the scroll over with Pilate's seal. "Read this."

Decimus dismounted, knelt by his son, and picked up his hand. "We have to take him somewhere that we can treat him. Marcus…Marcus. Wake up, Marcus."

Meskhanet knelt on his other side, weeping, holding the other limp hand.

Julius felt a sense of alarm radiate throughout his body. "No," he breathed.

Joanna beat him to Marcus's side, and she moved Meskhanet aside to place her head on his chest. "He's alive."

Julius released the breath he didn't realize he held. *Praise be to the One God.*

Joanna raised her head. "His heartbeat is faint. We need to get him to shelter. I have a salve to put on the wounds, but we should wash the dirt from them first."

The centurion motioned to a couple of guards. "The Decanus Domitius must go back to the guardhouse. He shall answer for his deception to the tribune and procurator. Throw the beam out of the wagon, and transport the man here to the procurator's house." He turned to Julius and saluted. "Pilate offers the use of the Fortress of Antonia to the centurion from Caesarea and all his friends."

Rebecca tugged on Julius's sleeve and whispered in Aramaic. "Please, sir, allow me to go to my son."

Julius turned to the centurion. "Where is Barabbas held? This is his mother, and she wants to see him."

The centurion shook his head. "I don't know. I was not informed of any other prisoner."

Domitius blanched and interrupted. "Barabbas is no longer a prisoner, sir. I released him in return for his testimony against Marcus."

Julius stiffened, and he repeated the information to Meskhanet, translating from the Latin they'd spoken.

She gave a small cry and turned a frightened look on Joanna.

Varrus, Joanna, and Rebecca tightened around Meskhanet, casting worried glances toward every boulder and tree.

Julius joined Decimus at Marcus's other side.

Even Brutus stood ready, his gaze raking the surroundings, his hand on the hilt of his sword.

"Let's get Marcus and Meskhanet to safety and shelter." The hair on the back of Julius's neck scratched against his cloak. Where could they hold Marcus to lift him? Hands and feet, maybe. Everywhere else had bleeding stripes.

Julius grasped Marcus's feet and nodded to Decimus, but Varrus brushed him out of the way and lifted Marcus by his wrists. Grunting, he lifted Marcus clear of the ground while Julius guided them to the wagon. They laid him on his stomach on his father's cloak.

Marcus moaned, but didn't wake. Meskhanet climbed in next to him.

Decimus tied his and Meskhanet's horses to the back of the wagon and clambered in on the other side of his son.

"Move the horses as fast as you can when we're on smooth ground, soldier," Julius said. "Let's go."

Meskhanet paced to and fro next to Marcus's bed in the Fortress of Antonia, praying. *Adonai, this man has become precious to me. Please, don't take this loved one from me too.*

For a fortress, this was opulent. Four walls and four towers, a courtyard. Pilate occupied one tower, two housed soldiers, and now one housed Meskhanet and her friends. But tapestries and ornately carved beds and tables couldn't heal Marcus, and thus far he showed little sign of improvement.

Oh, his wounds were healing a little, but after three days he still hadn't regained consciousness. She stopped at his door and peered through. Joanna stood by his bed pouring wine over his back again. She had asked for honey, but none had been provided yet. Decimus dozed on a couch.

Meskhanet stopped pacing near Marcus's head. *Adonai, will he wake?* But maybe it was better that he slept. The wine on his stripes would hurt.

Julius strode through the door from the stairway, followed by Tribune Rufus.

Julius nodded to Meskhanet, but the tribune didn't. He stared. *Another man with hungry eyes.* She turned her back to gaze out the window at the courtyard. She knew her large friend Varrus would be glaring at him, which made her smile to herself. Tribunes did not frighten Varrus.

"Who is the woman?" Rufus murmured.

Meskhanet couldn't hear Julius's reply, but she didn't mind. He wouldn't say the things other men did.

Varrus patted her on the shoulder and then patted his stomach. "Uh?"

"What, Varrus? Are you hungry?"

He nodded.

"Wait until Julius comes out. I don't know where you should eat. With the soldiers, possibly."

Varrus squinted into the room, scowling.

"I don't think the tribune is dangerous. He's just come to see Marcus."

Varrus nodded, but his scowl continued. And then he smiled. He turned to Meskhanet and pointed into the room. "Ungh."

Marcus had turned his head! He was awake and had turned from his stomach to his side to gaze up at the tribune with half-shut eyes. Marcus struggled to rise, but Rufus placed a hand on his shoulder, staying him, and Marcus dropped back to his stomach. How long until his back healed enough to bear his weight there?

A few more murmured words, and the tribune and Julius strode from the room.

"Julius." Meskhanet touched his arm.

He turned to her. "Yes?"

"Varrus hasn't eaten today, and we are out of the food we brought from Caesarea. Where may he eat?"

Julius pounded his forehead. "Of course. I hadn't thought. Come with me, Varrus."

Varrus shook his head and pointed at Meskhanet and then at Joanna.

"I'll stay here if the tribune permits." Julius bowed his head toward the officer. "Sir, Barabbas considers both Meskhanet and Marcus as traitors. May I stay here until Varrus returns?"

"Certainly. I'll show him where the men eat. What about you, young woman? Have you and your friends eaten?"

"No, sir." Meskhanet would not lift her eyes.

"My apologies. I'll see that meals are brought to you. And broth for Marcus."

"If you please, sir, my mother wants honey to put on his wounds too."

The tribune chuckled. "And honey."

Boots and sandaled feet walked away from them.

Julius laughed. "You have certainly changed since your days in Loukas's house. The young woman I saw there would scarcely have spoken to a tribune, let alone ask for honey."

Her cheeks warmed. "It is for Marcus. I would not have asked it for myself."

He put one arm around her shoulders and gave her a quick squeeze. She jerked back, shocked.

"That was the touch of a friend, Meskhanet, not a lecherous man." Julius stepped back.

Her faced heated even more. "Oh. I'm sorry, Julius. I should have known you would not—."

"No, I would not. Go in and see our friend. I know he wants to know you are here. I'll be in the hallway. Stay away from the outer windows."

Cyril yawned loudly and stood from where he'd been sleeping on a pallet. "I'll go stand guard outside the window."

"With what?" Julius demanded.

"Brutus left me his spear when he went to eat." Cyril lifted the spear from where it leaned against the wall and pointed it at Julius.

"On purpose?" Julius grinned and grabbed the staff of the spear, tugging it out of Cyril's grasp.

Cyril jumped to grab the spear back and wrestled it from his master. "Yes. It surprised me, too."

Meskhanet stared at them. She would never understand men.

Joanna walked up to them, a small scowl troubling her brow. "I hate to interrupt such important skirmishes, but have either of you seen Rebecca lately? When I went to sleep last night she was on a pallet next to me."

Julius ran a hand through his hair and shrugged. "No. She's not a prisoner. She's allowed to leave."

"I fear for her. I think maybe she went to find Barabbas." She turned toward the window.

Meskhanet shook her head, her stomach tightening. "Surely he would not harm his mother. At least not intentionally. Remember, Joanna, how concerned he was when his knife missed me and hit Rebecca?"

"But if he decides she is a traitor, too...." The creases between her eyebrows deepened.

"There's no way to know where she is. This city could hide a herd of elephants." Cyril thumped the spear's shaft on the floor. "I'm going outside. If you need me, shout."

Julius nodded. "I'll be in the hall just outside this doorway."

Meskhanet pulled loose hair away from her face and sent a quick petition to her Adonai. With an anxious glance toward the window, she walked to the bed. "How do you feel, Marcus? No, don't move."

Marcus relaxed and laid his head back on the bed. "I feel a little better. As long as I don't move. And as long as you keep that bottle of wine away from me." His grin was a little crooked. "It would be all right if you were going to let me drink it. Instead you pour it on me and you ask me to drink broth."

Meskhanet smoothed his rust-colored hair. "Soon, my friend. Now you need food easy to swallow. Broth. Do not argue."

Marcus chuckled and closed his eyes.

Voices sounded from outside. Meskhanet turned toward the window, but Joanna stepped between her and the opening.

"Hello in the fort—Rebecca is coming in," Cyril called.

Rebecca trotted into the room. "My son has been arrested again."

Joanna hugged her. "I'm sorry, Rebecca, but perhaps it is for the best. I feared for Marcus and Meskhanet."

Rebecca nodded and rubbed moisture from her eyes. "I know. I wish he could be free, but there is something wrong in my son's mind. He believes God has called him to kill all traitors, and he sees both of them as traitors." She turned toward Julius, who had entered the room behind her. "He wants to kill all Romans too. I did not know there were good Romans until I came to know you and Marcus and Decimus. My son still does not know it."

Chapter 41

Marcus sat on at the edge of his bed and dropped his feet to the floor for the first time in two weeks. He sucked in a breath and gritted his teeth as sharp pains stabbed his legs. He let them hang over the edge of the bed for a time then lifted them again to the bed.

His back itched, but at least it didn't bleed or weep any more. Sitting up hadn't been fun, but the dizziness passed. He wished he could walk, but until his legs would hold him it would remain a wish. He pulled his knees up, wrapped his arms around them, and lifted his gaze to the window and sighed.

"Marcus."

He jumped.

"You are sitting up. Good." Joanna strode to his bedside.

He laughed. "You might want to begin knocking before you enter, Joanna. I could have been unclothed."

She smiled back at him. "You might be feeling much better, Marcus, but I think you won't unclothe yourself today. Let me look at your back."

He turned his body, scooting his legs until that they hung off the far side of the bed. More stabs, but not as bad. Gingerly, he lifted the stained tunic up to his neck.

Joanna touched his back in several places and sniffed. "There doesn't seem to be any infection. Another week and you will be ready to rejoin your regiment."

Marcus snorted. "Back to being a foot soldier. My father will be so proud."

"Your father is happy you're alive and healing, and so is your youngest brother." Decimus stepped into the room followed by Septus with a kitten.

"Pax, little brother. When did you arrive? Did Papa bring you?" Marcus reached down to lift Septus to the bed, but Decimus pushed his hands away.

"What do you want to do, tear all your scabs loose?" He lifted Septus to sit beside Marcus.

Septus stroked the kitten but wouldn't look at Marcus.

He slipped his arm around the boy and knuckled his head. "What's unsettling your mind, little brother?"

Septus reached across and with one finger lightly stroked a scab on Marcus's other arm. "Who hurt you?"

Marcus hesitated. "It was a man who was angry and didn't understand the truth."

Septus looked up at him, tears streaking down his frowning face. "Do you want me to hit him for you? I'll hit him very, very hard."

Marcus swallowed the lump in his throat and pulled Septus to his chest. "No. Hitting him wouldn't help. It would not heal me, and it would not make him sorry for what he did. I think he is already repentant."

Meskhanet, who had followed Septus and his father into the room, patted Septus's shoulder, touching Marcus's arm in the process. Stimulating jolts ran from his arm throughout his entire frame. *Hmm. I must be mending even more than I thought.* He smiled at her over Septus's head. She smiled back. Another jolt. He took a deep breath and held it.

"I am glad you are recovering so well, Marcus. I feared for you."

Marcus wished everyone would leave the room except Meskhanet, but instead Varrus, Julius, and Brutus also entered. He sighed and turned to his friends. "Welcome to my chambers, all of you. I apologize for not having proper attire to greet you. Perhaps Julius would bring my toga?"

Julius chuckled. "Your tunic is stained and the toga filthy, but I think we can clean them up for you if you swear you won't bleed all over them again."

The tribune wanted to see him. Marcus paced the floor. Julius had brought all the trappings he needed, but even a bath and a shave did not quell the tightness in his chest. Rufus's last conversation with him had resulted in a journey to the flogging post and very nearly to his death. Julius said the man had come to see him once, but he remembered nothing.

His father strode into the room with Julius.

"Ready?" Julius asked.

Marcus swallowed. "Yes, I suppose I'm as ready as I can be. Thank you for coming with me."

His father nodded. "Let's go, then."

Why had she never noticed how attractive Marcus looked before? Clean shaved, hair trimmed short, fresh linen tunic, leather skirt—he looked handsome. His eyes said so much when he saw her come into the room. Perhaps she should not lift her gaze to his, but his smile pulled her forward and her eyes answered his.

A new helmet with a red crest and a bright red cloak had been thrown casually upon his bed. Julius and Decimus stood on his left, Joanna on his right. All of them smiling at her.

She stopped. She gazed from one to the other of them, puzzled.

Marcus stepped forward and lifted his hands, palms up, in front of her. His voice came to her, deep and melodious. "Meskhanet, daughter of Joanna, would you consent to be betrothed to a centurion?"

She caught her breath. A centurion—Marcus, a centurion. Her gaze darted to Joanna whose smile never wavered. To Decimus, who nodded. And back to Marcus.

She smiled, and she raised her hands and fitted them into his.

Made in the USA
San Bernardino, CA
21 March 2014